Paradise, Nevada

Paradise, Nevada

(This Town Wasn't Built on Winners)

Dario Diofebi

BLOOMSBURY PUBLISHING

NEW YORK · LONDON · OXFORD · NEW DELHI · SYDNEY

BLOOMSBURY PUBLISHING
Bloomsbury Publishing Inc.
1385 Broadway, New York, NY 10018, USA

BLOOMSBURY, BLOOMSBURY PUBLISHING, and the Diana logo are trademarks
of Bloomsbury Publishing Plc

First published in the United States 2021

ISBN: HB: 978-1-63557-620-7; eBook: 978-1-63557-621-4

LIBRARY OF CONGRESS CATALOGING-IN-PUBLICATION DATA IS AVAILABLE

2 4 6 8 10 9 7 5 3 1

Typeset by Westchester Publishing Services
Printed and bound in the U.S.A. by Berryville Graphics Inc., Berryville, Virginia

To find out more about our authors and books visit www.bloomsbury.com and sign up
for our newsletters.

Bloomsbury books may be purchased for business or promotional use. For information
on bulk purchases please contact Macmillan Corporate and Premium Sales Department at
specialmarkets@macmillan.com.

The crisis consists precisely in the fact that the old is dying and the new cannot be born; in this interregnum a great variety of morbid symptoms appear.

—ANTONIO GRAMSCI

And, you know, there's no such thing as society. There are individual men and women and there are families.

—MARGARET THATCHER

CONTENTS

Contents

Prologue

E verything was at once extraordinary and dull.
Dazzling and quotidian.

To the visitors, it was exotic and tantalizing and new and as inebriating as advertised. They were dizzied by the lights, addled by the sounds; the city had them in its thrall. But it was ordinary to us. Mundane and unremarkable. We'd grown accustomed to the lights, blinking out of darkened aisles. We were deaf to the digital treble of the machines, the laughter of the drunks. A visitor's once-in-a-lifetime was our everyday.

This is the first paradox about Las Vegas: the Positano Luxury Resort & Casino was the beating heart of Friday-night euphoria, and it was our home. It sat center-Strip, the city spreading round it like a widening spiral of magic and commonplace, strip clubs and college dorms, shooting ranges and Walmarts, private jet landing strips and bus stops to quiet distant hopeless suburbs. We can't explain about the fire without establishing this, that a town can be both fiction and reality, both paradise and home. We all here have to come to terms with it, sooner or later.

Then there was the money.

Inside the neon-lit darkness of the Positano, herds of visitors roamed our halls, chasing it. They bounced from wall to wall, from distraction to distraction, letting the room slowly guide them to its center, its raison d'être: the gaming pits. The colors of the playing chips turned money into a fantasy: blue for $1, red for $5, green for $25, black for $100, purple for

$500, yellow for $1,000, beautiful white *flags* for $5,000, their edges striped in patriotic red and blue. We still long for them after all these years. Behind glass cases on the tables' chip banks, in the hands of pit bosses and dealers, in the satchels of the high rollers. We look at them. We ache for them.

Everything here is about money; when it looks like it's not about money, then it's *definitely* about money. This is the second paradox. That the money too is both fictional and real, both exhilarating and tragic, both there and not there. The town itself embodies this, glittering and triumphant, but hidden away from prying eyes in the middle of an unforgiving desert. The one truly *free* market in America. Free of guilt. Free of shame. We cannot think of the fire without asking ourselves what role money played, how much of the night had its roots in those silly little disks of color-coded clay. The crowds in the casino hallways. The conversations in the cocktail lounge. The deals struck in elegant offices on the highest floors. The high-stakes Texas Hold'em in the upstairs poker room. You don't spend as many years in Las Vegas as we have, treated daily to the sight of fortunes changing hands, without learning to question the nature of these things. We can't help it.

Finally, there are the stories. The third and hardest paradox. Because the more Las Vegas seems but a loose collection of unrelated individuals— the more its inhabitants, both temporary and permanent, look like isolated segments of life that don't link up together, disparate narratives incapable of producing any meaning—the more the city demands that they connect. A city that wasn't built to be lived in, perhaps the only one in America, defined for us by the memories of pen-happy visitors and weekend drunks. The idea of a town. It's in the stories of those who stay that Las Vegas exists, in the low constant hum below the chiming and music, in the real city they created, against all odds, at the heart of a glorified theme park.

We cannot begin to explain the night of Friday, May 1, 2015, at the Positano, the bomb at the Scarlatti Lounge, the sound of the alarm, the blackout, who made it out and who, tragically, did not, without trying to summon, at least in fragments, the stories of the ones who were there. Their stories are part of our story, and ours is part of theirs. We wish we could do more.

This is not going to be easy.

PART I

FALL 2014

1

Ray

On the pinkish backdrop of Google Maps, the blue dot of Ray Jackson's car trickled down coastal California like a teardrop on a puffy cheek. Or, photographically, the car being white and the actual surface of California sometimes yellow and sometimes green or brown, more like a drop of milk foam flowing down a paper cup. But to the driver inside—who was about as far from sentimentalism and designer coffee as a native Californian can be—the whole thing resolved only into a suboptimal situation, the result of a string of suboptimal decisions yielding undesirable outcomes at every turn.

First of all, he disliked driving. Given the set of all plausible vehicles, the set function of his ability to enjoy the journey showed a conspicuous dip at the independent variable "car." To make things worse, in the aftermath of two weeks at home for Thanksgiving, he had accepted his uncle's advice to take the long way round from Marin County to Vegas, through Big Sur, without giving it much thought. This wasn't like him, but he'd told himself he could use some time to go through things again re: his moving-to-Vegas plan. Yet now that he was on it, the 101 to the 1 instead of the 580 to the 5, he could see how this scenic detour had been a mistake: he was a nervous driver, eyes firmly on the road at all times, too focused to take in the reportedly breathtaking colors of the Pacific streaming to his right. All he'd accomplished was turning a nine-hour straight shot on the interstate into a twelve-hour oceanside ordeal.

Secondly, while there was no doubt he would need a car in Las Vegas, he was not so sure that taking his dad's had been such an EV+[1] deal after all. True, his father no longer drove it to Sacramento twice a week on account of: (a) he didn't do career counseling for CSUS anymore, and (b) he had gone partially blind due to two successive retinal vascular occlusions in the last couple years. Also true, while Ray could technically still afford to buy a car, a large expense now didn't sound like a great idea, given his situation. Still, taking the white Chevy SUV provided his parents with an excuse to suggest visits that, coupled with how much closer to home he would be now as opposed to Toronto, could easily backfire.

The main issue, however, remained Las Vegas itself. When he'd moved out of his apartment in Toronto, Las Vegas had been a vague idea motivated mostly by a desire to get the hell out of there, asap. He'd figured his stay in Marin County ought to give him enough time to evaluate his options and derive the optimal living solution, but fourteen days of his parents, an incredibly old dog, and a fierce ping-pong opponent had ended up draining his computational stamina. He had been, he had to admit, unacceptably lazy. And now he was moving to Vegas without a real grasp on the mathematical landscape of the decision and with what a less analytical mind would probably call a "bad feeling."

For years, as a professional online poker player, Ray had regarded live poker and the world of brick-and-mortar casinos pretty much the same way a neurosurgeon would regard the game Operation: they were all very cute, with their chips, their drinks, and their serious faces, but let's be honest, they had no idea what they were doing. Ray's world, the world of high-stakes online poker, was a specialized haven of advanced math and tracking

---

1 Expected Value, meaning the long-run average value of theoretical repetitions of the examined decision would yield a positive outcome, as defined by $E[X] = x_1 p_1 + x_1 p_1 + \cdots x_k p_k$; where variable X can take value x_1 with probability p_1, value x_2 with probability p_2, and so on up to value x_k with probability p_k.

software, and the idea of moving to Vegas to play in casinos felt like an insult. Not to mention what his online peers would think. Was he maybe just overreacting to this whole thing, just running away from his problems without really thinking things through?

Surrounded by an excess of nature, he kept looking at the axis of the road ahead. It really had been naive to think time at his parents' could help: the house had a way of muddling his thoughts, stirring up a fog of prolixity and bad logic he was only now starting to come out of. He decided to concentrate on the new episode of one of the machine learning and AI podcasts he'd listened to nonstop during his last weeks in Toronto. That always made things clearer.

Two weeks before, Ray had arrived in Marin County at night. Having spent the cab ride home looking at his phone to discourage the driver from talking to him, and having had to wrestle his father for control of the heavier, more wobbly-wheeled bag on the way inside (so that "Seriously Dad, let *me* do it" had been his first words), he'd had no time to gradually reacquaint himself with his childhood town, neighborhood, and house. At the periphery of his vision, familiar shapes gave in quietly to the sameness of the night. But as soon as he was inside, the yellow glow of the low-energy light bulbs on the cherrywood bookshelves awakened him to his obvious mistake: he was home.

It took Ray a few days to readjust to the place where his precocious talents had been first noticed and nurtured. In the quiet jazz suffusing the rooms he knew so well, he could still hear the whispered expectations for his future his parents had gone to extreme pedagogical lengths to hide. It was in the living room, where they had insisted on throwing him house parties and, worse yet, surprise parties with the other, non-mathematically-gifted children. It was in the kitchen, where he had been recruited in all manners of *commis* activities by his French-cuisine enthusiast mother ever since he had been tall enough to reach the countertop, drawing him away from his desk and his calculus. It was in his parents' bedroom, where secret pillow talk about Ray's limitless potential must have taken place for years. The secrecy, Ray knew, was some hippyish hokum meant to alleviate the pressure and allow him to organically develop his dispositions. But behind the smiles and the encouragements to "go out and have some fun," Ray never doubted for a second the narrative his parents had always wanted from him. For him.

At the root of his problems with the house was a familiar and much more tangible contrast: the Jacksons' was a house of Letters. It was, in fact, in response to this axiom, transparent and irrefutable for anybody who traversed their labyrinthically bookshelved corridors, that young Ray had derived his own clear-cut identity as a man of Numbers. In the late 1980s, only a few years before his birth, Howard and Victoria Jackson had opened the Satis House Bookshop in San Rafael, a so-called independent little hideaway for the literarily inclined. Throughout Ray's childhood, the bookstore had been the object of his parents' endless profusions of love and endeavors, and had hosted readings by some of the most celebrated writers of the time. Ray himself, cute and well-behaved, had soon been a welcome guest at both the readings and the postreading dinners with this or that novelist, which accounted for the wealth of unnecessary synonyms and flowery phrases that still clogged his mental storage centers. And now that he was back, and corridors were once again something you *traversed*, and cutting a potato was called *batonnet*-ing or *allumette*-ing (two different things), and decisions were made because of how they *felt*, regardless of their optimality, Ray found himself utterly incapable of the very rational thinking that the future of his poker career demanded.

The days leading up to Thanksgiving became an elaborate game of domestic chess. Ray's king, who only wanted to castle short and mind his own business in a corner, was assailed by opposing forces from both flanks. His father, a short, thin, gray-haired man whose face had developed a kind of puffiness with old age and whose eyes had narrowed to small horizontal slits, haunted both floors of the house like a slow-moving, legally blind ghost. He had a way of walking into whatever room Ray was in, hands joined against his lower back, like a Parisian flaneur (his words), that always managed to drive Ray up the cherrywood-paneled wall: he had no reason to come in and made no attempt to hide the fact, he just walked in and sort of *loitered*. It would have been quite better, honestly, if his father had started chopping wood right there in the room—something Ray pointed out with the disgruntled *"What?"* that opened most of their conversations throughout the two weeks.

If sitting in one place, evaluating different answers to the question that kept vexing him (he simply *could not* stay in Toronto any longer, this much he knew), made Ray vulnerable to his father's loitering, moving around the house exposed him to his mother's own traps: simply running into her, the tallest and strongest-looking Jackson, entailed a project (usually kitchen-related) that would tie him for an hour in a collaborative activity he knew was only an excuse to have a chat.

It wasn't that Ray didn't want to talk to his parents (as much as he felt like talking to anybody at all lately). He was, he would have been ready to admit, acceptably fond of them, after all. It was more that he really didn't want to talk to them *now*, now that his impeccable decision-making had frozen, his future wasn't loading, and there were signs of an imminent internal personal OS crash.

And of course, as if on cue, his father started announcing that they needed to "have a talk" before Ray left, "just whenever you have five minutes."

Ray mentally outlined two possible scenarios: in the first one, his father having been a career counselor for decades + Ray having chosen professional poker as a way of employing his gifts + his being in the process of moving away from Toronto and (maybe?) reconsidering his career path, all suggested the heart-to-heart about his life choices and how they made him *feel* that he had so far miraculously managed to avoid. It wasn't anything personal, he just *really* didn't want to talk about it.

The fact was, the son of the career advisor had never really needed any career advice. Ray had been seventeen when he left home for parental-chest-swelling Stanford, and nineteen when he scandalously dropped out and moved to Toronto to pursue his online poker career. By then he had already been VFlnd3r, online poker prodigy and heads-up cash game[2] specialist, for quite some time to pretty much everybody he knew (except, of course, the people he knew in person). But while he had stayed enrolled through the early stages of his phenomenally fast ascent to poker stardom, the 2011 ban on online poker in the United States, known among initiates as Black Friday, had brought him to a crossroads. Stay in school, or follow the international diaspora of American poker pros? Stanford, or Pokerstars.com? It was the first time he had been able to apply his EV computations to a real-life problem, and it had been a simple, reassuring victory for math-based decision-making. Less than two months after Black Friday, he was signing the lease to an apartment in Toronto—sight unseen, based on an elaborate neighborhood scoring system of his own creation—by far the most rational way of playing the hand he'd been dealt.

It wasn't easy to determine how his parents had taken the move. What for years he had called their "being chill," he knew, was really a byproduct of their inability (his and theirs) to discuss anything of importance with each other. He knew they worried, suspected they worried a lot, but could never figure out how much the fact that their son was making nontrivial sums of money playing cards on the internet bothered them (the Jacksons' being one of those rare American households where moneymaking was not considered of value in and of itself). Still, their support had stayed unwavering. As for him, if the DoJ ban that had made him an exile had taken an emotional toll (as it seemed to have for most of his poker friends on Skype and Two Plus Two Poker Forum), he did not care to know: introspection was a guessing game he had no time for. His public persona displayed no doubt, having left only one lapidary comment in the "Black Friday/F*** DoJ/where next?" Two Plus Two thread: "Worry only about what you can control. Whining is for result-oriented *fish*. This is poker, adapt or die."

---

2   One-on-one poker played with real money, as opposed to tournament poker, the entry-fee-type sportified version of the game made popular by ESPN2 coverage featuring overweight insurance salesmen repeatedly saying "All in."

(This had been quoted and commented "so much this" by lower-stakes players even more fervently than his posts usually were.)

And so online poker had become his life: the monetary upswings and downswings caused by a capricious mathematical goddess called Variance[3] less and less capable of causing comparable swings in his mood; the validation he received from his graphs more important to him than the actual money he made (his words); the fact that his friends' names were sauce123 and OtB_RedBaron and that poker was quite literally all they ever talked about absolutely ordinary and fine to him. In the poker world, he was a pioneer. He was one of the first to systematically apply advanced game theory to real in-game decisions. He filled notebooks with decision trees before any software was developed to do it. He was even one of the four Brains selected to represent humankind in the historic Brains vs. Artificial Intelligence poker challenge in Pittsburgh last spring.

The second possible topic his father might want to broach scared him even more. Wasn't it possible, Ray considered, that what his retinally occluded, philosophically inclined father wanted to discuss with his only son was the issue of his own aging and mortality? Wasn't it possible that he wanted to talk about his health, "open up" about his "feelings," even sort of preemptively counsel his son through his future grieving? It would be entirely in character. Ray shuddered at the prospect. When had the human race gone so collectively wrong that they started to value the noise of the psyche over the signal of the brains? Where was all this sharing coming from? Introspection, again, was better avoided, a luxury application for underutilized servers.

---

3 Defined as the expectation of the squared deviation of a random variable from its mean and calculated through: $Var(X) = E[(X - \mu)^2]$ where $\mu = E[X]$ or, in layman's terms, how far spread out a set of individual observations can be from its theoretical expected value. Meaning for how long and how much a theoretically winning poker player can lose and vice versa (the answers being: a long time and a lot, which is the reason why poker has stayed popular with amateurs for years, the only game where a novice can beat the best player in the world pretty often and for heaps).

Introspection got the best of Ray by Overlook Point #2. It was the second cliffside rock he had felt compelled by the Big Sur road-trip ritual to stop at and sit on; he wasn't sure how long he was supposed to sit there by himself, or what kind of emotions he was supposed to experience in the process, but once there, he was dead set on doing it properly. Cobalt waves turned turquoise before dissolving into whispering spumes against the shore, the shallow waters shining in gentle light from the cloudless sky. The sea was underneath him, striped with brown algae, and from his protruding rock he could see the highway curling up like smoke around the cliff, like in that song Dad used to play in the car. Unable to shake the residual sentimentality of his weeks at home, he decided to allow himself a frank assessment of his thoughts and, well, *feelings* on the subject of his father's deteriorating health. Ray did not consider himself a cold person, immune to human emotion. He was just by nature very careful not to let any of it corrupt the linearity of his decision-making.[4] But now, his decision-making being on a dismaying hiatus, bluish waves of feeling found no rational cliff to dissolve against and there he was, looking at the ocean, thinking of his dad.

He had been dealing, he had to admit, with a certain anxiety about mortality lately. It had started the day of his father's first retinal vein occlusion, and had gotten worse with the inception of the treatments, the periodic injections, and the grim vascular landscapes described by several well-respected MDs. It was a sort of irrational inability to accept the precariousness of existence: a childish rage at it, and a black, unspeakable fear of the going-away of life. The realization suddenly hitting him that he would one day have to face mortality as mere lifelessness, the lifelessness of objects; that at some point he would be in a room where his father would lie on a bed like a book on a shelf or a rock on a cliff, bound by gravity and propelled by no sentient will. A thing. It scared the living shit out of him. Not the loss, nor the painful getting-used-to-it and recalibration of his perception

---

4   An asset that happens to be to professional poker what a quarterback's innate throwing arm is to football.

of a world that no longer included the man who had driven him to school and taught him ping-pong. That was okay, as long as it didn't get in the way of his personal plans. But no, as hazy as his decision to move to Las Vegas seemed, he was quite sure that being closer to his aging father had nothing to do with it. Thankfully.

"Stanford would be lucky to have you, Matthew," said Uncle Raymond. Matthew was the seventeen-year-old son of the Wongs, longtime neighbors and friends of Ray's family. Together with Ray's parents, Uncle Raymond, Aunt Lynda, and the twins, they made up the ten-handed full-ring table of their Thanksgiving dinner, filling with digestive conversation the interval between the deconstructed holiday turkey and the pumpkin Gruyère gratin with thyme and the salted chocolate caramel tarts everyone was too full for. In the corner, Uncle Raymond's old albino boxer Pushkin looked up toward the table, too old to walk around and nag for food; his strategy involved sad eyes and people's natural sense of pity.

"And when are you thinking of going back, Ray?" said Aunt Lynda. Ray's mother's jerked up her chin, detecting External Pressure being projected on her independent, free-thinking son. Ray would have found it funny, had he not resented the question.

"Ray is an extremely successful poker player, honey," said Uncle Raymond, apparently sans condescension. (It was commonly accepted that Ray had been named not after his uncle but rather after Northwest native and Jackson household all-time hero Raymond Carver, in the wake of whose untimely death and consequent parental sadness he had quite possibly been conceived.) "He will go back when he feels it's time."

"*If* he decides to go back," said Ray's mother.

"He's moving to Las Vegas tomorrow," said Ray's father, in a purely factual tone. Just offering information. "I'm giving him my car."

A full-ring table, typically nine- or ten-handed, is the standard setting for a live poker game, the higher players-to-dealers ratio being more cost-effective for casinos. Online games have over time shown a marked preference for shorthanded tables, six-handed usually. But to Ray, one of the purists of true one-on-one poker combat, anything more than two was a crowd. As a matter of fact, something could be said about one person being really all that was needed to . . .

"You know I just remembered, I read about you online some time ago, Ray," said Mr. Wong, out of the strategic blue. "You played against that supercomputer, right? Where was it, Philadelphia?"

"Pittsburgh," said Ray.

"The computer gave you quite a beating, huh?" said Mr. Wong, proving that people nowadays have access to way more information than they are able to comprehend.

"The experiment was not well conducted—," began Ray, formulating an answer he'd repeated a few dozen times since last spring.

"This artificial intelligence thing is really scary," said Mrs. Wong.

"We had to play twelve hours a day for twenty straight days—"

"I mean, what happens if computers become more intelligent than us?" said Mrs. Wong.

"—also, considering standard deviation and the effect of variance over the sample size, we had—"

"AI is the future, Mom," said Matthew Wong.

"—you could say my individual results against the bot were a statistical tie—"

"Whether we want it or not," Mr. Wong said, agreeing with his son.

"—although there's no question that the work the scientists have done is really remarkable," conceded Ray.

"I do wonder," said Ray's father, after a beat, "whether our blind faith in science and numbers is leading us somewhere we didn't mean to go. *Obsolescence.*"

With his last word, he knocked over a half-empty wineglass, which rained to his left across the white tablecloth. There was embarrassed silence for some time, while Ray's mother got up and dabbed a napkin against the spill, looking apologetically at Mrs. Wong, who sat next to Howard, seemingly unstained.

"You know what you should do?" Uncle Raymond said to Ray, after clearing his throat. "You should drive through Big Sur on your way to Vegas. I bet you've never been. It is quite the place for a man grappling with such weighty concerns."

"But that's not what I—"

"That is a wonderful idea," said Ray's father, who seemed eager to put the incident behind them. He was balling up some bread crumbs between his index finger, middle finger, and thumb, a sort of nervous tic Ray associated with squirrels, and houseflies, and himself. "There's nothing like sitting on those cliffs, watching the ocean."

"Like stout Cortez when with eagle eyes . . . ," began Uncle Raymond.

". . . he star'd at the Pacific—and all his men . . . ," said Ray's dad.

". . . look'd at each other with a wild surmise . . ."

". . . silent upon a peak in Darien."

In the study, Ray sat on the sink-in juniper-green armchair and rested his feet on the coffee table, which was covered in sheaves of paper. There were even more books in here, categorized by some inefficient, esoteric criterion that wasn't alphabetical, or by size or color coding. Books he remembered the cracked spines of, many books he had tried and abandoned after a chapter, sometimes after a paragraph, whole libraries of fictional beginnings that had contributed nothing to his knowledge or intellectual abilities. It was uncanny how little he had in common with the cult his childhood home was a sort of temple to, and still they had never pressured him into it, his mathematical inclinations always encouraged, cultivated, boasted like a trophy around friends. The little math whiz Jackson boy, who'd have thought?

The bot *had* beaten him. Badly. About eight months before, Ray and three other top-ranked No Limit Hold'em heads-up specialists had been invited to Pittsburgh to participate in an experiment, a twenty-day-long match between four human "Brains" and Artificial Intelligence, funded by Carnegie Mellon. The bot was a new and updated version of a poker-playing

program developed by the Computer Science Department, always interested in testing the limits of artificial intelligence through complex games
(the thousand-year-old game of Go had recently and famously been taken
over by a computer that had defeated—as in, pulverized—the best players
in the world). The twist was that the new software hadn't really been
programmed by anybody: the scientists had simply taught it the rules of the
game, after which the bot played trillions of hands against itself (self-play),
experimenting all possible mistakes and solutions, refining itself into near-
perfect performance. It was called reinforcement learning, and for the
past eight months it had kept Ray awake in the morning.[5]

He hadn't been lying at dinner: it was true, his own personal results,
however losing, had not been bad, and qualified as what mathematicians
called a "statistical tie." But that didn't fool him. He had been there, sitting
in a room where technicians who could have easily been classmates of his
at Stanford looked on as he made small mistake after small mistake, one
trivial human imperfection after the other accruing hand after hand to an
unbridgeable gap. He couldn't beat the bot. Not if he studied every minute
of his life until the air left his lungs, he just couldn't. He was human. He
miscalculated. He misclicked. He got tired, and grew frustrated, and
needed sleep.

That was his problem. It was stupid, really: the scientists at Carnegie
Mellon couldn't care less about using their software to win money in online
poker. As a matter of fact, they couldn't care less about poker in general.
Poker to them was just a blank set of rules, a case study in the field of game
theory, exactly like the prisoner's dilemma or tic-tac-toe. Nothing was going
to change in the world of online poker, at least for a while. And yet, getting
back from Pittsburgh, Ray had found himself haunted by an inability to
make the simplest decisions. A hesitation he couldn't seem to recover from.
That's how it had begun.

---

5   No self-respecting online poker player sleeps at night proper—closed-curtaining mornings are
to pros the middle of the REM cycle.

The dog Pushkin entered the study with the dragging limp of old age. He reclined sideways in that peculiar way of dogs and Greek deities and stared at Ray from the depth of his placid pink-rimmed eyes. Ray grimaced. For this dog, mid-single-digits-year-old Ray had once contracted an ardent fondness, like an extramarital affair made stronger by infrequent encounters and the heartbreaking awareness that Pushkin was, in fact, *someone else's dog.* There had been tears, he now recalled, blushing.

His sentimentality, his flawed decision-making—all his problems were rooted in his past. There was no escaping them. They were in these bookshelves, and in the way he'd been raised. Yes, he made mistakes. Just that morning, after two weeks of failed reasoning, he had finally told his parents he would be driving to Las Vegas the next day, committing himself to the decision on an impulse. On a fucking *whim.* How hopelessly suboptimal.

Recursive thoughts and emotions overpowered Ray's processors all the way past McWay Falls and Ragged Point and the tourists posing for Instagram pics. It was the day after Thanksgiving, the *other* Black Friday. Regaining control had been the whole point of agreeing to this scenic detour on the way to the desert: he knew he'd find himself alone with no phone reception, sitting on a rock above the turquoise waves or on the sun-roasted beaches of California, and what else could one do in such situations but parse decision trees? Yet now he just sat there, looking at the sea lions lying sideways on the beach in San Simeon like a whole pack of senescent albino boxers, admitting computational defeat. Waving the old white decisional flag. Yesterday's ping-pong had been the last straw.

"Do you want to play when they're done?" the Wong kid had asked, appearing at the top of the staircase.

While their parents were watching the postdinner football game in some ironic intellectual way, Ray was downstairs in the basement, watching his little cousins perform a parody of a ping-pong match. Both boys too short for the table, they had come to Ray to ask for permission to remove the small heap of correspondence resting on it and play. Now they were taking turns hitting the ball in the vicinity of the table and (in the impossibility of an actual back-and-forth rally) chasing it around the yellow-lit space cluttered with boxes of xeroxed, stapled files. Ray could see how Matthew Wong would predict this incredibly boring game to be short-lived. Yet he thought that if Mike and Doug, these kids he barely knew, were anything like him— if, that is, Jackson blood was a thing that extended beyond pale skin and short stature, and reached the nodes in the brain in charge of obstinacy— then there was a good chance this could go on for hours. At any rate, he'd given them the lousy paddles with the rubber pimples and no sponge between the wooden blade and the hitting surface, hiding the pro-level Killerspins he had bought in high school, in the heyday of his ping-pong career.

"Sure. Are you any good?" Ray said.

"I'm not bad. What about you?"

"I'm okay, like, average."

And then the kid had said something incredibly irksome: "I don't want to bet money, though."

Who knows what the Wongs had told him about Ray. The conversations they'd had. A standup neighborhood kid turned bad, poor Jacksons, imagine how hard it must be on *them*. And with all the problems they have, what with Howard and his eyes, and Vicky always there to take care of him, the thought of a son going around doing *that*! What bothered Ray wasn't the tarnish on his neighborly reputation, but the wild inaccuracy of depicting him as the gambling type, which couldn't be farther from the truth. In fact, he strongly disliked gambling. Hated it. What he did for a living, the way he looked at it, had absolutely nothing to do with it.

The kid turned out to be annoying. For starters, he moved weird: he squatted down to return serve in a strained, unnatural position, and then crab-walked sideways along the baseline during rallies, twirling both arms in odd, liquid gestures, like his body had more than the normal percentage of water in it. And on top of that he wasn't good, but he was flat-out night-marish to play against, his whole left-handed repertoire consisting of odious little chops and fiendish backhand spins that sent the ball flying a mile away from the table as soon as you so much as got near it to return them. His serve was a balletic backhand number involving a weird crossing of the arms in a wide scissoring motion that looked like he was trying to wipe something off his right forearm, or hurriedly swatting away a spider that had managed to crawl up his right elbow. As awkward as it may have looked, the first three times Ray approached the resulting weakish ball, his fore-hand returns landed on a stack of *Calaveras Station Literary Journal*s in an open cardboard box several feet behind and to the right of the playing surface.

Ray, on the other hand, was legitimately good. Like most ping-pong table owners, he had over the course of years of crushing amateur opponents developed an extremely aggressive, predatory style, his own centered around a lightning-fast inside-out forehand topspin that had taken him years of practice to master, and that had been the undoing of dozens of neighborhood kids. A stroke that, of course, just couldn't seem to ever go in tonight. Whatever he tried, it seemed like the table was at least a foot shorter than he remembered; even his backhand floaters finished out long. He was already sweating profusely during warm-up rallies and particularly aware of the fact that the Wong kid had very casually said "Ready when you are" at least four or five rallies ago. His cousins, who had given up the game but stayed in the basement, were now sitting on boxes of French cuisine magazines, annoyingly rooting for him to "win" the warm-up.

"Okay, last one, and then we play. Best of five, sets to eleven, two serves each?"

The truth was, Ray hadn't played ping-pong in years. Not after Stanford Table Tennis Club. Not after it turned out that the level of play he faced at home was an unreliable test of his ability with a paddle, and that the number of players who could render him a sniveling idiot in uniform-mandated short-shorts was indeed considerable, and weirdly concentrated in the Palo Alto–Menlo Park area. The realization that his years of undefeated streaks and cavalier handicap offerings had been a textbook case of the big-fish-in-small-pond scenario had not been a painless one. Despite what the Wongs would have guessed, it hadn't involved substantial money loss in misguided bets against stronger players (the idea of putting money in a situation the EV of which was unclear and potentially wildly negative was simply incomprehensible to him), nor had it been achieved after a stage of excuse-making and self-delusion; it had been a quiet landing on an island of small sadness. Weird as it was to admit, he had been forced to accept the loss of a source of validation and self-worth he'd somehow relied on for years. A thing people liked and at which he had been unquestionably good. The best. He had soon started to overcompensate, to exaggerate his assessment of himself: when somebody asked, "Are you good?" he would now shrug and say, "Average, I think." This was a transparent lie, and yet he felt that it would do him good to frustrate his ego in something he had really cared about. He perceived there was a lesson in it to be learned.

But this kid he could beat. This kid he had to beat. It was fine losing against really good players at Stanford, players who had put in the hours and trained more and better than him and simply deserved to win. But this kid wasn't good. This passive, risk-averse nit[6] with his chops and spins, Ray couldn't lose to him. Back in high school, he had beaten hundreds of kids like this. And yet today it seemed like nothing would fall in. All of his returns wandered off on unpredictable vectors, no matter how carefully he hit them, so it was like starting with a handicap, because he could never break serve unless the kid missed. After missing long a couple of topspin forehands, the first set was gone, 7–11. He smiled tensely in feigned disinterest as the twins cheered him on.

The Wong kid, though, seemed genuinely not to care: he was standing in his awkward kyphotic slump, long fingers fiddling with the rubber of

---

6   In poker jargon, a *nit* (adj. *nitty*) is an extremely careful, conservative player, whose winning strategy is to take no risks and just wait for really good hands. The term is mostly used as an insult among professionals.

the paddle, his bespectacled stare vaguely concentrating on one or two small areas around the curve of the racket, where over time the glue had started to give and the rubber was beginning to detach from the blade. He was wearing a white shirt with a yellow-and-gray pattern that reached far down his thighs outside his gray pants, and black Converse high-tops in an advanced state of decay. When the second set started and a focused, perspiring Ray found a way to return his serves more consistently, the kid complimented him with oohs of admiration every time an impressive forehand attack would go in, after which he would take an absurdly long time chasing the ball around the basement, much like Ray's cousins had done, oftentimes dropping it after having retrieved it or tripping and knocking over stacks of files. Ray hated him.

The dog appeared in the rectangle of light from the door above the stairs. He lingered, visible desire to join the downstairs scene contending with an old man's fear of falling down the steps. Ray had just won the second set, 11–8, and was getting ready for his first serve in the third, but the Wong kid seemed suddenly more interested in the children's efforts to help the stupid dog down the stairs. They played the third set amid the twins' cheering and patting Pushkin for having made it to the basement, and while his opponent had resumed normal play, it felt to Ray that his attention was still elsewhere, incredibly. Ray won the set 11–4, the only points he conceded having been mistakes of his on attempted attacks.

Ray had a 2-point lead in the fourth set when the parents arrived. It must have been halftime in the upstairs game, or maybe it was over—how long had they been down there?—but now Ray's mom and dad (who probably couldn't see much, to be honest) and Mr. Wong were standing at the head of the stairs, watching from above without coming down to join the kids and the dog. The weirdness of the situation was not lost on Ray: a grown man (which he was, wasn't he?) drenched in perspiration playing ping-pong in the basement of his childhood home against a smiling, distracted high-school kid, respective parents spectating at a distance and talking like their sons were on the swings at the playground; the dog still staring at him, a red triangle of tongue permanently sticking out from his resting face; Ray's little cousins shouting in encouragement. He missed a serve, badly.

And why was it that the people who turn out to be good at ping-pong were always these kind of like fake-nerds? Like this kid here. Clearly obsessive, but not cripplingly anxious; weird, but nonchalant. The kind of people who will stay at the table and play another game when everybody else has moved on to beers and mingling, but also the kind social enough to be around humans to play often. Essentially well-adjusted geeks. And, wait, did he think this guy was good now? This kid who was now doing his stupid oohs of admiration *mid-rally*? With the set tied at 8 after a missed return on another spin-heavy serve, Ray found himself so scared of losing and having to play a deciding fifth set that he started simply defending, sheepishly sending the ball over the net without trying to attack, just hoping his opponent would make a mistake. But the Wong kid did not attack, not even when provoked to. He just kept working his spins, switching his angles, hitting it short and then long, left and then right. And then Ray missed. And again. A lucky shot kept him in the game on his last serve, but now the Wong kid had a set ball on his serve, 10–9.

One thing anybody who has played any game with a strong mental component will know is that planning and strategizing is one thing, but executing, going through with it in the heat of the moment, is a whole different enterprise. Ray, who was known in the poker community as one of the best thinkers-under-pressure and keepers-of-one's-cool, did not understand why he was suddenly so aware of the joint in his right wrist, stiff, frozen as he tried to put weight on his forehand. He knew he needed to attack the loopy floaters the kid kept offering him, and yet he kept returning weak and flat, just to keep the rally going, just trying not to miss. As the rally got longer and longer, he felt himself drifting out of it, becoming aware of the dimly lit basement and the rhythmic sound of the ball and the smell of the dog, aware of being watched, of his parents, and the children, and felt sure he was going to lose it, he was going to miss the next forehand, or the next one, or the one after that. But he didn't. He somehow found his focus again, and all of a sudden his wrist was fine, loose and responding to his commands, and the next forehand was a strong inside-out topspin to his opponent's forehand side, right on the corner between baseline and sideline, perfect. And that's when the Wong kid stretched awkwardly and with an ugly move managed to chop a lame lob that just shaved the side of the table on Ray's left sideline and caromed away and landed on Pushkin's moist snout. Set Wong.

The uncontrollable shouting of the children, the excitement. Fifth set. Crucial not to look up toward the stairs, toward his parents, maintain some kind of dignity. The Wong kid taking forever to rest and get ready, all smiles and dorky voice-over bits, "It all comes down to this. This is where legends are born. Tonight we dine in hell." Ray shrugged, then did the thing holding the ball under the table in his right or in his left hand and asking his opponent to guess to assign the first serve. He showed the ball, holding up his right, nonguessed hand, then crouched down to serve.

Portions of scenic Pacific coast ran along the windows of the car like a hastily put-together music video from the '90s. Like someone from LA in charge of location had been lazy and just decided to go with the closest pretty sight available. The landscape equivalent of elevator music. So maybe Ray wasn't a well-adjusted nerd, he wasn't nonchalant. Maybe that was why he couldn't just let things go like everyone else. He couldn't play a game without caring like Matthew Wong, or make mistakes and suboptimal decisions and just be okay living with the consequences. Ray thought about things, and about the details of things, and about the reasons and advantages and disadvantages of every decision, and he cared, he knew that about himself. It was what had made him so good at the game. But now everything was confusing, slippery, and after Pittsburgh nothing had been the same. Back home, he had faced the worst downswing of his career, a vast, frightening amount of money lost because of his human flaws, and after a while he'd just stopped being able to play a single hand anymore, unable to live with another mistake. He'd stared blankly at the tables on the dual screens in his room in Toronto and waited, waited as the days went by, and the same fear that had frozen his wrist playing ping-pong had pervaded his whole body and taken residence in his brain. Waited without sleeping and without eating. Waited until he simply couldn't take it anymore. Until he just had to leave. And now the lease to the Vegas condo was already e-signed, the career of VFlnd3r effectively ended by law the second he'd crossed the border. A new chapter of his life about to begin. And when the blue dot of his car started trickling eastward on the map, swept sideways like a teardrop in the wind, and his father's white Chevy gained momentum through the Mojave Desert on the traffic-free I-15, and the sun set and the road ahead was darkness and silence and distant lights, Ray found himself hoping he could just get the ball over the net one more time, hoping he was not making a mistake.

Interlude I

(the story of a hotel)

In the eighteen full spins of the seasonal roulette wheel between the laying of the first stone and the fire, the Positano had been through a lot. It had opened, on prime center-Strip real estate, in 1999, at the tail end of an era of wild Las Vegas expansion centered on a single outdated and spectacular architectural concept: the theme resort. Legend has it that Al Wiles (né Alan Michael Wilinofsky, already owner of three of the ten biggest hotels in town) had dreamed of a monumental token of his undying love for his second wife, Swiss model and singer Sophie Heidegger-Fourier, with whom he'd spent an unforgettable honeymoon on the Costiera Amalfitana at the beginning of the 1990s. On a street that in a matter of ten years had already sprouted a black Egyptian pyramid, a fairy-tale castle, and ambitious large-scale replicas of the towns of Venice and Paris (complete with canals and a 1:2 version of the Eiffel Tower), the quaint pastel colors of the Italian coast could look like an almost unambitious project. Enter Al Wiles. What the eccentric billionaire envisioned, and what (one can only imagine) he firmly demanded upon meeting the Architectural Digest 100 six-time winners from Engels & Vogelsang Studio, was no mere postcard of a fishermen's village.

"I'm sorry, Herr Wiles, but what exactly do you mean, 'the whole fucking coast?'" asked Eli Engels, presumably.

"All of it, the whole shebang, *tutta*." Arms swinging outward, as if already dispensing the indecent amounts of money the enterprise was sure to require.

"But, Herr Wiles, the cliffs . . . ," Hendrik Vogelsang probably cautioned.

"The cliffs, the sea, down to the fucking *lemon trees*! I want Amalfi with the cathedral on the water for the lobby and the casino, and I want Positano with the little houses all perched up on the cliff for the suites and the three-star restaurant. And I want the breeze and I want the sunsets and I want the lights that turn the houses into a golden necklace around the hills and there's music from somewhere and everybody is in love."

And so building had begun. Ground had been broken in April of '97, on the birthday of a certain Swiss former runway queen, and immediately filled with 33 million gallons of salt water and seashells and authentic Mediterranean fish. Once completed, waves would gently lap real Italian sand. Children would go fishing in the early-morning breeze, legs dangling from the edge of a dock. Directly overlooking its twelve acres of Tyrrhenian Sea, a 700-foot hill had been erected out of surprisingly cheap Texas deep-rock, a by-product of fracking, and subsequently hollowed out and equipped with the most complex system of Otis elevators ever conceived.

The genius of the design was that, from the outside, the Positano wouldn't look like a building at all. At floor level, the seaside town of Positano, with its fish market, its cathedral, its town hall, disguised the facade of the large casino-and-shopping area; the rooms of the hotel were entirely contained by the houses on both sides of the cliff (sea view cost extra). Standard rooms in condos of eight, or even twelve, deluxe rooms in duplexes, and luxury suites in individual houses at the top of the compound. But if you stood outside, looking at the sun brushing colors on the Costiera, the houses wouldn't look connected at all. Just a village on a cliff.

From the Amalfi Lobby, or the gaming pits, or any of the twelve seaview balcony tables at the exquisite Mare cocktail bar, it was never more than a seven-minute walk to the highest luxury suites in the Hills of Positano tower, or to the exclusive, six-months-waiting-list Limoncello Restaurant. Gently guided by Wilesian hints ("Class, class, class out the

ass!"), Engels and Vogelsang reimagined Italy through the lens of unbridled German creativity. For the interiors, they borrowed the grandeur
of the Royal Palace of Caserta (only fifty miles north and inland of the
real Costiera, after all), the white-and-gold garishness of eighteenth-century
Baroque glistening above the marbled desks of a 24/7 concierge. With its
over twenty dining options ("from world-class celebrity-chef dining to a
quick bite on-the-go"), its miles of shopping venues ("featuring the elegance
of the designer boutiques in the Sorrento Promenade") and its 5,001
rooms (the odd one Wiles's own fabled private villa, the appearance of
which Engels and Vogelsang had to sign an NDA about), the Positano
was not the biggest but far and away the most luxurious and ambitious of
the Vegas hotels.

But alas, *tempus fugit.* The new millennium was not kind to the theme
resort, now suddenly considered old, kitschy, uncool. A new generation of

modern resorts appeared, shining prisms of glass and steel; their facades were dismissively un-Mediterranean, their interiors no-nonsense and un-Baroque, their souls sadly unthemed. Never again would the dreamy pencils of Engels & Vogelsang be allowed to shape the future of the Strip. Never again would a $3 billion rock-and-salt-water cultural appropriation be green-lit by investors.

"The tourist's taste has changed," someone may have got up the courage to tell Wiles one day.

"The world has changed. Everything changes. Everything dies," we imagine him reply, slowly retreating, in exactly seven minutes total, to his mysterious Xanadu atop the hill. The new millennium had not been kind to Al Wiles either. Sophie seemed to have changed; the impassioned Swiss who would laugh, and cry, and make love each time as if it were her last day alive, had turned into a cold, inscrutable businesswoman who Al could only talk to through the frigid punctilio of her team of Italian lawyers. She lived in Monaco now, and in summers would sail the *Sofia*, Al's 200-foot yacht, which she got in the settlement, to the real Amalfi and Positano.

Bereft of his beloved Heidegger-Fourier, Wiles felt lost, a man thrown into a world he no longer understood, he no longer could interpret. Among the sleek-looking new hotels that did not resemble anything else in the world but all resembled each other, built seemingly every year, every month, everywhere on the Strip, the Positano felt like a fortress at siege. Much to the dismay of his investors, Wiles himself was rumored to be going "full Hughes," an invisible hermit in a pink mansion surrounded by lemon trees. It was with considerable relief, therefore, that they welcomed MGM's multibillion-dollar offer to buy the Positano, along with a couple of smaller Wiles Group properties along the Strip.

It's hard to say what goes through the mind of a man who's lived the last ten years of his life alone on a fake hill overlooking a fake sea, tormented by all-too-real sorrow. It may have been that the Positano reminded him of the happiest years of his life, when the world was like exotic clay in his Brooklyn-born hands. It may have been that he wasn't yet ready to give up on his vision of Las Vegas, which to him had always been more than just a business but a dream come true, an idea and a hope for a better world. Some say that it was simply that Al Wiles, of all people, belonged to that rare breed of multibillionaires to whom money never really mattered, to whom love and care were the only tangible forces a man could cling to in the long, confusing project of life.

Al Wiles never sold the Positano. Weeks after he'd rejected the biggest purchase offer in the history of Las Vegas, he fired his chief financial advisors and hired fallen-from-grace, unqualified Eli Engels and Hendrik Vogelsang as his sole business advisors and all-around right-hand men. In 2010 work began on the biggest expansion a Vegas hotel had ever seen, an entire new wing on the north side, built on a gulf. The Sorrento Promenade was transformed into the Sorrento, an ancillary hotel with 2,002 additional rooms (Engels and Vogelsang now permanently anchored onsite in hilltop villas of their own). Luxurious sailboats ferried visitors back and forth between the Amalfi Coast and the new town, while VIPs could rent private skippered cutters and ketches with Michelin-star onboard catering for a romantic day at sea. Italy's most celebrated pizza chef promptly inked an NBA-caliber contract.

Completed in January 2012, the Sorrento once again made Wiles's Italian paradise resort the jazziest place in town. Visitors came and came and came back. The big man himself made a brief, smiling appearance at the opening ceremony, his triumph. Real estate gossip in town had it that his dreams of expansions up the Tyrrhenian coast might still not be sated: Naples, after all, was just a few miles up . . .

2

Mary Ann

She needed to get the fuck off social media. Enough. Things were going to get better now, that was the whole point, and Mary Ann felt like for sure there was no happiness online. She should delete her accounts. Sitting cross-legged on the floor, surrounded by boxes and empty gray carpet in her new Strip-side condo, she scrolled backward through her history. Social media was a swamp, a rank, slimy pond where people bathed in each other's need for validation, telling themselves stories about who they were. The whining and dining of the rich kids, hopeless folk from back home framing bits of their day to remind each other they're alive. No thank you. You guys can have it. Mary Ann was going to feel better, or at least stop hating herself, or at least try.

On its surface, the waitressing thing was nothing new. And if her previous flirtations with the job were any indication, there was not a lot to feel upbeat about. She'd been miserable as a lemonade girl at the Mississippi State Fair, ladling six-year-olds their saccharin-filled juice, trying to save money to be a #collegegirl; anxious as a mocha girl in Oxford, when she was scraping together rent money to move to #NYC; and as far as being a kombucha girl in Manhattan to pay for her first photo shoot, well, look at how *that* worked out.

But even she had to admit that this was different: cocktail server at a five-star center-Strip Vegas hotel. There's girls who would kill for a job like that, at least according to Aunt Karen. The job was demanding, yes, but the hours were manageable and the money great. Under the snuggly blanket of unionized labor, Mary Ann's situation was the waitressing equivalent of tenure track: flat-out too good to complain. And with the new apartment—where she might currently be using a cardboard box as a dining table, but which also marked her first time living on her own— she seemed set on giving Las Vegas an honest try. This was no temp job, there was no larger, all-redeeming goal she was working toward. This was it. Her work-life status was: in a relationship.

She slid a few feet across the floor to rest her back against the living room wall. The box/table was draped with Aunt Karen's Christmas lights, to supplement the faint yellow glow from the room's low-energy bulbs.

She still didn't feel good about it, was the thing. Maybe it was just her, like she simply wasn't made to be happy and that was that. She was ungrateful, incapable of recognizing her luck. Childhood friends in Jackson who, at twenty-five, had three kids, three jobs, and no hope, and here she still *wanted*, wanted hard, in spite of everything that happened. Maybe it was just her. But a lot of it must be the online thing. That draining, self-obsessive spiral that sucked her in for hours on end, leaving her angry and despondent on the other side. It just wasn't healthy.

It was Walter who had used the phrase to describe her generation— "infected with self." Evenings at the lounge, he'd go on about how they were "accumulating lives like currency," doomed to unhappiness unless they figured it out. A touch on the preachy side, Walter. He had a point, though. She had coated her life in lies and likes, doubled down on her ambitions and self-image, bought in on all the narcotizing bullshit the times had to offer. She of all people really ought to know better.

And so she began with Instagram. Of all those extra lives, that excess of self, the pictures were by far the worst. For sure. Her finger ran up the smudged, greasy screen as she traveled back in her own version of time.

Her phone was the brightest light in the room, and from the relative darkness it enveloped her body in a ghostly fluorescence. She was so *jealous* of her, the woman smiling in the photos. And at the same time she felt ashamed of her. Her carefree, hungry, #blessed self. She opened a few pictures here and there as she kept scrolling, a small farewell tour before she would finally get rid of this fucking @maellison person for good.

Trying on my first Positano uniform! #bestjob #nerdyframes

[Mary Ann in front of mirror, right hand holding up red iPhone 4, eyes checking picture on screen, long hair, center-parted, down to bare shoulders. Round, slightly dorky glasses. Tasteful makeup, red lipstick on playfully (?) frowning lips. Cheeks slightly puffy, unusual. Uniform is black miniskirt dress, Korean collar tied w/ serious-looking black ribbon, vast drop-shaped décolletage. Yellow granite vanity top displays minimal toiletries, white contacts receptacle, Visine bottle, aquamarine toothbrush, black coat hanger resting across white sink, crumpled-up purple towel, car keys. White shower curtains visible in background.]

88 people like this

Seriously, why had she even posted this to begin with? What had she been thinking, what could she possibly gain in sharing this with 1,142 followers in exchange for eighty-eight likes? The transaction felt so unnatural, dangerous. Toxic, that's what it was.

It wasn't surprising that pictures'd be her drug of choice. There seemed to be, among her modeling-days friends, a few ways you could react to your picture getting taken over and over: you could become really obsessive—about your appearance, who took the photo, and how, and for what, and were they gonna shop it?—and this way you ended up pretty much the stereotype of how people think of models; or you could start resenting it, feel inadequate, in pain every time you hear the shutter, hating your face and how it comes out looking, and of course it's not hard to see how this type doesn't go the distance in the industry. Mary Ann had been neither. And she hadn't been the type to just go along with it, always camera-ready and smiling and just mindlessly fine with the whole thing either. What modeling had done was make her completely numb. She just didn't care anymore, at all, because she had stopped believing the person in the pictures was her. Scrolling through her IG postmodeling, post-NYC, post-Episode, a lot of the pictures she had up were just shabby, almost intentionally bad. Barefoot in oversize pink scrubs and wet hair tied back and no makeup on spa day for Aunt Karen's birthday. Selfie in sweatpants lowering a mouse into Rodrigo's enclosure (Aunt Karen's pet python, Aunt Karen herself visible on other side of plastic snake case, fifty-two, dressed in her D-cup bustier for the waitressing gig at Circus Circus). And this one, from her first day working at the Pos. Where, really, you could see her freaking toothbrush, for God's sakes!

The job had come through Karen, after six months working at a Hawaiian bar right outside the hipster part of downtown, and less than nine months living in Vegas altogether. The Positano was for sure the classiest, most extravagant property in town, and interviews to work there were like Golden Tickets to the Chocolate Factory (which, come to think about it, the place kind of resembled: a massive replica of some part of Italy or other, with its own *sea* out front). A waitressing job there was a big opportunity, a rare one for a recent transplant. Of course, if Mary Ann had any doubt as to why this had happened to *her* (she didn't), stage one of the interview process had a way of clarifying that. Five hundred girls crowding the Positano ballroom, standing in a bikini lineup, turning to get body pictures taken. But at the time, waiting with the others to be evaluated, and even later, in front of the mirror, trying on that ridiculous uniform, she hadn't felt angry or sad. Or much of anything really. She lacked the energy to even care, honestly, that's just how things went. Hell, if her likes and comments on social media were any indication, she was probably starting to look at people that way herself. (Seriously, she needed to quit.)

Working on the Strip was strange. The place was clearly designed to be *different*, a break from whatever people were used to in everyday life. It was meant to be extraordinary, new, and dazzling. But there it was, day after day, always the same. The absurd buildings, the usual amazing lights. It reminded Mary Ann of one of those people you see in movies with short-term memory loss who introduce themselves every time you meet. Frozen in a first impression. Working there made her feel like she was in on a secret, seeing the real face of Las Vegas and expected not to give it away; but it also made her feel like an intruder. Like all the lights and spectacle were a picture on someone's timeline. Not her daily routine. She hadn't thought she would ever get used to it, this oddity she lived in day after day. And yet it felt like yesterday that she had started, posted the picture in front of the mirror, yesterday that Aunt Karen had talked her into taking the interview. Like everything else, this too had faded into numbness.

How did people do it? How did they make sense of lives without desires larger than survival and stability? That's what she could never figure out: How did they get rid of the hunger and the foolishness?

She was a fool all right. Somehow she had failed to pick up the one lesson humble origins have to teach, the lesson Aunt Karen had elevated to a personal manifesto: take what you can get, shut up, make it work. Instead, she had lived most of her life at the bleakest intersection in contemporary America, that of Poverty and Ambition. She was a living insult to everybody back home who wasn't #blessed with good enough looks to build a nice, effortless life for themselves. Selfish. Ungrateful. Awful.

Walter was right, self-loathing really is just another excuse to think about yourself.

She scrolled farther down.

#TBT to my first job in Vegas, serving tiki cocktails at Lei'd Back with Hawaiian belle @lilynori #DowntownLasVegas #NewportCasino #sisters #aloha

[Mary Ann by nondescript glass door, carrying a tray of piña coladas (?), little yellow umbrellas on top, pineapple wedges on rims of hurricane glasses. She is wearing a blue Hawaiian shirt with lighter blue accents, purple/orange lei around her neck, red mid-length A-line skirt, a smile. Behind/to left side of her, girl hugs her, unreciprocated (Mary Ann's hands both on tray), kisses her on left cheek. Same outfit, a few inches shorter, Asian, hair tied in chignon held by black rubber-tip pencil.]

59 people like this

Mary Ann had been working the Lei'd Back bar, left of the main slots in the big room at the Newport, for almost six months by the time this picture was taken. It was a nice bar, if a bit cramped, with tasteful little round tables and unobtrusively joyful decor. It evoked beachside mai tais and the Maui sunset, and Bloody Marys at dawn on the immaculate beaches of Kauai.

Aunt Karen had worked there herself almost ten years in the 1980s and early '90s, before finally landing a Strip job (albeit at the wildly unfashionable and peripheral Wiles Group Circus Circus). She had maintained enough contacts to all but promise Mary Ann a job if she please please please got herself on a plane and came out here, already. By then, Mary Ann had already overstayed her welcome on her cousin's couch in Batesville, MS, and was really in no position to refuse. Her return to Mississippi after the NYC mess had been a long shot anyway, doomed from the start, and short of actually going back to Jackson to look for whatever was left of her dad, she had already exhausted all possibilities. She let Aunt Karen book her a flight.

The first couple of months had been challenging. Aunt Karen had an extra room in her apartment on Pecos, in East Vegas, but the space was so cluttered with junk that Mary Ann sometimes missed her cousin's couch back in Batesville (the bed before that, she didn't miss at all). Her aunt's hoarding drove Mary Ann crazy: in a house with a sleek-looking home theater and a never-used Blu-ray player, hundreds of unplayable VHS tapes were stashed in hazardous, Jenga-like towers, along with stacks and stacks of old cassettes and records. Her aunt's sweet but obvious plan to keep her busy, assigning her care of the pet python Rodrigo, horribly backfired when the slithery little shit developed stress-related anorexia and pretty much stopped eating entirely, sometimes killing the mouse and leaving it there to rot and stink, sometimes flat-out refusing to have anything to do with mice in the first place. The look of guilt and embarrassment on Aunt Karen's face when the veterinarian mentioned the word *anorexia* was memorable. Mary Ann, who had lately become used to people's misplaced compassion about what they assumed had been her problem, had not given it much thought. But all the same the incident had put a major dent in Operation Back-on-Your-Feet. Finally, after taking its sweet time, Lei'd Back had called.

"Sweetie, this is such a great opportunity," Aunt Karen said six months later, just a few hours after Mary Ann's picture with Lily and the piña coladas was taken. "You know how long it usually takes to get a job on the Strip? And it's such a classy place, real A-listers. It could really be great for you."

They were sitting at a rough wood table, the kind that can be found at rest stops near the mellower hiking trails, inside a new cocktail bar in East Fremont, downtown, the heart of new hipster Vegas. The cocktail list included smoked rosemary Manhattans and some weird concoction of Japanese whisky with rice syrup and sake, but Happy Hour only covered beer and gin and tonics or other basic highballs. Aunt Karen's battered leather jacket could have maybe passed as hipster, if it weren't for the embarrassing Guns N' Roses graphic with the skull in the top hat on the back and the obvious feeling she emanated of being not quite vintage as much as flat-out old. Her fashion sense, like her apartment, seemed stuck in the year she'd moved to Vegas, but in a way that struck Mary Ann as unintentional rather than statement-making. Like, she didn't even notice.

"But what did you tell them about me? I mean, why did I get this interview, if it's so hard?" asked Mary Ann.

"You know I have friends, sweetie," said Aunt Karen. "The shift manager for all the bartenders at the Sportsbook was real good friends with Rick back when we were going out." (Rick having a recurring role in Aunt Karen's stories as her on-and-off boyfriend for a real long time, in what looked like a potential love-of-her-life-type situation she either never fully recovered from or was secretly still in the midst of.) "Rick's friends would never deny me a favor." (Rick sold weed et al.)

"But why don't *you* take it, then, Karen?" asked Mary Ann.

"Because *the Positano*, sweetie. *The Pos.* Center-Strip, five-star shit. They don't hire fifty-year-olds with skin that goes like *this* on their neck, even though I could still run circles around all those girls who've never lifted a tray in their life. But you! They would *scoop you up!*"

Aunt Karen looked a lot like Mary Ann's mom, but she also didn't. Mary Ann couldn't help thinking that the features that had looked lovingly chiseled on her mother looked on Karen like they'd been tossed like a jacket over a bedroom chair. It was the kind of spontaneous observation that Mary Ann caught herself making, a ruthless evaluation of female aesthetics that, she realized, came from not an inflated devotion to beauty but a resigned cynicism, a veteran's indelible awareness of the ways of the world. Karen had always looked, even younger, just some indefinable *something* shy of pretty. It was only when she stood next to her sister that the connection became painfully evident, like when you look at the thin, ghostly pencil lines of a sketch next to the finished painting and realize that yes, I guess that bit there *did* look like a horse's leg, and oh, *that's* what those weblike things were. The sad thing about it, of course, being that the finished canvas had been lost over ten years ago, and the sketch was all that was left for people to make sense of. Her and Mary Ann, who looked even more beautiful than her mom.

"But I like the Lei, Karen, it's okay, it really is. It's very easy work," said Mary Ann.

"You work three shifts a week with no benefits and make peanuts, sweetie. Do you even know how much those girls make? This is Vegas—being a cocktail server at the Pos is like being a surgeon. And waitresses there are union, unlike us bevertainers at the Circus." Mary Ann shrugged, unimpressed, and Aunt Karen's voice dropped to a more serious key. "It's what we do, Mae. We adapt, we find a way to make it work. Little at a time. This town, people like us can find work here—and *keep* it—good, reliable work. That's all there is to it. You take this job, you'd be able to get a nice place in one of those condos by the Strip, where you don't have to feed mice to a snake. Then at the Pos you could meet the right man, the kind wouldn't be caught dead at the Newport. And before you know it, you have a little life for yourself, you know? You've made it *work*."

Her mom used to call her Mae. It always felt strange hearing Karen call her that, but she let her. Mary Ann was so unfair to Karen. She judged her simplistic worldview, the way she'd internalized the narrow perimeter of a woman's life in a city like Vegas. But even so, how could she tell Karen that the one thing she thought her niece should want—love, marriage, sex probably—was something Mary Ann just had no inclination for, at all, and perhaps never really had? (Something else, by the way, that proved she was just irrevocably fucked up as a person, just wired wrong or something.) She needed to redirect the conversation.

"I'm just . . . I'm not too comfortable with all this smiling and looking pretty for the job, you know? Or not yet, maybe."

"It's gonna be fine, sweetie. You are fully qualified. The way you look is a plus, just something to get you through the door. From then on, it's *you* they're gonna love, trust me."

"Yeah, I mean y'all are in for a real treat, guys," said Mary Ann.

"They are, if you hold the sarcasm and smile for fifteen minutes. And maybe if you rehearse your answers for the test a bit."

"What test?"

"It's nothing, a formality, really. It's just that the Pos is so high-class, and they have to do everything by the book."

"What test?" Mary Ann asked again.

"Well, these big-shot hotels require a little talk with a psychiatrist as part of the interview process. But I've talked to people who have taken it, it's like a ten-minute thing, tops."

"Karen."

"Trust me, Mae, please. It's going to be fine. Everybody lies on that thing. *Everybody.*"

Casual Friday! #modellife #NYCmodel

[*Mary Ann on her side on unmade bed, white linen creased and ruffled, no cover or pillows visible. Wears open black shirt buttoned in middle, no bra, black underwear (mostly covered by shirt). Skin looks tanned or darker than usual. Left elbow propped against mattress, left hand holding head upright, waves of dark brown hair running through fingers. She looks directly at camera, no smile, eyes meant to convey all expression, desirability, mystery, sexual voracity. Also looks: young, uncomfortable, sad (?). Photograph is clearly work of professional.*]

428 people like this

New York. All backscrolling ends up in New York. Had she even wanted to be there? Had it been hers, the original impulse that led her into trouble, or was she pressured into it somehow?

She wanted to be an actress, this she remembered for sure. What was the link between herself as a drama major at Ole Miss and the face looking at her from those photos, a face that would appear in *Cosmopolitan*, in *Maxim*, and then at Mount Sinai Beth Israel Hospital on a December night? It wasn't that she had been voted Most Likely to Become Famous in high school in spite of marginal popularity and thankfully unrecorded displays of robot-dancing at socials. It wasn't that she had been a prominent Ole Miss Tri-Delt despite only ever going to the House for the free black bean patties and salads she would eat by herself on the pigeon-infested patio. But somewhere along the way she must have started to want things, really *want* things. To want them like she was entitled. Progression: student, model, actress. In New York, she had given herself rigorous daily schedules in black Moleskine notebooks. Timetables, plans, weight goals. She'd do a photo shoot on Gansevoort in the morning, a shift at Fits to a Tea on the Upper West side in the afternoon, then ride all the way to Battery Park for acting classes and finally back to Astoria to sleep. The facts were simple enough; the feeling seemed impossible to retrace.

Trouble started as a sense of nausea. Her family and friends all seemed to assume her career had taken some kind of downturn. She wasn't getting jobs anymore, they kept hiring younger girls, maybe a Meryl Streep–type director of the modeling agency demanded she lose weight, more weight. Frustration, dysphoria, anorexia of course. But did they bother asking her, really? It had been nothing like that. She *was* booking jobs, decent ones too. She wasn't gonna be rich, no, not a supermodel, but she had a career. Besides, being a model had never been the goal. She had known episodes before, her family history was like an IKEA catalog of them, and that wasn't how any of it worked. It didn't come from the outside. It was all you. The nausea came first, a sense of her body telling her something was wrong. And along with it dread: a sleepy, blank dread that made every stupid little thing seem complicated and useless. Later, when they defined anhedonia for her, she wasn't convinced: they made it sound like laziness. But she knew laziness, and laziness didn't hurt. This was a laziness that hurt. It was like that sense of having forgotten something really important, or the feeling of having made some huge mistake and not knowing what, except it was always there. Everything she did. She got up from bed, and her body seemed to tell her it was wrong. She took the subway, and she felt the dread. She lay on a bed in an unbuttoned black shirt posing for a creepy photographer for a shoot she didn't want to do anyway, and there it was. Progression: bad, worse, the worst.

It's not like she thought she was original, like her way of feeling bad was unique and nobody could grasp it, no. She had never thought that. She just had issues with the blanket definitions they threw at her, until they tired themselves out and signed for the meds. There were doctors in New York that if you agreed to listen to them describe to you how *you* felt for twenty minutes they'd be pretty liberal with the Rx pad after. And when she thought back about her time there, it seemed like all she did by the end was think about how she felt. How was it today? Was it maybe a little bit better than yesterday? Was today the worst of the week or had Monday sucked worse? Mom had been like that too, so definitely she wasn't original at all.

Deleting an Instagram account is surprisingly difficult. Maybe not surprisingly; they don't want you to do it. There's no option in the settings menu, and Mary Ann had to google it; she thought that was probably enough to discourage anybody not really dead set on extricating themselves from the social trap. But she was done with that shit, all of it. Enough. From the Google search page she landed on a separate, almost secret Delete Account page, a page inaccessible from the app. She was just a click away. Isn't it ridiculous? Even when you've made it so clear that you want out, they're still trying to keep you in: "If you're just looking to take a break, you can always <u>temporarily disable</u> your Instagram account instead."

The afternoon when Mary Ann deleted all her social media, she went out to take pictures of the Strip before her shift. Walter, who she would see tonight, had been suggesting she "cultivate a creative outlet" for some time. It might be New Age bullshit, but it did stand to reason that if she hoped to feel better and finally turn a psychic corner, having interests of her own would be a necessary stepping stone. At least he hadn't called it "self-care." She had never thought of it before, but now that she felt free of those pictures of herself, she realized she actually enjoyed photographs. Of places, people that weren't her. Photos she wouldn't *post*. So she went out.

She wanted to take pictures of the Strip during the day, when the lights were doused and the buildings weren't wearing any makeup. She decided that if she couldn't find a way to make the place look beautiful without the neons and the colors, then a strong argument could be made that the place really wasn't beautiful at all. That it only *looked* beautiful through lies, tricks of light, and low visibility. After over a year living in Las Vegas, she hoped to find something she actually liked beneath all the fake, to reach some kind of personal understanding with her new home. That'd be a start, at least.

As she got near them, the casinos seemed to lie along the Strip like a troupe of actors who've gotten drunk after rehearsal and fallen asleep on couches and rugs, boring, explicit sunlight revealing the cheapness of their doublets and corsets. The colors had the blandness of scorched metal, the reds and greens of the night fading into tired browns and yellows. Maybe she would throw in some Hefe filter after all.

The first annoying thing about being flagged as suicidal after a failed attempt is that there's no way to tell the truth. Or rather, you can try, say that you are almost definitely sure that you really hadn't meant to, really, that all you felt was a deep, stronger-than-anything-before desire to be sedated, nonthinking, finally not wanting and not hurting. You can try, and Mary Ann had tried. But it seemed like every time, people assumed that she was lying. That this was exactly what someone who really *had* meant to would say. Which was infuriating, really. Plus pretty much everybody, medical or not, with the exception of the two MDs she'd talked to in the psych ward in NYC in the days following the incident, had readily jumped to the anorexic-model conclusion with a lack of attention to what she was actually saying over and over that she found quite scary. Why listen and try to understand, when you could just settle for the nearest cause-and-effect cliché you could find?

To accommodate the needs of the ever-congested car traffic, pedestrian crossing at street level was severely limited on the Strip. Aside from a couple of hazardously brief green lights, tourists were required to use the ubiquitous overpasses to get from side to side: escalator-serviced turrets that appeared at every corner, projecting skeletal white bridges across the street.

The resulting elevation, coupled with the ability to stand still in the middle of the Las Vegas Strip without being run over or yelled at, turned the over-passes into magical places where people ended up spending a lot more time than what was required by simple point A —> point B. Phone in hand, Mary Ann leaned on the glass railing and watched as sober groups of tourists arranged themselves in drunken disorder to take pictures against a questionable architectural backdrop. Frozen drinks in Eiffel Tower–shaped plastic containers were proudly displayed. Tongues outstretched. Breasts occasionally bared.

The second annoying thing about being permanently marked as suicidal is that well-intentioned people around you seem to assume that the fact you're alive should be enough of an accomplishment to call yourself happy. That after that, any kind of dream or ambition or desire you had or still have is put in perspective, and as such is forever to be considered a very optional cherry-on-top. Which is real bad, because if you are the kind of depressive who's not only able to experience longish stretches of being okay but also maybe feels like she really might be out of the woods this time, for real, then all those desires and dreams of more than just day-to-day endur-ance *will* pop up again, and when they do, they'll make you feel like there's something fundamentally wrong with you, like you're an ingrate and an awful person. And so the whole well-intentioned attitude of just helping you settle in a routine of reliable small things and "making it work" may not really be helping a lot. Meaning: clinically depressed people and even allegedly (once-)suicidal people are still going to have dreams and ambi-tions and are still going to be childish about it. And they kind of have a right to, don't they? Which is something that Mary Ann had tried to explain several times to several well-intentioned people before finally giving up and starting to lie about either her past or her future.

She walked the bridge to about two-thirds of its length, then stopped and turned her gaze and phone camera to the right. Out back, the Positano sprawled along the Strip in the unruly shapes of nature, more landscape than architecture, its peaceful sea shimmering in the desert sunset. Farther north, the shield-shaped amber of the Wiles Tower, hit by the descending sun, reflected a single ray that swiped the Positano like a tender stroke of light. Mary Ann tapped the screen.

She would be fine. It would get better now. She had made it through. It was okay that she still wasn't *happy*, it was okay that she wasn't even sure she liked the town, or her new job, or her new empty apartment. The laziness that doesn't hurt is okay to live with. Her life could still be *good*. Most people she knew were terrified of the meds, like meds would change them, they wouldn't be *themselves*. Like they were so precious and great to begin with that they needed to be preserved in their original, unadulterated form. She could never see what the big deal was, really. Of course she was still *herself* (too much herself, according to Walter). It was just the same. And really, how fucking spoiled by life must you be to think emotional numbness is a *bad* thing?

It would get better now.

Soon she would walk to the end of the bridge and enter one of the connecting galleries between the hotels. And she would walk the large hallways inside the hollow hills, peering out of large windows from one of the fake overlook houses to see the waters underneath. And in no more than seven minutes she would reach the staff changing room and slip into her black miniskirted uniform. And through more hallways inside what looks like nature from the bridge, and through the neon-lit darkness of the casino floors, she would reach the Scarlatti Lounge and begin her shift. She was excited to tell Walter about her day.

Interlude II

(the story of a neighborhood)

Gentrification in Las Vegas was impossible and inevitable. With the coming of age of a large population of second-generation locals, coupled with up-and-coming UNLV luring more and more young nongamblers in town, an arts-and-crafts district with password-protected speakeasies, home-brewing festivals, and kale salads had soon become all but a necessity. People needed their almond milk. Yet the town's very nature, the 24/7 tackiness of the Strip for the tourists and the quiet suburbs peppered with strip malls for the rest, seemed to work against it. The first attempts, sad little specialty coffee shops around the UNLV campus in the half-developed east side of town, where the financial crisis had hit the hardest, never amounted to more than college hangouts. Men in checkered shirts and long beards who looked weirdly old to be students diligently stared at the screens of their MacBook Airs, but the feeling just wasn't there.

It took the help of the only Vegas-born Silicon Valley billionaire, Zach Romero, founder and CEO of market-leading gift-making-and-shipping service Gifty, to turn a town's hipster dreams into reality. After years mining social media profiles with its gift-matching algorithm, Gifty had become more or less the international standard for gift outsourcing. Now, on the brink of Fortune 500–ness, the company was ready to take the next step, moving to a location where space was not an issue, and stocking and handling could be expanded with virtually no limits. The slogans practically wrote themselves: the old and reliable "It's the thought that counts. Let us take care of the rest" was quickly paired with "What happens in Vegas travels anywhere you want" (image of very recognizable brown-paper-wrapped martini glass with a decorative umbrella and mail tag to Greenville, NC) and "From Sin City, with all our love" (image of unwrapped pink box opening to reveal smaller heart-shaped chocolate box and pair of black five-inch stilettos). A few bloggers at TechCrunch.com cynically pointed out the advantages of relocating "way the fuck away" from the Bay Area's surging prices, but Vegas locals never doubted that this was a gift to them. A gift from Gifty. And as soon as the company headquarters and all subsidiary facilities were moved en masse from Emeryville, California, to the run-down and by now sort of sketchy streets around the old downtown, anything became possible. Investments poured in to renovate the garish old casinos of Fremont Street (now rebranded the "Fremont Street Experience"), while the low buildings and miserable parking lots around it were quickly turned into the cool district of "East Fremont." Reports of quinoa sightings multiplied. Drinks meant to be sipped instead of chugged became socially acceptable. Dilapidated pawnshops turned into kitschy-but-cool Pawn Museums. Witty one-liners appeared in chalk on small blackboards outside craft beer and tapas bars.

With Gifty blazing the desert trail, it was only natural that a number of small-but-ambitious startups would soon follow. A VR-based transcendental meditation app called HappyPlace; a single-dog-parents dating app called Woofer; a coding bootcamp called DCS (Desert Coding School), whose biannual yield of skilled young graduates boosted the appearance of several Bay Area–style startup incubators, which in turn increased the demand for available real estate. Soon North Vegas was a place people *moved to*, instead of ending up there at the tail end of a weekend of debauchery, yelling at a diner waitress. It grew an identity of its own. The neighborhood was suddenly alive.

The Newport, however—the dusty hotel and casino where Mary Ann had her first job in Las Vegas—found itself just a couple of blocks north of this unprecedented gold rush. The Gold Rush too, its sister hotel. They had sadly both been built in the 1970s, just outside the Fremont Street Experience, in a derelict area of downtown right off the I-515. It was a grim-looking, depressingly overpassed block that no amount of bohemian flair was ever going to salvage. Hipsters wouldn't go there to park their cars. Yet to its affectionate clientele, the Newport (/Gold Rush) was not just the most beautiful hotel in Vegas: it was the only one. After over a decade languishing as a cut-rate alternative to the already cut-rate hotels downtown, management had cleverly reinvented the property to suit the needs of a specific, small but loyal niche: Hawaiian tourists. Floral motifs appeared. Pineapples were purchased in bulk. In a matter of a few years, close to 90 percent of all Las Vegas visitors coming from the Eight Islands stayed at the Newport, thanks to advantageous flight+hotel deals secured in collaboration with charter airlines and even flagship company Hawaiian Airlines. A last-ditch marketing move unexpectedly developed into a real community, with real-life Hawaiian immigrants moving to the desert to open tiki bars and Maui-style barbecues. They even had a name for it: Las Vegas had become the "Ninth Island."

Just north of the classic Vegas casinos of Fremont, and northwest of the small web of streets taken over by Silicon Valley nerds, Vegas's own Hawaiian district was by choice unpretentious and peripheral. It never tried to win over the hipster crowds with trendy ahi poke bowls in shabby-chic bars, but contented itself with serving oxtail soup to real Hawaiians in actually shabby casino food courts. It was a real, local, unflashy alternative to Fremont, which was itself a real, local, unflashy alternative to the Strip. Real exclusivity in Las Vegas always a matter of doing less than.

3

Ray

As with many iconic, tourist-intensive places in the world, common knowledge about Las Vegas tends to crystallize around a handful of nicknames and fixed adages. "Sin City." "America's Playground." "Lost Wages." These snippets of coagulated wisdom mostly serve as experiential guidance for travelers; they provide them with reassurance that they are enjoying the city exactly as it's meant to be enjoyed, that they are not missing out on some crucial part of their expensive holiday fun. The most famous of these is naturally "What happens in Vegas stays in Vegas," a real crowd favorite despite truistic logic and, at the same time, complete inaccuracy (Las Vegas being a contender for most Instagrammed, Snapchatted, tweeted, and otherwise recorded location worldwide). What it promises is the mirage of a life away from one's daily, boring self, an escape into an avatar whose actions, no matter how outlandish, and alcohol-fueled, and adulterous, are reliably and permanently consequence-free. It is an invite: come to Vegas, leave yourself at home.

Perhaps lesser known is the old saying "This town wasn't built on winners." This one is usually deployed as a consolation tactic, a sometimes affectionate and sometimes ironic there-there to the fresh victim of gambler's remorse, and in all its curt cynicism, it does have the advantage of being true. *Don't worry*, it says to the guilt-ridden tourist awakening to dehydration, headache, and dread of poverty, *it's all part of the game.* This is Vegas; what you lost was the price of your fun.

Yet if the whole town had in fact not been excavated, erected, and miraculously provided with water for the advantage of winners, it sure as hell looked to Ray like the high-limit poker room at the Pos contained a whole lot of them all the time. Save for the few hours every night during which nobody was playing (usually between four and nine a.m., though this oscillated a lot—often play stopped much earlier, sometimes it never did), it seemed like it'd be impossible to enter the living-room-sized space upstairs at any time without finding there anywhere between five and twenty young professionals, smiling, chatting, *winning.*

Upstairs was where the real money was. They called it "upstairs" out of implicit reverence, a silent nod to the distinction between ordinary tables and high-stakes, but it was actually just two steps separating the elevated space in the top-right corner from the rest of the room. Above the decorated opaque glass of the screens, a no-nonsense black-on-white inscription simply read "High-Limit Poker," and that was it. It was what he had come here for: the room where the best live pros made their money, day in and day out, twelve months a year.

It was his third day in Las Vegas, and Ray had yet to play a single hand of poker.

Each day so far he had put his name on the waiting list (kept by staff with aristocratic pen and paper, while the downstairs tables obeyed the whims of an automatic seating software called Maestro) and waited. Observing the higher-stakes games was generally discouraged, but being on the waiting list to play seemed to provide him the credentials he needed to loiter a bit. There they were, all of them, young, with the conspicuous looks and attitude of the lifetime poker winner, unmistakable in their expertise before Ray even saw them play a hand, sitting at the elongated oval of the nine-seat table and sliding their chips across the orange baize to bet or call, craning their necks to look at their two hole cards under the protective cup of their left hand: reg, reg, reg, reg, maybe spot[1]?, reg, reg, reg, reg he recognized from Facebook as a successful tournament player. For the first two days of his waitlisted spectatorship, the ratio had never gone above 7:2, more often 8:1.

This he had sort of expected. In spite of the haughtiness with which online players dismiss live poker as online's dimwitted uncle, he knew that wherever large amounts of money were in play, professionals abounded. It would have been naive to imagine anything different.

Still, he had fled. Twice. His name finally top of the waiting list, he had felt a familiar anxiety resurface, the same paralyzing fear that had left him sitting at his desk in his Toronto apartment, mouse in hand, staring blankly at his dual thirty-inch monitors, watching others play. Contemplating the impending Tragedy. He had felt it surge again through him, and without much thinking had rushed back down and out, down the two steps and out into the gaming pits, out toward the lobby and self-park and home. Speed-walking among the rows of dead-eyed seniors rusting at the slots, making and losing his way through the seemingly tesseract-shaped layout of the casino, he had finally emerged out of the Pos feeling almost physically sick.

But not today, he thought. He was waiting, sitting at one of the empty tables,[2] making sure to spend enough time scrolling on his phone so he wouldn't look weird, but close enough to glance at the action. In the room's low lighting, the speakeasy glow that fills space and dims vision, the sound of colliding poker chips was constant and ubiquitous, a dull clatter in the background. Far above Ray's head, the coffered ceiling was dotted like a scatter plot by the dark bulbs of the eye-in-the-sky cameras. Not today. Today he would play. He battled a feeling of disgust as he watched the

---

1 *Spot* being the technical term, carefully whispered among pros (or "regs"), for what was once known as "the sucker." A somewhat gentler synonym for the openly derogatory *fish*, the proper politically correct equivalent of which is *rec* (short for "recreational player").

2 The five tables in the high-limit area were almost never full outside peak-season events such as Superbowl Weekend, March Madness, and, of course, the World Series of Poker in June.

dealer, center-table in the cornflower-blue satin shirt, spread the three communal cards of a flop.[3] While his brain evaluated the resulting texture,[4] defining ranges, optimal balance, frequencies, his stomach groaned and twisted. He tried hard to ignore it. Today he *had* to play. He had to play to stave off Tragedy.

When Carol, the smartly dressed fiftysomething floorwoman, finally spoke his name into the microphone—"Twenty-five/Fifty No Limit Hold'em: RAY. Ray, I got a seat for ya, Twenty-five/Fifty No Limit Hold'em"—he made his way to seat 3 with the apologetic tiptoe of a late house-party guest looking around the room for a familiar face. He was glanced at, briefly, as he sat down, but the arrival of yet another reg, which he so obviously was, hardly constituted news here. Early twenties, casual clothing, inquisitive brown eyes, a shy demeanor about his thin, short frame: he looked just like any other pro. The player directly to his left, seat 4, yellow-haired and sturdily built and with arms so short Ray wondered if he could reach far enough to collect his chips when he won a pot, offered a quick nodding *hey*, while seat 2, head bobbing slightly to the music from his high-end German headphones, didn't seem to register his arrival at all. Both were sitting with massive stacks of chips,[5] as was the intimidatingly huge jock in seat 8, while the rest of the players at the table, including the toupee-wearing, golf-cap-sporting middle-aged spot in seat 5, all played

---

3 In Texas Hold'em poker, every player is dealt two facedown cards ("hole cards"), followed by three communal cards ("flop"), a fourth ("turn"), and finally a fifth ("river"). Bets are allowed at every step, the winning hand resulting from the best five-card combination that each player can make.

4 Poker-geek jargon for the composition of a flop (high cards, low cards, cards closely "connected," like 7 8 9, or spread far apart, like K 7 2, etc.). Ranges, balance, and frequencies are fairly advanced concepts relating to the so-called game theory optimal (GTO) approach to poker.

5 While alternative strategies exist, 100 big blinds are usually considered the minimum amount it makes sense to sit down with (so $5,000 for a $25/$50 game), 200bbs being the usual average choice. In high-stakes games, where there is no set maximum buy-in, some Vegas professionals choose to sit down with extremely large stacks; this is part status signaling, part unspoken challenge to the rec player to keep up and match their buy-in. A trap of sorts.

between $5,000 and $15,000. Ray slowly stacked $10,000 in chips on the felt in front of him and waited for his first hand.

He folded: 7 of clubs, 2 of hearts (in pokerspeak, 72 off-suited, or "off").

It is a common misconception that professional poker is at its heart a game of reading people; that knowing the opponent to the point of guessing the cards they hold is the ultimate goal to pursue. In reality, while the so-called exploit-ative approach[6] does offer certain advantages, proper math-based poker is essentially a quest for perfect play, an ever-elusive game theory optimal (GTO) strategy that transcends the need to adapt to a specific opponent, always profitable (or at the very least break-even) against anybody. In other words, Ray wasn't at all worried about playing new, unknown opponents. It wasn't their confidence, their status as house veterans, or their money that induced in him the sense of gastric hollowness he was trying to combat with green tea, courtesy of the miniskirted solicitude of an M-starting name-tagged cocktail waitress he had thanked and tipped without daring to look up at her face. No, Ray's battle, as always, was against himself. His brain, his decisions, the dauntingly smooth surface of mathematical perfection.

He folded: K5 off.

He folded: Q2 suited (Q of spades, 2 of spades).

He folded his big blind: 82 off.

---

6   Based on the detection of patterns and mistakes, or "leaks," in an opponent's play.

The first hand he finally did play was a big bluff. He raised $150 from the small blind with KJ off and was called by the plump reg in the big blind. The flop was Q 8 6 rainbow (all different suits). He bet $100, big blind called. The turn was a 10, which gave Ray's KJ an open-ended straight draw.[7] He bet $500, the size of the pot, and his opponent quickly called. Ray looked at the dealer's hands as he slowly, with a bit of flourish, turned over the river card. A card is just a card, he thought; it makes no difference whether I make the straight or not. Artificial intelligence wouldn't be rooting for a 9 or an A here, it would just be processing the right move for every possible river. But yet he did hope. There was $1,500 already in the pot. The river was a jack. While Ray now technically had a pair, his two jacks were most likely worthless against an opponent who had called his flop and turn bets. He knew as soon as he saw it: with the hand he had, the perfect play here was to bluff *big*.

Seat 4 was staring at him, like all live players do, in hope of gaining information through some physical tell. The whole idea was laughably primitive to a player of Ray's proficiency, but that didn't solve his problem. He hesitated, not for fear of getting called and losing the money but in silent, dreadful anticipation of going over this hand in postgame analysis and finding it flawed, imperfect. Right and wrong were useless old concepts, smelling of sin and judgment and all that sort of nonsense, but optimal and suboptimal terrified him. He reached for three of the yellow chips resting on top of his stack and released them across the betting line. He had bet $3,000, twice the size of the pot.

How he hated himself. Years of playing, millions of hands, endless hours in pursuit of a perfect machinelike neutrality toward outcomes, of a complete, productive concentration on the process of decision-making. Result-oriented poker is the death of a poker player, he used to say; result-oriented thinking is the death of all rational thinking. But as he waited for his opponent to make his decision, to fold and offer him a $750 profit, to

---

7   He would make a straight with an ace on the river (10 J Q K A) or with a 9 (9 10 J Q K).

call and deliver him a $3,750 loss, there he was, staring blankly into the space in front of him, wondering, hoping, human.

Seat 4 folded.

Ray knew better than to feel good. The very idea of playing cash games professionally hinged on the ability to ignore individual wins and losses. No one hand mattered, no one *day* ever mattered. Everything had to be transient, everything was noise; the game was the only signal, the way his choices fared against theoretical perfection the only meaningful measure. Besides, if you start allowing yourself to feel happy after a good hand, how do you stop yourself from feeling terrible after a big loss? And if Ray was still far from perfect when it came to ignoring the sadness of losing, he was a very accomplished professional at denying himself the pleasure of winning.

"I almost called, you know?" said seat 4. The hunt for free information. But also: the information he himself was unwillingly handing out. *Result-oriented.*

"I see," said Ray, uncomfortable in spite of his sense of superiority.

"It's always interesting when someone new makes a big bet early on, you know?" seat 4 continued. "You start thinking like 'Would he make a big bluff right away?' but also like 'What if he thinks that I think he wouldn't make a big bluff on the first hand, and so he bluffs?' you know?"

Ray said nothing. These people had no idea, no idea at all. *Feel players.* They had made their money, a lot of money from the looks of it, playing live against retired lobbyists and real estate developers and bookies; they had guessed their way to the high stakes, made millions on a hunch, but they had no idea. This was the way they thought about poker: *What if he thinks that I think he wouldn't make a big bluff.* What an idiot. It's a good thing they probably think I'm one of them, he thought, a good thing they also have no idea who I am.

"My name is Logan, by the way," said the feel player, open hand extended forward, the little he could.

"I'm Ray."

"How long are you in Vegas for?" asked Logan.

"I just moved here," said Ray.

It was unclear if this last remark had piqued his attention, or whether he had been listening the whole time and Ray was only now noticing, but the broad-shouldered, steroidally buff reg in seat 8 had freed his left ear from the acoustic isolation of his earplugs and was observing their exchange with a disapproving look. He stared at Ray without turning his head toward him, eyes strenuously left-leaning, lips pursed.

"That's cool," said Logan. "Where from?"

"Northern Cali, Marin County," said Ray. A cautious half-lie, just to be safe.

"Well, welcome to fabulous Las Vegas then, VFlnd3r. You're gonna love it here!"

When Matthew Wong, perfectly unperspiring and seemingly untired from their monumental Thanksgiving five-setter, head tilted down in age-appropriate if out-of-character sheepishness, ping-pong paddle still in hand in the now-empty basement after the children had managed to get the dog back upstairs, walked up to Ray in the covenant of postmatch gregariousness asking for career advice, Ray had to work hard to stifle a laugh. They were in his father's house, after all; his father, the professional career counselor.

"You've got the wrong Jackson, Mr. Wong," said Ray, in his best Indiana Jones impression. "Why don't you try my father?"

"This is different—I don't want to hear 'Find out what really makes you happy,'" said Matthew, daring to mock his host in his own home. "I just want to make a lot of money, like you."

It may have been a winner's benevolence at work, but Ray was starting to warm up to the kid. It took some guts to talk that way, out of pure, uncoated adolescent desire and ambition. He may have been an irritating adversary and an unpleasant houseguest, but his heart was clearly in the right place.

"I should have made much more, believe me," parried Ray. "And anyway it's too late to get into poker now."

"So what should I do?"

Turns out Ray *was* the right Jackson to ask.

"I mean, take a look at what's happening in the world," he started, sitting down with professorial gravity on a cardboard box, he too paddle-in-hand, playing a round of invisible ping-pong for emphasis. "Look at any field you like, any business. It's pretty clear that the strongest trend in the last say fifteen years has been the systematic application of real hardcore math to everything that used to be done empirically, using experience and, like, having-done-something-over-and-over"—paddle moving in circles, a series of minimal backhands—"as the key approach to getting it right.

"All those play-by-feel types who thought themselves good at what they did and made a bunch of money off it, but were too lazy or too plain dumb to *really study it*; if you asked them, they'd tell you that's just how you do things. Marketing copywriters: thought they knew what people wanted because they had a mediocre statistical survey and this kind of *feel* for what the right slogan was. And they did all right, I mean they were better than most. Or taxi companies, booksellers, movie studios. All pretty decent at their jobs, because they'd done it so many times and nobody else had, and up until our parents' generation, that was more than enough.

"But then, bam!"—forehand topspin in the air—"Big Data marketing, and Uber, and Amazon, and Netflix, algorithms for everything, math everywhere, and they blew the competition out of the water. A real fucking hostile takeover of the nerds." Backhand slam.

"You sound like a Silicon Valley VC," said a snickering Matthew Wong, who apparently just couldn't help being a dick, regardless of the correct placement of his heart.

"It's not just Silicon Valley, Matt." He called him Matt now, in the heat of his lecture. "It's everywhere. This is the world now, this is the real effect the internet has had on society—real market meritocracy—it just took a while for it to manifest. Because if all information is available at any time, it also means that everything you say and do in business has to be able to, like, withstand serious trial. And the competition is *huge*.

"If you have a business and want to be at the top of your industry, you can't just wing it based on experience and on your-daddy-having-done-this-job-for-fifty-years, because (a) nobody cares and (b) someone somewhere will be smart enough and have enough time on their hands to prove you wrong, outsmart you, and put you out of business for good. We are completely nerdifying the business world. Maybe the world in general."

"We?" asked Matt. Sarcasm-free, sounded like.

"Well, I and others have done it with poker, yeah, exactly that," said Ray, returning an imaginary serve with a defensive backhand chop.

"And what about me? How should I do it?"

Which was his original question: How do I make a lot of money?

"Look, these are just *bubbles*. Poker was a bubble, and not even a big one. There's more, there are others. Granted, they're probably growing fewer and fewer by the day, but they still exist. It is our mission, it's what we do. We go to war against the feel players. We call them out on their bullshit, we call their bluffs. We compete, we play fair, and we win. You want to make a bunch of money? Find a field that's still ruled by feel players and go GTO on their asses. Nerdify it. There's gotta be some left."

The day after his first session, Ray resolved to drive to the Pos early in the morning. So early, in fact, that upon leaving his apartment he found himself waiting at the gate behind the obtrusive volume of a school bus picking up the neighborhood children, a sight that struck him as uniquely bizarre for a town like Vegas, but which he found oddly soothing, decidedly untragic. He made a mental note of the time. (It's in those early days in a new town,

Ray knew, that our disoriented brain turns to pattern recognition in search of comfort, and every little gesture acquires the potential to morph into habit, the habit into ritual.)

The apartment he had rented was on the upper level of a duplex in a nice residential complex in Spring Valley, west of the Strip; a gated community with small irregularly shaped swimming pools, a sparsely equipped gym, and security guards bicycling around the quiet streets encircling the houses. It was a large one-bedroom with fluffy carpeting, good Wi-Fi, and an overall prevalence of beige, a reasonable enough choice for a town surrounded by a desert. On the outside, it was basically indistinguishable from the other apartments if not for a bronze mailbox in the shape of a smug-faced owl, which gave a satisfying bong when Ray patted it on the head.

Out of the gate and past the web of driveway-lined residential streets, he made a left on Tropicana. He was not going to give this leftover anxiety any more thought. He had felt fine yesterday, getting up from seat 3 after his first session as a Vegas reg, professionally unfazed by the monetary loss his nine hours at the table had yielded, confident, calm. Sure, he had not anticipated the added pressure of having to live up to his own screen name and reputation (which that snoop Logan, albeit a know-nothing feel player, had somehow dug up through obscure Facebook triangulations before he even sat down to play, as it turned out). And sure, his first live table had hardly been the recreational-player free-for-all he had envisioned as a beacon of hope from his Canadian Fortress of Solitude. But none of this had seemed to matter as he got up and replied to Logan's see-you-tomorrow, and as he quickly looked away after meeting for a moment the hostile stare darting at him from seat 8 (the Navy Seal–looking reg, who was called Bryan, he'd learned through certain triangulations of his own).

The night, however, had been a different story. Sitting cross-legged on his bed, hunched over his laptop in the well-known position of the dying lotus, he had spent hours staring at the minimal gray interface of Postflop Solver, the $1,990 game theory software no online pro worth his salt could live without, reviewing hands from the day. Mistakes. A river call against the table's spot he could have easily avoided. Suboptimal decisions. A big pot against Bryan, where he had folded his missed draw on the river but should clearly have bluffed all-in. Even his first bluff against Logan, a shameful display of mathematical imprecision. By the end of it, he'd had to shut his laptop, shaking with an anger he had never known in the days of his poker triumphs. This wasn't working. Whatever it was that he was trying to do by swapping mouse clicks for clay chips and round-cornered cards and cocktail waitresses you couldn't even bring yourself to look at wasn't working. It had been one day, and just a few really big hands, and one hand *never* mattered, one day was *never* important. But what if his mistakes were not an accident? What if he was slipping, what if something was broken and couldn't be put back together again? What if VFlnd3r had been the accident, his entire poker career the result of a combination of weak competition in the early days of poker and his own monumental, undeserved, fraudulent luck? Months and months of recursive thoughts exploded back into his head again: the Chinese water torture of loss upon loss upon loss, the exponential acceleration of his doubts and fears in his last playing days, his final, immobile contemplation of the imminence of Tragedy. Sleep had been brief, and fraught with dreams of ping-pong.

He was determined not to think about it today. He made a left on Rainbow, prettily brick-walled and quiet, then a right onto traffic-heavy Flamingo. He looked around: to the sides of the road, residential areas were splayed at a comfortable distance from one another, arranged with an orthogonal ease that, Ray found, suited his desire for morning calm. Everything seemed spacious, unconstricted, free to breathe. It was the ordinary-looking magic of architecture with too much room. Even the strip malls, aggregated centers of all southwestern human activity, lazed along Flamingo like the zeroes on Riemann's line, far apart, their buildings short and wide. No need to build up, just spread out some more. Only the buildings on the Strip, appearing at a distance in their unilluminated morning quiet, looked huddled up together, almost touching. But that, Ray thought, was just because they'd agreed on a small parcel of land that was worth more than the identical land next to it, artificially creating the cramped space that begets great architecture.

He parked his car and walked past the hotel lobby, where a crew of yellow-hatted men were disassembling Fall, the maples and oaks and pumpkins and squirrels and heartwarming colors of the falling leaves, and getting ready to install a snowy Christmas village. In the farthest corners of the yet interseasonal room, isolated groups of tourists posed for last pictures amid the residual foliage, progressively cordoned off by visibly annoyed staff. The poker room was on the opposite side of the casino tesseract, all the way across a labyrinth of dimly lit corridors designed to confuse and disorient. It was one of the well-known ploys casinos developed to trap their visitors in a state of suspended will: first, discourage the thought of going home by dissolving time (the no-clocks, no-windows rule); then make it physically hard to, by stretching space beyond the confines of Euclidean geometry. At least that's what it felt like to Ray, whose mind today begged for the simplicity of light and linear space. And maybe a winning day.

"It's a whole 'nother skill-set, being out here," said Logan, silk-shirted and gray-blazered and wearing the kind of pointed leather shoes Ray's mother said were only good if you needed to squish a spider in a corner. "You gotta be good at different things. You might be great at all the numbers and the stats and whatever you guys use, but sometimes out here it's more important to know the difference between a Hublot and an Audemars Piguet," he said, pointing at the octagon of dark steel resting on his left wrist, the intricate maze of wheels and springs fully visible in a way that, Ray thought, made it quite challenging to tell the time. "You know?"

They were sitting at an empty table upstairs, Ray eating complimentary breakfast from one of the large, white-clothed, show-offish trays the hotel's room service delivered food on (three-egg omelette with fruit and a bowl of oatmeal), Logan "just hanging."

At the table next to them—number 14, always the first one to fill up by virtue of the privacy afforded by the large glass screens—five sulky regs were playing an almost parodically slow game of waiting-for-a-spot poker. That Bryan dude, the Asian reg who had been seat 2 yesterday, the Euro tourney player Ray had recognized without remembering his name, and two more he hadn't seen before who couldn't pass for spots if they tried, with their bored expressions and backpacks and baseball caps.

The rules of a full-reg game are simple: the table must never be full (so the spot can instantly sit down), play must never break (so the spot sees a game running instead of five vultures in German headphones just waiting for him/her), and, of course, nobody really wants to lose. The result was a weirdly tense atmosphere, where even a short bathroom break would be seen as treacherous and play slowed down to bare-minimum speed; the game would break very fast if, deep down, each of the professionals involved didn't hold the strong, secret, delusional belief of being the best, the only one for whom playing this hard, high-variance table really made any sense. *Why are the others not quitting?* they were all wondering; *If they don't leave, why should I? I'm the only one who would make money in the long run here.*

Ray, who in his day had battled[8] more than his fair share, and who could honestly say he probably really *was* the best player in the room right now, was too inexperienced in live poker to pick up on the elaborate game of chicken that was taking place next to him, and kept eating and listening to Logan's preachings and ignoring wardrobe-chested Bryan's not-at-all-friendly stares. If he had known, he could have illustrated at length the game theory implications both of the actual game of chicken and of the even more interesting group dynamic at play here. But he didn't know.

"Really rich people," said Logan, "they don't want to think about the money. It's not just vulgar to them, it's *boring*. There's this whale who used to come here, the man won a fucking Nobel Prize in economics, ran a national bank too or something like that. This one time he lost a million *in a month*. People like that, money is not why they're here, and if the regs remind them of it too often, they leave. They're after the competition, the challenge, maybe just the fun. The money is incidental. But this is true only

---

8 Online jargon for pro-only, devilishly tough games.

of the really rich spots, the whales.[9] Your average spot *will* care about money, and you should learn to recognize that. Do you know your watches?" he asked. Ray didn't. "I didn't think so. I shouldn't even be telling you these things, but I like you, you know? Mr. Value Finder, am I right? Honestly, I think you'll crush here, I do. See all those guys? They're all hoping you don't sit down with them: they know you're better."

Logan's friendliness had a purely vectorial urgency: it wasn't so much an exchange as a one-way stream of electricity that seemed to need nothing in return. Ray, conversationally impaired by a mouthful of oatmeal, felt that he hadn't really done anything to deserve it, but was by nature very welcoming of no-strings-attached praise, which he regarded as the only form worth his attention.

"A watch is the most surefire way to tell how much money someone really has," Logan went on. "Granted, it's not one hundred percent effective, but it's always your best bet." He introduced the difference between various materials, designs, movements, and explained to Ray how any idiot can wear an Omega, and any idiot with some taste a Rolex Submariner, but that it takes the kind of money you can't fake to be sporting a different Audemars every day (he himself had five, he mentioned in passing), or a Patek Philippe, or a Richard Mille (if you swing that way). "Because ultimately," he concluded, with the serious tone of the teacher reaching the conceptual core of the lecture, "the golden rule of poker, and of life, is that everybody has a lot less money than you would think."

This Ray knew. All phenomenally fast ascents to poker stardom involve a degree of recklessness and disregard for risk-of-ruin projections the mere thought of which now made Ray shudder, but which Stanford-Ray had possessed in spades. You had to play big, bigger than you could afford. Of course, for every VFlnd3r who made it, there was a whole cemetery of nameless failures: players who had flirted with danger just

---

9   As in "big fish," get it?

like him, but had been less good or less lucky or both. They sold insurance now, or worked at their parents' car dealership, their noms-de-guerre forever forgotten in the dusty corners of the internet. Survivorship bias at its best.

But the dirty little secret to phenomenally fast ascents to poker stardom was that, a lot of the time, these newborn stars didn't actually end up having *that* much money. There just hadn't been enough time. Sure, they had enough to play high stakes and almost never ask for the price of their day-to-day expenses; but still they were the proverbial grasshopper, and their working-ant counterparts, slowly and patiently trudging up the ladder to the top, always wound up having saved much, *much* more. And if, for example, one of these stars were to enter a horrific losing stretch at the big games, and lose confidence, and maybe after that find himself suddenly unable to play due to AI-induced mistake-dread, such star would most likely find his net worth thinning to the point of maybe not urgent financial worry, but of a fairly stringent no-more-room-for-fuckups scenario.

"Are you going to play today?" asked Ray. Logan's sitting posture, the angles of his knees a bit more obtuse than advisable, a good portion of his lower back touching the seat of the chair, contrasted with the primness of his outfit considerably.

"Nah, I don't really play much these days. I'm just waiting for some friends to go to lunch together," said Logan.

"You don't play much?"

"No, man, this game gets boring, you know? I mean, of course you know, you've played like a billion hands." Logan chuckled. "Have you thought about what you'll do after poker?"

Ray had. He had thought and thought about it. After poker was a void, a humiliating defeat, a dishonorable discharge from the last clear-cut source of validation he had left. It was a leap into an unknown where he would have to prove himself anew, and perhaps fail. He had worried and obsessed over it. He had thought about it enough to eventually lump the whole multifaceted terror under the label of "Tragedy." The whole point of this morning was *not* to think about it.

"Not really," he said.

"I guess you online wizards can just think about it later," said Logan, "you'll always land on your feet with that brain of yours. *Us*, we need to work at it."

Ray finished his breakfast. At table 14, the M-starting-named cocktail waitress was going around dropping off little clocktower-shaped Fiji waters. Safely at a distance, Ray could finally look at her, confirming his impression from the day before: she was, in fact, the brand of beauty a guy like him would do well to erase from his mental image folder as soon as she landed there. Her white hand brushing auburn strands from her forehead, her thin lips parting in a smile that sent delicate, lovely waves to the hazelnuts of her eyes, gave her the air of refinement that no doubt had convinced an army of less-rational men that she was a discreet beauty, the kind that requires particular sensitivity to be able to appreciate. Perfect, but approachable, perhaps even *attainable*. It was a game Ray knew better than to be sucked into. The strains of heartbreak and desire that had plagued his vulnerable teenage years had now been folded like a sweater in the summer and put back in his emotional closet, waiting. He didn't rule it out as a possibility, love, sex, affection, but until the war against the feel players had been won—the adult world finally conquered, Tragedy averted—the whole thing felt like a particularly suboptimal use of his time, productivity-wise. One day, maybe. And anyway, she was far from perfect. There was a certain precariousness in her stride, not altogether graceless, but more impelled by inertia than one would have hoped. Her figure was too linear. Yes, maybe one day.

Lost in his thoughts, Ray hadn't noticed Logan getting up to greet a couple—he in his seventies, she somewhere over fifty. He hadn't noticed the man's thickly green-and-red-striped shirt, or his aviator prescription glasses, or his oversize gold cufflinks. He hadn't spotted her pearls and her ring and her purse. He hadn't carefully evaluated (nor would he have, had he seen them) their respective left wrists, dutifully Richard Milled. Eyes still wandering around M.'s neckline, he had failed to acknowledge the gigantic SPOT firmly impressed across their foreheads. He just saw the back of three heads, white and black and blond, slightly bouncing exactly twice on their way out together.

He sat down to play.

4

Tom

By the time the cop pulled him over on Tropicana, Tom had been an illegal immigrant for fourteen months.

Back home, cops who were assigned routine roadside checks carried a sheet of paper with a grid progressively filling up with names and information. They were prescribed to stop a certain amount of people and write down their license numbers: once they reached the bottom of the page, they got to go home. They really had no incentive to be prejudiced about who they pulled over.

Tom didn't know how it worked in America, but in all honesty, if he were a cop he would have waved his truck down too. He drove a '94 Ford F-150 with what he considered a good three hundred thousand miles of life experience. Twenty years of unprotected exposure to the desert sun had left their mark on the red paint, which had faded to an opaque shade, with large pink areas surrounded by whitish borders, like dead skin starting to come off in bits after a bad sunburn. The front license plate hung at an angle. A family pack of Jack Link's Beef Jerky was visible through the windshield, sitting to the side of the steering wheel. Yes, he would have waved his truck down just like the cop had, and he would have asked the driver for license and registration, and he would have frowned over the laminated blue foreign card the driver offered with a tense smile. After the frowning and the head-scratching, he would have taken the card back to the cop car to run it. Which is what had happened, and now he was waiting.

His license, his real driver's license, had expired four months ago. He didn't have it with him. He figured having "forgotten" his license at home would be a less serious offense than carrying around a long-expired one, somehow. He hadn't thought this through; being pulled over in Vegas seemed too unlikely an event to really take into consideration, given his lucky streak. He did, however, have his Social Security card from back home, an official-looking navy-blue thing with a confusion of foreign words on it, which qualified him to receive free public health care in a whole other country, but said nothing whatsoever of his ability to drive a college-aged Ford pickup. In an inexplicable reflex, when the cop had asked him for his license, he'd just handed that to him without really understanding what he was doing. And so now he was waiting in the truck for the cop to find him out and for everything to end.

His fingers twirled his driving pen around—the white complimentary-looking pen with the tangerine cap and "Rio Hotel & Casino" written in rainbow letters on its side that was an essential part of the pickup's engine. The way it worked was, you stuck it firmly at the base of the gear shift to hold it in drive, otherwise it would slide back into neutral while the vehicle was moving, which wasn't ideal. He'd paid $2,100 cash for the truck, but the pen had come included. The driver's seat had recently got stuck in a semi-reclined position, after one day his roommate Trevor had borrowed it (Tom didn't really care to know how the damage had occurred), so that driving now presented a choice between limited visibility and an unsupported back. Other than that, though, the truck was basically okay.

The cop was taking his time. He was a gray-haired man of maybe forty-five, greasy-skinned and beer-gutted, and he'd walked the few meters separating the two vehicles with what Trevor would describe as the confident, relaxed stride of the natural alpha. Like Tom Cruise in *Top Gun*. He was a good American cop, and pretty soon he would come back with the SS card and follow-up questions, and start the process that would ultimately result in Tom's expulsion and lifetime ban from the United States of America.

Tom's heartbeat didn't have the thump of genuine fear. It was a fast, hummingbird-like pitter-patter against his ribs he associated with memories of schoolyard derision and classroom stuttering through reading aloud. It was the heartbeat of shame. He wanted to run out of the truck and tell the officer that he was sorry. That he never meant for this to happen, and this wasn't like him, not at all. That he was truly, utterly, indescribably sorry. Go explain to him that he had never done something like this before, that he was so very aware that U.S. Customs and Border Protection was no joke, and that he knew and accepted what needed to happen now. Confess to him, even, that all this standing up for himself, being a man, making his own decisions for once and taking risks, all of this had not come from him (he realized that now); that he had just been imitating Trevor and listening to all he had to say, and that he was just as much of a follower and a "helpless beta" now as he had been when his plane landed at McCarran seventeen months ago. All this he wanted to run and tell the officer, get it over with. And he would have, but for the sole, strange bit of advice his mom had given him when he'd hugged her goodbye before his ten-day prize trip to Las Vegas. She had sat up on the blue couch with the ripped white linen cover where she was lying down, turned down the TV, put out her cigarette in the ashtray she had painted herself, next to the iron bowl with the little glass bongs and used-up lighters, and told him: "If you are driving in America and they pull you over, remember: *never* get out of the car; they're allowed to shoot you if you do." He had reassured her that he wouldn't need to drive there—only ten days!—but promised her (his mother, who'd seen America only on TV) that he would nonetheless remember this. So now he stayed in the truck.

The cop sauntered back with his card and a smile. Maybe this wouldn't take too long. Tom looked at him with a sheepish look Trevor would have called him out on: stay in control, unfazed in the face of adversities, poised. But all Tom wanted was for this to be quick.

"Rome, huh? *Bella Italia!*" the cop said. "Was there with the missus couple years back. Loved it. Huh, is that beef jerky? I really shouldn't, but . . . thanks! The food in Italy, man, so good! And the women, but like I said, was there with the missus. *You* know what I'm talking about!" Tom nodded, dumbfounded. "All right, man, enjoy Las Vegas, okay?"

Because after all, Tommaso Bernardini really was a lucky man.

Tom's luck had begun almost two years before, in a garage-turned-back-alley-cardroom off Via Tiburtina in Rome, no more than three blocks away from the only apartment he'd ever lived in.

The East Rome neighborhood of Rebibbia was by and large all Tom knew of the world at twenty-four. His father, a low-level cubicle worker at the Ministry of Internal Affairs, had died when Tom was five, leaving him to grow up with an older brother and a quietly depressed, pot-smoking mother. He was a shy, incredibly polite young man, just above average height and with a face that would have been perfectly forgettable if not for a long diagonal scar across his lower lip he'd got as a kid, trying to eat leftover chocolate cream off an unsupervised plugged-in stick blender in the kitchen.

The neighborhood had a strange, rural feel to it. Small houses, diminutive gardens, a shabby forgotten village at the edges of the city. Tom's mother's side of the family had lived there since the 1970s, and she was fond of it. She cooked, laughed, and painted. But Tom's father, who even before his untimely death regarded his own life as a spectacular failure, had grown to hate it. He found it suffocating, numbing. It was no coincidence, he said, that the neighborhood's claim to fame was for hosting Rome's largest correctional facility. "Hopeless calm," he would say, quoting from a book he loved. "*Quiete nella non-speranza.* Calm in the midst of hopelessness."

After his death (heart), nobody complained anymore. As their mother no longer painted and worked what jobs she could keep (school janitor, selling flowers outside the city graveyard), Tom and his big brother Francesco developed their own distinct relationships with that handful of blocks where everything seemed to have started as a garage—the arcade, the supermarket, even the neighborhood church. Francesco worked hard, convinced that a serene and determined disposition was required to hold up his end of the social-mobility bargain. Calm in the midst of hopefulness.

Tom, on the other hand, a quiet child made even quieter by the trials of high school, slid into adulthood like a feather on a pond: not a sound, barely a ripple. His brother encouraged him to chase his dreams, as far away from home as they would take him, but it seemed to Tom like the more one wanted, the more one stood to lose. And so, through his years of uneventful domesticity, Tom grew into the kind of man who wants nothing for himself, trusting that if he hid at the margins of the world, without bothering or inconveniencing anyone else, the world would want nothing from him in turn. Not happy, but not unbearably unhappy, poor, but getting by, twenty-four-year-old Tom lived in the calm, hopeless conviction that he would grow old in his home neighborhood of Rebibbia, and didn't quite feel one way or another about it. That is, until the night in the illegal cardroom (formerly a garage).

Like many young Italian men, Tom had dabbled in poker at the height of its popularity circa 2008–2010, when cowboy-hatted professionals could be seen gambling for millions on prime-time TV, and newspaper-hatted construction workers could be heard talking about pocket aces and big blinds at the counter on their espresso breaks. It had been a fad, and Tom had taken part in it as much as his limited resources and lack of any real competitive spirit had allowed. A fan, more than a player; a diligent spectator, but a lazy student of the game. And when poker gradually lost its mass appeal, and the public had moved on to legalized sports betting and right-wing populism, Tom too retreated to his world of comic books and video games, nominal university enrollment and work. By the time he won his ticket to Las Vegas, he had barely played any cards in years.

It was a February night. Francesco, by now a systems technician for an IT firm in Shanghai, had taken two unpaid weeks off around Chinese New Year to fly home to his mother and little brother, and was leaving the following morning. The two of them had been drinking €2 beers sitting on a fence in the neighborhood square, where a wooden Christ rested wailing on the cross in a tacky glass case. The noise of speeding cars from the multilaned Via Tiburtina, one of the major arteries of the suburban east side of Rome, reminded the neighborhood of its role at the periphery of the metropolis. Tom had grown to a few centimeters taller than his brother, but his thin pencil-drawn features and acute angles left him unremarkable and invisible in a way Francesco's stout physique and large shaved head did not. In their conversations, it was somehow Tom who seemed to be constantly looking up. At some point, while reminiscing about their mother's get-rich ideas and her afternoons getting stoned on the living-room couch, or about the gray neighborhood building where both of them had gone to grade and middle school while their mom worked there as a janitor, Francesco declared he was cold, and suggested they go play some poker, "for old times' sake." They made their suburban way to the downhill alleyway that led to the cardroom, signaled by a dozen poorly groomed men smoking cigarettes outside. Live poker was illegal in Rome, but tame establishments such as this one were more or less openly tolerated by the authorities, as long as they kept the stakes small and their mouths shut. That night, the tournament had a €30 buy-in and promised a "Vegas package" worth €2,500 to the winner. Tom only had €20 in his pocket, and wasn't looking to part with all of it at once. But Francesco, who sent money home from China every month, volunteered the difference and convinced him to play. It was his last night in Rome, after all.

In that damp fluorescent-lit basement packed with 184 players, Tom's luck manifested for the first time. One by one his opponents fell, losing chips to bad river cards, bluffs, or mistakes, but Tom's stack kept growing. He wasn't doing much to deserve it, he felt, it just seemed like he was being dealt good hands a lot more than anybody else. After hitting yet another full house on the flop, he started to feel genuinely sorry for the other players. Around 2:00 a.m., Francesco was knocked out of the tournament on a bad beat. Surprised to find his brother very much still in, he got a beer and started waiting for him at the small bar inside the cardroom. But Tom wasn't done hitting good cards.

It was 4:00 a.m. when the final table started, and the tournament director, a fifty-year-old of gladiatorial size and grade-school hairdo, proudly rolled out a tray of ancient-looking snacks for the last players standing. By the time Tom finished his first Yo-Yo, a sugary bun with chocolate stripes he hadn't seen since the late '90s, three of the nine players had already succumbed to his unstoppable rush. Two more by the second one. And when he first bit down on the five-cereal disappointment of a Kinder Colazione Più, he was heads-up, two players left, playing for the big prize. Flight and hotel for ten days in Las Vegas, plus the buy-in for one of the smaller, secondary (but still highly desirable) events at the annual World Series of Poker. A $1,000 tournament paled in comparison with the fabled $10,000 Main Event, but it was still a world away from Via Tiburtina, the glass-cased crucifix on the square, the neon lettering outside the garage door advertising "Pool Club" (no pool tables visible anywhere inside).

Thinking about it a year and a half later, now that he'd played almost 3,000 hours of poker and undergone Trevor's invaluable (and free) coaching, he knew he'd played embarrassingly bad that night. It was eerie to consider how close he'd come to jeopardizing this life-changing opportunity, and everything he was to learn and experience as a result of it (though also, come to think of it, the whole immigrational clusterfuck and blackmail ordeal soon to follow). In the end, he'd called his opponent's all-in with a measly pair of sixes, cracking his pocket queens via a fateful six-on-the-river. He won. A 6:00 a.m. meal of beer and Yo-Yos with a beaming Francesco, and the news that the prize could absolutely not be converted to cash, concluded the most surreal night of Tom's life to date—though a rather average one, compared to what was to come.

The Rio. Red-and-purple, off-Strip, vaguely Brazilian-themed architectural faux pas, location of Tom's ten-day free stay (in a lowest-rate smoking room, the furniture of which nonsmoker Tom found outstank even his mom's TV couch—which he didn't complain about at all, thankful and overwhelmed as he was by his first experience abroad), and proud home of the annual World Series of Poker. The Rio, hotel and casino, and so much more.

By the time Tom arrived, on June 16, the month and a half of daily poker tournaments ranging from a $1,000 buy-in to exorbitant prices ($50,000 that year, but with a $1,000,000 buy-in special event penciled in for the following Series) was already in full swing. The place was packed. But as much as the Rio's garish decor suggested carnival and revels, a large part of the crowd roaming its halls had not come to Vegas with parties in mind. Past the casino area, up and down the corridors of a spacious convention center, poker celebrities, young wannabe pros, and starry-eyed dreamers alike hopped from one table to the next with the common goal of snatching one of the coveted—and frankly unwearable—gold bracelets awarded to the winners. Fifty-plus tournaments a year, fifty-plus winners taking home the trophies, thousands of losers taking home experience.

The World Series of Poker was, in fact, the diamond-encrusted carrot that set the whole poker industry in motion at the beginning of its very own golden age. The rags-to-riches tale of one Chris Moneymaker, of Atlanta, Georgia—a no-name comptroller who in 2003 turned $40 deposited online on Pokerstars.com into a ticket for the $10,000 Main Event, and then went on to shock the world by winning the whole thing for $2,532,041—was the spark that triggered an unprecedented poker boom. An old game for card sharks and Vegas gamblers suddenly turned into a sport, and an improbably democratic one at that, in which anybody, *anybody*, could dream of beating the world's best, and make a fortune in the process. A month-long circus that fed on the all-American dream of making a quick buck, a living, breathing monument to the comfortably-sitting-down pursuit of happiness.

Tom was amazed. It wasn't just that everything was extraordinary, outlandish, rich—growing up in Rome has a way of immunizing locals to the effects of ostentatious architecture. It was a brand of magic particular to the Rio that awed Tom. The center of Rome, which Tom had to take a long subway ride to see, was extraordinary to *look at*, in a purely spectatorial way that made you feel small and insignificant; inside the Rio, the extraordinary was *inclusive*, it was there for you to be a part of. It had the same kitschy pink neons that punctuated the squalor of Tom's neighborhood (buzzing 24/7 over the doors of dive bars, cash-for-golds, even a "Las Vegas Club" with 70 percent cash-back slot machines); but here, surrounded by visitors laughing, wolfing down wings at the All-American Bar & Grille, ordering Jack and Cokes from boa-wearing cocktail waitresses, here they were *fun*. On his first night in Vegas, in the casino at the Rio, Tommaso Bernardini stumbled on his first ever traveler's epiphany: not all that glitters is sad.

His tournament set to start at noon, Tom thought it best to honor his mission by calling it an early night. He had flown in on a middle-row seat and been shuttled to the hotel on dimly lit backstreets: Las Vegas, to him, was still entirely contained within the purple walls of the Rio. The following day he showed up at the Brasilia Room, table 64, seat 6, with more than an hour to spare. He walked around the hallways of the Las Vegas Convention Center, getting smooth-talked by concession stand vendors about products he couldn't possibly be tempted by. In fact, the $1,512 in crisp airport money-exchange bills he kept in an envelope wedged between his underwear and his right butt-cheek amounted to all the money he'd managed to put together in the last three months, by picking up extra shifts at the dog wash where he worked, by calling in any present, loan, and potential inheritance he could think of, and by subsisting solely on €2 *pizza e mortadella*—white focaccia with what he would later learn was inexplicably called "bologna" in the US—for way longer than medically advisable. Yet once the vendors started talking, he didn't have the heart to interrupt them. And so he waited patiently, asking pertinent questions and feigning interest in overpriced phone chargers, mystical balance bracelets, and $7 oxygen shots (here some interest was real: he figured his mom would be keen to know more about the potential business of selling air—it was just her kind of thing). Finally, after a long, hungry reflection, he decided to invest in a bag of the protein snack that sponsored the event, something he'd never seen before called Jack Link's Beef Jerky.

When the tournament started, Tom was pleased to find out that it wasn't that different from the back-alley game off Via Tiburtina. He had been afraid of being out of place, but his videogame-based English was more than enough to say "bet," "raise," "all in." Besides, he wasn't doing much of that anyway: in contrast to his Roman triumph, for the first two hours at the table Tom didn't seem to get any remotely playable hand. It felt like the deck had been stripped of all picture cards, and Tom realized he had no idea how to play poker when you weren't hitting at least two pair at every hand. He just kept folding, trying not to disturb the players who were actually trying to win. His table was lively and lighthearted, and everyone was a little older than he'd expected: thick mustaches, thick bellies, thick American accents he had some trouble following. He had barely played a hand by the time the first player, a friendly sixty-year-old to his direct right, was eliminated. Two things caught Tom's attention: first, the man smiled, shook the hand of the player who had busted him, and bid a warm goodbye-and-good-luck to the whole table upon leaving (proving to be much less bothered by this $1,000 setback than a lot of the cursing, yelling players Tom had knocked out in his €30 tournament win); second, the new player who was sent to table 64 to take his seat was a young man.

"That's my luck for you," the new recruit whispered to Tom with a conspiratorial wink. "Softest tourney of the Series, and I get seated out of position against an online *wizard!*"

He looked about Tom's age, maybe younger, with a short, fit frame, a big head that struck Tom as vaguely bobblehead-doll-like, and bright red hair styled up and back in unabashedly leonine fashion. He was wearing a loose-fitting white linen collarless shirt, baggy olive-green pants, and rubber-soled shoes with individual toes that Tom had never seen or heard of before (and was fully fascinated by).

"I . . . a wizard?" Tom said.

"Check that, a *Euro* online wizard," said the stranger, theatrically shaking his large head. "How bad can I run?"

Tom caught up: statistically, any young, introverted-looking kid sitting at a WSOP tournament was likely to be an online professional (the higher the buy-in, the higher the certainty). Euro pros, unhindered by the legal ban of online poker that had befallen their American counterparts, and therefore still able to grind millions of hands per year and refine their play, were considered an even more dangerous elite. Especially if seated to your left, in position, always acting after you, reraising you, putting pressure. The misunderstanding, from a poker perspective, was a clear win/win for Tom: the only likely professional at the table had mistaken him for a Euro reg, meaning he would probably not only avoid playing big pots against him, if possible, but would in general not antagonize him and perhaps even play fewer hands overall because of his bad position. It was a major advantage that fate and a stranger's prejudicial profiling had dropped on his plate. But of course, this last part was not the kind of thinking Tom had the experience to make.

"No, no, no, I never play. I am recreational."

"Yeah, right, I'm sure you are," smiled his confirmationally biased neighbor.

As the tournament progressed, with Tom languishing below the average chip count but somehow managing never to get knocked out, many people had come and (mostly) gone from their table. Yet with less than an hour to go in the first day of play, the room was still packed full of people. The clickity-clackety sound of poker chips being shuffled or fiddled with by thousands of restless fingers (official soundtrack of every poker room in the world) was still white-noiseishly pervasive. Cocktail waitresses delivering purified water and watered-down coffee still had to zigzag around the tables, squeezing through the curved backs and butt-out postures of the players enjoying a massage. While the screens with the tournament clock and info announced that over two-thirds of the field was gone, the room appeared just as bustling with activity as it had been in the morning.

Tom's neighbor had pretty much talked to him nonstop throughout. It might be because of simple proximity, or their similar age group; but, as Tom was soon to learn, his conversational affinity with Trevor (as he'd introduced himself) ran much deeper. On the one hand, Tom was a natural-born listener. As a consumer, he enjoyed nothing more than to witness other people's displays of expertise. He loved documentaries, cooking shows, streams of people playing video games or even just writing code. He had listened to his father for as long as he'd had the chance, then to his brother. He'd even listened with sympathy and undivided attention, for afternoons on end, to his mother's half-baked ideas about quitting her job to sell her homemade ceramics, be a freelance tour guide for tourists picked up right off the streets of Rome, buy an abandoned farm out of town and live off the products of the earth. He listened to anybody, with joy. In conversation with him, people at times slowed down, embarrassed to realize they'd been talking about themselves for so long; they paused, waiting for Tom's turn to begin. But it never came. After a couple of seconds of silence, Tom would smile and simply say "And then?" And on they went.

As for Trevor, as soon as certain obvious lapses in Tom's play made it clear that he was, in fact, *not* a fearsome and not-to-be-fucked-with online wizard, a dynamic took shape. Trevor was a talker, a lucid, effective (if unsolicited) explainer of things. He said so himself, claiming that his understanding of human experience was bound to his ability to articulate it. He was brilliant. Among the many things Tom learned about him that first afternoon were: that he was from LA County, California; that his father was a professor at the most prestigious school of magic in the world; no, not like Hogwarts, like stage magic; that he himself was of course well versed in close-up magic and pretty neat chip tricks such as *this, this,* and "*this one* that I call 'antigravity' and that took me three weeks to master"; that he had majored in psychology at UCLA, which was a wonderful field of study because it gives you a real understanding of what it means to be a human being, of how we are such fascinating, complex creatures, and of how we behave and why, and what challenges this knowledge presents; that afterward it'd turned out he was a man of praxis rather than theory after all, and he'd sought to apply his newfound knowledge of our shared behavioral mechanics in a field more relevant to his demographic, i.e. getting girls; that he had, in fact, been involved with the world of PUAs (pick-up artists) in LA, and been the protégé of this now-retired master who, like, invented most of the moves a lot of these kids today swear by; that he had been a PUA coach himself, as a senior and fresh out of college, but that he'd by now grown quite tired of that whole spiel; that all the while as soon as he'd turned twenty-one he'd started to hit the Bike, and Hawaiian Gardens, and of course that shithole Commerce (which, he explained, were the main casinos in Los Angeles) to put to use his people skills, so to speak, in yet another, more remunerative field, i.e. poker; and that these here were his first WSOP, but that he was loving Vegas so far, and if games were so fucking soft, he'd be crazy to keep grinding those crummy cardrooms in Cali instead of just moving out here already. And so on.

When Day 1 of the tournament ended, 487 players were left to come fight for the bracelet the following morning—among them, Trevor, with a healthy, above-average chip stack that made him confident and hopeful for what was to come. Also among them, super-short-stacked Tom, who was left with the equivalent of seven big blinds (the average was at 35bbs, and in general, anything below 15bbs is considered "danger zone," a likely candidate for swift elimination). In Tom's situation, any professional worth his salt would already be studying the schedule for a new tourney to late-reg in the morning, after being predictably ousted from this $1,000, two-thousand-person lottery (these side events, with cheap buy-ins, fast structures, and infinite entries, are, more than any other, subject to absurd amounts of luck-based variance, and are usually regarded as little more than warm-ups by serious pros). Tom, who of course had put all his chance-acquired eggs in this tiny, pro-snubbed basket, went straight to bed to get a good eight hours, and woke up early the next day to read up on short-stack play in tournaments from an old poker book his brother had bought and left in Rome years before. In the margins, next to a paragraph about not being in a rush to double up and waiting for the right spot to go all in, his brother had scribbled and underlined three times "PAZIENZA!!!," which Tom repeated aloud and took on as his personal mantra for the day.

The Brasilia Room was a beehive of activity. The seniors event (fifty-plus) had been scheduled for an early start, 10:00 a.m. versus the usual noon start time, and its tables, abuzz with a swarm of four-thousand-strong geriatric bees, took up a good two-thirds of the gray-carpeted space, and just as much of the adjacent Amazon Room. A room full of poker players is a sight to see: hangar-large, neutral-colored, a static choreography of seated strangers elliptically arranged around identical tables; past Main Event winners smile from banners hanging on the walls; knocked-out players mutter to themselves through their walk of shame to the exit doors; massage girls excavate curved backs in search of who knows what treasures. A room full of *senior* poker players, though, possesses a people-watching charm of its own, one that the depressingly homogenous crowds of twentysomething wizards could never aspire to. Wide-eyed as only a real first-timer can be, Tom took in cowboy hats, collegiate baseball caps with Sunday-golf sunglasses resting on visors, tableside oxygen tanks, snakeskin belts, tweed jackets, TD-sanctioned aides for the visually impaired (sitting behind them, whispering flops in hairy ears: "Seven of spades, deuce of clubs, king of diamonds"). So many stories he would love to hear (but would be rude to ask). Stories of the real America he knew from TV, and never thought he'd get to see.

The tournament restarted with the tournament director's official "Shuffle up and deal!" at noon. Of the 487 players remaining, 245 would "make the money," meaning reach the roughly 10 percent of the initial field that received a prize for their efforts. In-the-money (ITM) scores usually started at little more than the original buy-in for the tournament, and climbed up to substantial amounts approaching the final table of nine players. The first prize, which Tom hadn't allowed his mind to linger on for even a second, was a whopping $355,000.

The first news of the day was Trevor's bust-out. Tom had folded for no more than one round, his small stack eroding to less than six big blinds, when he saw a pair of five-toed shoes walk toward the exit doors. As he looked up and made eye contact, Trevor smiled, looking oddly relaxed and unfazed for a twenty-five-year-old who's just lost $1,000, two hundred people shy of an ITM finish. What had happened? He'd had such a comfortable stack to begin the day; how had he lost all of it? Had someone played a bad, reckless hand and sucked out on him? Had he gotten too cocky and bluffed it all off against a good player? Or had it been the other way around, him hero-calling what he thought was a bluff and being shown the goods? Tom decided he'd take a short break to find him in the hallway and ask him, to tell him he was a really good player and it was such a pity he hadn't made it to the final table, he certainly deserved it.

But he couldn't. Just as he got ready to get up, the dealer dealt him his next hand. His hands instinctively reached for it, making a little hut or shield around the two cards so that he could lift them up by a corner and look at them. Two black kings. There was no getting up now. After the first two players folded, he took a few seconds to fake-think about it (he thought acting too quickly might give away the strength of his hand), then announced "I'm all in." Immediately, the player to his left called. No suspense there, but a long wait before the cards would be turned over and his fate decided. Five more people had to act. Four of them folded more or less quickly, but the kid in the big blind didn't move. He was a young profes-sional—or at least looked like one—an Asian kid in black Nike clothes and white Apple earphones who had spent the first orbit of hands barely looking up from his phone. He didn't move a muscle, just stared intently at the chip stack of the player to Tom's left, a young, blond, foreign-accented pro (as in most tournaments, the demographics of the field shift dramati-cally in favor of young wizards in later stages of play). The big blind took what felt like an awkwardly long time, then reached for chips. A lot of chips. More chips than were necessary to call. He slid them past the betting line with deliberation, and the dealer announced "Reraise." The potential Swede went in what in pokerspeak is known as the tank, the identical, silent state of thinking about a decision that his opponent had only just come out of. Tom felt like an interloper. His measly, hopeless stack, a stack that had no ambition of making it to the money, let alone snatching a good prize, had triggered a clash of the two biggest stacks at the table. Two pros, two great players who had the skills and the chips to see this through to the national-anthemed, eighteen-carat end, were fighting and endangering their tour-nament life over his sacrificial bet. He wanted to apologize, somehow, for putting them in such distress. For eliciting such deep, clearly complex, and (for him) inscrutable thoughts. He had completely forgotten the fact that he had a great hand, the second-best hand in No Limit Hold'em, in fact, and could be in great shape to not just double but more than triple up his short stack. None of that mattered. He just hoped he hadn't caused too much trouble, is all.

"I'm all in," said the Viking-faced pro. Tom didn't have the time to turn to the Asian kid in the big blind and wait for him to go in the tank. Everything happened in a second. The big blind folded instantly, and the player to his left tabled Tom's tournament's death sentence: two beautiful red aces. The only starting hand in poker better than the one he had. A hand so good, in fact, that his opponent was now an 81.2 percent favorite to win once the five communal cards of the board were revealed. Turning over his sorry-looking kings, Tom nodded. In acceptance? Admitting defeat? Everything was suddenly so confusing. The dealer knocked softly on the green Jack Link's Beef Jerky–sponsored felt, then spread the flop. For all he was able to understand, in his trancelike state, he may as well have needed an aide for the emotionally impaired, whispering the cards in his ear as they rolled out: "Seven of spades, deuce of clubs, *king of diamonds*." He couldn't even say what the last two cards, the turn and the river, were. His heart had stopped at that king of diamonds.

It's easy to underestimate the amount of self-indulgence that celebrating alone requires. Like most acts of consumerism, it takes practice. At 11pm on his third night in Vegas, Tom was sitting on a round stool at the bar of the All-American Bar & Grille, a total of $21,064 in separate envelopes uncomfortably moved to the sides of his underwear, second-guessing his decision to splurge on a $6 side of mashed potatoes to go with his $15 chicken wings and $6 domestic on draft (imported was $7). It just wasn't in his nature.

The suggestion that he celebrate a little had come from Francesco, who he had Skyped first thing after his tournament exit, on shaky casino Wi-Fi.

He had made the final table! Ninth place! No, no, super short all the time, incredible even getting that far, no regrets at all! Yes, yes! Okay, ready? $19,600! At lunchtime in Shanghai, his brother had yelled with happiness and given a spirited performance of an AS Roma stadium chant (probably a first, on a Shanghai–to–Las Vegas phone call). He firmly refused to accept a third of the winnings, which Tom felt he owed because of the €10 Francesco had given him to enter the satellite tournament in Rome.

"And don't give it to Mom either, okay?" Francesco had said. "This is *your* money. Use it for *you*."

The food was perfect. The wings dripped a reddish sticky grease that got on Tom's fingers and seasoned them with salty delights. The meat was tender, flavorful, and Tom had to gnaw it off its bones in messy bites that reminded him of childhood Sundays, when his dad bought rotisserie chicken for the kids. The mashed potatoes, which he'd been afraid might be too much of a luxury, turned out to be an absolute bargain considering the generosity of the portion and the wonderful creaminess of the puree. His brother had teased him about how bad the food would be in America, but this meal—and the glorious discovery of beef jerky yesterday—proved him absolutely wrong. This was a land of abundance, where even the simplest of foods dared you to want more, to eat to the last full-bellied bite. A land for the *hungry*.

Yet all through this culinary triumph, Tom was in the grips of a train of thought too insistent to ignore: What was the true meaning of the phrase "life-changing money"? What did it entail? Was the money itself the active party in the transaction, altering the life of its recipient whether he wanted it or not? Or was it rather a guiding light or GPS of sorts, a road map he'd been given to change his life ultimately on his own? Was it really a responsibility? Was he ready?

It stands to reason that someone with Tom's background and experience with money would quickly delude himself as to the proportions of his windfall. That he'd think that less than $20,000 could, in today's world and in an expensive city like Rome, be even close to life-changing would support that idea. Yet in his mind, Tom was in no way exaggerating his present situation.

For one thing, he never dared call himself poor in the first place: like many working-class Italian families, his too had inherited the luxury of home ownership thanks to the frugality of the postbellum generation. Granted, the already small apartments his grandmothers lived in (grandfathers, in keeping with a tragic Bernardini trend, had both died young) would one day have to be divided among a ridiculous amount of siblings (his aunts and uncles) and were therefore, to Tom, worth virtually nothing. But at least the apartment off Via Tiburtina, blocks away from the gray menace of the Rebibbia penitentiary, was entirely his mom's, and therefore his and Francesco's. And as little as it was worth, it was enough for Tom to know that he would always have a roof above his head. And still this money *was* life-changing, any way he looked at it. Having a bank account with funds in it, more funds than he would need to spend in the immediate future, would be a shocking new experience. And it would raise some questions. Example: Was he, approaching twenty-five, still living with his mother because he couldn't afford not to, or because he secretly wanted to? Was he washing and grooming dogs instead of going to classes because he needed the €500 a month or because, deep down, he was really done studying computer science, and had kept enrolled only because for his income bracket it was free to do so, instead of having to disburse the hefty €1,100 in yearly tuition other students paid? Finally, once survival was not an immediate concern, what did he *want* to do? If having to come up with answers for all these conundrums wasn't life-changing, Tom didn't know what was.

"Mashed potatoes with wings? Man, I have so much to teach you," said Trevor, straddling the stool to Tom's left with rubber-toed dexterity. "Mind if I sit?" Tom nodded and gestured with his upturned palm, which in this case meant "Please," and absolutely not the equally possible "Well, you're sitting already, aren't you?" (Italian gestures, once famously flamboyant, have shrunk to minimalism in younger generations, but still maintain a variety of subtle nuances.)

"How are you gonna bring that money home?" asked Trevor.

Tom looked quickly down at his crotch, where the envelopes bulged slightly against his pants. Did Trevor know?

"Bring?" he asked.

"You know you can't take twenty grand to the airport, right?" said Trevor. Tom didn't know, in fact. How on earth could he know?

"I can't?"

"No, and you can't wire it either, or else you're going to pay thirty percent taxes on it, plus whatever international wires are," said Trevor.

"I don't know," said Tom, shaking his head. "I don't know." Of all the money-related problems he'd ever imagined he would face in his life, having too much of it had never once come up.

"That's what I figured. But here's an idea," said Trevor, pausing to order a light beer and show his ID to the bartender (Tom hadn't been asked). "What if you stayed here a bit instead?"

"I don't desire to spend it," said Tom, again looking down and instantly back up. Had Trevor noticed?

"Of course not, no. But see, I'm moving here myself, to grind live poker full-time, you know? And I need a roommate. Why don't you stay for a month or two, put your skills to good use, make four or five grand on top?"

Tom didn't follow. "But I don't desire to spend it," he repeated.

"No, dude, Vegas is dirty cheap. We'll get a two-bedroom for nothing and then just crush the cash games. You can push back your flight for sure."

What was Trevor saying? The thought of extending his prize trip seemed like a betrayal, a breach of contract with the good people at his friendly neighborhood illegal cardroom. Besides, there was just no way he was good enough to make money playing poker every day, once his obvious lucky streak ran out. And yet at the same time, the thought of playing more, of raking up more chips from the center of a table (and real-money chips, this time, not worthless tournament tokens), the thought of winning, of becoming a reg, of producing real wealth, more than he'd ever thought of making, and maybe over time getting better, moving up stakes, making even more . . . but no, wait, this wasn't right. He was going back anyway, eventually. What was the point?

The All-American Grille was a warm, murmuring organism whose multiple eyes focused on the screens above the bar counter. An ESPN highlight reel of game 6 of the NBA Finals was playing, an instant-classic overtime win for Lebron's Miami Heat that had concluded hours earlier, around the time Tom traded a creased slip of paper with his name and seat number for real-life wads of American cash wrapped in gold-rimmed bands with "$5,000" written on them in Old West serif. He had not taken a picture of the money for social media, or held it in his hands to feel its weight, or fanned himself with it. He had asked for envelopes, please, and quickly placed the "bricks" (as the woman at the cage had called them) inside, licked the paper shut, and dashed for the restroom to hide them in his boxer briefs. No, he did *not* desire to spend it, let alone lose it at a poker table.

"But verily I am no professional," he said. "You have seen me play! In the cash games I will be pwned forcefully."

Tom's English, passively refined by years of gaming into a sharper tool than he gave himself credit for, presented the successive layers of the epic escapism of *Zelda: Ocarina of Time* and *Final Fantasy IX*, and the colloquialisms of internet message boards and MMORPG chats.

Trevor gave him a broad-smiling look that Tom interpreted as kindness. Over time, he would learn to attribute it more precisely to the sense of real gratitude Trevor felt anytime he was offered an opportunity to explain, teach, or otherwise impart a modicum of his wisdom.

"I *have* seen you play, yes," he said. "And sure, you could use some advice here and there. But you have no idea how freaking *easy* games in Vegas are. You just wouldn't believe how bad people play. Besides"—an even broader smile—"you'd be living with a really good coach, Tomsky!"

Tomsky?

Interlude III

(the story of a secret meeting)

Out on the golf course spreading behind the Hills of Positano™, shielded from the sun by the ruins of a Roman temple, Ada Tingey-Peterson was drinking water in a cocktail glass. The wedge of lemon that had come skewered to its side lay on a diligently folded, $\mathcal{P}$-emblazoned napkin in front of her, the thin black straw next to it. The big advantage to fake temple ruins versus real ones is air-conditioning, a breezeless cool coming from well-disguised vents on the heavy-looking marble plinths in the eight corners of the room. Ms. Tingey-Peterson was the secretary-treasurer of the powerful Workers in Hospitality Organization of America Local 2201, which at over 80,000 registered members, all employed in local hotels and casinos, was the de facto voice of the Las Vegas working class, and as such loathed, feared, and begrudgingly sucked up to by both casino owners and Nevadan politicians. Which she knew. And enjoyed.

"You can tell Mr. Wiles that I find his absence here today hardly excusable, compulsive hermitism or not. The matters at hand concern the very roots of his business, as I'm sure he knows, and there's really no explanation—"

"But absolutely he knows, Frau Tingey-Peterson, absolutely," said a preoccupied Hendrik Vogelsang, shifting on the plush red velvet of his chair and nervously looking around.

"We can assure you that nothing is more present to Herr Wiles's mind than the well-being of his many, many employees," a composed Eli Engels explained, "and that we at the Positano and all the Wiles properties around the city are happy to welcome the help of WHOA in the always delicate matter of making sure the rights of the workers are ensured, and respected, and valued."

"That is all well and good, but he still should be here to say so himself. Frankly, I'd be tempted to leave if it weren't for the cats," said Ms. T.-P., pausing to extend her right arm and do the tongue-clicky *ds-ds-ds* sound that is common feline shorthand for "Come here, you little cutie" in the direction of an admittedly adorable red tabby Siberian. "Which I assume I have *you* to thank for: it's rare one gets to have a business meeting with the very people who have built the meeting room."

This last jab did not fail to elicit an effect. While proud of their architectural successes, Engels and Vogelsang found it sometimes hard to be taken seriously in their new roles as central figures in the economical and political landscape of Las Vegas, and were therefore particularly sensitive to what they perceived as condescending hints at their professional past. The cat compliment tasted particularly sour for Vogelsang, who had originally opposed the project with all of his well-mannered might, and had got to the point of almost making a scene, even as the ominous shipment had been golf-carted to the temple and released meowing and purring around the marble shafts of the Corinthian columns.

"They are Siberian cats, Frau Peterson, all of them," Engels was explaining, "elegant, beautiful, and hypoallergenic, and more agile and intelligent than . . ."

It had been one of Wiles's notorious architectural intrusions, this one based on a memory of happier days strolling around the ruins of the Forum in Rome, where cats roamed free among the pebbles and open-sandaled tourists. "Let's have a bunch of cats around," had been his words. "All over the temple bar, but like really high-end, well-behaved top-shelf cats, classy cats." Engels had found it lovely, and so it had come to Vogelsang alone to object that felines would do more harm than good to the enjoyment of the Ruins bar by their target demographic of largely male, middle-aged-and-up golfers with very little interest in round-eyed Siberians. (The fact of the matter being: Vogelsang was hugely afraid of cats. As in terrified.)

"They are, however, a very exigent breed," continued Engels. "These ones are brushed five times a week and have their teeth cleaned daily by a dedicated Cat Squad. As for their nails . . ."

The meeting was actually important. On the heels of a scrupulously researched *Las Vegas Sun* report, a secondary center-Strip resort (part of the Wiles Group) had lately faced a major shitstorm on account of a series of suspicious layoffs of nonunion female employees, rumored to have done nothing wrong other than either putting on a few pounds or simply aging. Strong words had been deployed. The infamous concept of model-server was once again discussed in raised tones. A picture in the article had shown a smiling thirty-six-year-old reportedly let go for "not looking like she had the day she was hired anymore" (this turned, on LVSun.com, into a whole slideshow featuring Instagram pictures from the profiles of all the women who had lost their jobs).

The article, which Engels and Vogelsang were in pregame agreement not to mention, especially as it was signed by a Lindsay Peterson, and one can never be too careful, had already caused enough low-level managerial heads to roll in reparation that a good portion of Las Vegas execs were developing genuine phobias of the sound of their own vibrating phones (the others being too busy cursing this or that Peterson and all their preachy, better-than-thou Mormon lot). The situation called for swift, professional handling. Regrettably, Engels and Vogelsang specialized in large coastal excavations.

"But see, Frau Peterson, the very idea of the model-server rests on specific studies that have shown—"

"Specific studies that your boss has paid for, and that are completely irrelevant anyway, because we have no data concerning customer response to alternative staffing policies," Ms. Tingey-Peterson interjected matter-of-factly.

"Alternative . . . ?" asked Vogelsang, on the edge of his chair and stoically avoiding the blue-eyed stare of a solid pearl-gray a couple feet to his right, a spiteful-looking animal who seemed like he or she could probably be the leader of the clowder.

"Have you ever even *tried* to have male waiters along with the girls, for example?" This was a transparent gambit, but Wiles's German delegation was too inexperienced and pathologically cat-worried to read through it.

"Male?" said Vogelsang, by now completely at the mercy of the lovable little creature.

"But no casino in Las Vegas . . ." said Engels, taking the bait with a gullibility he would hours later come to realize while narrating the incident to his wife in their villa overlooking the gulf of Sorrento.

"Wrong. Bally's has two. Both homosexuals, too."

"But, Frau Peterson," said Engels, "the model-server has been a legally accepted figure in Las Vegas for . . . for . . ."

"For longer than you two have been here," concluded Ms. T-P. She would almost feel sorry for her hosts, blindly sent into battle by their lunatic boss, if their very presence at this meeting didn't so flagrantly betray Wiles's well-known disdain for all organized labor, and his desire to have as little to do with it as possible. Behind their helpless display, he was still the one calling the shots. "Look, you don't need to give me your spiel about bona fide occupational qualifications, I wrote a doctoral dissertation about them at BYU. The bottom line is, we both know, or at least I hope we do, that these workers have been wronged, and that EEOC would probably agree with me."

Engels did know it. He had prepared for this meeting with care and diligence, but Ms. Tingey-Peterson seemed to be, like his brother in their decades of mail and now online chess games, always a couple moves ahead. Together with the slow decadence of the theme resort, the '90s had seen the end of the ill-fated attempt to turn Las Vegas into a family-friendly destination. It was around this time that the Las Vegas Convention and Visitors Authority had debuted the well-known "What happens in Vegas stays in Vegas," in a clumsy but surprisingly effective effort to relaunch the image of Sin City as a place where *young, hip,* and *sexy* happen round the clock, 365 days a year. The model-servers, along with a number of similarly outrageous legal subterfuges, had been the spearhead of an overall resexualization of the Vegas experience, which most casino owners had more or less privately welcomed as a return to the good old days of Sinatra and scotch and sodas, and solemnly accompanied with I-told-you-sos in the act of giving family-oriented marketing advisors the much-anticipated boot.

The other side of the chip was not so glamorous, though. The whole concept of hiring sexy young girls to work as waitresses, bartenders, and dealers (and justifying their need to stay fit, and young, and sexy throughout their employment) hinged on the trick of qualifying them as "models," therefore calling into question the notorious BFOQ of which Ms. T.-P. was apparently *eine verdammte Expertin*. This put the casinos in a laughably weak position in the face of Equal Employment, and WHOA always one successful organizing campaign away from the "maxi-lawsuit to end all maxi-lawsuits" (as Engels's private and definitely secret legal advisors liked to refer to it). And this even before a suspiciously named journalist decided to splatter the whole thing across a little-read paper's front page and, more importantly, a locally quite influential news website. Things were ripe for a game of cat and mouse, Engels knew, and, looking at his business partner hysterically fretting in his seat for fear of a twelve-pound Siberian, he figured it didn't take a great stretch of the imagination to know where they stood in that scenario.

"Model-servers, model-bartenders, bevertainers, dealertainers, trust me, I've heard it all," said Ms. Tingey-Peterson, with the same expression Engels imagined his brother to have, even after all these years, in the act of clicking in his checkmate. "I'm not trying to tell you how to run your business, or rather Mr. Wiles's. And these of course are not our workers, or our conversation would be quite different. Your customers want the pretty girls, you say. Fine, I can't stop you. But we know Las Vegas, better than you ever could, and what I *am* trying to tell you—call it a personal courtesy—is to fix this mess. Because things cannot . . . Hey, you little cutie, come here!"

5

Tom

According to Trevor, few indicators are as reliable, when it comes to assessing a man's status, as his demeanor upon walking into a room. Alphas are confident, entering new territory with slow, long strides. They assert dominance over the space around them through a relaxed yet attentive stance, still and poised, no leaning or swaying or rocking back and forth. Aware of people's attention being irresistibly drawn toward them. Taking their time. At ease. In command.

But having rushed into the Positano poker room with a stumbling speed-walk past the registration podium, wide-eyed Tom, sweat gluing his T-shirt to his chest and drying fast in the AC cold, neck moving around in quick jerks like that of a small bird as his eyes scanned the tables in search of the familiar pepper red of Trevor's hair (invisible so far among the rows of unremarkably-hued heads of hunched-over poker players and straight-backed dealers in blue Positano shirts), confused counsel-seeking Tom, still in the midst of a major panic attack in the aftermath of his epiphanic close-call with the Italophile officer on East Trop and pacing the inter-table space in short vectors impeded by backpacks, purses, and the occasional life partner railbirding a poker player from an additional chair arranged for him/her behind the spouse's own (the nervous pacing resulting from a combination of Tom's urgent need to tell Trevor that he could no longer, no longer go on living illegally and at constant risk of being found out and deported, and his genetic and often embarrassing inability to make out faces at a distance), poor Tom, was acutely aware of how everything in his demeanor appeared hopelessly, screamingly beta. He needed to calm the fuck down.

If Trevor wasn't at the tables, as it seemed, there were only a few places he could be. Outside the door of the Moda nightclub, the older and larger of the two clubs at the Pos, studying the line of people waiting to get in? Nothing gave Trevor more delight than watching the suited-up bros struggle to put on their game faces—stiff-shouldered, eyes mean, insecure, like lion cubs fumbling a play-hunt in the savannah, endearing in their complete misunderstanding of what confidence really is. The Moda was closed on Tuesdays, though, so he wouldn't be there. In the Via del Nord (formerly part of the Sorrento Promenade), the hotel's north-side shopping district, maybe? A compulsive sweet tooth in perpetual struggle with himself and on a strict diet-and-workout regime, Trevor had lately resolved to cut all added sugar from his diet with the exception of breakfast cereal, his favorite. As a result, he'd made a habit of standing by the window of the French patisserie, watching the chocolate fountain for minutes on end in a fearless test of his strength of will. As an added temptation, he would go in and buy Tom some rich, decadent treat—chocolate eclairs, caramel and fudge layer cake, a double-chunk cookie—an experiment that Tom was quite happy to participate in. But Trevor didn't know Tom was here, and he wouldn't dare go to the pastry shop without being able to tell himself he was going for someone else. No, Tom thought, Trevor was most likely taking one of his frequent breaks from the grind in the place that above all he found relaxing: the Positano Sportsbook, just to the right of the poker room.

He found him there, splayed on one of the brown-leather lounge chairs. His foot, resting casually on an LCD-monitor table, partially covered the voiceless talking face of Charles Barkley, who according to the bottom-screen TNT graphics was analyzing Lebron's "second first month" as a Cleveland Cavalier.

"Trevor, I need to confer asap, man."

His roommate, it seemed, was talking to himself: "On a break from our two/five session at the Pos. Our table is, surprise surprise, very good, and the poker gods have been kind so far. A few hands worth taking a look at together in these first couple hours of play—"

"Trevor, dude, man, I'm in dire need of your counsel."

"But first," Trevor said, "I guess I may as well introduce you guys to my real-life Italian roommate." Trevor reached forward to the back of the lounge chair in front of him where, Tom now realized, his phone lay horizontally wedged above the chair's own LCD screen. He was recording a video. "All right, Tomsky, say hi to the awesome people of YouTube! Folks, this is Tom, Tomkins, T-Bone, Tomasso, Tom*ah*to."

"Trevor—"

"I'm sure you'll see plenty of him in future episodes. I promise you'll love him, he's the best. No really, this dude's the bomb. Tom-the-bomb!" Trevor stuck the phone back in the chair. "Okay, so in the first hand we open pocket jacks from the cutoff—"

Tom resolved to wait. He settled on an empty chair a few feet away from whatever Trevor was shooting and decided to try to regroup on his own, without a little help from his friend. The problem was, of course, that as much as Trevor loved it, the Sportsbook was to Tom the least relaxing place in Vegas. In an attempt to remind patrons of every sporting event taking place around the world at any given moment (to induce vig-heavy bets and ambitious cross-disciplinary parlays of, say, men's college basketball, women's tennis, and dog racing), virtually every flat surface in the room was equipped with a hi-def LCD screen of its own: eight megascreens enveloping the room's walls broadcast the marquee events, while vertical strips of smaller square monitors propagated less mainstream competitions; the tables, all built in the televisual golden ratio of 16:9, offered fully customizable sports coverage through highly sensitive touch-screen technology (although Trevor's rubber-soled foot had no visible effect on them); additional video feeds came from mini-screens mounted on the back of each chair, from old-fashioned TVs behind the betting booths, and, naturally, from monitors hanging all over the bar. How could Trevor find peace and quiet in the midst of this video assault was to Tom a complete mystery.

Any way he thought about it, the incident with the cop looked more and more like a miracle. A miracle that wouldn't happen twice. He felt that once again he had been absurdly lucky at a crucial juncture of his life, as seemed to be par for the course in the last couple years. But now he really needed to take action to avoid throwing it all away. A year and a half in Vegas had changed him. He felt changed in ways he would have never been able to predict the night of his WSOP score, when Trevor had left him at the All-American Grille counter to mull over the strangest, most exciting offer he'd ever received. He dared want things for himself now, he dared to dream. Hell, sometimes he even felt like he deserved his unbelievable luck. His years in Rome had been pure survival, dreamless, hopeless sleepwalking, a flavorless meal. Here, he had a life.

He was a different man all right. But not different enough to go on like this. This was reckless, stupid: being an illegal immigrant meant gambling with his future, it meant putting the idea of a life away from the sad neons of Rebibbia and into the awe-inspiring neons of Las Vegas in serious, all-or-nothing jeopardy. Once you got caught, there was no coming back. This was the real surprise: for the first time in his life, Tom felt like he really had something to lose.

"I'm starting a vlog!" announced Trevor, arms open wide, joining Tom where he was sitting. "Isn't that neat?"

"Is splendid," said Tom. "Kick-ass! But so, Trevor, I wanted to tell—"

"Right, your thing, I heard you. Go for it, I'm all ears."

"I was driving on the Tropicana earlier, I was coming here—"

"In the Tomsmobile, is what you're saying."

"Yes."

"The old Ford Tomster."

"Yes. And also, you know, the driver's seat still doesn't come up," said Tom, who a couchside maternal education had rendered very patient with conversational detours. "Which I'm sure you didn't do anything bad, but—"

"By the way, you're cool with appearing on the vlog from time to time right?" Trevor reached back into his pocket to check something on his phone or do something to his phone. "Like, I know I didn't ask, but I just thought it'd be okay for sure—"

"So then I was on the Trop, Trevor, driving here, and this cop tells me to halt—"

"—I'm anticipating a pretty solid following, so that could be good for both of us, I think."

"—And he requested documents, you know? Trevor?"

"I'm with you, he asked you for ID, go on."

"Yes, the ID," said Tom, reaching into his black nylon cardholder bulging with his Wiles Group player's card, his Italian SS card, and the ten $100 bills he needed as daily bankroll for his poker session ($300 for his buy-in, the rest if he needed to reload). He no longer kept money in his underwear. "I don't have a license, Trevor, man. And I am illegal, remember? My passport has an expired tourist stamp on it."

"Right. Shitty spot," conceded Trevor. "What did you do?"

"I had a panic. I gave him this." Tom handed over his SS card.

Trevor laughed. "What is this thing? No wait, more important, how are you not in jail right now?"

"He was Italophile," said Tom.

"Come again?"

"Italophile. An admirer of Italy."

"How you know these words, I'll never figure out," said Trevor.

"We have the same. Also, Trevor, bro, man, really sorry to say, but my name is Tommaso. T-O-M-M-A-S-O. Not Tomasso. Strong *m*, weak *s*."

"Right. So all good then?" said Trevor.

"Not good, no, not good," said Tom. "This was . . . a wake."

"A wake?"

"Like an alarm clock."

"You mean a wake-up call."

"A wake-up call."

"A wake-up call to what?"

"I can't stay illegal, Trevor," said Tom. "I don't wish to be deported. My life is here now, I want to stay. Is really important to me."

"But it took almost two years before you got pulled over once," said Trevor. "You know how slim the chance is that happens again?"

"But I am frightened," said Tom.

"Shit," said Trevor, looking back to the lounge chair Tom found him in.

"Should I not be?"

"No, I just realized something. You probably shouldn't be in the vlog now, should you?"

"No, verily I shouldn't," said Tom. "I was trying to tell earlier—"

"Showing an undocumented immigrant on YouTube and all that," said Trevor. "Shit, I'm gonna have to shoot that whole bit again."

"I'm sorry," said Tom.

"It's okay, we'll figure it out."

"We will?"

"Yeah, it's fine. We'll come up with a fake backstory for you, so you can be in videos. Like, a movie character, you know? We'll say you're a Euro wizard." He winked.

"Oh."

"I think I should really buy a new camera for this," said Trevor. "You know, phone cameras really suck when it comes to video-making. Professional equipment is so expensive though, ugh."

"But Trevor—"

"Don't worry, bro, I'm thinking. We're gonna find a solution to your problem, easy."

"I am frightened we won't."

"Yes, yes, I'll start thinking of a plan right away. You're not getting deported anytime soon, I promise. Do you trust me?"

And so maybe once again if Tom hadn't been a follower, a listener, a beta, if he'd learned to take the reins of his life like Trevor had tried and tried to teach him to do, maybe he wouldn't have put the matter of his immigration status and ultimately his whole future in the hands of someone else. If he'd listened to Trevor when he taught him how to stand up for himself and be a man, maybe now he *wouldn't* have listened to Trevor, and he wouldn't have set in motion the relentless chain of events that would lead him to crime, danger, and clear-cut responsibility over the sudden disappearance and very possible death of an adorable little Pomeranian called Pepperthedog.

It had taken about a week of sweltering Las Vegas summer for Tom to decide against stashing his money in mail envelopes in his underwear. True as it is that the desert heat is, as they say, a dry heat, having a tight packet of heavy paper pressed firmly against the skin of one's ass and/or thighs is hardly a pleasurable experience on a 115°F day (or, rather, 46°C, as it was and would always be for Tom). Summer heat in Rome is a moist veil that covers the city—a wetness that alters shapes and textures, a psychedelic prankster that makes inanimate objects sweat and the world go sticky. The sun in Vegas has no sense of humor whatsoever. It is a hyperefficient oven that leaves the world well done and juiceless. A wallet seemed like a reasonable compromise.

So he had stayed. With a three-month tourist visa, a respectable bankroll for the live games, and an inebriating sense of potential, Tom had decided to call home for advice. His brother loved Trevor's idea, and even his mother, who had more or less always encouraged him to find a way to *svoltare* (turn things around, mostly financially), had fully endorsed his poker trip. Tom had worried she would miss him, but she'd sounded so genuinely thrilled at the idea that both her sons were "making their fortunes abroad" that he decided she probably wasn't lying.

The Strip was a revelation. After spending his first, life-upending four days in Vegas all within the purple confines of the Rio, the discovery that the city had more, non-samba-themed wonders left in store came almost as a surprise. Of course Tom had seen images of the Strip before: he had seen *The Hangover* and *Ocean's Eleven*, and he'd conquered the township of Las Venturas playing *GTA: San Andreas*. But as Trevor walked him around, showing him the different places in town where one could profitably play low-stakes NLHE ("The Mirage, the Shibuya, the Wiles Tower: this town is our oyster, my friend"), the visual impact of the real deal was almost overwhelming. On the curved surfaces of commercial buildings, gigantic screens bounced video teasers off each other for *The Phantom of the Opera*, *M&M's: The Musical,* and *Robosex: Burlesque of the Future!* A 1:2-scale Eiffel Tower and an 800:1-scale neon-lit Coca-Cola bottle rose to comparable heights. The idea that lights and billboards and brand names could be used not to make the financial best of a sorry real estate situation but to create something truly beautiful was to Tom exhilarating.

It was the Positano, however, that attracted Tom most of all. Having never been to the real Costiera Amalfitana himself, Tom had no real claim of familiarity with the postcard prettiness of the (fake) seaside hotel. And yet he did recognize in it something that seemed to include him. Something he felt he belonged to. He loved how the artificial waves muffled in a watery sound the distant drum and bass coming from a shopping center farther south along the Strip. He loved how the nature-filled distance between the street and the hotel compound created room for rare gusts of wind to dance in. He was very happy to learn, from Trevor, that the Pos remained, even just for small stakes, pretty much the place to be for Vegas poker.

They had started grinding some serious hours at the tables right away, while Tom was still enjoying free hospitality at the Rio. While Trevor's primer about live cash games hadn't gone much beyond "play *tight*, don't *limp*, and don't fall in love with Ace-King," Tom's transition to the world of ten-hours-a-day professional poker was an incredibly smooth one. He was winning, and winning easily. The $1/$3 tables he sat at were almost entirely made up of tourists trying to have a good time, and even from the limited reach of his expertise, Tom could see how they were making very basic mistakes. It really did all come down to playing tight and waiting for good hands.

Trevor himself, judging from the times they happened to play the same table, favored a much more risk-prone style, taking fuller advantage of their opponents' blunders by being more aggressive. He told Tom this took time to master, and that it'd be better for him if he played more conservatively until he had more hours of experience under his belt. His plays required a grasp of the language of the table—peoples' subtle emotional and psychological cues—that Tom wasn't yet ready for, but if he kept watching Trevor and asking him questions, he was sure to eventually achieve fluency. Tom nodded at this, but secretly didn't quite look forward to it: deep down, risk-proneness and aggressive play scared him, and he felt that a quiet, tight approach suited his personality a lot more. Nevertheless, he studiously asked questions and wrote down hands he played to have his coach look them over and give him advice. A couple of weeks in, he even asked Trevor if he could railbird some of his sessions to take notes, which Trevor apparently enjoyed quite a bit. When he knew he was being watched, Trevor showed a tendency for even fancier play than usual, with impressive bluffs and brave hero-calls and the like.

The apartment they rented for the summer was a small two-bedroom on South Valley View, between Harmon and Flamingo, just west of the Strip and fairly close to the Rio. On paper, it was also conveniently close to all center-Strip resorts, which was the reason for Trevor's choice. In practice, since Trevor didn't have a car, and since the apartment was located just beyond the pedestrian nightmare of the Las Vegas Freeway, going anywhere to play turned out to be tricky. Tom's refusal to splurge on taxis (he had been in a taxi exactly once in his life, a story he would eventually share with Trevor, many months later) forced them to settle for the bus, a solution virtually unknown to tourists, but not too much of a hassle.

The compromise, however, had come at a cost. It was on one of their first days in the new place, on a cloudless Vegas noon, that Tom and Trevor decided to try out what on Google Maps looked like a leisurely fifteen-minute blue-dotted walk to the north entrance of the Positano. Out of the door they found themselves in the large concrete backlot that spreads just past the Strip: short service buildings, parking lots, and lanes upon lanes of sun-scorched asphalt undulating in the distance. Sunlight bounced off the curved glass of the hotel windows, projecting a kids-ants-and-magnifying-glass scenario they were roasting at the wrong end of. At Trevor's suggestion, they decided to climb up the ramp to their left to cut through, but the shortcut soon landed them on the sidewalkless overpass to the Las Vegas Freeway, with cars speeding by and signs that threatened Salt Lake City and Phoenix. And it was there, as a herd of black Impalas cruised by, missing them by centimeters, that Tom for the first time experienced the slightest of doubts about his roommate's managerial policies; he realized, as he looked at himself, stranded on the overpass with no clue as to how to get out of there, the straps of his backpack drawing two awkward stripes of sweat on his T-shirt, that he'd clearly let Trevor claim for himself the role of the decision-maker of the two. That his reluctance to assert his views too strongly and his chronic fear of any form of confrontation had once again, like so many times in his life before, landed him on the weak side of a dual dynamic. That he had once again, this time much too literally, taken the high road.

He didn't say anything that day, as they retraced their steps back toward Valley View, and after that they never talked about shortcuts again. Tom's doubts never built up to any kind of real resentment. They found the right way, and at the end of the day they came to the serene shared conclusion that walking to the Pos was quite out of the question. And as the weeks went by and their friendship grew deeper, Tom less and less questioned the nature of his role in it, or wondered why it was that his younger roommate had taken the helm so naturally, without any fuss.

A day in the life of a poker player, turns out, is remarkably predictable. They woke up in the early afternoon, ate milk and cereal while talking about hands from the day before, then left for the Positano, or the Rio, or some-where else. On the way they would call in for the waiting list, something Trevor would generously do for both, sparing Tom the embarrassment of speaking English to a stranger on the phone. Then they would play, Trevor taking frequent breaks, Tom barely ever, logging in hours upon hours in the unchanging light of the poker room, unaware of afternoons turning to sunsets, sunsets to nights. Tom would listen to the same few albums on his Walmart-bought headphones over and over, shuffle a stack of $1 chips the same way almost constantly, experience the same emotional roller coaster as he won and lost daily. He had soon started to identify the desperate, angry feeling of getting stuck early in a session, the irrational desire to make it all back right away, the dangerous tendency to try to get involved in more big pots than usual in order to get even. Likewise, he soon started to recognize the natural high that came with a big winning session: the feeling of power, boundless potential, pure invincibility. It was only in moments like these that he could see a way to the alphaness Trevor kept talking about.

For sustenance, Las Vegas low-stakes poker grinders depended on casino comps. The discovery that for every hour spent playing cards he would earn $2 redeemable at select restaurants in the casino was, for Tom, perhaps the most stunning in a series of jaw-dropping Las Vegas wonders. He came to treasure his sapphire-blue Wiles Group player's card (valid at all Wiles-owned properties in town) like a magic artifact. He never gave anybody any money for it, it wasn't linked to a bank account, and yet anytime he swiped it, it materialized free food and smiles all around him. American, Chinese, almost never Italian. Those first weeks in the desert became for Tom, the son of a land of hardened food snobs, a veritable honeymoon with American cuisine. Everything was *more*, the salt, the sugar, the portions. His hunger. His metabolism, the only fearless, risk-taking part of him, stood up to the challenge admirably, and he stayed deceptively thin. But he grew voracious. Once he found out that the snack bar stocked plenty of varieties of beef jerky bags, it became hard to see him anywhere without an emergency stash. That too became part of the routine.

Meanwhile, things at home were less predictable. Tom's mom, the chronically sad, couch-ridden woman who had depended on her son's help relentlessly for nearly two decades, now beamed an enthusiasm strong enough to overcome any Skype lag. When he was growing up, other children had stolen the change from their parents when they were sent out to buy milk round the corner; Tom added money from his pocket when his mom didn't give him enough to buy her weed at the housing project down the street. Yet this woman, faced with a long Roman summer alone for the first time in maybe her whole life, seemed to have found something she could get excited about: she had apparently cleared as much stuff as she could from Tom's room, and had started Airbnb-ing it for stunning, easy profit.

The delighted voice with which she went on and on about how cute, just how flawless and sweet and pretty, this Brazilian girl she had over now was gave Tom pause. It wasn't the thought of a stranger living in his room, going through his stuff, impinging on his privacy: Tom had little-to-no sense of personal property when it came to himself (though he valued and respected that of others, naturally). And it wasn't the fear that his mother could enjoy her sweet, pretty new roommate more than she enjoyed having him around (jealousy being a sentiment, like most self-concerned ones, utterly foreign to him). It was, rather, the thought of going home at the end of the summer and taking this joy away from his mother; this one thing that seemed to be making her more active, energetic—dare he say happy?—than ever before. How horrible would it be, to be the one causing it all to stop?

They had become fast friends. Which, as Trevor explained, didn't actually mean they'd become friends *fast*, though that was true too. But their friendship had developed roots of familiarity and care that extended much deeper than Tom would have thought possible. He *liked* Trevor, he was a good friend; and, as completely undeserved as it seemed, Trevor really seemed to like him too.

Throughout the summer, on their time off poker together, they explored Las Vegas. These long, unpredictable nights led them halfway across town, from one casino to the next, talking to strangers, playing elaborate drinking games, or just waiting for the sun to rise above the desert. While Vegas looked scientifically designed to siphon as much money as possible off its patrons, Trevor turned out to have an arsenal of tricks up his sleeve that made their fun pretty much free of charge. Since poker-room waitresses tended to remember and recognize him, he could score comp drinks in every casino even when they weren't playing (Tom, who up to that summer had been a fairly lousy drinker, developed a real love for the most sugary concoctions on the menu—piña coladas, frozen daiquiris, and the like). Trevor could even get them into clubs and pool parties for free, using a technically expired Platinum VIP player's card he claimed to have found in a bathroom, but they didn't go often, and usually didn't stay long. The town just had so much more to offer.

What Tom discovered early on in their friendship was that, beneath all his charisma and his obvious social talents, Trevor was actually much more down-to-earth and straight-up fun than he seemed. Sure, he was confident, charming, and from what little Tom could tell, very good with women (on uneventful poker days, when Tom took the bus home and Trevor stayed just a little longer and got a cab, he would show up at the apartment four or five hours later, unknown tourist girl in tow, and make a wordless beeline to his room—turns out that Walmart headphones have better noise canceling than you'd think). But in spite of all that, he still enjoyed having silly fun with someone as socially inept as Tom. He liked to come up with complex games for their nights out: scavenger hunts of variously intoxicated tourists (drunk, tripping, stoned) or specific clothing ("find someone playing slots in sweatpants"), or the all-time favorite "hooker-not-a-hooker," played at the counter of the fancy cocktail lounges. Tom found that they laughed together more frequently than he ever had with anyone else. Trevor was like an ideal, better version of himself, he felt: the man he could have been if he hadn't been so damn scared all the time.

Then, of course, there was the teaching. The initial spark of compatibility that had brought Tom to listen to Trevor's entire life story at the very tournament table where they'd met—while telling him close to nothing about his in return—had flourished into a dependable interplay, a perfect synergy of two complementary dispositions. It was understandable that

Tom would have a lot to learn: about poker, about America, about life. What came as a surprise, perhaps to both, was how neatly and serendipitously Trevor's areas of expertise matched Tom's needs, and how smooth this unilateral transmission of knowledge would turn out to be. It hadn't taken long for Trevor to figure out that it was Tom's personality, more than his poker game or his linguistic fluency, that most needed fixing. He was, at the time of his first Trevor-advised decision to prolong his stay in the US, a hopeless beta. And in a town like Vegas, and in a world like the poker world, nothing could be more damning than that. And so Trevor had set off on a journey of education of his roommate, not just out of desire to groom for himself a better wingman and partner in crime of sorts but out of real, fast-growing affection for this ill-equipped video-game nerd on an unlikely quest to conquer Sin City. He was rooting for him, was the thing.

In a few weeks, Trevor's lessons—conducted over 2:00 p.m. Lucky Charms in the apartment, on bus rides, or on their drunken nights property-hopping around the Strip—had ranged from the philosophical to the technical to the nitty-gritty and jargon of pick-up artistry. He wasn't trying to teach him to pick up girls (though Tom would often meekly try to steer the conversation that way) so much as offer him a new perspective on life and the underlying forces that rule human interactions. A new understanding of the power of the self. He explained the struggle for dominance, the pursuit of happiness, the invisible hand, the selfish gene. He mentioned Joseph Campbell and Aleksandr Solzhenitsyn, Carl Jung and Ayn Rand. There was no reason, he said, someone as cool as Tom should relegate himself to the corners of existence. He deserved so much better.

"That's why I'm a bit worried," he said, the night of their last dinner together before Tom's flight home. His ninety-day tourist visa would expire in less than a week.

"Worried of what?" asked Tom, dipping a shrimp from his brimming buffet plate in a splotch of gravy next to his steak.

"I'm worried about you, Tomsky. About you going home," said Trevor.

In his view, Tom's obvious sense of inadequacy, crumpling self-confidence, and impaired sense of self-worth stemmed from some deeply rooted feeling of guilt. Very Euro of him. Very Catholic. The solution, without suggesting he picked up the innate entitlement of the American, still had to begin with a new and powered-up belief in himself. Tom needed to stand up for himself. Put up a fight.

"What should I fight?"

"That's what I wanted to talk to you about tonight," said Trevor. "I've had a great idea."

It was a Wednesday night early in September, and Trevor had taken Tom out for dinner at the Positano buffet. They needed one last real dinner together before he left, he'd said: not their usual tableside meals from aluminum boxes and styrofoam plates, a real feast. Though Trevor had said "I'll take you out to dinner," nobody was actually paying: they'd both been saving up for a few days to pay for the $35 buffet pass with their casino comps. It was their big send-off for Tom, after all: proper celebration was in order.

After they skipped the long line at the entrance by virtue of their pass (something Tom found slightly uncomfortable, just walking right past all those people waiting—Trevor, on the other hand, seemed to enjoy it a good deal), a waiter had shown them to their table, and filled their tall glasses with a dozen cubes of ice and water.

"I've kept this as a surprise for a special occasion," Trevor said, getting up with his plate. "Here you go, Tomsky: your new favorite place in the world!"

The room was huge. Fifteen, maybe twenty manned stations offered individual specialties—from where he was standing, Tom could see prime rib, beef filet, sirloin steak, all carved right in front of you and to your specifications—while mile-long self-service displays hosted anything and everything a digestive tract could one day dream to process. Children crowded the massive dessert island in the middle of the room, squealing in delight at the steel udders releasing globs of ice cream in their bowls, while behind them red-faced men filled their plates with more cuts of meat than Tom could name, regardless of the language. The sheer vastness of the buffet was hard to believe, and Tom realized he was only seeing a small part of it. There was no telling what else this cave of wonders had in store.

"A great idea?" asked Tom, after finishing his first glorious plateful of food, mainly from the meat-carving stations right across from their table. He would have explored further, but Trevor had got some lean chicken breast and broccoli and quickly returned to their table, and he felt bad about making him wait. The shrimp he'd found close by, cascading over an ice bed upon a two-meter-long table, and he piled as many as he could fit in the last available square centimeters of plate. That all of this would be *free*, available to him especially as a valued regular customer of the Wiles Group's resorts, was baffling. It didn't seem possible.

"Yes," said Trevor. "A real game-changer. Total light-bulb moment. Had a serious revelation over here, is what I'm saying. By the way, had you ever tried surf 'n' turf before? Or did you just figure that out all by yourself?" He pointed to Tom's plate.

"Is this servant's turf? The shrimps with the gravy?"

"Never mind. Tell me this: How do you feel about leaving?"

Tom sucked his ice-cold water through a straw. Two American ideas, the ice and the straw, he was immoderately fond of.

"I don't know," he said. "I have not thought about it a lot."

In fact, Tom had tried hard not to think about it at all. As June had turned to July, July to August, August finally to September, his life in Rome had started to appear so distant, so different, that he didn't quite recognize it anymore. What he did, what he wanted, who he was back there. There was a drowsiness to his thoughts of home, a sort of underwater feel to them.

"Are you afraid?"

"Of Rome?"

"Of thinking about it."

"Not afraid maybe," said Tom. "But my life is very different there. Is like, you would not recognize me there."

"Of course I would, Tomsky."

Tom looked down at his empty plate, action-painted with trails of brown gravy, and shook his head. "You would not be my friend."

"But what about you?" said Trevor. "Which of these two lives do *you* like? Which one do you want?"

Still staring at the thick splotches of sauce on his plate, Tom considered this. He had never been good at it, figuring out how he felt about his life as it was happening. The last three months had gone by in a blur, certainly aided by his newfound love for tropical cocktails, but he realized now he'd never really noticed how happy they'd been. Perhaps it's because that's how happiness works, we let it glide by us while we're not watching, and when we finally see it, it's when it's about to end. Or perhaps all his life, the good and the bad, had this way of sliding past him, leaving no impression until it was over. He should think more about this someday, he thought. And yet he *had* been happy this summer, he saw now. The rush, the mix of confusion and fear and excitement that had spurred him on day after day, the endless discoveries. And this feeling, this childish idea that maybe there was something about America, something intrinsically different, better. A land where every small thing, like the ice and the straw in his water glass, had the uncanny ability to strike him as decidedly typical, absolutely American. A land where shrimp cascaded by the tableful, just there for the taking. A land, he thought, where even someone like him could find the courage to take it.

"Is not important," he finally said. "I don't have a choice. I must go back."

"Yes, that's what we thought," said Trevor. "But here's the twenty-four-carat, five-star home run of an intuition I had: What if you didn't?"

"I didn't?"

"Stay here."

"Trevor, man, I don't follow."

"Stay. Overstay. Fuck you, tourist visa! Stay right here. Live in America. Be a professional poker player."

"But is illegal!"

"Then be an illegal, renegade professional poker player in Las fucking Vegas. How's *that* sound?"

According to Trevor, very good. Piece of cake, really. He'd done the research: Las Vegas was home to over 150,000 illegal immigrants, which percentagewise was over twice the national average. Not only that, it was also by far the best city to live in with no bank account or any credit whatsoever, what with the gaming industry being a well known currency-based system, and the desert sun being way too hot for anybody to worry about due diligence. He'd personally met several local tinfoil-hat weirdos at the tables who'd been living off the grid for years, 100 percent cash, easiest thing in the world.

"*You* could be one of those weirdos," said Trevor. "Besides, have you not noticed that we've been paying our rent in cash since day one?"

Tom wasn't sure whether Trevor was joking or not. Surely he couldn't be suggesting that he become a criminal, not him! Yet by now he'd learned to recognize Trevor's uncontrollable excitement about personal, self-affirming decisions, whosever they be. The same passion in his voice as the night he'd suggested they be roommates, or as he analyzed true alpha behavior in *Top Gun*. Could it be that he valued individual empowerment even above the confines of the law? Could he really be serious?

"Look," he went on. "I get it, it's scary. It's supposed to be, the system is designed that way, to keep you in your place. You were born poor and in the boonies, in one of the countries with the lowest social mobility in the Western world. I understand what it must be like. You start feeling like it's that way *for a reason*, you go along with it. You give up hope."

"Hope?" said Tom, raising his head.

"Hope," said Trevor. "You grow hopeless."

"Calm in the midst of hopelessness."

"Calm . . . sure, that too. But it doesn't have to be that way." Trevor's energy was taking on a courtroom feel. "You don't have to let everything be decided for you by someone else, or by the arbitrary circumstances of your birth. You can make decisions, decisions that are *yours* and yours alone. Take a stand. Take *responsibility*. If you go home, you're saying you're okay with things the way they are. That you don't deserve this, that you don't deserve America. But that's the whole point of America, that you *can* deserve it if you just dare *want* it." He paused, satisfied with his delivery. "And speaking of wanting, I'm going to go get us something, give you a little time to think about this."

When Trevor got up, Tom's fears quickly filled the void left by the end of his speech. He watched his roommate disappear beyond the sitting area—into the realm of thrilling abundance he knew lay just around the corner—dreading the thought of having to disappoint him when he was so full of enthusiasm. He had been wrong not to stop him right away, to let him think he was seriously considering this. This was madness. He needed to go tell him right now.

He left the table in a hurried stumble, scanning the room for the familiar pepper red of Trevor's hair among the hungry tourists crowding the food displays like survivors at a postapocalyptic shelter, or animals at a fresh spring in a drought-stricken savannah. He walked past the meats and the desserts, past the shrimp and far into new uncharted territory, grilled vegetables and salad bars, entire tanks of unspecified white condiments, maybe yogurt or sour cream. There was no way he was staying in Vegas illegally. No way. The optimism Trevor was selling, the standing-up-for-himself, the social market of all human interactions, the wanting, wanting, wanting, it just wasn't *him*. Things didn't happen to him. Trevor wasn't just a better version of him, no matter how much he changed. There was a fundamental difference, a predisposition to the act of wanting, of taking, something primal, genetic, or too deeply ingrained to fuck with anyway. It was time to stop this daydream and go home. Past the meats and to the left, he discovered an ample bread region, stocked with an overwhelming variety of baked goods: ciabatta, sourdough, baguettes, several types of bread rolls, breadsticks, garlic bread, olive loaves. He realized he was holding his empty plate; he must have grabbed it when he'd stood up to chase Trevor. They had those puffy, soft, shiny buns he would eat as a kid—known in Rome as *panini al latte*. He picked up five. Go home. Go home to Rebibbia, to his quiet corner, where the world could forget about him, to the calm hopelessness that made his father gasp for air, but where he'd always felt a certain sad sense of safety, the safety of not choosing, of accepting his fate, of just surviving. There was fried rice, sticky rice, brown rice, saffron risotto (he scooped up a good helping). He would go home to his mom. She had always needed him, counted on him all those days when leaving the living room couch was too much to undertake. And yet, if he had to be honest, a case could be made that she was really better off without him. If she could keep renting out Tom's empty room, she wouldn't have to go back to washing hallway floors and scrubbing toilets once the school year started. She would have time for herself, get off her couch, maybe pick up painting again. He'd told himself it wasn't his fault that she would have to give that up, that his tourist visa was expiring and that he just *had* to go back; but now that Trevor was showing him another way, a way for him to stay if he only had the guts to go for it, was it not his cowardice that forced her to keep working? There was a whole huge sushi corner too! Hectares of nigiri, spicy tuna rolls, California rolls, sea urchin rolls, rolls with fish he had never even seen before, and supple pink slabs of salmon sashimi, and wine-red chunks of tuna, and four different kinds of soy sauce, and he couldn't find Trevor, and he picked up a lot. And honestly, why not? Why not, *really?* Why not stay? He rolled out his mental legal pad and began running down a tempting list of pros: (1) Money in his pockets. Enough to pay rent, maybe enough to buy a shitty car, enough to cover the virtually non-existent expenses of living in Las Vegas. (2) A job. A remunerative job, nothing special right now, but in a kind of business Trevor had called "scalable." (3) A source of income, serenity—maybe happiness?—for his mom. One that was entirely and conditionally dependent on his absence from home. (4) A friend. A friend who cared enough about him to research the really quite easy-looking scenarios of undocumented alienhood in town, and to push him, for once, to make a decision, take a stand, be a man. (5) An improbable, exhilarating streak of good luck. (6) A future? And after fears and changes of heart, fresh omelets and fried fish and mashed potatoes, and Trevor nowhere to be seen, he walked back toward their table with a storm in his head, and a plate so full he had to wrap an arm around it to keep his food from falling off, and wishing the decision would once again not be in his hands. That it would be made for him.

"Piña colada with whipped cream, Tomsky, how about that?" said Trevor, already back. "What do you say, should we toast to your new life?"

6

Mary Ann

O nly idiots get lost inside casinos. It's because they follow the lights, like overweight moths with a gambling problem. They wander around looking for the exact spot to lose their money, like it makes any damn difference. A reverse treasure hunt. But you can tell they're confused; they don't know where they are anymore. All it would take would be a look from above, then they'd see it for what it really is: a large room, filled with tables and boxes and not enough light. The air-conditioned basement of hell.

To maximize floor-level gaming space, most of the service tunnels at the Positano stretched out underground, midway between the tourists and the impenetrable vaults underneath. Above, the casino's main cage was a large floor-to-ceiling structure, banklike tills of marble and gold outside, reinforced steel inside, extending downward like a solid trunk all the way to the lowest levels, funneling money down deep. Over the years, increased demand for computer monitoring and hi-tech security prompted the development of the Donut, a multilevel round office encircling the casino-to-vault elevator and hosting the heart of the Positano control system. To make room for the Donut, all female staff changing rooms were moved in 2011 to the mezzanine, a hidden level wedged between the fake town's rooftops and the hillside slope of the hotel above. There were no windows facing out, but the hallways of the mezzanine offered a rare elevated vantage point on the casino aisles below.

Outside the north-side changing area, Mary Ann leaned against the banister, pressing the inside of both forearms to the cool metal bar, peering through the concealed glass slit at the gaming pits downstairs.

This wasn't working.

It wasn't getting any better.

She was still in her street clothes, dark blue Levi's over white Keds, a white sleeveless top, but already wearing full, heavy makeup for her Friday-night shift. Past the soundproof glass, swarming little visitors trekked silently along the tables and slots in groups of two to six, their drunken laughter and the obsessive ringing of the machines on mute. The town was theirs. Without sound, the idling and backtracking of the tourists by the boat-shaped twelve-seat Treasures of the Mediterranean Jackpot Bonanza! 3D slot, or by the lantern-lit blackjack tables with seashell-brassiered dealers at the Siren's Cove, looked positively insane. Young men and women dressed for a night out walked alongside European families in shorts and sandals, seniors in short sleeves and walkers, hotel guests in spongy white complimentary slippers. All looked ahead and around. A choreography of silence. The ballet of a madhouse.

It's what they want, isn't it? To get lost. Stretch themselves to the corners of the city, grow large, shapeless. Engulf more life than a single self can contain.

Little happened during weekends in Vegas casinos that would have been unusual on any other day. And yet it was as if someone would biweekly bend over the background noise console and crank the volume of the wackier and more irksome tracks. The lights seemed shinier, the drunks drunker, the shouting higher-pitched and louder. Everything got headachy. Looking down at the silent-film version of a Las Vegas Friday, Mary Ann counted herself all kinds of lucky that in the carefully egalitarian, union-sanctioned shift rotation of Positano waitstaff, Fridays and Sundays were her assigned days at the upscale and harpsichord-soundtracked Scarlatti Lounge. Advantages included quieter surroundings, less mileage to cover back and forth in heels, and Walter. Her colleagues at work down in the pits made more money, of course, but her seniority status could only land her one mediocre shift there a week, on Wednesdays, along with two morning poker-room snoozefests on Mondays and Tuesdays. Thursdays and Saturdays off.

"You sure look at them a lot for someone who doesn't like them," said Gabrielle, announced by the discreet analog chime of the service elevator reaching the mezzanine.

"Hi, Gab." Mary Ann turned around. "Tables night?"

"You look like you're watching Netflix."

"Yeah, *Planet Earth*."

"Tables, yeah," said Gabrielle, patting her large red designer-knockoff handbag. "You at the lounge?"

Mary Ann nodded. She was back staring at the silent casino aisles below.

Gabrielle joined her along the banister. At least a decade older than Mary Ann, Gab was taller and more imposing. She was from Northeast Texas, on the Louisiana border, and had worked at the Pos long enough to have used the old underground changing rooms. They only had a couple shifts together, since Gabrielle got way more prime-time tables action, but she always addressed Mary Ann with a warm, slightly overbearing friendliness that Mary Ann felt bad about reciprocating poorly. Like all resolute, energetic people, Gabrielle made her extra conscious of her downer sad-sack nature.

"It's not that I don't like them," said Mary Ann after pausing a beat. "It's strange . . . I've been coming here early a lot."

"They're just having fun, Mary," said Gabrielle.

Downstairs, a flock of massage girls in black yoga pants and tops were making their way from North Valet (a side entrance to the Pos on West Flamingo Road) to the poker room, where their evening shift stroking affluent hairy backs was about to begin.

"Someone won the jackpot at Treasures earlier," said Mary Ann. "It was eerie to watch."

"Wait—how long have you been here?"

"I was looking right there when it happened," Mary Ann said, voicing the train of thought she'd been on before Gabrielle's arrival. "This woman . . . she was playing the slot, and she was so lost in it; you could see it in her face. It's like she didn't exist anymore. She was a *thing*. And then the winner lights started going—"

"Who was on the floor? Nick?" asked Gabrielle. "Did he come over to sign the papers?"

"Her eyes—it was like she wasn't ready—"

"How many people were there when it happened? Was there a crowd?"

"Gab, she looked so *scared*," Mary Ann said. *Sedation*. Waking up from deep sleep. Coming to.

Meanwhile Gabrielle was distracted by something downstairs.

"Look at that," she said. "They're at it again."

Mary Ann looked, but no jackpot seemed to be going off anywhere in sight.

"Where?"

"That chip runner, look!" Gabrielle pointed, weirdly animated. "She's bringing a damn *frappuccino* to the poker room!"

"So?" Mary Ann asked.

"So?" said Gabrielle. "That's *our* job! Chip runners can only get players chips and food orders, not drinks. Don't you know?"

"Does it matter?"

"She's stealing your money!"

"I mean . . ."

"We had a whole meeting about this when the goddamn Starbucks opened. WHOA said they'd take care of it, but I knew this shit was gonna happen."

"I didn't know you cared about this stuff," said Mary Ann.

"You should too. We're under attack here." Gabrielle paused to look around.

The elevator bell sounded, and the doors opened. Two incredibly short women emerged, pushing a cleaner's cart. They walked in silence past the changing rooms, following the mezzanine toward one of the utility rooms, a quick look of complete foreignness between four women of different age, race, clothes, lives.

"Let's go get changed," said Gabrielle.

The changing room's decor was not on par with fancy Positano standards. White fluorescence, pimpled black rubber carpets, and damp wooden benches. A distinctive high-school-swimming-pool vibe pervaded the vapor-fogged room. Someone was using the showers in the back, but other than that, the place seemed empty. Mary Ann caught up with Gabrielle and chose a hanger five away from hers, which she instantly regretted. Seven or eight would have been a better distance.

Gabrielle pulled out of her bag her own personal shift tray, a large, heavy-looking rectangular leather-strapped black contraption. The Positano provided waitresses with trays, but the flimsy round things were snubbed by most: it was clear that whoever designed them never had to make the rounds with eight Captain and Cokes, a tips jar, and a napkin box. When it originated, years before, BYOT was neither discouraged nor even really remarked upon by higher-ups, and gradually got so commonplace among staff as to spawn an actual niche industry, catering to different waitressing preferences in shape, weight, and portability. Mary Ann had one herself, which Aunt Karen had bought for her when she started out at the Pos. Thin straps, lighter weight.

"The union needs to do more to protect us," said Gabrielle.

"My aunt always told me the union's pretty great," said Mary Ann.

"Then why is all of this happening?" said Gabrielle, in the tight-lipped voice of someone applying Chapstick.

"Maybe if the free coffee didn't suck they wouldn't pay to get it from the Starbucks down the hall."

"It's bigger than that. We're getting screwed by the system left and right."

"We are?"

"*Yes!* We're not paid enough. Inflation goes up, but our one-dollar tips stay the same. People gamble less and shop more, and it's all the same for the owners, it's only us who suffer. And every year we lose jobs to automation and stupid new technology. This is our future we're talking about."

"Gab, the job is good."

"It *was*, maybe. Stay here long enough, and you'll see it get worse and worse. I got a kid, you know? I can't afford to let all this slide. And have you read about the layoffs?"

Mary Ann looked down. Gabrielle could be real grade-school-teacher scary sometimes. And Mary Ann didn't know anything about anything. Too busy thinking about herself even to read the news.

"We have a group to discuss these issues," said Gabrielle. "You should come to a meeting sometime."

Conversation drifted into lull as they slipped out of their street clothes and into uniforms. Both were black-and-silver minidresses, but the Scarlatti Lounge outfit Mary Ann was putting on had a more formal look, and was slightly less revealing, while Gabrielle's table uniform looked aggressively tight. It was the union-fostered compromise for the tiresome mileage of a shift in the pits: lower heels, sluttier dress (see *WHOA Vegas Waitressing Handbook*).

The image of the woman who won the Treasures jackpot kept coming back. The look of bewilderment at the noise and lights erupting around her, as if she'd been pulled from the womb of Vegas's amniotic daze. What had she seen? Waking up from deep sleep, coming to. Nobody ever talks about what happens after.

"I think she needed help," she said out loud.

What a dumb thing to say.

"The chip runner?" said Gabrielle. She was wiping away Visine tears from beneath her eyes.

"The woman," said Mary Ann. "The jackpot."

Gabrielle appeared to be considering this. From the showers, a young woman made her barefoot way across the fungally hazardous floor to a bench on the opposite side. A uniform Mary Ann didn't recognize lay in a dismissive heap beneath her hanger, indicating she had just finished a shift and was ready to go home.

"Hi, Maidon," said Gabrielle.

"Hi," said the girl.

Her uniform glittered and clinked as she put it away. Modeltainer, thought Mary Ann, maybe a dancer. The pretty face and barely clothed body of some nautical-themed pageantry or other. A reminder that things could always be worse.

"I can tell you, if I won that kind of money, I wouldn't need any help," Gabrielle said.

Mary Ann bit the inside of her cheek. "Yeah, I could use a jackpot too." She forced a smile.

"Maybe you should start playing the slots."

"I should get better shifts, is what I should do."

Gabrielle, now fully dressed, adjusted the straps of her tray. "Oh, you'll get there soon." She sized Mary Ann up with a full-on NYC-model-agency stare. "You're Friday-night-tables material all right. But come to a meeting sometime."

Desire for complete, real, no-joke sedation gets a bad rap. Probably because it looks so much like its melodramatic cousin, suicidal ideation. Especially in hindsight, and especially to other people. Truth is, at the time, in December of 2012, Mary Ann had come to covet a kind of relief from herself sleep always seemed to come up short of. In the very little she remembered of the Saturday night that effectively ended her time in New York, her career as a model, her life as a person-trying-to-make-*something*-of-herself, there was this original sense of wanting to not want, and not feel, and not dream. Not in the peaceful, confusedly Buddhist way her mom had pursued at age nineteen, right after Mary Ann was born—moving her around the East Coast with the Plus One Theater Company, a doe-eyed bodhisattva in training—no. More in the urgent, life-or-death (and ultimately death) way her mom had wanted at age twenty-seven, back in Oxford, when she promised to take her daughter out to the 4 Corners Chevron for chicken-on-a-stick if she behaved at the AA meeting. "I just want a break," she used to say, "someone to take care of me."

That night, in the fifth-floor-walkup prison of her new SoHo apartment, it was Mary Ann's caution and ultimate attachment to life that precipitated the mess. She had recently moved from her more spacious, cheaper, and all-around nicer apartment in Astoria. Her new roommate, Vika, from the agency, was a much better suited specimen for life as a New York City model, at least as stereotypes go. She was Ukrainian, enjoyed going to clubs, and when she got back home and asked Mary Ann for a Xanax to come down from the blow and go to bed, she crushed it very neatly and snorted it with a $20 bill. Alone in the apartment on a Saturday night, Mary Ann was curled on the living room couch, a hand clasped against her mouth, with the absolute certainty that she was a horrible, horrible human being.

Had Mary Ann given in to that rising feeling of terror, of piercing, hurtful worthlessness, all at once, she might have been better off. She might have gulped down a few too many 1 mg blue footballs, dragged herself to bed just in time to fall into a dreamless vacuum, woken up sixteen hours later, on a rainy Sunday afternoon, dehydrated and numb, to the sound of Vika's laptop-speaker EDM. Instead, a novice drug abuser prodded by psychic pain like slaughter-bound cattle, she was, at a level perhaps deeper than her self-hatred, really quite scared of hurting herself. Without making a conscious plan, she decided to microdose herself into the stupor she sought. Pouring the last half glass of water from the red-capped Brita Vika kept in the fridge, she took 1 mg and went back to the couch.

There was absolutely no doubt she was a horrible person. She had driven another devoted, adoring boyfriend to desperation through her utter inability to even pretend to love someone (the first one, back in high school, had coped using acoustic guitar breakup songwriting as a gateway drug to the opiates of his college years, eventually graduating from prescription to street, which surely, she could tell herself, she had nothing to do with, but the evidence was incriminating and who did she think she was fooling, really?). Sloppily, she had missed him (this last one, John, a full-stack developer at Google NY), and gone back to him in August, just a month after breaking up with him, only to find that the sheer act of him walking into the same room made it hard for her to breathe and made her forehead sweat, which he noticed and privately cried about, all the while letting her stay at his place while Vika looked for an apartment, even when it was clear she didn't love him, probably never had, and had no inclination to have sex with him or anybody else anytime soon. So maybe she hadn't really missed him. But she *had* eventually snuck out of his studio in the middle of the Hell's Kitchen night and never answered his calls again, because the truth was, she really didn't care about him. He was a lovely, good-hearted man, and she had hurt him so much, and so deliberately, and she didn't care *at all*.

She allowed herself another Xanax. Unfiltered tap water is supposed to be bad for you, or so Vika said, but footballs are small enough to just swallow dry. She tried placing the blue pill in the middle of her tongue, fewer tastebuds there, then geysered as much saliva as she could muster from the sides of her mouth. The motion dislodged the pill from its seat, and a bitter taste exploded everywhere in her palate as she gulped the little fucker down with her own warm spit. She turned on CNN. Something soothing about the flat-toned streams of professional speech, the blank-eyed stares into the nothingness ahead.

That second and final breakup with John had come almost three months earlier, and while it might have triggered the onset of the Episode, it certainly hadn't been its main motif. No way she would spend a week in bed because of *that* (which, not to be the cry-for-help kind of depressive, just out of real, small-apartment/impossible-to-miss-it curiosity, had Vika even noticed?). And yet a week and then a month had gone by of near life-lessness. Emotional nausea. Wanting to metaphorically vomit herself out of her body (though not at all wanting to physically vomit, or anything literal and predictably weight-related). Real depression is a lot like therapy: it is a path of self-discovery, a learning process with its peaks and valleys, its breakthroughs and epiphanies. That night, things finally felt clear: throughout her life, Mary Ann had caused nothing but pain to each and every person who had the misfortune of knowing her. This latest stunt of emotionally torturing an engineer into talk therapy, then psychiatric help, then even in-house employee assistance for serious Googley support, was no one-off. And horrifyingly, the real reason she cared about it so much was just that people would know, that he would know, that *they* would know, and judge, and not like her anymore, and *that* was the only thing that mattered. She was just a bad, bad person, and always had been.

In her very limited drug experience, Mary Ann had come to understand 2 mg of Xanax as a threshold of sorts. She couldn't remember whether this was something she'd read online or heard from her complacent prescription-signing NY doctor, but the feeling remained. It seemed like 2 mg of Xanax carried enough sedative power to wrap the panickiest depressive in a warm chemical embrace, numbing the mind, relaxing the muscles, impairing movement. It was *supposed* to work. However, there appeared to be an unspoken, tricky caveat to benzo pharmacology, one seldom mentioned in the pertinent literature: you kinda have to *will it* to work. As muscle relaxants go, anxiety meds are a too-polite guest, one that makes sure to repeatedly ask for permission to fuck you up. Xanax blackouts, within standardized dosage, need to be annoyingly consensual.

Still shaking from psychic pain, Mary Ann was in no condition to help the drug do its job. She needed to be taken against her will. She was also starting to worry that the second pill, the one she'd swallowed dry, had never really found its way down and was uncomfortably (and dangerously) lodged somewhere in her esophagus. She resolved to take more, a few more, washing them down with some of Vika's inexplicably top-shelf scotch (tap water is supposed to be bad for you), and adding a couple Tylenol and finally two omeprazoles to the bluish handful for good gastric measure. She could still taste how good, clean, elegantly sweet the Macallan eighteen-year-old felt, which vouched for her lingering, unwelcome lucidity.

If an unwanted creature comes into this world, wreaking havoc upon the lives of one innocent, loving mother, and one maybe guilty, but just-doing-his-best father, and her entire, self-serving existence unfolds for over two decades as a black hole of desire for attention, love, praise, and everything she perceives of said world she perceives in terms of how it affects *her*, how it is good or bad for *her*, and at no point during those over two decades has she ever had a sincere, nonmanufactured passing thought for the well-being of anybody else, and still this undeserving, unloving, unlovable child has lucked into a life well above those of all others around her and certainly any life she could have expected, this child, who still manages to feel achingly unwanted and unloved and alone, still manages to perceive her charmed life as hollow and meaningless, still manages to want more for herself and look with hatred and rage at a world that doesn't devote every atom of its attention to *her* and her alone, this incorrigibly selfish child, would this child be wrong for thinking of herself as a bad person and wanting to shut down the wretched engine of her self for one night? She wouldn't be.

Through the mosquito-netted window, freezing cold New York wind swept the room as Mary Ann made her way back from the kitchen countertop to the couch. Compared to her previous trip, her walk lacked coordination. She moved with the cross-legged convexity of amateur skiers, but the couch turned out to be quite far. She settled for the orange living room table, sat on the one slender IKEA chair (opposite a low, uncomfortable wooden bench with no back support), and lay her whole torso on the cold metal surface, arms crossed, facedown, eyes closed. She started crying. Soon she realized she was thinking of how this would look to others—like a movie audience or something—her sad, beautiful body arched and moving up and down from the sobbing, a picture-perfect image of scripted pain. Then she realized she was still thinking of herself, performing for attention, demanding to be looked at; that even in absolute, heartrending suffering she was still a prisoner of her desire to be seen, she was still fake. That no matter how much she hurt, she was still so much a piece of utter shit that she couldn't access one true, genuine feeling, and if she couldn't now, defenseless and weak, then when? Then she started crying for real.

Fuck it, she'd take sleep at this point. It wasn't the original plan, but fuck it, this needed to end. She thought of Vika and her breezy comedowns on that very table. She'd snort Mary Ann's pills, then saunter off to bed with an amphetaminic spring in her step, and sleep off her upper-downer high in loud snores. Mary Ann had never done it, not even coke, but she'd observed the procedure enough times to understand the basic mechanics. She grabbed Vika's heavy marble ashtray and, in a late resurgence of her micro-dosing instinct, decided it'd be best to try just one first. Except crushing the motherfuckers wasn't easy, with tear-fogged eyes and shaking hands, and she felt like she was wasting more than she was lining up. Besides, one pill didn't really produce much of a line, and her spectatorial experience with drug-snorting had all involved horizontal length and the trademark head-sweep one sees in movies. Fuck it. She crushed the entire last handful of 'em. Looked like a line all right.

And so if her clumsy dealings with the ashtray, and the pills, and her $20-bill-less nasal vacuuming hadn't taken a pathetically long time—long enough for the whole multistepped intake to kick in and truly and finally fuck her up good—and if upon getting up from the table to get to the couch and sleep she hadn't found her body now fully beyond any attempt to stand, let alone walk, and had she not almost immediately hit her knee against the fucking low wooden bench and fallen down, hitting her forehead against the hardwood and passing out there and then, blood more scary-looking than actually dangerous, signaling to even the most absent-minded of Ukrainian roommates getting home after a night out that something was definitely not okay and that medical help was necessary with the highest degree of solicitude, had she instead somehow gained the couch and passed out there, bloodless and asleep-looking, all muscles and respiratory system relaxed to the point of near-complete shutdown, what then? What then? She had only wanted a break.

The way the Scarlatti Lounge worked was that it was *boring*. It had been one of Hendrik Vogelsang's most brilliant sociological intuitions: the only way to achieve real exclusivity in Vegas, the only way to make a lounge truly aristocratic, was not exorbitant pricing but understimulation. Money couldn't deter the cowboy-hatted oddball who'd just successfully "let it ride" at craps, nor the twenty-first-birthday boy out to impress his friends, and not, of course, the hookers. What Wiles had asked for was a quiet nook, a secluded island of elegance for the relaxation of the high rollers, the corporate retreaters, the high-class escorts. And so the Scarlatti worked by subtraction. Minimalist, silent, tuxedoed Koreans took shifts at the harpsichord, a strictly Baroque and mostly Italian repertoire (although Vogelsang had managed to occasionally lift the regional restrictions to include his life's one true love, the music of J. S. Bach). A series of unostentatious paintings hung on the walls, scenes of nineteenth-century Roman aristocracy, the work of an obscure Italian neoclassicist bought in bulk from a museum in Copenhagen that seemed oddly glad to deaccession them. The room's decor was elegant and bland, expensive-looking and lame, like what would happen if you gave your grandmother unlimited budget to buy you a prom dress. Mary Ann liked it there.

On her tray, the standard-issue, nonreplaceable Scarlatti tray, Mary Ann was arranging two glasses, a bottle of Beluga Gold, and $500 worth of caviar in different varieties. These tasting menus, the pièce de résistance of the Scarlatti drinking experience, had the sinister tendency to attract the most obnoxious elements of the lounge's clientele. Your cigar-wielding businessmen, rich waitress-winking creepers, and the like. Today was no exception: on a couch at the far side of the seating room—all the way across from the bar, past the largest painting above the archway that divided the lounge into two separate areas and the harpsichord—a man in his seventies sat morbidly near his twentysomething date. He was wearing a dark blue satin suit with real-life heraldry embroidered on the chest. She was wearing a strapless yellow cocktail dress with black heels, belt, diamond-bearing choker. As frequent as the sight was, the Las Vegas convergence of supply and demand in the field of moneyed seniors with a DD/lg fetish and young movie-star lookalikes with pliable morals, Mary Ann still had trouble dealing with it. Look at him, and he might smile with pride, Freudian savoir faire, perverse beckoning; look at her, and she might give that we're-not-so-different-you-and-I look that drove Mary Ann insane. She concentrated on the gestures, the feel of her fingers around the gold-crowned metal sturgeon on the bottle as she poured the vodka, the lining up of the little plates and spoons and forks, the napkins, soft. Then she smiled to no one in particular and turned around.

"No dear, I wouldn't," said Walter, idly chasing a maraschino cherry around his glass with the elongated $\mathcal{P}$ of a Positano stirring stick. "But we still should refrain from judging them."

"I know, I know I should," said Mary Ann, balancing her now-empty tray with one hand against her stomach, back resting on the marbled wall. "It's just hard, in a town like this."

"That I understand," said Walter.

"I've been trying, I swear. I wanted the new apartment to be a turning point. Remember the day I told you about deleting Instagram? I really thought things would get better after that."

"And they will, in time."

"Well, they haven't so far. I keep blaming the town, or the fact that I don't have friends and spend too much time alone. But the truth is, it's my fault."

As a rule, Mary Ann would nip most conversations with patrons in the bud. While the kindhearted southern belle remained her character of choice in their nightly play, prolonged chitchat was still a waste of valuable time. Plus, it was better to deter customers from getting the wrong idea, or rather from reinforcing their arbitrary assumption that all Vegas cocktail waitresses turned tricks in the hotel rooms after their shifts.

Walter, however, was different. Not only didn't she interrupt their conversations quickly, she actively *initiated* them. A well-kept sixty-five, Walter had the weekend habit of reading at the lounge while drinking old-fashioneds for exactly three hours, between 7:00 and 10:00 p.m., an after-dinner ritual that coincided perfectly with Mary Ann's shifts. He never met anyone there, and didn't seem to be waiting for anything. He just sipped his drink, nose in a book, always kind to his waitress and never seemingly bothered by interruptions. Mary Ann was instantly fascinated.

During the first nights of their acquaintance she had discreetly inquired about his life, on account of his behavior being slightly odd for a tourist and completely unrealistic for a local (no local would drink regularly on the Strip, what with the crowds, the traffic, and prices being anywhere from one and a half to three times higher than at any other bar in town): turns out he was, in fact, from out of town, Laguna Beach, California. He was in Vegas for business.

"And what is it that you do, sir?" she had asked one Sunday, as soon as mutual confidence allowed.

"Oh, call me Walter, love, by all means. Walter Simmons," he said. "I ghost-write unspeakably dull memoirs for the rich old men of Orange County. Frightfully pedestrian, I know, but it does earn an honest living." He sighed. "Alas, one of them has a real passion for baccarat, so I'm here most weekends lately. Says I bring him luck, if you can believe it."

She wasn't sure what it was that quickly made her look forward to their biweekly meetings. Maybe the posh British elegance of his tone, something out of a theater production, or a documentary, or a Mazda commercial. He had a kindness to him, a willingness to listen to Mary Ann patiently and forgivingly. She wished their meetings were farther apart, instead of clumped so close on Fridays and Sundays. The weekend would come, and she would binge on his presence, taking special delight in sowing discursive threads on Friday that she could pick back up on Sunday, not worrying about the passing of time. She'd spend her Saturdays off in a warm sense of comfort and personal improvement, protectively bookended by what she'd started to consider their two regular appointments. But then Mondays came, and she found herself stranded at the wrong end of a Walter-less week, impatient, longing, *bereft* (Walter's word).

(If she had to be really honest about it, Walter's obvious queerness must have had something to do with it as well, her unguarded, spontaneous trust in him in an environment where everybody else seemed to operate on the assumption that she was available for purchase.)

At the harpsichord, behind them, the last-shift player was taking his leave in deep bows. For the rest of the night, music at the lounge would come from the instrument's digital auto-play. They were eerie, these player-less sonatas—like some restless Baroque ghost fated to practice Bach for all eternity.

"Do you really have no friends?" asked Walter.

"Maybe that's not true either," said Mary Ann. "I have Aunt Karen, even though I don't call her all that much since I moved out."

"Nobody your age?"

Mary Ann thought she saw Walter give the slightest, politest glance at his watch resting on the table. Though maybe she'd imagined it. People always assume the worst, when sharing and watches are involved.

"You see what this town is like. It's weird," she said. "And it's not just the men. I know this woman who's a doctor, like a serious hospital doctor, but then I talk to her and all she cares about is her looks, and money."

"Money does appear to be a theme, yes."

"It's all everyone here cares about. Making money. And if you're a woman, it's finding a rich husband. It's the story everybody will tell you, if you let them."

"Las Vegas is a city of stories."

"And they're all about money, and power."

"Oh, come dear, I'm sure you're being too harsh."

They turned their heads in unison to the mismatched lover's table in the back, where daddy was feeding caviar to his girl by the spoonful. When the man looked back at them with a smile, eyes moving from old gentleman Walter to young, beautiful Mary Ann, the grossness of the misunder-standing made her shudder. They were the only other patrons in the lounge that night. Mary Ann looked away.

"I had a friend at my old job," she said. "Lily. But I haven't kept in touch with her either. I liked her, she was smart, but see?—she was pretty sad herself. She needed help. I think that is why I stop calling her, really. Isn't that just awful?"

"Do you feel that it is?" said Walter. She could see how he enjoyed this role, how he playfully acted the couchside clinical repertoire. A library of gestures and pauses of which he probably assumed Mary Ann had no experience at all.

She paused, her gaze lost somewhere to the left of the table, lips tight shut. The image of a woman gathering her thoughts. Which were: Am I overdoing this thinking pose? Does it look fake?

"I think it's awful that I don't really care, yes. That I'm aware of it, and I still let it happen. That I can forgive myself for something so shitty this easily."

Walter smiled.

"It doesn't quite look like you're forgiving yourself, does it?"

She could be honest with Walter. Real honest. She opened up to him, the ugly truths of her, and he accepted them without judgment. There was a relief to it, letting herself think out loud, no matter how circular, or abstract and detached from any real-life consequence, her thoughts might be. But sooner or later Walter would leave, like everyone else in Vegas, and then what? She would be alone again. It wasn't getting any better. She really should call Aunt Karen more often.

"Maybe I'm not," she said. "But maybe I like giving myself a hard time on this so I can avoid the real issue."

"Which is?"

Her eyes again widened in the far-off look of deep reflection she felt was appropriate. "That I feel *invisible*. I don't feel *seen*. I mean, me of all people! I feel utterly, truly *unseen*, and I'm afraid *that* is the real reason I'm unhappy. That every time I try to be less selfish, like deleting social media, learning to live without ambitions, even just *noticing* the lives of the people around me, all this stuff is just effortful, it's just me *trying*, you know? It's not real. That deep down this town is making me miserable because I don't feel *seen*, and I keep trying to be better and I can't."

It felt good to say it. What she'd been thinking, peering down from the hidden personnel hallway at the people Las Vegas was *really* meant for.

"But isn't this human," asked Walter, "all too human? We go to church to ask God to look at us, to judge us guilty or good. We get married and vow to watch each other do the dishes, take the trash out, to give each other's days meaning. This seems hardly your fault."

"Well, I don't have either of those things."

"I'm sorry?"

"God, or a husband."

"Would you want them?"

"No, I wouldn't."

Really wouldn't. Admitting to herself that she had never truly desired sex or relationships—and that this was okay—had been maybe her biggest post-Episode realization. At the time it had felt so momentous, so liberating and powerful, that for a few weeks she'd believed it the solution to all her problems, the one single breakthrough that would turn her life around for good. But then time passed, and she hadn't talked about it with anybody. She'd seen it go from secret happiness, to secret worry, to secret shame. And, honesty or not, she never told Walter either.

"The problem is, I see what the path to being a better person would be: trying to help others, truly caring, for once, about something outside or bigger than myself. I see it, but I don't *feel* it. Inside, deep inside, I don't *really* care, it doesn't move me, it doesn't hurt. But I do feel unseen, and insignificant, all the time, and *that* hurts, it physically hurts. It's like I've learned nothing from everything that happened to me. Don't tell me everyone is like that, I know they're not. Karen thinks about me, she worries. And all I really think about is how irrelevant this city makes me feel, how it's not all about *me me me*."

A distinctly therapeutic pause ensued, a kind Mary Ann had experienced before, and learned to attribute to a clinician's self-satisfaction at a patient's progress. A small nod. Walter's hand reached for his watch, fiddled with it, and placed it back on the table facedown, which Mary Ann registered with some pleasure. Then she felt ashamed that this might be all she really wanted from him.

"That is remarkably lucid, dear," Walter said after some time. "What you just said takes courage."

She smiled.

The first notes of Scarlatti's Sonata in D Major, K. 491, trilled merrily from the harpsichord, with no human fingers touching the keys.

Getting home from work in the middle of the night is not nearly as bad as getting home from work in the middle of the morning. Which was another reason why Mary Ann's shifts at the Scarlatti were a rather favorable arrangement.

On her way out of the Pos, round-the-clock darkness in the casino, round-the-clock fluorescent lighting in the Staff Only hallways, Mary Ann walked in the self-indulgent daze that follows most therapy sessions. It seemed to her like a heightened degree of self-involvement was the one constant in her interactions with legitimate and cocktail-bar counselors alike. Which was strange, since nothing had ever made her feel worse than thinking, but like really thinking hard, about herself. And especially strange now, since Walter's whole therapeutic spiel seemed to revolve around a certain *withdrawal* of the self, relinquishing the idea of herself as the protagonist of an extraordinary story and embracing participation in a larger, if not higher, structure, i.e. life itself. Of course, Mary Ann could smell the hippyish whiff of his words, like burning incense. A familiar smell. Like something her mom would say. Yet coming from Walter, it didn't feel as vague. It felt like a road map, with a goal almost within reach.

The elevator's doors shut out the yellow-lit hallway and opened up, after a dizzy takeoff and downward rush, on the parking-lot gray of the staff underground lot. She wanted to feel better, or at least stop hating herself, or at least try. And maybe Walter was right, maybe her honesty, and the courage it took to admit her desire to be *seen*, really were a necessary step in the right direction. Maybe in order to open ourselves to others—and really mean it—we have to first stare at the bawling child at the center of our being, and make our peace with her. Something that for all she'd been through, she'd never truly done. Maybe she *was* being brave.

Out of North Valet she made a right on Flamingo to drive the couple of really large blocks that separated her from home. When Strip-crossing is involved, Vegas becomes the kind of place where it can take twenty minutes and several ramps of stairs to walk two blocks. Her condo was part of a gated residence on Koval and Flamingo, a nice citadel of beige apartment buildings with enough trees around to afford some shade to the cars parked outside. But to get there from the Pos, one had to drive through the kaleidoscope of kitsch that was the Las Vegas Strip on a Friday night. And so it was on the long red at the traffic light on West Flamingo and the Strip, her car facing the pink-and-white tackiness of the Flamingo Hotel, that her thoughts took a familiar turn for the worse.

Because if being shockingly, unguardedly, stupidly honest was her way of dealing with her self-obsessed nature, of keeping herself functioning and, really, surviving in the world, was that honesty, at least, *good*? Could she have this one thing, and be sure of it? And like a hot wave rising up her chest and throat, came the realization that perhaps all her attempts at self-lessness and self-improvement, her honesty too, had not just been effortful and hard—as she'd told Walter—but really just more advanced, more devious tricks to subtly manipulate others and be seen. That by offering up these vulnerable sides of herself for others to see and judge, she was winning over their trust as a thoughtful, deeply empathetic, self-aware woman, while at the same time only scratching the surface of the really deep, ugly shit. That she was truly *addicted* to approval and validation, would do *anything* to get it, and whatever she got would never be enough. That she didn't care about these people as people *at all*, in spite of her efforts. That she wasn't really trying to empathize with anyone, so long as they thought she was, because what empathy she had was entirely procedural, a means to an end.

If she had her way, she would switch people on and off like household appliances, flipping through human-shaped channels like a TV addict. Wasn't *that* really fucking horrible?

Her fingers tapped the wheel like the fingers of a wireless operator from a black-and-white movie. Her sweat turned cold, drawing rivulets on her skin. What her mother had wanted was for someone to take care of her. *A professional, someone who's paid to do it.* She used to say that every time things got bad. Maybe what she wanted was the right to be honest about not giving a fuck about a single other living thing in the world, *at all.* Just like her daughter.

And so as she waved hello and drove past the night guard and into the parking lot, Mary Ann waved hello also to full-on panic—her old friend—and drove on toward her building like an inmate on death row, blood going cold with real, primal fear. And when she found her assigned parking spot occupied (somewhat diagonally) by Aunt Karen's old Impala, she barely registered the extreme unlikeliness of the circumstance, and the very possibly worrying nature of her aunt showing up just like that on a Friday night. Her body was shaking, her mind screaming with the certainty she was the worst person in the world.

And out of the car and up the short, non-dizzy elevator ride to her second-floor apartment, and sliding the keys into the hole, and up until the very moment before finding her loving, only-family-in-the-world Aunt Karen lying unconscious on the living-room floor, her thoughts were still racing, her selfish brain still oblivious to the likely emergency, her whole being incapable of concentrating for even a second on something that wasn't about her her her.

PART II

WINTER 2014—2015

7

Lindsay

RED CREST TOMATO ASPIC

1 package strawberry Jell-O
2 ¼ cups cooked or canned tomatoes
2 ¼ teaspoons prepared horseradish
1 ¾ teaspoons scraped onion
1 ¾ teaspoons salt
Dash of cayenne

A favorite of mine! A delicious red salad, perhaps served with some asparagus and sliced eggs, that will make everyone think you've been hobnobbing with famous chefs! Gay, sparkling, quivery, luscious-looking, it will lend appetite appeal to any meal!

Start by dissolving the Jell-O in the hot tomatoes. Add horseradish, onion, salt, and cayenne, then force through a sieve into a bowl, giving a good squeeze to the solid bits. Turn into individual molds, then chill until firm. Don't forget to garnish with rich, creamy Best Foods mayonnaise!

Serves 4 to 6.

This was later, after Grandma Peterson had sold out. Stick blender in hand, ready to cream the asparagus, Lindsay eyed the book open on the counter with her great-grandmother's Jell-O recipes. Her first books, in the late '40s, had been a delight. Her prose was witty, energetic, unconventional. Midrecipe, she would suddenly take long detours—winding sentences, peppered with modifiers, urging her readers to "mix furiously," "stir like crazy." She had been a rebel, in her own way. She told women that whipping up a ham and celery loaf dinner in less than twenty minutes didn't make them bad mothers, that the food at their table could look good and taste good and still allow them not to spend their whole day in the kitchen. Had she been a progressive, independent woman in Manhattan, it would have been audacious. For a young mother of six in the Mormon Southwest, it was downright revolutionary.

On January 21, on the eve of what would have been Grandma Peterson's hundredth birthday, Lindsay was working on an aspic for the next day's celebration. She was twenty-eight herself, standing a broad-shouldered five-eleven in a not entirely ironic chef's apron. Dark hair, blue eyes, the build of the serious teenage athlete still visible in the sedentary adult. Her personal version of the aspic was ambitious, involving at least three culinary procedures she had never attempted before, and all the instructions she had to steer by were the rather simplistic ones in Grandma's corporate best seller. The older, cooler books were hard to find, and the copies Lindsay had read over and over as a child were at her parents'.

By the mid-1950s, on a generous contract with Jell-O and Hellmann's/Best Foods, Grandma Peterson had authored five branded cookbooks and almost single-handedly stirred a gelatin craze throughout the Southwest. Carrot and cabbage salads. Molded crabmeats. Piquant tongue loaves.

This was way before the clichéd association of Jell-O with Mormon cuisine—something the Petersons had actually resented, as they felt it cheapened their family heritage. But Grandma herself had loved it, the late-'80s resurgence of the almost-forgotten, unfashionable gelatin in the form of Bill Cosby–endorsed wobbly deserts. Jell-O pudding. Pudding Pops. Jell-O Jigglers. Days after her eighty-seventh birthday, her last one, as it

turned out, she had been one of the guests of honor at the festivities for
the proclamation of Jell-O as the official snack of the state of Utah, in Salt
Lake City. She even appeared in several smiling, happy, celebratory
pictures with Cosby himself (something else the Peterson family had
lately come to resent).

"I still maintain Grandma would not sanction this." Her brother Orson's
voice came through the baby monitor, clear as if he were five feet away. The
bed in his room was certainly at yelling distance from the kitchen, but this
was simply more practical.

"You just don't like that it's vegan, as usual," shouted Lindsay, who had
bought the monitors herself as a gesture of goodwill and understanding,
and was still getting used to them.

"That's not what it is," said Orson.

"I'll have you know, I would have used vegetable alternatives to Jell-O
regardless, for chemical reasons," said Lindsay.

"I'm sure you would have."

"Instead of just a side of asparagus, I'm making a warm asparagus cream
that the aspic will be immersed in," said Lindsay. "Agar-agar molds can hold
up to like a hundred and sixty degrees, gelatin melts. So there."

"I'm sure animals have nothing to do with it," said Orson.

"Gelatin is made from bones and hides and pig skin," said Lindsay. "It's
so gross."

"Pig skin and bones bought the house we live in, sis," said Orson. "Don't
be casting *asparagus*, please."

Not a big house, but really nice. A really nice house, with really nice
neighbors, in a really nice part of Henderson. And all this niceness no more
than ten minutes away from their parents, in the prettiest corner of the Las
Vegas Valley. Technically, the affluent, vaguely Californian palm-treed
boulevards of Henderson were not part of Las Vegas. Though no rural land
separates the two townships, Henderson proudly calls itself a city. The
second largest city in Nevada, as a matter of fact. Then again, even Las Vegas
isn't technically part of Las Vegas, the casinos of the Strip, the airport, and
the UNLV campus all belonging to the adjacent and virtually unknown

unincorporated town of Paradise, Nevada, so exact nomenclature gets a bit dicey. The way most Hendersonians navigate the ordeal is to say "Henderson" whenever talking to a fellow Nevadan, and "Las Vegas" to anyone else. The way the Petersons and most LDS-residents handled it, what with the mental images the name Las Vegas summoned in people's minds, was to say "Henderson" no matter what.

It was no secret that the house had been meant by their parents for Lindsay and her future husband. No pressure. Really.

But as the years went by, a feeling seemed to spread in the collective Peterson-brain that Lindsay might be, unpredictably and even a bit stubbornly, not interested in marriage at all. Her brother Wallace, who was two years younger, and who had retired from professional swimming at twenty-four, had married the nicest girl in Provo and was on the BYU swimming team coaching staff. Even Dallin—who at twenty-five was still pursuing his very successful career in the pool and training hard for his second Olympics—had tied the knot just after London, and now split his time between Utah, Arizona, and wherever in the world people were racing each other in chlorinated water. And so when Orson graduated from college, the first Peterson to snub BYU for local UNLV in three generations, an empty bedroom at Lindsay's and an unspoken but rather unanimous desire for him to leave the parental nest had made the present living arrangements look like the obvious choice.

"Besides," said Orson, his words coming through the monitor displaying his room from his bed, floor cluttered with books and crossed-out drafts of his own messy writing, himself not onscreen, his voice like a voiceover, "I think Grandma would object to your recipe on more . . . conceptual grounds."

"Meaning?" said Lindsay.

"Meaning, Lin, that her whole pedagogical deal was making it quick and easy and if-you're-done-with-cooking-fast-maybe-you-can-go-read-a-book-or-something. And here you are, conducting what I believe is a test run for a skill-intensive highbrow revisitation of her ten-minute classics."

"The temperatures are tricky," admitted Lindsay. "I want to make sure I don't mess it up tomorrow."

"Case in point," said Orson.

"You're welcome to come help, you know?" said Lindsay. *Worth a shot.*

"I don't feel like getting up right now," said Orson. *Right now.* "What are you using to replace the eggs?"

"How do you even know there's supposed to be eggs in this?"

"I'm a reader, Lin," said Orson. "Never be surprised I've read something."

"You read great-grandma's recipes for fun?"

"Are you gonna use those gross vegan eggs? Or do you just skip them?"

"I'm making spheres of cashew mozzarella, thank you very much."

"You're kidding me."

"Which I made from scratch."

"Spheres?"

"Spherification, yes."

"I know what it means," said Orson. "I was just expressing disbelief."

"And flour and herb chips," said Lindsay. "For texture."

"Oh my."

Getting Orson to leave his bed was extremely tricky work. The youngest in a line of tall, strong, athletically gifted Petersons, little Orson Beckette's growth had been stunted at age 8 by the onset of a rare condition called Guillain-Barré syndrome. In GBS—a cause-unknown neurological mix-up in which the immune system unwittingly attacks the body's own peripheral nerves, causing rapid and severe muscle weakness—adult Orson had come to see a microcosmic metaphor of the sorrows of the world, where men fail to recognize each other as parts of the same body and attack the weaker, more peripheral groups. Be that as it may, child Orson's physical recovery had been swift, but imperfect. While only about a third of all patients retain permanent damage from GBS, his rehabilitation still registered in the lower end of the disability spectrum: he wouldn't become a star athlete, but he could walk without a crutch most of the time and had no serious respiratory deficit. Way shorter than his brothers at five-ten, he had grown into a somewhat wild-looking but not unattractive man, strong Peterson bones a bit too visible through his skinny frame, the trademark black hair/blue eyes family combo taking on him a much darker, Gothic-novelish air.

What glued him to his bed for unhealthily long hours (when not days) was therefore to be found, according to the doctors, in his mind rather than his minimally atrophic muscles. It was, one doctor had announced, as if he'd given up on the physical world. As if the disease had left him with a deep-seated mistrust of his own body, to which he had then elected to assign as little work as possible, for fear it might betray him again. This textbook diagnosis of long-term trauma, quickly stamped on a shy and exception-ally well-behaved teenager, had been upheld by the cream of the south-western psychiatric crop, prone to regarding his smiling and candor as defense mechanisms and denial. Yet Orson wasn't depressed, antisocial, or unambitious. If asked, he would just smile and say he didn't feel like getting up just now, that everything he was truly passionate about involved his brain and not his body, and could be better conducted from a relaxed, effortless position. Coaxing him out of bed always involved, for his loved ones, an awkward moral compromise between compassion for his doctor-validated psychic wounds and their sneaking suspicion, only once famously uttered by his father in an uncharacteristic and much-regretted temper, that "the boy's milking it."

"Here, skeptic brother, tell me what you think," said Lindsay in her in-person voice, appearing at the open door of Orson's bedroom carrying a gay, sparkling, quivery, luscious-looking mold softly sinking in lime-green cream.

"Looks fancy," said Orson.

"You know, I was thinking about it, and I think you're wrong," said Lindsay, while her brother theatrically dug in. "I don't think this contra-dicts Grandma's philosophy."

Orson raised a questioning eyebrow.

"It wasn't really about quickness of preparation," said Lindsay. "It was about freedom. Which yes, for a woman in the fifties for sure meant that. But adjust for context, and you'll see how for an overworked and underpaid young journalist, freedom is taking my sweet time getting this right. Right and fancy."

"You go, girl!" said Orson, a mouthful of chewed-up red undercutting his quip, a raised fist overcompensating.

"Why do I even try?" said Lindsay.

"This is delicious, by the way," said Orson. "White balls are insane."

"Spheres," said Lindsay.

"I'm aware," said Orson.

ON THE FLOOR IN ORSON'S ROOM—"PERSPECTIVES OF MORMON HISTORY OF NEVADA (WORKING TITLE)," BY ORSON BECKETTE PETERSON; CHAPTER 1, DRAFT #9

Imagine a desert.

Land stretching, pale, uncharted. Unowned.

Desert.

Sound the word in your head, question the images it summons. Inspect them.

To you, a sliver of southern Nevada wedged between California and Arizona. Colorless, ~~boundless~~ useless, lifeless under a cloudless sky. Defined by what is not there. To you, an empty corner of the Mojave resting before the Dawn of Man.

Your idea of death.

Look around.

The mighty tardigrade, invisible, invincible, survivor of apocalypses. The minuscule, numberless thermophilic settlers, dwellers of wastelands, thriving. Hyperthermophiles. Extremophiles. Ask them what they see.

Look, if you can, at the shadows of the sagebrush, the creosote, the Joshua tree, not as relief from a merciless sun but as the vertical claim to existence of a life other than your own. The prickly menace of the cacti (hedgehog, beavertail, barrel, pincushion) a struggle for survival. A fear of the unknown not unlike the one that keeps you up at night.

Think, but really think, of the western rattlesnake and diamondback, the gopher snake, the red racer; think of the sagebrush, the western fence, and the leopard lizard, of the banded Gila monster and of the short-horned lizard; think of the noble desert tortoise. This is not for you.

Forget the word. ~~Forget yourself.~~

If you can't see the desert breathe, feel it alive, greeting the ~~very~~ sun that scorches your cream-basted skin like you would a cool summer breeze, you will never understand Las Vegas.

Las *Vegas*. The *meadows*. Unknown explorers on the Old Spanish Trail, their tongues beginning to swell, their eyes starting to recede into their skull from extreme thirst and dehydration, must have seen the water rising from the ground like a miracle from Heavenly Father. The timid, lonely patches of green clinging to life around it like a veritable Celestial Kingdom. Mormon Apostle Orson Pratt, mathematician, theologian, first Saint to see the meadows in 1847, said the springs appeared "at the termination of a 50-mile stretch without a drop of water or a spear of grass." We can ~~perhaps~~ forgive those unknown Spaniards for their grandiloquence. Las Vegas. A name born out of desperation, of unexpected, ~~intoxicating~~ exhilarating relief.

But ~~think of remember~~ consider the desert. Alive. Breathing. Vibrating with a life you don't understand. When William Bringhurst's missionaries arrived in 1855 (see chapter 2), the ~~inhospitable~~ unforgiving soil forced them to eat nothing but bread for weeks. A land unfit for human life. When you think of Las Vegas, and its human history of sacrifice, and heroism, and ambition, and triumph, never forget: to the desert, the springs are a gushing wound, the meadows an infection. We shouldn't be here. We are the interlopers.

The way Lindsay saw it, firstborn children can never truly rebel. Of course, they can surprise their parents, make different choices, blaze their own trail. But parents can always chalk it up to generational differences, their own parenting inexperience, *kids these days*. It's the firstborn who sets the script for the next ones to follow, or not. And in largely multiprogenic families such as the Petersons (and most of their friends and acquaintances), this script keeps reinforcing itself through every iteration—leaving, say, the third- and fourth-born children to deal with a narrative so set that only world-class success or spectacular failure can nudge it off its tracks.

Yet in spite of her perceived freedom, the secret thought that kept nagging at her, ever since her first piece of real investigative reporting for the *Las Vegas Sun* had been picked up by CNN, felt to Lindsay like nothing short of betrayal.

Her unsparing account of the ways nonunion labor was taken advantage of in right-to-work Nevada had been a big deal. It had come, almost by accident, at the end of a string of short SEO-optimized pieces about mall openings and minor local police ops that had filled her first two years at the paper. It had been praised. What it truly meant for Lindsay, though, was that her fantasy of moving to San Francisco, to join her college friends who had started a small literary journal there, suddenly felt less far-fetched. She wouldn't just be following her impractical, parentally discouraged lifelong dream of being a fiction writer, no. She would be making a smart career move, a completely reasonable relocation to a bigger market on the heels of her success. Was it her fault that there were no Petersons in California?

She had been in high school when she'd betrayed her family for the first time, with her decision to quit swimming. Two full years after her training schedule had increased to three hours a day, six times a week, and less than one year after her most meaningful success at the Junior Regionals (gold medal in the 100-meter backstroke, silver in the 200-meter IM, in May 1999). The realization, as she curled against the locker-room toilet of some pool she didn't even remember now, throwing up from the anxiety before yet another race, the realization that she didn't want to do this anymore was both liberating and damning. Incapable of keeping it a secret from her parents, she had come clean on the drive home. *I think I'm done. Is it okay that I think I'm done?*

Her parents had been understanding, kind, loving. But after that, betrayal had further ramifications, a next step implying a moral double bind the contours of which she could already foresee: How would she tell her coach? Because on the one hand she knew for certain that fear would not be a reason Coach would accept for losing his best swimmer; on the other hand, lying and saying, I don't know, that she couldn't keep up with her homework anymore now that she was in high school, that she really cared about swimming, but her education had to come first (all of which wasn't true; she'd never had any problem in school at all), that felt clearly wrong. For sure. And so the following week, in jeans and not carrying her bag—so that she knew she was definitely *not* going to swim—she had walked with her father up to her coach, and the three of them had sat on the small white plastic bench poolside, Coach in center, the tiny bench creaking under unusual nonprepubescent weight, the sound of two dozen pairs of young arms breaking the water and the smell of chlorine she already felt like she missed, and she had quietly sobbed and looked down at the red-tile floor while her father did the half-lying for her. She had never seen an adult enter the pool in civilian clothes before.

Many years later, when the moral weight of her dad's lies on her behalf appeared less significant, she still regarded her retirement from the pool as the watershed moment of her youth. It had been the one time in her life she had taken a decision clearly against what was expected of her, against a community she belonged to, against family tradition. And it had felt horrible. In a way, all her life since then, her gradually decreasing but still joyful involvement with the Church, her luminous years in Provo, her budding career at the *Las Vegas Sun*, her rooming with and pretty much taking care of Orson—all of it could be described not as a forced adherence to an externally set, premade mold, but as a conscious, happy convergence of her personal wants and needs with the expectations of her community. Really, she had *chosen* all of it, and it all fit. It felt *right*.

And that's what made the last months so hard to make sense of. Because the confines of her community and her upbringing had never felt narrow.

Because being a Latter-day Saint, and more than that, a Peterson, had always felt to her like something affirmative, rather than an imposition. Because she had never turned down an official Calling before, let alone an important one like the Young Women Presidency. But now her love of stories, both true and finally fictional—the breathtaking rush of connecting to a real readership, people who cared, listened to *her*—the stories now called her away from Henderson, on her own. So how could she want both? To disappear willingly, happily, to stay and give herself over to the needs of a community, a family. And this thought, this secret, scary desire she had been harboring ever since her friends had called her from the Bay. To drop everything. To drop everything and leave, and write, and *become herself.*

The Petersons' living room table was a vertical line, a dozen colorful mounds of cooled, acid-extracted animal collagen (and, in one case, agar-agar) wobbling at what appeared to be its right (to Lindsay) or its left (to Orson). A crescent-shaped, pimento-olive-eyed red Jell-O fish (containing fish), a concave emerald-green mold precariously holding a mountain of shrimp, two white mayonnaise-filled prisms lying in a Tetris bed of Jell-O cubes. And that was just the first row. The oldest and youngest of the Peterson siblings lay head-to-head on two couches opposite the table, watching new dishes being brought out to the living room. Dinner would be soon.

"I really wish you would get up before they arrive," said Hannah, their mother, looking at the impartial angle between the two couches where her equally loved and deserving children lay a tad inappropriately.

"But why?" said Orson. "I would argue that there's nothing more distinctive of the Peterson children than a predilection for the horizontal. I just prefer couches to water is all."

"I didn't mean . . . ," said Hannah.

"Do you need help with anything, Mom?" said Lindsay.

"Maybe come say hello to your uncle when he gets here, though?" suggested Hannah, already walking back toward the kitchen.

"Sure thing, Mom," said Orson.

"Why do you always have to do that?" said Lindsay, once they were alone.

"Do what?"

"Trip her up like that. Make her feel guilty."

"Another advantage of lying down," said Orson. "You can never trip up."

In one's twenties, welcoming guests to one's parents' home is a balancing act. The memory of living there is fresh enough to awaken a proprietary feeling, the small pride of watching familiar objects through someone else's eyes ("But of course we have an old grandfather clock in the living room! That's *the* living room clock, how can she not know it?"). At the same time a lingering fear of still appearing as the child who used to live there with her parents—maybe of still *being* that child—dictates some degree of distance, a clear publicizing of the fact that those rooms have in time grown remote and strange to us too ("No, I'm afraid I don't know where *they* keep the paper napkins, sorry"). And so it was this tightrope of hospitality and foreignness that Lindsay and a dutifully standing Orson were walking, as three generations of Petersons were gradually video-buzzed in and poured into the living room, complimenting knickknacks, tablecloths, and complexions.

"Hello, Uncle John," said Orson.

"Hey, Orson boy, how've you been? Clara told me our star athlete is here too. Haven't seen him in *years!*"

"Yes, Dallin is coming. And Wallace too, with the baby. They're just a little late 'cause they've been driving all day from Provo."

"Let's hope they didn't go for a world record on that one, huh boy?"

"Oh, they would never!" said Orson, pretending not to understand the joke. His uncle had already moved on to greeting his mom anyway.

Uncle John Tingey, husband of Aunt Clara, Lindsay and Orson's father Jacob's sister, was the Petersons' claim to municipal prestige and wealth. Not for anything he had done himself, as Orson had pointed out to Lindsay earlier in a belated objection to his mom's obsequiousness: he was just your garden-variety law firm partner, with a nice suburban family and a fairly nominal role in the bishopric. Certainly nothing warranting royalty treatment. Yet John Tingey was the son of Senator Ammon Tingey, arguably the most powerful and influential man in Nevada for the past twenty-odd years, and that was not something you could just ignore. Lindsay had met the man himself a few times at Uncle John's, back when she used to babysit Aunt Clara's daughters: tall, the kind of thinness you could tell was a life-long trait, the goofy smile of a high school geek capable of stiffening into profile-on-a-coin severity in a matter of seconds. His whole family, with whom the Petersons had way fewer interactions than Lindsay's mother would have hoped for, emanated an aura of solemnity and success: Spencer Tingey, the senator's first son, was commissioner for Clark County (where the Las Vegas/Paradise/Henderson cluster was located) and had not-so-secret gubernatorial ambitions. His sister Ada Tingey (who weirdly enough had married a guy named Peterson, from Utah, no relation) was secretary-treasurer of the notoriously tough-nut workers' union in charge of standing up to the boys' club of the casino owners—something that Lindsay regarded with unabashed fangirl admiration. And so yes, Lindsay had conceded to her brother, a lot of Uncle John's charisma had rubbed off on him from unearned familial clout. But that didn't mean he wasn't still a nice man, with a nice family, and three very nice daughters. And it didn't mean that Orson should make such a production of complying with their mother's request that he be nice to him.

"Can you believe she didn't cry *a minute* of the way?" asked Wallace, pushing a dark-blue stroller through the wide doorframe. "She was just lying there, playing with her *bee*, smiling at Uncle Dallin while Daddy drove. Isn't she the best?"

The stroller's seat was backward, and the thick vault of a parasol covered it, so that Lindsay had to more or less dive in to greet her six-month-old niece. Wallace, on his part, had left the handlebar and moved forward chest-first, arms out wide, to hug his sister hello. The misunderstanding resulted in an inertially robust headbutt to the sternum.

"Oh no, she's not here," said Wallace, managing to catch his breath and laugh at the same time. "I'm just carrying this in. She's with Madelyn, they're still out with Dallin."

"Then why did you—"

"Hey, little brother!"

"Hello, Wallace. At what age do former athletes usually start to get fat?"

"We're here, we're here," said Dallin, Wallace's baby girl resting on his left arm, her mother Madelyn having to sort of stretch up on her tiptoes to wipe saliva off her mouth.

"My favorite Olympian!" said Uncle John, who had returned to the living room with both of Lindsay's parents in tow.

"Hi boys, welcome!" said Hannah.

"Hi Madelyn," said Jacob Peterson. "And hey you! How are ya, little one?"

The living descendants of Grandma Peterson, the fruits of a tree with Grandma's name (Clara Gardner-Peterson) at the top and six branches for her six children, came in, since the birth of innocent little Ashtyn Kate Peterson, at a staggering and highly impractical 114. And that was not counting spouses, fiancés, and nurses for the elderly. Barring a monumental Facebook-powered organizational endeavor, it had soon been clear that an all-Peterson celebration of the works and days of the gelatin-molding ancestor would have been a practical impossibility. Even in Uncle John and Aunt Clara's large golf-course-side property, it would have been tricky—and, namesake or not, it didn't look like Clara had a particular interest in trying.

In truth, the real engine behind the whole hundred-year memorial birthday party had been Hannah, who had merely married into the Peterson legacy, but who took a genuine personal interest in the life and books of her grandmother-in-law, and was quite eager to celebrate her with a tableful of wobbly entrees. The compromise, happily endorsed by Jacob, had been to limit the party to the family branch that lived in Nevada, where Jacob and Clara's father had moved in the '70s with his mother's financial help, and to take as many pictures as possible to post online for the benefit of the hundred-plus Salt Lake City Petersons. As a result, a reasonable twelve adults plus a baby in a stroller were sitting around the living room table when Wallace started the blessing on the food.

"Dear Heavenly Father—," he began. It had seemed right for Jacob to have Hannah say the prayer, since she had done so much to make the evening possible; but Hannah, whose prayers were family-famous for surpassing the ten-minute mark to include a painstakingly detailed account of everything the Petersons felt thankful to the Lord for, said she was no good at it, and maybe Uncle John would want to speak instead? At which point Uncle John had said that by all means a Peterson should do it—which Lindsay thought was fair, it should definitely be Aunt Clara—and asked "our champion Dallin" to do the honors; and Dallin, who growing up had had the undisputed Peterson record for fastest food blessing at 04.86 sec, had maybe perceived a certain trepidation from his mother and sister and passed the baton along to his "big bro and new daddy Wallace." Which Lindsay didn't blame him for, but honestly it really should have been Aunt Clara, or Mom, or worst comes to worst, herself. But no matter.

"Dear Heavenly Father, we're grateful for this day, and that we can be gathered together to eat, and share our love with one another, and remember the amazing life of Grandma Peterson and her many accomplishments, and eat her admittedly strange but I'm sure delicious food; and we're thankful for Mom's enthusiasm, and perseverance, and her kindness in convincing us to drive from Utah for this, which we should really do more often; and we're thankful that my little brother Dallin chose to skip a bunch of training to be here instead of supporting his wife, who just today broke the NCAA record in the 200-yard freestyle in Greensboro in 1:39.10, which okay, it isn't an Olympic distance, but I still think it's pretty impressive; please bless us to be kind and help us to obey the commandments, and please bless Aunt Clara, and Uncle John, and their beautiful daughters who we can't wait to welcome in Provo when they graduate high school starting I believe next year, yes?; and please bless my parents, and my little brother Orson, who thinks I'm getting fat, and my sister Lindsay, in whom the spirit of Grandma Peterson truly lives on; and please bless my wife and little Ashtyn Kate, light of my life, who make me the luckiest in a string of very lucky Petersons, and whom I hope I can one day, with all the love I have to give, pay back; please bless this family, and our continuing care and love for each other, because it's as a family that our divine nature is revealed; we are thankful for the food, even the vegan stuff, and pray that it will nourish and strengthen us, in the name of Jesus Christ, amen."

"This is really good!"

"*Really* good!"

"Have you tried this one?"

"Thanks."

"But seriously, can you believe they actually ate this stuff every day?"

"Wallace!"

"No, I mean I like it, I do, it's just—"

"Carbs mostly, but it depends."

"I remember an article about how much Michael Phelps eats every day, it was unbelievable."

"I think I saw that one."

"Do you have to eat that much too?"

"I mean it depends, it's not always the same—"

"It depends on what I tell him to eat!"

"Sure, can you pass me the breadsticks, though?"

"Who decides how much *you* get to eat, *Daddy*?"

"This one."

"Correct."

"See, Jake, *he's* fine with that."

"Is Michael Phelps nice in person?"

"And I swear they didn't know until I told them."

"That's okay, it wasn't their fault."

"But like they wouldn't *believe* me when I told them."

"I remember a lot of girls got their ears pierced twice where I grew up. A lot of people just don't know."

"I mean it's not that big of a—"

"So they took off the second pair?"

"Well, yes, what else were they gonna do?"

"You know I heard *someone* might be a Young Women president soon."

"That's amazing!"

"That's a very important Calling."

"—"

"Look at her, she *loves* those!"

"Yes, look how concentrated she looks, it's amazing!"

"Look, look—she grabbed the whole box!"

"Honestly, I could never do it."

"Oh, that I believe!"

"Dad sure loves his steak."

"I suspect there's something unnatural about it."

"Unnatural?"

"Well, it goes against tradition, and what we've always done."

"Have you *tried* that, though, John? It's so good!"

"But of course, no, I don't want to judge. It just feels like there's value in the food a community shares together for a long time, no? Isn't it kind of the point of eating *these* tonight?"

"No, but you're right, Uncle John, I do believe there's value in tradition, too. I just—"

"The Word of Wisdom has *got* to be the most misunderstood, misapplied piece of Scripture there is."

"To be honest, I'm starting to warm up to this stuff. Is it okay if we include Jell-O in my diet, Coach?"

"What do you mean?"

"Well, it explicitly says that meat should be eaten *sparingly*, and only in times of winter, cold, or famine."

"Orson, it's fine, there's no need to—"

"I'm sorry, I meant *Daddy*."

"Which, considering it was published in 1833, and winter and cold and famine were, like, *real*, I don't think technically today there is much reason to—"

"Waaaaaaaaaaaaaa."

"But really it's fine, Uncle John. Really, I'm not trying to convince anybody to do it or anything."

"I didn't know you had such an interest in Scripture, son."

"I'm a reader, Uncle John. Never be surp—"

"Waaaaaaaaahaaaaaaaaaaa uh?"

"Wanna go look at the clock? Let's go look at the clock! Oooh that's a pretty clock, isn't it? Oh, look at the little circle! What's the little circle doing? Swing, swing, swing, swing, swing, swing."

"Your aspic is amazing, sweetie. Grandma would have been so *proud*."

"Hear, hear. It's a pity you never got to meet her, she would've loved you!"

"Waaaaaaaaaaaaaaaaaaaaaaaaaaaaaaaaaaaaaaaaaaaaaa."

"Nope, Daddy, I think that's all she wrote. We need to take this one straight to bed. Can you get the bunny from the purple bag?"

"Oh."

"As long as it's healthy, I guess I can't really object."

"Oh?"

"Dallin, did you take the purple bag when you came in?"

"Nope."

"Then I think it's still in the car. I'm sorry, honey, I'll run get it."

"Are you sure you get enough proteins?"

"Waaaaaaaaaaaaaaaaa."

"Okay, but quick. And get the baby monitors too."

"John, I'm sure Lindsay knows—"

"Can I ask you guys what model you got? No reason, I'm just curious."

It was cold outside. Not desert-town-what-do-they-know-about-real-cold cold. Just cold. Or so it felt. Getting into the car, Lindsay thought that no matter what numerical description lit up on the dashboard once she pressed the ignition button, it still wouldn't give her shivering any extra validation. To someone, somewhere, in some snow-covered northern state, this would still feel like spring. People born in resolutely warm climates can only ever perceive cold as a function of their weak predisposition to withstand it. Not so much an atmospheric phenomenon as a personal weakness, a shortcoming of theirs. How would a winter in San Francisco feel to *her*?

"You know what's funny about vegans?" said Orson, while palm trees started moving in and out of the light on both sides of the car. He was sitting in front, but even for such a short drive, he had reclined the passenger seat to an almost satisfactory approximation of horizontality.

"Thanks for sticking up for me tonight," said Lindsay. "You didn't have to, but it was sweet."

"When they say they want to 'save the planet.' Or that they're 'doing it for the environment.'"

"Wait, what's wrong with that?"

"Well, this presumption that the planet is something we have the power to *save*, or *damage*, when really all we do is *change* it."

"So you have a problem with semantics?" said Lindsay, flashing the lights twice before approaching a right turn.

"No, Lin, I have a problem with the idea that veganism is this noble self-less act we can do to 'save the environment,' when really what we want is to maintain the environment in the most ideal conditions for human life, i.e. for *us*."

"Are you going to talk about tardigrades again?" asked Lindsay.

"Well, yes, tardigrades," said Orson. "Extremophiles. Bacteria. They would all be quite happy if we torched the entire place. And there's billions of them. Billions of billions. Who's speciesist now?"

"I think Uncle John does it on purpose, sometimes," said Lindsay, trying to swerve car and conversation at once. "Make me look like a rebel or something."

"There's this view that the world as it is now is *right* and must be *preserved*, maintained status quo, underneath all of it. Like we are so important, the planet wouldn't know what to do without us. But it's all relative. There's always someone happy when everything burns."

"I think he gets it from the paper. He thinks I'm some kind of political activist."

"Well, he's definitely read your article, if that's what you mean."

It was Orson and not Lindsay who was the real family apostate. His disengagement with the Church was evident even to his family, but as a result of his condition, nobody had ever dared question his desire to stay home on Sundays. After all, his dedication to the study of Mormon history was enough evidence of his own private devotion to alleviate any suspicions. Only Lindsay, in the whole world, knew how deep her brother's lack of faith ran: he was a reader, a researcher of facts. A born skeptic. In Mormonism, which he really did love, he saw a cultural heritage, a rare collectivist tradition in the heart of a selfish world. Lindsay's conversations with him would often dance along the fault line of her belief and his doubt, yet neither of them really hoped to persuade the other. They never tried to win the argument.

"Mom seemed really excited about the Young Women Presidency thing," said Orson.

"Yeah, they all are," said Lindsay. The car turned onto the driveway with the smallest of bumps.

"When are you gonna tell her?"

"You know that's not why I'm a vegan," said Lindsay, turning off the engine. "You know that. I just don't want to kill stuff. I don't want to hurt things, I don't want things to have to die because of me."

"Not even bother them," said Orson, smiling.

"Barely be there at all," said Lindsay.

Interlude IV

(the story of a vlog)

FADE IN . . .

A rocky cliff, blue waters, we HEAR waves crashing softly against the shore.

Behind it, a palm-lined street with few CARS, farther beyond a JAPANESE PAGODA. We realize we are looking at the view through a GLASS, the sound of the WAVES coming through small SPEAKERS.

On the left we recognize the WILES TOWER, amber-colored and crescent-shaped, the MIRAGE, the FLAMINGO; to the right, the Eiffel Tower of the PARIS HOTEL and the silvery doughnut-shaped INDULGE SHOPPING CENTER.

SEMI-EXT. HILLS OF POSITANO VISTA BALCONY—SUNRISE

Debussy's CLAIR DE LUNE starts to play.

TREVOR, 25, linen shirt, red hair, thin athletic build, moves into view, looking at the SEA beyond the glass enclosing the balcony.

TREVOR

Las Vegas. You know, 41 million tourists come here every year. Sometimes I almost forget. You live here everyday, everything becomes so ordinary, you barely even see it anymore.

(beat)

So here's what I thought. We've been together for a few episodes now, but we've never really experienced Vegas like tourists do. Just goofing around, talking to strangers, losing some money. So why don't we take a day off from our usual stories today, and just hit the Pos like we're only here for the weekend? Really *see* it for once, is what I'm saying. We'll take this $100 bill and do our best to lose it, real Vegas style. What do you say?

Debussy's CLAIRE DE LUNE reaches its climactic piano sweeps, then fades out.

CUT TO:

INT. POSITANO CASINO, NORTH SIDE—LITERALLY ANY TIME OF ANY DAY

A brown-carpeted hallway, the tables of a nice-looking RESTAURANT to the right, the slot-lined aisles of the CASINO to the left. We HEAR chimes and sounds coming from the SLOTS, muffled by Lana Del Rey's YOUNG AND BEAUTIFUL on the casino speakers. Beneath it all, a faint, deep rumble,

barely audible, like the distant sound of traffic
from the top of a high-rise.

TREVOR

So this is the North Entrance to the Positano
Hotel and Casino. Loyal followers will recognize
this as the door we always come in from on
our way to the poker room. But let's look
around today, explore the place a bit instead.
The North Entrance is the lower tip of a
huge diamond-shaped room. The way I always
pictured it is you walk onto a baseball field
from the home plate, so that's what we're
going with.

TREVOR sits on a nearby penny slot's leather chair.
He uses his finger to draw the shape of a baseball
field in the air, with the HOME PLATE at the bottom
and the OUTFIELD at the top.

As his finger moves, white chalk LINES appear
onscreen, superimposed on the shot of TREVOR sitting
at the slot machine (as in the iconic scene from
Pulp Fiction).

TREVOR

So, let's see . . . this is where we are now . . .
poker room's right here on first base . . .

(he keeps drawing, filling up the perimeter of
the map with arrows and names)

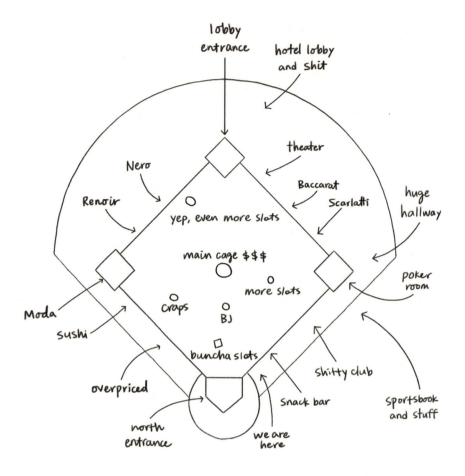

We got that . . . that . . . whole huge hallway on
this side, with the shops and the east-side
elevator . . . couple lounges here, the
theater . . . you get the idea.

(he starts drawing small circles in the
middle of his drawing)

And then everything infield is the gaming pits,
with the Main Cage pretty much where the pitcher's
mound would be. What do you say, make sense?

TREVOR makes a brushing motion, erasing the onscreen drawing, then gets up and resumes walking.

TREVOR

So then, we're tourists, we just got here. We're itching to play. Where should we start?

CUT TO:

INT. AZTEC GOLD: WONDERS OF TENOCHTITLAN SLOT—SAME

We see a massive SLOT MACHINE shaped like an AZTEC TEMPLE built of solid (fake) gold. Resting against all sides of the pyramid are four huge brightly lit SCREENS with rows of rolling SYMBOLS (ritual masks, feathers, temples, golden nuggets, profiles of Montezuma). TREVOR is sitting on one of two gilded THRONES in front of each screen, idly tapping the gem-shaped buttons that control the game. Next to him sits LARISSA, 23, short, green-eyed, long hair tied in a ponytail, casual clothes.

TREVOR

The slots, of course! I mean, where else? To a large chunk of the Vegas tourist population, slots are the number-one attraction in town, by far. Now, personally, I never *really* understood them. The appeal of them, is what I'm saying. So today, I found us a mentor to walk us through the ins and outs of the adrenaline-filled journey that is the life of a slots player. Wonderful people of YouTube, this is Marisa.

LARISSA

Larissa.

TREVOR

Larissa.

LARISSA

Hello.

TREVOR

Larissa is from Mexico.

LARISSA

De Chihuahua.

TREVOR

Right, from Chihuahua. Now Larissa has agreed
to show us how to play this culturally awkward
gaming device, while we have a little chat and
maybe a drink. We put in $20, and we're going to
see how long it takes us to lose it all. Is this
the one I press? Great. And I have to select how
much . . . okay, that's easy.

(They start playing.)

So tell us a bit about yourself, what brings you
to Sin City?

LARISSA

I come to Las Vegas with my friend, for chopping.

TREVOR

Chopping?

LARISSA

Buy clothes? Las Vegas Outlets, Indulge Chopping
Center, Ross Dress for Less.

TREVOR

Shopping.

LARISSA

Yes, sorry for my English. In the region where my
family come from, we say like that, different.

TREVOR

And you took the opportunity to do a little
gambling on the side.

LARISSA

Is funny, I know, I say *chopping*, *suchi*, *Chakira*.

TREVOR

Am I doing this right?

    (in turning to her, Trevor's knee brushes
twice against Larissa's thigh; it's involuntary, this
deployment of the well-known PUA strategy of "kino escalation," the
establishing of a base of innocuous physical contact, in stages.
A reflex. A memory from a distant life.)

LARISSA

Sí, you are winning!

TREVOR

Look at that, I'm a natural. Now what happens if I press here?

(He presses the button.)

LARISSA

No no! You bet all the money like this!

TREVOR

Haha, great, no gamble no future! So how long are you and your friend in town for?

LARISSA

We don't decide yet, maybe tomorrow we leave.

TREVOR

That's too bad.

LARISSA

Look look! Pay attention now, lot of money on this.

(SPARKS go off all over the game's screen, the words "TREASURE OF CORTEZ" flashing in gold.) Now you have the bonus round! Triple points! All or nothing!

TREVOR

Damn, that's too much pressure. Why don't you press for me?

(Trevor takes Larissa's hand and places it on the big ruby button. When he lifts his own hand away,

it is with a gentle, lingering movement: quick
enough to look perfectly normal on camera,
slow enough to feel deliberate to Larissa. For
some time now, he's felt ambivalent about it, this set of rote
behaviors he's no longer in full control of.)

LARISSA

You win $75! Is amazing!

TREVOR

Woohoo!

(Turns to the audience.)

Damn, so that's what high-stakes gambling feels
like! My heart is pounding! Well, it looks like
our plan to lose our $20 investment failed, so
what do you guys say we move on to another game
and see if we get lucky there? But first, of
course, let's thank our lovely Larissa for her
invaluable help. Thanks, and good luck with your
chopping!

(LARISSA looks surprised, but eventually waves
goodbye to the camera.)

CUT TO:

INT. SIREN'S COVE BLACKJACK TABLES—SAME

Four BLACKJACK TABLES with ocean-blue felts.
Behind them, a large platform with two metal
POLES, upon which beautiful WOMEN in revealing

siren costumes are dancing to remixes of classical
music. The area is lit in the yellow glow of faux-
antique candle LANTERNS. TREVOR stands, holding a
full drink, two feet away from one of the tables,
where a young DEALER in a seashell brassiere is
dealing cards to two other PLAYERS. There is a
stack of CHIPS in the empty seat right behind
Trevor. Next to him, MARY ANN, 25, in full cocktail
waitress uniform, is delivering drinks from her
tray, smiling.

TREVOR

Alright, bad news first: we are still winning,
unbelievable. More bad news: they won't let me
shoot a video at the blackjack table. Verboten.
I'm pretty sure even this that I'm doing right
now is not allowed, but we'll do it anyway, just
for a quick update.

MARY ANN

Wow, you're such a bad boy.

TREVOR

(grinning)

Hey, we got a live one! Which brings me to the
good news: I haven't actually been playing much,
because I've been chatting with my friend here, who
is super fun, so at least part of our plan for the
day was successful. Now what do you say we ditch
this dumb game and go take this martini for a walk
around the shops, like the good tourists we are?

(We see him turn his head for a second, noticing MARY ANN leaving. The art of seduction, something both exhausting and addictive about it. The endless performance, the evaluation of the IOIs and IODs, the practiced, refined use of a certain brand of misdirection, like a proficient stage magician, like his dad.)

CUT TO:

INT. VIA DEL NORD SHOPS—SAME

A large HALLWAY, full of PEOPLE walking up and down, stopping at windows, eating ice cream, laughing. TREVOR is looking at the CHOCOLATE FOUNTAIN in the window of the pastry shop.

TREVOR

Isn't this great? I say no town could call itself Sin City without a fountain of real molten chocolate, don't you agree?

(And perhaps he, more than anyone else, was primed to see it. From his father, the magic teacher, he'd learned firsthand and from a very early age the more elaborate forms of misdirection; not just a library of rehearsed, perfected gestures, but an almost scientific devotion to the audience's experience. Its anticipation, manipulation.)

I have to confess, in the past I've had a bit of a weakness for the stuff. Chocolate. Sugar, really. Not the steadiest of wills when it came to desserts, is what I'm saying. But hey, I'm only human. And this here looks really damn good.

(He was fourteen, TREVOR remembers, when he wrote and underlined
three times in his notebook: "I only know what I can tell;
I only am what I can show.")

Anyway, as you see, the place is always packed.
Morning to closing time. One of the best spots in
Vegas to people-watch, definitely. And I really like
it, watching people. It's such a beautiful,
uplifting, human experience . . .

(Humans. These flesh-draped boxes of goo hallucinating a reality,
delusional and pathetically easy to fool. Pick-up artistry, and its
teaching, gave him codified, repeatable access to what he craved
most, the purest, noblest form of human contact: performance
and control.)

LARISSA comes out of the shop, eating a mint-green
macaron. Walking next to her is ANA, 24, tall, in
jeans and sneakers.

LARISSA

Trevor!

TREVOR

Larissa! How cool is this? Couldn't have scripted
this better!

(He'd seen early on, of course, that the same misdirection and sleight
of hand was being used on the PUAs themselves: presenting banal
human traits, like the attraction to the more desirable specimens, as
exclusively gendered and harmful, and then hiding the trick under a
sciencey-sounding moniker, hypergamy; making blanket statements
about human relationships, like acknowledging sex drive or the desire

to experiment with a variety of partners, and repackaging them as epiphanic, so-called red-pill dictums, much like the Barnum statements of horoscopes and fortune-tellers; turning what's at best cultural circumstance, say internalized submission, into genetic predisposition, the exact same trick memorably performed by the propaganda experts in Nazi Germany. He could see it spiraling out of control too, taking on a philosophy of its own, engulfing—or being engulfed by—a broader discourse, one he wasn't sure he could be a mouthpiece to.)

LARISSA

Is great to see you again.

(She greets him with a hug and a kiss on the cheek.)

TREVOR

It is! Las Vegas feels like such a small town sometimes!

(He'd chosen exile. A brilliant solution. In Vegas, the emotional desert of America, a city predicated on the suspension of judgment and a real self-indulgence of the soul, he would finally be the purest version of himself: unfiltered, guilt-free, real Trevor.)

LARISSA

This is my friend Ana.

ANA

Hi.

TREVOR

Hi. Trevor. People of YouTube, this is Ana.

(Except he'd been back to his old tricks almost immediately. Upon
meeting Tom, this impossibly perfect clean slate of a man, this
type-O-negative listener. He couldn't resist himself. And just like
an addict, once he cracked the door, it had swung open to the flood,
and he was back, all the way back. Tom was so receptive, so
spasmodically, endearingly starved for guidance, that Trevor gave
him everything he knew. And after a year or so, when it became
clear that Tom was nearing the top of his admittedly limited potential,
Trevor's hunger overflowed to the nameless masses of social media.
YouTube, his final classroom.)

ANA

Wait, could you turn that off? I'd rather not be
on camera really.

TREVOR

Of course of course, in a minute. I just have to
remind my friends to like and subscribe, and leave
a comment below to let me know what you guys
think.

(And there too, now, he saw misdirection, sleight of hand. A huge
voluntary marketing survey disguised as an act of communication,
the user-product relationship flipped on its head. The illusion of
saying something to someone, while really just declaring yourself
as a potential buyer for a certain class of products, be they
physical, cultural, or even political. Magic was everywhere, if you
knew where to look.)

Wait, where is your accent?

ANA

I grew up in Texas, family moved back to Mexico
before I went to high school.

TREVOR

Moved back? Amazing. Did Larissa tell you we were playing the most culturally offensive slot machine in Vegas earlier?

LARISSA

Sí, I said it. I think it was funny.

TREVOR

It's really too bad you guys are leaving so soon.

ANA

Yeah, I'll probably book the flight for tomorrow. And hey, is that thing still on?

TREVOR

Wait, so you haven't booked yet though?

(And who was he to say no? If this was the way of the world, just tricksters fooling each other, layers upon layers of them, why not him? What else could he do, being able to see all this, but take advantage of it? And who knows, maybe he would do some good along the way, too. Maybe he could start by helping Tom.)

Because I think I just got a really great idea.

ANA

Seriously . . .

TREVOR

Like total once-in-a-lifetime, paradigm-shift, slam-dunk of an idea. Just really really good stuff.

(He turns to the audience and winks.)

ANA

What the hell was that?

TREVOR

That, my friend, is how you set up an expectation
for your audience.

                                              CUT TO:

8

Ray

Reviewing his hands after a session was, for Ray, an exercise in self-mortification. The software on his laptop showed a square chart of all available 1,326 permutations of two-card starting hands in No Limit Hold'em. As he advanced the cursor on the tree graph of the hand he had selected, different parts of the square lit up in bright colors, indicating which hands he should bet, check, call, raise, fold. This constituted the optimal balanced range to play: if Ray were able to bet exactly those green hands here, and check exactly those red hands there, his play in the hand would be perfect, unexploitable. It would force his opponent to play perfect too, and break even, or diverge however slightly from the optimal, and lose.[1]

The problem was, he couldn't do it. He couldn't *exactly* do it. At the start of the great mathematical revolution that forever changed the world of poker (and that he among others had spearheaded), he had thought it possible. Given a deck of fifty-two cards, there were 22,100 possible three-card flops Or rather, 19,600, if he discounted the two known cards he was

---

1   This is known in game theory as a Nash equilibrium, after Hollywood's favorite mathematician, John Nash.

dealt. But poker hands didn't end with the flop. There was a turn, too, and a river. And if he considered full five-card boards, the combinatorics became simply staggering.

It had been immediately evident that learning to play each of his starting ranges[2] on every possible flop, turn, and river would be a task no human brain could ever accomplish. However, it had occurred to Ray that if he managed to group flops into a few basic textures, then treated those as approximately equivalent, the numbers wouldn't look quite so daunting. If he considered an {Ad Jd 5c} flop the same thing as an {As Js 5h} one— which in practice they were—and treated all similarly interchangeable permutations the same way, the number of possible flops decreased to a human-sized 1,755. With that number, he could set to work:

- there are 13 basic three-of-a-kind flops: {A A A}, {2 2 2}, {3 3 3}, {4 4 4}, etc.
- there are 312 basic one-pair flops, of which 156 are *rainbow* ({Ad Ah 5c}, {Qs Qd 9h}, etc.) and 156 *two-tone* ({6d 6s 7s}, {8h 8s As}, etc.)
- there are 1,430 basic high-card flops, of which . . .

The first year of in-depth study on the so-called GTO strategy had been feverish, ecstatic, frenetic. Ray would start a day analyzing how to handle his big blind range on a low paired two-tone flop, and find himself still assigning combos eighteen hours and three skipped meals later. Back then, software had been his great ally. He knew he couldn't possibly memorize or—harder yet—compute an entirely perfect strategy. But with the help of decision trees and software simulations, Ray could apply his human cleverness to shortcuts and viable approximations. It was beautiful. It was

---

2 The percentage of all possible hands one should elect to play instead of just folding varies according to the player's position relative to the dealer's button. Meaning: the more players after you, the fewer (stronger) hands you should play, and vice versa.

empowering. Like watching his dense, flawed matter refine itself into the ethereal elegance of pure math. It didn't matter that a computer could do it much better and faster when given the correct parameters by a human, because no computer (yet) could even come close to doing it on its own, without input. And it didn't matter that Ray had to approximate—to compromise—because he was still miles ahead of even the best humans. He was the least-human human.

But as with all feverish, ecstatic, frenetic ventures into the realm of science, the more Ray studied, the more he realized how little he knew. Cracks appeared in his approximations. Boards that he had considered essentially interchangeable showed resistance to his grouping and simplifying ambitions. And most of all, his trusty GTO software kept refusing to give him clear-cut ranges, providing him instead with problematic frequencies. It was never

- [bet: AK, AA, KK] and [check: QQ, JJ, AQ]
- but always something like
- [bet: AK 73% of the time, AA 84%, KK 62%, QQ 20%, JJ 8%, AQ 22%] and [check: AK 27%, AA 16%, KK 38%, QQ 80%, JJ 92%, AQ 18%]

Provided that he could even remember or derive the correct play with his range in every situation, how was he supposed, in real poker, to bet a specific hand 8 percent of the time and check it the remaining 92 percent? He could ballpark some of the percentages using suits,[3] or even through some ridiculous gimmick like looking at his watch,[4] but he knew it still

---

3 For example, if one decided to bet AK every time *except* when holding the ace of hearts, one would automatically be betting 75 percent of all possible combos of AK—twelve out of the total sixteen.

4 When needing to randomize a 33 percent frequency, a particularly diligent poker player could decide to bet if the second hand of their watch is between 1 and 20, and check if it is between 21 and 60.

wasn't nearly enough. And the deeper he plunged into his studies, the clearer it was that even subtle changes in frequencies could dramatically alter the resulting optimal countermeasures. If the software said 42 percent, it wasn't just as well to consider it 50. It had to be 42, or the whole thing was pointless.

It was around the time that these revelations had started to curb his mathematical optimism—and in the middle of what was turning into a pretty ugly monetary downswing—that the invitation to play in Pittsburgh arrived.

He had been aware for a while of the recent impressive advances in the field of machine learning and AI, but nothing noteworthy had so far appeared on his radar. The first poker bots he'd had the chance to play were pathetically flawed. To compensate for low computational power, their creators had simplified ranges and decisions to a ridiculous extent, making them much easier to beat than many mediocre human players. But the CMU bot, named Cardanus[5] by the PhD student overseeing the project, was different. It did everything Ray had done with notebooks, software-run simulations, and joyful intuition, and it did it on its own, without human input or supervision. And once it devised an optimal strategy for the hand in progress (a feat from which it derived no pleasure or personal satisfaction), it applied it relentlessly and impeccably, without ever fucking up its frequencies by even a tenth of a percent. Cardanus was everything Ray was, and a lot more than Ray could ever dream of becoming.

When he got back from Pittsburgh, there was nothing left to do. Outside, Toronto was shedding its winter coat and gearing up for an abnormally hot summer, its elms and oaks and maples silently sprouting the green silk of life. In Ray's minimally furnished apartment, light

---

5   After Gerolamo Cardano, sixteenth-century Italian physician, mathematician, chemist, physicist, astronomer, and inveterate gambler, author of the 1564 study of games of chance that effectively founded modern probability theory. Also, it had the word *card* in it, which the grad student in question found remarkably neat.

flooded the living room windows and illuminated his computer screens, turning them into Petri dishes of dust and smudged fingerprints. Even though the bot itself had not achieved perfection, and had to use small approximations of its own, there was nothing Ray could do to reach its level; it just couldn't be done. Deep inside, machine learning systems were not individuals, Cardanus was not one brain: the evolution of artificial intelligence had lately converged toward multiagent systems, nets of individual nodes working simultaneously and collaborating in a kind of swarm intelligence. Tasks that could proceed separately, with no mutual dependency or even communication, were called "embarrassingly parallel." The difference between an agent's performance results and optimal performance was called "regret." Cardanus, with its myriad interconnected cells working by trial and error, free of the shackles of corporeity, had brought to the table a game-changing regret minimization technique that Ray, alone in an apartment filling up with summer, had no way to possibly emulate. It wasn't a fair fight. And it was over.

Sitting in his West Vegas bedroom, laptop screen covered in the leafless, lifeless trees of game-theoretical analysis, live-pro Ray looked defeated. As he idly moved the cursor on the graph of a hand from the day's session, a 3bet pot in which he'd faced a difficult river decision, different parts of the starting-hands square lit up green and red, yellow and blue, indicating the combos and the frequencies of his optimal calling range. He didn't need to care this much. None of the other players in Vegas cared this much, those experienced thirty-year-old pros who made a very comfortable living at the tables, and golfed in the morning, and posted pictures of water-skiing on Lake Meade with their sons and wives. If he could just let go of his desire for perfection, Ray knew there was an easy life waiting for him in the Positano poker room. He would slowly turn into a real Vegas reg, one of many, making small-town-dentist money by showing up every day to grind his repetitive job. Maybe he would have to swallow his pride and play downstairs for a bit to replenish his bankroll. If he could just let go, let go and go back to winning by making fewer mistakes than the others. By minimizing regret.

OOP decision BOARD: {7h 3h 8c 8h Js}		
	BET 1.5x pot 21 combos / 33.3%	CHECK 42 combos / 66.6%
	value: [AA; KK; QQ 16%] — 13 combos	[Ah Ks; Ah Kc; Ah Kd; Ac Ks; Ac Kc; Ac Kd; Ac Kh; Ah Qs; Ah Qc; Ah Qd; Ac Qs; Ac Ac; Ac Qd; Ac Qh; Ah Jc; Ah Jd; Ac Jc; Ac Jd; Ac Jh; Qc Jc; Qd Jd; Ac 2c; Ac 3c; Ac 4c; Ac 5c; QQ 84%; 99; TT] — 42 combos
	bluff: [Kh Qs; Kh Qc; Kh Qd; Kc Qs; Kc Qc; Kc Qd; Kc Qh; Ac 9c 50%; Ac Tc 50%] — 8 combos	vs pot-size bet call 50%: [QQ; Ah Jc; Ah Jd; Ac Jc; Ac Jd; Ac Jh; Qd Jd; Qc Jc; TT; 99 50%] — 21 combos
		vs 2x pot bet call 33%: [QQ; Ah Jc; Ah Jd; Ac Jc; Ac Jd; Ac Jh; Qd Jd; Qc Jc; TT 33%] — 14 combos

Regret, regret, regret.

After two months of living in Las Vegas, Ray's relationship with other professionals and, to be precise, human beings in general remained embarrassingly parallel. Save for occasional conversations with Logan, who seemed to hardly ever play and yet still always be around upstairs, Ray could count on the fingers of one hand the interactions he'd had away from the poker table. He wasn't exactly trying to make friends, but even for him this conversational embargo was starting to wear.

On a late January morning, sitting in seat 6 at an eight-reg/one-mediocre-spot $10/$20 table, he was ready to enter the social fray. As the other regs debated the proper odds for a side bet involving the tossing of a plastic bottle, he decided to weigh in.

"I don't think there's a difference in aerodynamics, given consistency of shape," he said, surprising the others, by now used to his silence. "But of course the wastebasket diameter-to-bottle size ratio increases with the smaller bottles, which gives you better odds regardless."

"That's true," said JJ, from the right side of the table. He was a former East Coast reg who had moved to Vegas a couple years prior and who, it seemed to Ray, had managed to be accepted as a bona fide Vegas reg, if still a somewhat marginal and fringe-orbiting member of the upstairs group. He was now pondering the physics of Fiji bottle throwing.

"Meaning with a relatively larger target, the toss doesn't need to be as perfect with the three-thirty-milliliter bottle as it would with the five-hundred-milliliter," said Ray.

"Yeah, seven to one is way too much with these," said JJ.

"Why do they use milliliters anyway?" asked Calvin, the Korean reg from LA sitting in seat 2. Rumor had it he had made millions playing in Macau back when the Chinese games were ridiculously soft.

"Three hundred and thirty milliliters is like twelve ounces," said Ray. "More or less."

"What you say," said Eike, the German seat-5 reg who was offering the bet, "is correct, but only if we assume that throwing the smaller bottle works the same as throwing the larger one." He was a tournament player by trade—the one Ray had recognized on his very first day—but he was based in Vegas and logged in some serious hours at the upstairs cash games. "Which I'm not convinced." The fact that he had a transparent interest in driving the price up was openly acknowledged and accepted. This was not a hustle.

"You mean the influence of size on your grip and throwing technique?" asked JJ.

"Yes, especially on a backward throw," said Eike.

The bet was simple: without moving his chair away from the table, just turning his back to the wastebasket in the far corner of the upstairs room, Eike had to sink a shot with a mostly empty Fiji bottle (a little water left in for balance). Bank shots accepted. It wasn't a new bet, but the newly introduced smaller bottles forced the players to re-evaluate the odds.

(Ray folded: A3 off-suited.)

Ordinarily table chitchat proceeds in subsets. There are always a few silent players, either quietly listening to others or acoustically isolated by noise-canceling headphones. A matter of personality, more than actual need to focus on the game. Simultaneous conversations get carried out in low tones at opposite sides of the table, 1 to 3 and 7 to 9 typically becoming friends by proximity. Seats 4 to 6 have options, but seat 5 will usually talk louder than the others, feeling a kind of toastmaster's responsibility. Dealers, needless to say, are conversational nonfactors.

"So my three hundred bucks to your twenty-one hundred?" said Eike, eager to close the deal and gamble.

"How about your three fifty to my two thousand?" asked JJ.

(Ray played and won a small pot with Q9 suited against the table's spot, a round-faced car salesman from upstate New York.)

"That's less than six to one," said Eike. "No way!"

"I'd take a piece of that at six to one too," said Calvin.

(Ray folded: K4 suited.)

It is quite common, at exceptionally good tables, for all the players to participate in the same conversation. It happens everywhere. It usually means a big fish is at the table, and all the pros are going out of their way to be nice to him and create a friendly atmosphere that will keep him at the table longer. It's just common sense.

What is much less frequent is for a *bad* table, such as the one Ray was playing (and marginally winning at) now, to engage in lighthearted collective banter like the bottle debate. Logan had pointed it out to Ray in one of their first conversations as "what makes Vegas regs the best in the world." And Ray, in spite of the little credit he gave them, had to admit that it did make a difference. A thoroughly entertained spot is a more active spot. Even a tourist who was actually okay at the game would be much more inclined to loosen up a little, gamble it up (and inevitably make more mistakes), upon seeing a bunch of twenty-five-year-olds tossing around $1,000 chips on silly bottle-throwing bets. It was basic psychology. And if the odds were calculated fairly, the regs knew these bets were long-term breakeven, and therefore irrelevant. Just a bit of variance. In the long run, nobody was making any money.

"Okay, six to one is fine," said Eike, handing Mary Ann—who'd just come around with a trayful of 330 ml Fijis and coffee cups—a $1 tip in exchange for his shooting gear. "You guys are splitting it? My three fifty to your twenty-one hundred?"

"I honestly can't believe they switched to these smaller bottles," said JJ. "I feel robbed."

"What's hard to believe?" asked Bryan, removing a white earpiece to join the conversation.

He sat to Ray's left, in position, with his trademark monochrome T-shirt and imposing chip stack. "Less water per bottle, same one-dollar tip, you order more bottles, they make more money. Seems pretty straightforward to me."

A pause. Bryan waiting for JJ's answer. Mary Ann too, tray in hand, standing behind him, waiting to deliver water and receive her tip. But JJ, oblivious, stared blankly into space after having put in a sizable preflop 4bet[6] against Ray's button squeeze.[7]

---

6 In the betting round that takes place before the flop, posting the blind is implicitly considered the first action. A raise (or open) is the second action. Any further action, any reraise, is generally indicated by its successive number, for clarity, thus 3bet, 4bet, 5bet etc.

7 A reraise (3bet) after a raise and one or more calls. The original raiser is metaphorically "squeezed" between the new aggressor and the possible ulterior reraises coming after him from one of the callers. Older poker terminology abounded in such imagery and flourishes (limp, donkbet, trap), whereas the lexicon of the GTO generation tends toward the dryness of pure mathematics (overbet, range linearity, range elasticity).

Most of the time, poker action has a way of flowing unobtrusively through and around the exchanges at the table. The two or three players in a hand take a short break from talking, the conversation freezes—then they naturally flow back like nothing happened, regardless of who won or lost. The idea being that everybody is just here for fun, that the money in play doesn't matter to anybody at all.[8] Cocktail waitresses, though, are generally much less attuned to the stop-and-go of a poker player's attention span, and often find themselves involuntarily underlying, with their lingering, those rare moments of complete absorption and professional concentration regs would rather not make a big deal of. It's not their fault, of course; they have a job to do. It's just the way it is.

(Ray folded: AJ off.)

"It's a pretty sick marketing move," said JJ, collecting and stacking close to $1,000 of profit from the hand and finally handing Mary Ann a blue $1 chip.

"I don't know, I think what it does to me is I just drink less," said Calvin.

"I doubt that," said JJ. "I'm pretty sure we order water thirty-three percent more often now. Which not only costs us more tip money, it also slows down the game."

"But it also means I get to see *her* thirty-three percent more often," said the spot with a broad, flirty smile. He was short, with thin graying hair, and wore a blue blazer over his khaki sweater and Rolex. He handed Mary Ann an unprompted $5 chip. "Here you go, honey."

"That's very true," chimed in Calvin, his face, and those of JJ and Bryan too, relaxing in a smile at the realization that they'd let their love for table-side math get the better of them. They'd sounded cheap and calculating. Reparation was in order.

"So this bet, we are booked?" said JJ.

"Booked at six to one," said Eike.

---

8 Of course, Vegas pros are a group so conspicuous and homogenous that the idea of hiding their status would be absolutely ridiculous. Spots know perfectly well they're surrounded by sharks. Still, it's an issue of manners, and Vegas regs are far and away the best-mannered regs around.

"In for half of twenty-one hundred," said Calvin.

"Booked," said JJ.

And so as Mary Ann walked away, and the car salesman debated whether to focus his attention on her departing ass or the much-awaited throw, and as Ray folded 78 off, and the dealer took longer than usual spreading the three-card flop, distracted as he was by the sight of three men half his age wagering a month of his salary on grade-school tomfoolery, Eike took a final generous swig to get the water to the desired level, turned his chair around, and after one or two practice swings let the bottle go, all eyes at the table now fixated on him, and held his hand aloft long after the release, like a cocky NBA player after a buzzer beater, and didn't even turn around to watch the 33-percent-smaller-than-usual transparent prism rattle noisily around the square metal rim of the wastebasket, and gloriously sink in.

There's an etiquette to live poker, that's a given. You don't cheat, you don't collude with other players, you don't steal another reg's seat. But also: you don't berate the spot for the way he plays,[9] you don't blame the dealer for your losses or forget to tip regularly, you don't make a scene when you get unlucky. These are the tenets of basic tableside decency.

In an ecosystem as structured and delicate as the upstairs room, however, the unwritten rules of poker conduct stretch much deeper, covering all bases of potential behavior: you don't slow the game down; you never say no when other regs (or, God forbid, a spot) suggest raising the stakes; you don't try to lure spots to a different game[10]; you *don't* slow the game down. In light of that, what JJ was doing now—using the spot's bathroom break to talk shop with the other regs about a sensitive issue—was not full-on wrong, but certainly something a real Vegas veteran would never do.

---

9   In simpler, more poetic times, this was referred to as "tapping the tank" (as in fish tank: disturbing the fish), a tendency microstakes regs have never fully outgrown.

10   Known as *poaching*.

"I ran into Logan yesterday," said JJ, looking at Bryan once both players had folded their hands. "He's over there, you know?"

"I don't wanna talk about it," said Bryan.

"It's like three times a week or something," said JJ.

"I don't wanna talk about it."

This interested Ray. Ever since moving, Logan had been the only other reg who'd been friendly and kind to him. He was a naturally charming and funny kid, and was the only one who had not made him feel like an unwelcome threat to the upstairs environment, a foreign interloper who nobody wanted around. Logan didn't seem to care. Maybe it was because he didn't play much anymore, and had moved on to other business ventures or something (which, considering the way he played, was probably a smart career move). Or more likely he was just an equanimous, chill dude, with his expensive watches and pointy shoes, and had no interest in fretting over the increase in competition brought on by these online exiles. Which Ray respected, in a way.

Yet in the past weeks he had started to notice a certain degree of tension at good old table 14 whenever Logan's name came up in conversation. A foulness of mood. Even Bryan's ill disposition toward Ray seemed somehow connected to Logan, which was quite strange. It was as if the upstairs regs strongly disliked the only fun member of their little group. Like he had done something to them. What it was, Ray could not fathom, and since his interactions with any potential sources were still severely limited, he didn't dare ask. Besides, it was pretty clear that Bryan *did not want to talk about it.*

"Well, someone should, at some point," JJ managed to sneak in, just before the blue-blazered spot got back to the table.

"How much pressure?" asked the girl in standard all-black massage-girl attire.

"I . . . medium? Maybe?" said Ray.

"Is it okay if I use a little oil?" said the girl.

"I guess," said Ray. "Maybe not a lot?"

"Great. Let me know how it feels," said the girl.

The massage was a first for Ray. He found the whole procedure, a group favorite among the upstairs regs, baffling: the turning around the chair, the awkward and vaguely clinical chest cushion, the leaning forward over one's stack of chips, powerless, conspicuous. It had always looked to him like an extremely undesirable situation to be in while sitting at a table, surrounded by more-or-less strangers, trying to focus on a card game.

Next to him, Bryan was already straddling his chair backrest-forward and bending head, neck, and broad shoulders over the cushion on his allotted portion of playing felt. A muscular Hungarian lady named Irina was working on his back. Like many of the high-stakes pros, Bryan had preferential phone contact with his favorite masseuse, and how-are-the-kids?-type conversations with her mid-massage. Professional live poker is made of habits, and Vegas regs had over the years perfected theirs to a form of art. Table massages were not cheap ($2/minute plus tips), but in the microcosm of the upstairs room they were viewed more as business expenses than luxury.

This too, of course, Ray saw differently. Spending $2.40 a minute (tip included) would slash his expected hourly win rate by an unacceptable $144 per hour. At a bad $10/$20 table like this one—where it would be challenging (if not impossible) to make $200/hour—that meant that for the duration of his massage he was a barely-above-breakeven player in terms of expected value. Like, he might as well go play a $2/$5 downstairs for a half hour, for all it mattered. Yet he was starting to look at live players with different eyes. They seemed to rarely think in these terms, which are obvious and sort of bread-and-butter to online grinders, but they still thrived. Jockish and incompetent as they looked, it was clear that they were math-driven, rational people at heart, who'd learned to ignore their more analytic impulses and take things a little easier. They'd been around for years, made way more money than he had, and seemed to live a more serene life than his. Maybe there was something to what Logan had told him about required skill sets being different here. Maybe live poker, much like ping-pong, was really meant for well-adjusted nerds. Of course, reason suggested they'd also just had it unbelievably easy until now, and were about to be wiped out as soon as the online pros started migrating en masse to the live tables. Like happy, oblivious picnickers relaxing on the shore before a tidal wave. Still, while waiting for their downfall, he had a sense he would do well to give their experience a chance and see if he could find something useful there, before discarding the whole thing as feel-playerish hogwash. Hence the table talk. And now the massage.

The therapists's hands were already digging deep, fast-fading trenches in the skin of his back. It wasn't exactly painful so much as extremely uncomfortable. He was acutely conscious of the contact between the girl's fingertips and his bones, his barely covered, frail, exposed ribs, and quite unsure what to do with his arms, which he still needed to move, to reach back over to the edge of the table to look at his cards or grab a handful of chips to bet. He was sure he looked ridiculous.

"Maybe," he finally said in a low tone, after remembering he was actually *paying* for all this. "Maybe let's do soft pressure, maybe?"

"Of course," said the girl. And again: "Let me know how it feels."

And suddenly it was great. It felt great. More than great. It was what he'd wanted, what he'd not known he really needed. Slow, comforting movements, sweeping across his back, and shoulders, and neck, and arms, warm and safe. Like the built-up tension of the last few months had found its home deep within his sinews and muscles, and only slow, gentle stroking could melt it away. Like his sense of discomfort and displacement, and feeling lost, in the wrong place, doing the wrong things, the compounding of a thousand mistakes, all this could maybe be eased and somehow *understood* by the hands of this stranger, softly telling him it was okay, everything was okay, everything was going to be . . .

"That's how I like it too," said Bryan in a whisper, for the first time ever addressing Ray with a friendly smile. "All these bros that want to be hit hard, like, with the elbows and shit. And I'm here and I'm like, 'Softer, please!'" He laughed. "I think basically we're just paying to get cuddled."

Which perhaps if you weren't the son of a lit mag editor at a small but proud college—professional metaphor-unpacker—if your self-awareness had not been honed into razor sharpness from the earliest age, if you were instead, say, a thirty-two-year-old professional live poker player from Montana, who loved the gym, his wife, his two-year-old daughter, maybe the implications would be lost on you. Maybe you'd laugh about it. Wanting to be cuddled. Paying to be hugged. Maybe it was okay, when it wasn't something you needed, when it wasn't something you found instantly and almost unbelievably . . .

(Ray raised from the button: AA.)

The Shibuya. Once you enter, turn left at the huge fake-traffic intersection where people take selfies, follow the hallway past the restaurants, past the poker room, all the way to the shops. The Shibuya is going to be crowded, and everything will look different. Look around, it's nice there. There's an amazing ramen bar on the mezzanine, right above a Hello Kitty store. There's a secret whisky lounge too, with all these great Japanese whiskies by the glass, it's above a posters-and-memorabilia place on the left side of the hallway; you have to find this secret door disguised as a Tokyo subway map, and then you go up this tiny elevator, it's pretty cool. While you're there, take a look at the poker room, I mean why not. It's mostly micros, but they have this awesome private room with glass walls where sometimes they'll run a big game if you ask them. The whole room is just gorgeous, it's brand-new.

To be fair, the idea of walking that far just to hit a CVS for Chapstick and Visine had sounded quite absurd to Ray. While the intricate web of overpasses and hallways that connected most Strip casinos did ensure little to no time outside with the tourists, it was still a twenty-minute walk at best, and that was provided he could actually follow JJ's directions on the first try. Still, JJ had made a convincing case about the importance of boycotting the Positano gift shop and its criminal prices. It wasn't the couple of bucks he was going to save. It was the principle. He had made it sound important, a rite of passage for a new wannabe-Vegas reg, buying his first desert starter's kit—various moisturizers—at the Shibuya.

The intersection was a thing to behold. A tennis-court-sized square of asphalt all inside a building, both bordered and diagonally cut by the white stripes of a preposterous but very real pedestrian crossing. A continuous flow of people waiting, walking, Instagramming, regulated by large shiny traffic lights in the corners. The fake buildings surrounding the fake square, plastered with bright colors and big-font Japanese kana with the occasional westernized "Joysound," "Hisamitsu," "Uniqlo," "Starbucks." The statue of a sitting brown dog was photographed with paparazzi-like intensity.

The sheer size of the crowd was daunting. Understandable at 5:00 p.m. on a Las Vegas Friday night, but still impressive. Ray lingered a bit to do the math. It looked like at least eighty crossers (twenty per traffic light) were required at all times to guarantee the authenticity of the Tokyo experience. Postulating that no one in their right mind would cross more than once (since the diagonal stripes allowed all corners to be reachable from every-where), and that crossing had taken him a couple minutes tops, it stood to reason that to keep the intersection busy for twelve hours per day (10:00 a.m.–10:00 p.m.) would require a bare minimum of 28,800 indi-vidual crossers. And that was not taking into account the fact that, at those rates, arrivals at the intersection needed to run like clockwork, perfectly staggered at the same concentration throughout the day. So real-istically, the numbers were like double that.

Yet, as Ray stood there taking stock of the implied benefits in terms of casino revenue, certain observations forced him to reconsider these figures. First of all, the number of people (children mostly, but not exclusively) who seemed to like nothing more than crossing and recrossing over and over, giggling at red lights and then sprinting across through the sea of people, was honestly concerning. Second—and this took Ray five red-to-green cycles, phone stopwatch in hand, to figure out—the traffic lights did not follow a consistent, time-based pattern: red lights *waited* for a crowd to gather before turning green. Meaning there was a guy somewhere, presumably in a control room watching the eye-in-the-sky feed, whose job was to manually direct traffic to ensure the opposite of what people directing traffic usually go for: congestion, blockage. Sardines-in-a-can.

This is the point where even an above-average nerdy personality would call it a day. Give up on the whole pedestrian-counting deal. Not Ray. If there was one thing that had made the difference in his career, one thing that made him shine over thousands of other smart, talented button clickers, it was his dedication to riding his mathematical trains of thought to the rigorous end. He was thorough. Yet the reason Ray was still at the top-left corner of the Crossing at the Las Vegas Shibuya—reevaluating the average crossing time (T) to account for serial crossers (ACPP[11]) and elastic red light duration (ARLT[12])—was more personal in nature. He *needed* this. After the end of today's session, when the brief relief of the massage had dissipated and his muscles had frozen again, his heart pounding, Ray craved the tranquility that only the most gratuitous, finicky math could provide.

One of the things he'd learned about live poker since moving to Vegas was that the close monitoring of his emotions he'd mastered in the days of VFlnd3r now took on different, more introspective forms. In online poker, the level of constant focus demanded by the simultaneous action on multiple tables[13] made his emotional landscape a black-and-white affair. He was good to play while in "A-game" (fully concentrated, alert, and responsive brain reflexes, imaginative and perceptive play, complete indifference to outcomes); and in "B-game" (less than optimal focus, average brain reflexes, dependable ability to execute known strategies, complete indifference to outcomes); anything from "C-game" (sense of distraction and/or anger, tired and/or anxious, poker auto piloting and irrational, impulsive play, result-oriented tempers) and below was a reason to quit the session

---

11   Average crossing per person.

12   Average red light time.

13   Four to six once he got to the high-stakes, even ten to twelve back when he was climbing up the poker ladder. Which is a lot more feasible and less superhuman than it sounds, but still pretty intense.

immediately, or at the very least take a break. He either was playing well, or he wasn't.

Live poker turned out to be much more nuanced. There was just too much time between one action and the next, what with all the folding and watching other people play, and keeping a constant ECG scan of his psychic state had soon proved impossible. The mind was bound to wander. In any given session, he found out, he was likely to experience a dizzying range of emotions: from unwarranted feelings of omnipotence to fatalistic self-pity and existential dread. He had discovered and mentally charted at least ten different types of distraction: from mild preoccupations (say a text from his mom exhorting him to call his dad more often, or an article about independent bookstores in the age of Amazon) to more serious worries (an absorbing clinical study about retinal vascular occlusions, or a minor epiphany about his willingness to pay a stranger for a half-hour of physical comfort and tenderness); from small discomforts he could soldier through (a stiff neck or a leg cramp from sitting in the same chair for nine hours) to urgent concerns dictating immediate action (physiological needs and panic attacks); and so on.

In short, he had lost. Through no fault of his own this time, just clear, unequivocal bad luck—his two aces losing a preflop all in for a pot of over $10,000 in horrific fashion. But he hadn't quit then. He kept on playing. And after more than two hours had passed, he still couldn't shake the feeling. The sense of loss and despair. It was still there, fifty, a hundred hands later. Influencing his play in the most human and suboptimal ways. He wasn't angry, or frustrated exactly, yet lately every successive loss had the power of awakening in him the whole string of bad outcomes that had led to where he was, sitting with poor posture in a Las Vegas poker room, playing with physical cards and chips. With live games getting shittier by the day. With scary-little money left in his bank account. With Tragedy ever so close. He'd lost the ability to erase previous stages and start a new session like a clean slate (which, of course, is what an AI like that fucking Cardanus would do). The ghosts of mistakes past haunted his every move.

He had made the lame excuse about needing to buy Visine and Chapstick, a necessity Vegas regs respect so much that nobody questioned his motives, and just left. And now he really, *really* wanted to know how many people walked the Shibuya crossing per day.

Left of the crossing he'd entered a mock subway station, pink-walled and home to one of the city's best sushi bars, which in two hundred feet let out onto an izakaya-lined street in nighttime Tokyo. The illusion was remarkable: it was still a hallway, broad and for the most part straight, connecting the shopping center to the crowded crossing at the heart of the hotel-and-casino area; but the night sky stretching high above contrasted with the low white ceiling of the "station" so much that Ray really felt like he was stepping outside on a crisp summer night in Shinjuku. They even simulated the wind-in-your-face effect of resurfacing into the open air, somehow. Paper lanterns hung from the doors of restaurants and blackjack and pai-gow lounges alike, and a large opening to the left signaled the alley entrance to Cirque du Soleil's kabuki-themed show *Zakura* and its red theater, fronted with perpetually blossoming cherry trees.

The poker room spread behind a golden balustrade to the right of the hallway. It was tinier than the one at the Pos, but noticeably newer and, to be honest, nicer. The tables were spaced farther apart, and the chairs looked comfortable. The walls had Japanese paintings of trees, birds, and peaceful landscapes. But more than anything, it was the light that made the difference: a soft white glow refracting gently against the pale blue walls, making the room exactly the right degree of bright. The dark, orangish gloom of the Positano poker room had nothing on it.

Ray passed the balustrade and the main floor-staff podium, where the waiting lists for the micros were punched in the auto-seating system. He walked around. The chips had a more minimal design here, a solid monochrome with no-nonsense numbering at the center, but the colors were the same. People played with blues, lots of reds, the occasional green $25. He figured he should enjoy watching them, these grinders who played as many hours as him, suffered the same crushing swings (at least in the number of big blinds won or lost), and all for nothing. Just for the dream of making it to where he was. For love of the game. It should give him a sense of purpose, Ray thought, a sense of pride in what he'd achieved. Yet somehow the cocky look in the eyes of the kid in shorts and five-toed shoes—who was stacking up his chips after a "big" pot at the table in front of him—only made Ray uncomfortable. Queasy, almost.

He almost didn't notice the private room. It was all the way in the back, past two low-stakes PLO[14] tables, with its own smaller podium in front and an elegant glass wall. And it wasn't empty. Someone was playing, sitting around its one table, with stacks of black $100 chips indicating that this was no small game at all. He got closer, almost all the way up to the glass divider. Five crystal-clear spots were playing what was unmistakably a big No Limit Hold'em game, laughing, drinking red wine, tossing big chips in the pot like nothing. A private, secret game. Two of them were a couple Ray had seen at the Positano three or four times. He remembered the man's gold cufflinks and striped shirts, the gold aviator frames; he remembered the woman's pearls, and their flashy, oblong watches. And then he remembered he'd never seen them actually *play* at the Pos. They'd only enter the poker room for a moment and then leave, only to look for someone, only ever to meet up with . . .

The sixth player at the table, seated with his back to the glass door, turned around and saw him. Ray thought Logan's smile was surprisingly affable, given the circumstances.

---

14 Pot Limit Omaha, a widespread and successful variant of poker where each player is dealt four cards instead of two and bets can't be bigger than what's already in the pot. Many pros have a love/hate relationship with it, since the effects of variance are even stronger here than in Texas Hold'em. Ray was not a fan.

Interlude V

(the story of a deal)

Rick was a man if you ask him he'll tell you you can know all you need to know about America from the first five songs on *Nebraska*. Not that you'd ask him. Or that he'd tell you. Matter of fact, you probably wouldn't be talking to him at all, and certainly not about music. Just things are not always as they seem, simple as that.

The thing with the kids downtown had started a while back, and honestly, he'd had enough of them. You wouldn't think you'd get to pick and choose much in this line of business, but in some ways you do, and he didn't like them. He didn't trust them. Things are not always as they seem. They said they'd gotten together to pick up girls, and maybe that was true. Or maybe that was true *at first*. But Rick could smell obsession from a mile away, and these kids reeked. They were fanatics.

Rick never had trouble getting girls. Like if there's a national average he'd feel sorry for the four or five dudes who'd have to die a virgin to make up for his numbers, you know? And it wasn't any harder to do now that he was fifty. There's enough girls who come to Vegas to work in casinos, or strip joints, or porn, and he knew everybody around. So, see? Not hard to do. The difference was that Rick had been in love with the same woman for twenty-five years, and that's what mattered. You can fuck around as much as you want, but that don't change how your heart feels.

But with these kids it's not about what's in your heart. Used to be all about the girls, now it's all about whatever the hell they're talking about now. They were good business, bottom line is. Hard to turn down good business. They needed all this stuff, equipment, and they paid lump every time. But the stuff they'd been asking for recently, Rick didn't understand what they'd need it for. And it was starting to scare him. Karen told him he needed to *empathize*, and that we're all just doing the best we can, even them. That they may be bad apples, but they were also just kids who got beat up in school a lot, and no girl'd ever let them undress her if her clothes were on fire. That she didn't like them too, but she could see where they were coming from. Maybe so, but Karen didn't know what happens when you put a bunch of miserable pissed-off kids together and tell them whose fault it is that they're miserable and pissed off. Rick had seen the writing on the wall. Like, at that *lair* they had, Rick had seen the shit they'd written around, when he'd brought over their stuff. And the flags too. Karen hadn't seen the flags. At least, Rick didn't want to be the one who put a gun in their hand.

He was meeting this kid Trevor in the empty lot behind the Paris, on Koval. He liked the Paris. He and Karen would go eat there sometimes, he liked the apple pie and she laughed that he couldn't say "tarte tatin." Even though he wasn't so bad, it was more like a joke the two of them had. This was out front, at the restaurant under the tower. *Bistro.* Whatever.

This kid Trevor wasn't exactly one of them, though. Rick had done his homework. LA kid, moved here a couple years back. It didn't look like he was involved with them much lately, but all the others seemed to respect him. Said he was a "legend." How someone who doesn't look old enough to buy a beer can be a legend Rick couldn't quite understand, but he seemed okay. A Santa Monica rich kid maybe, but not crazy. A while ago, he'd given Rick $1,700 for this pickup that wasn't worth the gasoline to light it on fire. He said it wasn't even his money, it was for his friend. Some friend he was.

Anyway, whatever he needed all the filming gear for, it didn't look bad. It didn't seem like he'd ever done shit, really, the legend.

And really what bothered him most about these kids was how they acted like he was stupid. They were afraid of him, of course, and tried not to cross him, but it was clear they thought he didn't know shit. Like if you're older than fifty and wear leather, then you can't use goddamn Google. They thought they had him figured out, that they had this superior knowledge because they were on the fucking internet. Did they know Rick read all their bullshit posts? Did they know Rick loved Billy Wilder movies and wanted to learn French? Did they know Rick was on Usenet groups before a lot of them were even born? And still they acted like he couldn't figure out what they were about. Like he couldn't see right through them. And the thing with Rick is, you could hate his guts and let him know, just flat-out tell him you think the world'd be better off without him, and that's fine; but treat him like he's stupid, that really drives him up a wall.

The lot was empty except maybe two or three cars and a truck, and Rick's van. Koval is like the backstage to the Strip. It's not even trying to be its own thing, it's just the back of the casinos on one side, and Motel 6 and shit like that on the other. It doesn't have another purpose. Vegas starts again next block.

"Can you get me a drone too?" the kid said. Rick was counting the bills, snapping his fingers fast like a bank teller. "Like for aerial shots."

"For what now?" said Rick.

"Just a drone, can you get me one?" said the legend.

"Kid you know this ain't Amazon, right?"

"No, I know," said the kid. "If you can't get it, it's fine. It's just that I'm doing this thing down by the Mexican border, and I thought it'd be cool to have one."

"Why are you even telling me this?" said Rick. "Fuck it, I don't wanna know!"

"All right, all right, sorry," said the kid.

"Christ, shit!"

So he was with them too now. Who knows how they'd talked him into it. Kid'd get killed in Mexico, bet your ass on it. The problem these days is you can't trust what you know anymore. Kids look like nerds, talk like nerds, then get together and shoot up a Walmart. People like Rick, they were born in this, they knew the rules, you knew how to deal with them. But now everything was online, your money, your ride, your girls, and maybe all the crazy'd gone online too. Nerds took over the crazy. Things are not always as they seem.

"Did they really use these for porn?" the kid was saying, checking out the boxes.

"Some," said Rick.

"That's so cool."

"Yeah, so maybe don't talk with your mouth right into them microphones, you know?"

The kid laughed.

Rick never wanted to hurt anybody. He did what he had to, but he didn't hate anybody. He was the guy who fixed the AC in your home in Summerlin last summer during that heat wave, you know? He liked that. He was good with people, and he had friends. A lot of people owed him favors. A town like this, things were bound to get ugly at times, but he'd never started them. This business with the kids, hell, he just didn't understand it. Didn't know how to deal with it. But Rick couldn't turn down work now. Not after what happened to Karen. Fuck it, kids, go get killed if you like, I won't say no to your money anymore. *Sir, I guess there's just a meanness in this world.*

"Look, kid," said Rick. "I don't know what you need a drone for down there, but if you give me a couple days I'll see what I can do."

"That's great!" said the kid.

"Right."

"Oh, and Rick?"

"Yeah?"

"If you find different models, could you maybe text me so I can choose?" said the kid. "Like, take a picture with your phone and send it as a text, you know?"

Empathize.

"Sure," said Rick. "I know."

After the deal he was sitting at the bistro with his earphones on before the waitress came, and he was listening to a woman on the internet say "tarte tatin." Rick was a man if you ask him he'll tell you the internet is a goddamn miracle. Sometimes he got lost on his phone for hours, just reading and reading, Karen sleeping next to him, and he'd just follow these links through the craziest stories while the night flew by, learning all he could, trying to make sense of this world. He loved that. He felt it was his privilege, to live in a time when someone like him could know so much. He touched the screen and played it over and over, mouthing the words: *tarte tatin, tarte tatin, tarte tatin.*

"I'll take that apple pie, please?" he said to the waitress. She was pretty. Sweet eyes. Kinda like Karen's.

He was going to have to leave soon, good client needed two more diamond rings. But he'd promised himself he'd make time for this today. Tomorrow he could tell Karen about it, make her laugh. The waitress with the big sweet eyes came back with his pie. He put his earphones back on and played some music. The afternoon sky was turning a pretty pink out west, behind the Strip and lots on Koval.

Well I guess everything dies, baby, that's a fact
But maybe everything that dies someday comes back . . .

9

Mary Ann

". . . So that when the true count is high, they start betting bigger. Because of this thing called the Kelly criterion, that says bets need to increase proportionally to the player's advantage."

On Gabrielle's Formica living room table, cards lay in the shape of a sample blackjack hand: Mary Ann and Gabrielle were the players, Erica the dealer. The cards had two rounded-out corners that identified them as belonging to one of the table-used "canceled" casino decks you could buy for $2 at the Positano gift shop or any 7-Eleven in Vegas. On a large checkered play mat on the floor, Gabrielle's two-year-old, Mike, was frying plastic eggs in a plastic frying pan over a plastic induction-cooking stovetop that folded up into a suitcase. Sunlight filled the room.

"But . . . how do you know all this?" asked Mary Ann, surprise overriding her fear of sounding offensive. It seemed rude to imply that a Siren's Cove dancertainer was unlikely to know advanced probability theory—especially since she'd just met her—but the question sort of came out anyway.

"You think the nerds in the poker room are the only ones who can do a little math?" said Erica, pushing up the bridge of her black-rimmed glasses. She looked as young as Mary Ann, short and gym-rat fit (as per Positano quasi-exotic blackjack dancing requirements). Her cheeks had that puffy porcelain quality that you could just tell they got pinched by strangers all the time when she was a kid. She didn't look offended by the question.

"It helps if you teach math in college," said Gabrielle. She tapped the table next to her 5-3 eight, asking for another card.

"It's community college, Gab," said Erica, dealing her a king for an eighteen stand. "And I'm an adjunct."

Mary Ann wasn't sure what to do with twelve against the dealer's six. It didn't matter, of course: the point was showing her how to count cards, not how to play. Still, when she tapped the table and saw Erica shake her head with a smile and wave her hand facedown to tell her to stand, she felt embarrassed. It felt like school.

"The numbers are easy," said Erica. "You can learn all you need to know in an afternoon on Wikipedia."

"And what *do* I need to know?" said Mary Ann.

"Not a lot. The basics of Hi/Lo counting, just to understand what I'll be doing from the platform," said Erica. "But mostly you'll be acting."

"To tell them when to bet more?" said Mary Ann.

"To distract them when the deck is cold," said Gabrielle. "And to get them excited when it's hot. The reason card counters get caught is they need to be looking at the cards and change their bets a lot, and supervisors spot them. But the guys we're helping won't even be looking at the table. They'll be drunk, chatting up their waitress, staring at Erica's a—*tushy* on the platform." She glanced at her toddler, who seemed concentrated on his cooking. "Pit boss will be *happy* to see them bet big."

"What happens if they get caught?" said Mary Ann.

"Nothing. They get asked to not play blackjack anymore," said Gabrielle.

"And what happens if *we* get caught?" said Mary Ann.

Gabrielle looked down at the cards.

"We go to jail," said Erica, with a matter-of-factness Mary Ann found concerning, but kind of inspiring.

On his mat, Mike had grabbed the handle of his trusty frying pan to lift it from the stovetop and give it a couple of expertly back-and-forth shakes. Play food rattled plasticky against the edges. He turned his head, calling "Mommy!", and received a smile from all three women. He put the frying pan back down with a satisfied grin.

"But we won't," said Gabrielle, turning back over to Mary Ann. "We're not trying to make money here—these guys are still gonna make a ship-load of mistakes. We just want them to lose a little *less*, maybe slow the game down a bit. This ain't a heist."

"It's a strike," said Mary Ann.

"It's a strike." Erica nodded. "Now let's go over this again. Tens, jacks, queens, kings, and aces are minus one, everything from deuce to six is . . ."

The night Aunt Karen was let go from her job of over twenty years at Circus Circus, she had done two things she'd later come to regret a great deal. They'd said something vague about downsizing, some long-winded legalese from the bevertainer contract about "occupational qualifications as relating to the dominant service provided," or some such nonsense. But she knew she was just getting replaced with a younger, blonder model. In light of the circumstances, she could then maybe forgive herself for getting blackout drunk on well vodka at the Super 8 karaoke bar off Koval, even at her age. But what she did after that was unforgivable. Because, yes, Mary Ann's new condo was just a block away, while her apartment on Pecos was a good five miles out east, and she was in no condition to drive; and yes, her name was on the lease, so the night guard at the gate would let her through, no problem; but having her niece find her in that state on the living room floor, forcing her to pull her up, nurse her, and eventually drag her to the car and drive her to the Desert Springs Hospital on Flamingo, that was one of the worst things she'd ever done. Poor Mae. To do this to *her*.

Truth was, that was the night Aunt Karen's world had stopped making any sense. Las Vegas was supposed to be a place where you could make it work, no matter who you were or where you were from. A place where if you kept your head down, and didn't mind people living large around you while you sweated and forced a smile through overlong shifts, there would always be a job for you, and everything would be all right. Aunt Karen had built her entire adult life around this lesser American dream, never complaining and never asking for more. She hadn't had children, hadn't traveled, hadn't dragged a daughter halfway around the country to be a *stage actress* in the goddamn '90s. She had just worked. And now she'd lost everything, and it didn't make any sense.

And so the following weeks, which she had spent largely in bed, with Mary Ann visiting her twice a day and more often than not staying overnight, Karen had found herself trapped in the conundrum of desperately needing help and feeling awful about receiving it. In her room, she'd worry about how horrible she was being to Mae, which all the more made her want to stay in bed with the lights off and in need of constant care, which in turn made her feel *even worse* about Mae, and so on. And any time Mary Ann managed to assure her that she was fine, that it was okay, really, that she loved her and was just happy to help her get back on her feet, then the prospect of an imminent future *out there*—in that world that had lied to her and discarded her like spoiled food—triggered the whole ugly thing all over again. She couldn't break out of the loop. It was as if her family's mental health history had finally managed to track her down, a runaway all the way from Mississippi, and presented her with long-overdue psychic bills.

As for Mary Ann, the most perceptible consequence of the incident had been that her life suddenly felt extremely *busy*. On top of her work shifts, she now had two apartments to keep more or less habitable, groceries to get for two people, plus an aging and cranky python, several drives on a commute that involved crossing and recrossing the Strip at peak traffic congestion as she drove to and from the Pos and her aunt's. The sudden spike in daily activity had made her eager to jump out of bed in the morning in a way she hadn't been since long before the Episode. The setting aside of most of her hobbies, from people-watching to self-loathing, from daylight photography to relentless self-blaming, had been spontaneous, seamless. And as much as she turned it over and over in her mind to find it flawed and self-serving, her anger too seemed genuine: she was furious at Them, the people who did this to Karen. The people who ran a billion-dollar industry on technicalities and loopholes to preserve the lucrative status quo. The people who, she now realized, had maybe hired *her* as part of that same process of ageist turnover, putting good workers out of a job for not looking twenty-three anymore.

By the end of January, Karen couldn't deal with her domestic situation anymore. The American lie of honest hard work had shown its true colors, and it was no use pretending everything would be all right again soon. But she couldn't bring Mary Ann down with her. Poor, vulnerable, generous Mae, she deserved better. She was almost starting to resent her help, forcing her to hide the pain of her disillusionment from her impressionable niece. In the end, she had shaken off the outer coating of her malaise—started to take care of herself (and Rodrigo) again, even talked about looking for a new job—just to get Mae out of the house.

She dragged herself to the interviews Rick could get her (she'd been seeing him again for some time since Mary Ann moved out, but felt too ashamed of this childish relapse to tell her). But in the meantime even the once-down-on-their-luck, now flashily revamped casinos of the Fremont Street Experience had implemented stringent policies about dangling arm fat, dermal imperfections, various signs of the passing of time and of poor nutritional habits. At the Stagecoach Casino, a pit boss in full John Wayne getup had tapped the screen of a Geronimo's Fury penny slot throughout their five-minute interview, then told her they were looking for more of a Claire Trevor type. At the Grand Diamond, they could maybe get her a couple shifts a week with the Services Sanitation Team. She resorted to her last hope. A week later, she was ladling oxtail soup at the tiny Hawaiian buffet of the Newport, green florals on her shirt, orange plastic flowers on her hairnet.

Relieved of her daily nursing duties, Mary Ann found in her anger a natural way to channel her newfound energy. Karen's bedridden languishing might have been over, but the patent injustice that had caused it, the evil that had threatened the life of her lifesaving aunt, sure wasn't. While her earlier, effortful attempts at self-improvement had done nothing to make her feel better, helping her aunt became a welcome distraction from self-centeredness. It was a reflex, something that just seemed to *happen.* Opening herself up to the possibility that what made her feel marginal and used about Las Vegas might come not from her but from the city itself suddenly made her less alone in her struggle. And doing something for them—the thousands like her Vegas hurt and exploited—maybe really could help her too.

Opportunity presented itself with incredible punctuality. In the staff changing room at the Pos, where an overlapping of schedules enabled her weekly encounter with Gabrielle, Mary Ann found herself suddenly receptive to her colleague's usual brand of locker-room talk about the exploitation of the workforce. Finally willing to listen, she discovered that her anger was not unique to her. That after years of what they perceived as too-cautious compromise with the powers that be—with the new CBA years away in the future, and a staggering number of nonunion professions still at the mercy of Wiles's whims—a small, more intransigent group of waitresses, dealers, and various employees had decided they'd had enough, and formed a Shadow Union. Most importantly—and here, thought Mary Ann, lay the perfectly timed coincidence—she learned that this group of rebels now needed *her.*

"The waitress is key, you see?" said Gabrielle. "You can talk to the players a lot more freely." At the table, the rounded-out cards still displayed Mary Ann's last blackjack and Gabrielle's twenty against Erica's 6+6+10 bust, but they weren't playing anymore. The card-counting lesson concluded, Erica flicked distractedly on her phone. "If a dealer started telling players when to bet big, she'd get fired in like a day. But a flirty waitress chatting up a customer is just trying to sell more drinks. There's no way she can be suspected of trying to influence play."

"So I don't have to keep count?" said Mary Ann.

"No—actually the less you look at the cards, the better. Erica's doing all the counting. She'll give you the signals."

"And the dealer's not in on it?"

"Very few. Most of them aren't with us; this is not their fight. HR Committee's trying to get our girls more dealing shifts at the Cove so we have backup counters. But their hands are tied anyway."

"What do you mean?"

"Supervisors look at them all the time. You know how many dealers get arrested in Vegas every year for cheating or stealing or colluding with players? It's too risky—"

"Mommy?" said Mike from the floor.

"Cameras are on twenty-four/seven, they're not just for watching, they record *everything*," said Gabrielle. "If we muck it up, they have immediate, incriminating evidence—"

"Moooommy?"

"But like I said, nobody is lookin' at dancers and waitresses," said Gabrielle. "Y'all look too hot to be smart enough to pull something like this. That's why we can only do this at the Cove."

"Mommy, breakkie?" said Mike, who'd finally got up from the floor to bring over the pseudo-eggs at which he'd worked hard at his fold-up kitchen. He offered up the perfectly odorless content of his frying pan for the women to smell.

"Mommy can't eat now, honey," said Gabrielle. "She's talking to her friends, see?"

Mike, Mary Ann thought, took this surprisingly well, retreating toward his play mat seemingly unfazed by the absence of maternal validation. Still, Mary Ann couldn't help feeling bad for him.

"Those smell delicious, Mike," she said. Mike didn't turn around.

"Erica is the one looking at the cards," Gabrielle went on. "So she's the only one with her tushy on the line. That's why you shouldn't even look. It's for your protection."

"So how's Erica gonna give me the signal?" said Mary Ann.

At this, Erica put her phone down on the table and started getting ready to imaginary-pole-dance the predetermined exotic codes.

The Siren's Cove, a four-table set with scantily clad dealers and a pole-dancing platform above it, was by far the most successful blackjack venue at the Positano—maybe in all of Vegas—and Erica was one of its stars. She was beautiful, her dancing was appropriately mesmerizing, and her blond hair and blue eyes looked perfect with the teal and azure of her siren costume. The idea was quite clever, Mary Ann thought: hiding in plain sight, letting the thing all security personnel are trying their best not to be distracted by be the one thing they really *should* be looking at.

The rebels' stated goal for the so-called strike was "to systematically shrink the owner's profit margins by means of nonconfrontational casino-wide sabotage, including but not limited to slowdowns, instigation to sobriety, noninvasive advantage gambling coaching et al., both as retribution for and as leverage against the unfair and discriminatory treatment of the workforce and the industry's demeaning and unconstitutional staffing policies." What it meant in practice was that, in the CBA-sanctioned impossibility of an actual strike, the Shadow Union (SU) had elected to go stealth. Cocktail waitresses were, as the recent wave of layoffs had abundantly proved, one of the most replaceable job figures in the country, given the intersection of low skill requirements and high rewards/desirability of position. Bartenders and hotel staff had it just as bad, with technological advancements threatening the very existence of their jobs and making redundancies easily justifiable. And, of course, models and dancers had it worst of all. The CBA's generic arbitration clause, covering a broad nondiscrimination provision, rendered legal action against the layoffs more or less impossible—even discounting the obvious difference in firepower of the legal teams involved. In short, the only way to get back at Wiles effectively was to do so invisibly.

By keeping the strike secret, the SU could collect data to offer to WHOA as leverage in the future renegotiation of the CBA, while at the same time hitting Wiles where it really hurt: his wallet. If the strike was successfully carried out for a whole quarter, revenue charts would show it, proving once and for all that fucking with the workforce was not just unethical but a poor business decision.

To plan the strike, the rebels had divided into committees: slots and keno (SK Committee), roulette and craps (RC Committee), poker and sports betting (PS Committee), blackjack (Blackjack Committee), and so on. The idea was to impair every source of casino revenue, but to harm each one only slightly, almost imperceptibly. Surveillance staff in the Donut would easily thwart attempts to cheat at any one game, but they were far less likely to pick up on ubiquitous microsabotage on every activity in their jurisdiction. And at the end of the quarter, Wiles wouldn't be able to blame any specific employees, and would have no legal recourse that didn't involve publicly and very embarrassingly admitting he'd been outsmarted by the collective brain of his workforce. Win/win.

The first meetings of the blackjack saboteurs, before Mary Ann's recruitment, had been a complete failure. The Committee had wasted weeks on a wild goose chase involving gift-shop decks like the one Gabrielle had cracked open for Erica's lecture. A bold plan. The two rounded corners on each card were all that distinguished recycled decks from the otherwise-identical real deal in play at the tables, thus preventing gift-shop customers from getting funny ideas. Without the canceling corners, cards could be furtively reintroduced in play by any close-up magic enthusiast to get a substantial—and very illegal—advantage over the house. So the committee had debated the possibility of acquiring noncanceled decks from collaborationist inmates at High Desert State (Nevada Department of Corrections, Clark County), the unwilling labor force in charge of the actual rounding out of the used cards for mass souvenir-market introduction. While, as it turned out, there was no shortage of SU members with close (sometimes very close) personal ties with more or less every prison in the state, the idea was voted against by the Board of Directors of Strike Modalities (the Board, for short) and officially ruled "dumb as fuck." A bit *too* bold. Chances of saboteurs ending up themselves shaving aces of diamonds at High Desert State projected in the high 90s. The committee had gone back to work, looking for something more subtle.

"And you can keep count of the cards while you're doing *that*?" said Mary Ann. The dancing alone seemed hard enough. Erica's grace, her effortless gyrations around the pole in seductive moves, the well-disguised but clearly visible muscular exertion in play. To do that while never losing sight of the playing cards laid down for only a few seconds, a good seven feet below her moving gaze? And do *math*, on top of all that? It looked impossible.

"I can do two tables at once," said Erica with a wink.

"That's amazing," said Mary Ann.

"This is exactly why this will work," said Gabrielle. "Nobody gives us credit for sh . . . tuff like this."

"You don't *have* to do it, if you don't feel like it," said Erica.

"But we really think you should," said Gabrielle.

"You should see what the RC people are doing," said Erica. "We have one girl at roulette who can use her voice and the spin of the wheel to hypnotize players. You have to see it to believe it."

"It's the people you never look at who can really surprise you," concluded Gabrielle. And Mary Ann couldn't help a smile as little Mike put down his unappreciated offering of fried eggs to methodically empty Mommy's purse of all her makeup, and change of clothes, and Visine dispensers on the floor—the more cylindrical or otherwise geometrically predisposed items rolling around the living room and dispersing under couches and coffee tables and TV stands.

New York is the kind of city where people who have a compulsive need to live at the center of things, and be *seen*, always end up moving. This gives birth to the common misconception that New York is a particularly lonely town, when in fact it's one of the most densely populated areas on the planet, and just has the misfortune of attracting a particularly whiny and narcissistic crowd. When she lived in SoHo, and had photos of herself taken daily, and ran into people she knew in the streets and commercial establishments of downtown Manhattan with small-town frequency, Mary Ann too subscribed to the mass delusion that nobody ever *saw* her. That she was a forgettable afterthought in the collective memory of a cynical metropolis.

But the puzzle of visibility in New York had nothing on the mindfuckery of being a cocktail waitress on the Las Vegas Strip. A hot piece of ass on display, but under no circumstance a distraction from the games; under constant eye-in-the-sky surveillance, but completely unnoticed; her every move recorded, but only as an extra in shots focused on the tourists. It was amazing how little she'd thought of it so far, the myriad ways her physical presence was simultaneously watched and ignored pretty much all day every day. By security, visitors, colleagues, everybody.

The strike opened her eyes to it. For a resident employed in a center-Strip casino, the city was like one big joke about the idea of being seen. She'd never really considered it, but Mary Ann now realized that during the better part of her day-to-day life, it was someone's *job* to watch her. And someone else's job, probably, to manage and archive all the footage of her going about her invisible daily things. What was it her mom had said? To have a professional look after her, someone who's paid to give a shit, purely transactional. Well, she had that now, didn't she?

In the days after she learned of the Shadow Union's shadow activities, cameras became Mary Ann's new obsession. Black and bulbous, they constellated the ceilings of the Positano with no apparent attempt to conceal their presence. Donut security personnel needed them ubiquitous and equidistant from each other, which resulted in their becoming a motif of sorts, a discreet polka-dotting that receded into the visual nothingness of all decorative patterns. Now Mary Ann really saw them. They were everywhere: lidless, sleepless, relentless. As she walked with Erica by the symmetrical rows of craps tables, she looked at her fellow conspirators on the RC Committee in the act of perpetrating full-on felonies and recoiled. How could they do it? Did they not see the cameras? How could they possibly hope not to get caught? The whole enterprise was madness. And, she had to remember, she still had time to back out.

"You're looking at it backward," said Erica. They were wearing street clothes, ordinary visitors taking an ordinary stroll before their respective Wednesday-evening shifts. "You're thinking of the cameras for what they *mean*, instead of what they *are*."

"And what are they?"

"Proof this thing can work." Erica was bold and tender, with no trace of Gabrielle's rougher edge. A kindness to her. "Now you're scared, and when you look at them you see the eye-in-the-sky, the fat mean security dude watching us from somewhere down below."

Mary Ann looked up.

"But think about the actual cameras for a second. Think of them as *objects*. They're everywhere, identical, and we never even *see* them. They're right there, doing this incredibly invasive thing, but they're invisible. And we are just like them."

"But Security get paid to look, it's their job."

"They're just people, Mary, and they live in Vegas, just like us. They have Vegas-vision: in their eyes, we're part of the furniture. If we steal chips from a table, they'll see *that*. But if we look like we're basically doing our job, then we disappear. We're objects." Erica smiled. "Have you never felt completely invisible in this town?"

She had. *Unseen.* Hearing Erica say it sent a cold spark down her spine. She wanted to feel bad about it, like the thoughts that kept her up at night were not even deep or original, and she was making a big emotional deal of the most ordinary Vegas thing there was. But it felt so damn good to know someone else felt it too.

"Look at that," said Erica. "What do you see?"

A waitress was chatting with a player by a craps table. She wore too-heavy makeup, and looked just the prescribed amount of flirty.

"I don't know her," said Mary Ann. "She's not with us, right? She's just getting that guy a drink."

"Cayleen is in grad school for clinical psychology at UNLV. She talks gamblers into not chasing their losses, call it a night instead. She's amazing at it. And it's completely invisible."

She was right, it was. Just a waitress smiling at a visitor to get a better tip. Vegas-vision. She squinted, noticed something comforting in Cayleen's eyes, motherly.

"It looks so normal."

"What did I tell you? It's like my friend says: in this industry, the individual is unfailingly subsumed under her social function."

"Whoa!"

"Sure, them too."

"No, I mean . . . *subsumed*?"

"Yeah, Maidon's wordy like that. You should meet her sometime, she's great. Let's keep going, there's something else I want to show you."

Past the craps tables, crowded with small huddles of the cheeriest and most social casinogoers, lay the quieter roulette region. Pinot-sipping couples, unbuttoned shirt necks, feverish young men scribbling numbers on gift-shop notepads. They passed the first two aisles of tables; at the third, Erica nudged Mary Ann to go on and take a look.

She knew something must be up here too, but she could see nothing. Six or seven players stood around the spinning wheel, placing chips on the felt in gentle, deferential movements. Erica smiled. It really did look ordinary. They got closer, their eyes and those of all the players fixated on the shiny pearl whirling against panels of varnished mahogany.

Maybe they could get away with this. Maybe they really were invisible. Even Mary Ann's appearance, the thing that had made her stand out throughout her life and filled her head with foolish ambition, became part of a pattern, repeated and ubiquitous like the cameras overhead. This could work. She felt a sense of calm wash over the preoccupations of the last few days. The dealer announced the numbers softly, with a slight, endearing lisp: twenty*th*ix, black; *th*irteen, red. Alongside all of it, Mary Ann could feel a growing desire not to disappoint Erica, an urge to make her proud. Erica seemed to like her, to believe in her contribution to the cause; to think she was worth something. The glossy white ball sank into the number pockets with a satisfying *click*. She wanted to help, she really, honestly did. She could *feel* it now. She wanted to be part of something bigger and do something for Karen and for all the others here. She'd been selfish for far too long.

"Isn't it great?" said Erica, pulling Mary Ann back from the table.

"What?"

"Vicky. I could see it was working on you too."

Mary Ann felt herself blush. She wasn't sure how long she'd stared at the roulette spins. Her head felt suddenly lighter, like it was filled with air.

"What was it?"

"She doesn't always do it. Just a few a day. She calls it soft group hypnosis."

"I didn't even realize—"

"Makes the players feel calm, sleepy. Lowers the heartbeat. Happy about themselves, but ready to go home. I told you you had to see it to believe it!"

In the week before her first Wednesday-evening shift at the Siren's Cove—swiftly arranged by a woman named Carla from the HR Committee once Mary Ann agreed to her role—she tested the limits of her invisibility.

On Thursday, already in uniform, she took a long detour on her way to the poker room: through the high-stakes baccarat club, the Banco Lounge, security personnel hallway C, all the way to the north-side convention center, and back inside the casino through the shops. As far as she could tell, nobody noticed her, and nobody said anything when she showed up five minutes late for her shift. She even stole one of the fancy butter cookies arranged on silver trays for the baccarat players. Nobody cared.

She did it again the following day, in extra eye-catching Scarlatti uniform, pausing for fifteen whole minutes by a penny slot to chat with a nice old lady who asked her for a water. She was from New Prague, Minnesota: three kids, all grown up, four grandkids (pictures). Mary Ann was real pretty, did she know? She had *driven* all the way to Vegas with her husband, who loved to play limit poker, they did it every few months. They were staying at the Shibuya this time, but she found it crowded and confusing. She had loved the Neon Museum downtown, though, had Mary Ann ever been? Mary Ann was almost expecting a supervisor to come ask why a lounge waitress was running drinks for a penny-slot player during her shift, but once again, nobody cared. The nice old lady didn't tip her for the water.

Only on Monday, finally, somebody noticed her. She showed up for her morning poker-room shift without makeup, and was immediately pulled aside by the shift manager. Many upper-tier casino staff looked like bored small-town cops from a movie, Sunday-barbecue guts stretching yellow pit-stained shirts with loosened black ties. The morning shift manager in the poker room, though, was fucking terrifying, an overzealous high school principal with a spry, angular, six-foot-two frame. Mary Ann stuttered an apology, quickly put on some makeup in the bathroom, and was on her best behavior the rest of the day.

So no makeup was a step too far. All the same, Erica was right: as long as she looked pretty and acceptably busy, nobody cared if she was there.

The casino was at war. Mary Ann saw it now. Everywhere she looked, workers in Positano uniforms were putting their job on the line by performing highly specialized, imperceptible acts of sabotage. Erica knew all of their names. Wraith-thin, mustachioed Ultimate Texas Hold'em dealers "inadvertently" lifted the corner of one of their hole cards just a little too much, hoping the player to their left would be smart enough to use the information to their advantage. Bartenders laced the drinks of the most unrestrained losing players with chamomile and herbs (and, Mary Ann hoped, nothing else). There was an electricity in the air, a current buzzing over the casino's perpetual background swoosh.

And she was part of it. It was her energy too. The one she'd been feeling ever since Aunt Karen's incident, the spontaneous, effortless drive toward others and away from herself and her obsessions. She'd traded in her personal hunger for social anger. In just a few weeks, the energy had won her a new friendship, filled her weekly schedule, given her something real to look forward to for the first time in years. She went out to East Fremont with Erica. She studied Hi/Lo counting on obscure probability theory papers, then settled for Wikipedia. She listened to visitors' stories of lost loves, lost jobs, found fortunes, exotic travels. Las Vegas is a city of stories. She could be part of it. She could help.

On Saturday she spent her evening off at Aunt Karen's. They watched *The Apartment* on VHS. Aunt Karen cried at the opening credits, when the music swelled up and the title appeared in white against the windows of an Upper West Side apartment building; she cried at the office scene with the broken mirror halfway through; then Shirley MacLaine overdosed on sleeping pills, and after that there was no stopping her crying. Mary Ann figured she'd probably forgot about that scene, or she wouldn't have suggested that movie. She felt bad for her feeling bad for her. Aunt Karen had somehow acquired an old but fancy-looking VHS player, so at least she could finally watch all those tapes. Mary Ann wanted to do more for her. She wanted to help. Personally, she thought *The Apartment* was really damn good.

"Do you think it could be?" she asked Walter at the lounge the next day. "Do you think it's possible that helping others becomes this kind of reflex, this energy that sort of just *happens*?"

"Is that how you feel?"

"I feel like if I could really *want* something, but then it's not just for me, maybe that can be enough? Enough meaning?"

"Something bigger than yourself."

"Something bigger than myself."

Walter said there are many ways of helping others. Some are easier, straightforward, and others more tortuous. And some make us wonder whether it's really ourselves we're helping. But there was value in them nonetheless. It's as if he knew.

"I really want to help."

"And what about being *seen*? Is that still a concern, then?"

She couldn't help a smile. The harpsichord plucked a hearty allegro.

"It's a concern all right."

The Neon Museum was unsettling. It was the eve of her first day as a saboteur, her Tuesday off. Erica was being really sweet, she kept making sure she was okay to do this, didn't want her to feel forced into it. But she didn't feel forced. It was her decision. A wiry hipster got close and offered to take pictures of her with the backdrop of the old Vegas neons. He had contacts, he worked for an agency. People are the worst. The marquees of the past shone like dying stars, consumed by a million eyes, looking looking looking. Old lights of casinos long gone. You'd think they'd let them rest now, in peace and darkness. But there they were, plugged to a wall, hooked to their electrical IVs, still performing, again, and again, and again.

Interlude VI

(the story of a breakfast)

Deluxe rooms at the Positano were hosted in charming stuccoed duplexes of pink, white, or cream. Brightly colored window blinds on the outside and stunning ceramic tiles on the inside gave off the signature maritime vibe of the nicer Mediterranean towns and bigger productions of *Mamma Mia!* They didn't have the in-your-face expansiveness and opulence of the hilltop suites, but still provided much-sought-after distinction from the ordinary five-star fare of the standard rooms. Discerning guests found them "cozy."

The room had been booked by Larissa's father, the governor, and it had been the subject of her parents' lengthy, caring consideration, as they tried to assess the correct amount of luxury to bestow on their daughter and her friend. Given the circumstances, it was the least they could do. In situations like these, it was important not to appear ostentatious. Sympathetic and generous, yes; grief-stricken and considerate, yes; but an excessive display of munificence would be improper and even send the wrong message. Even long after the governor's last term as an elected official, much of the emotional life of the Portillo household was conducted through nuances of monetary expenditure, subtle calibrations in gift-giving. The situation with poor Ana (so tragic!) was no exception, and Larissa's characteristically generous idea that the two of them take this trip together, now that some time had passed, had been approached with all the composed, well-measured enthusiasm it deserved.

Larissa always had a sunny personality. Consensus was, she got it from her great-grandmother on her mother's side, who'd been the kindest soul, always concerned with the well-being of the miners in the family quarries. She, Larissa, was so devoted to making the life of those around her better, so selfless and full of life, that the thought she would be moving to the Distrito Federal—where her boyfriend was already in law school—at the end of the school term, to study to be a fashion designer, had already cast a minor damp on the household, and on her mother especially, who would miss her so. But that, of course, is motherhood for you, a long lesson in smiling in the face of one's diminishing importance. She was smiling now, at the other end of the phone call, at this bizarre new idea that her daughter should take an absurdly long road trip back home instead of flying. She would swallow her fears about the road, smile, say yes dear, what a lovely plan. Larissa always did have a sunny personality, after all.

Ana could see Larissa on the phone out on the balcony, by the breakfast table. For the deluxe rooms, breakfast was served in gorgeous sea-view semi-balconies, enclosed by glass screens, on round white tables. Someone filled the centerpiece basket with fresh lemons every day, but Ana remained convinced that the lemony sea-salt scent in the air must be sprayed on, or otherwise artificially conveyed to the room, via the vents or something. God forbid there be anything close to sincere in this town. Something that actually was the thing it looked like.

Larissa's relationship with her parents should be studied in labs: maybe composition analysis or testing on guinea pigs could explain what the hell was going on. As close as Ana and Larissa had been since Ana arrived in Chihuahua, it was the one thing—a lot more than the abyss of wealth separating them—she had always found hard to adapt to in their friendship. Sleepovers in a thirty-thousand-square-foot mansion, being ferried around and chaperoned by the family chauffeur, Larissa's dad on the news, it was all rather screwy, but there were ways you could tune it out. Not always, but often enough. And anyway, none of it was Larissa's fault, and she was incredibly chill about it, considering.

But the stuff with her parents was a different matter. That they could be this close, talk to each other this much, and yet so clearly and so fundamentally misunderstand each other on a daily basis, it made you want to bang your head against the wall. She'd grown up watching this clan of emotionally stunted plutocrats fumble around the most basic human interactions, removing themselves from each other through so many layers of precaution and passive-aggressiveness they'd become effectively strangers. The mother most of all, but the governor too, with sweet, guileless Larissa constitutionally unable to see any of it for what it really was. They'd managed to protocol themselves into noncommunication, turning their charmed lives into stalemates of loneliness. Honestly, it made Ana want to scream.

As for herself, there wasn't a whole lot to say. The sun kept rising, the stars kept shining, the world kept spinning, though maybe a few inches off its axis. Enough time had passed for her character to reboot itself, her fighting instincts to kick back into gear. She was a survivor, always had been. She didn't need any help, definitely not the governor's.

A funny side effect of her parents' accident had been the souring of her relationship with Gerardo. They'd been seeing each other for a little over a year, she a talented twenty-four-year-old medicinal chemist, he forty-seven and married and a civil engineer. When they met, he had been exactly double her age, and he'd joked he'd be sixty when she turned thirty, then a hundred when she turned fifty. Larissa was the only one she'd told; her mom would've lost it if she'd found out. They had been instantly, madly in love, and with him she'd felt sheltered and cared for in a way she never believed she needed, and was almost embarrassed for. So naturally, when everything happened, she'd imagined falling onto him like a shipwrecked sailor on a raft, as if that were the natural thing to do. Gerardo had thought so, too, it seemed, and redoubled his attentions while also pulling away just enough to give her the time she needed to grieve, proving his innate ability to always do and say the right thing. And yet. And yet what in the end did happen was she'd cooled off, toughened herself up to survive in a world where everything you loved got revoked from you like *that*, and it was better not to need anything outside of you at all. Weird how these things go.

This trip, too, was an exercise in futility. Not only did it not help her (and how could it? To spend a week buying name-brand clothes in the ugliest city in America?), it also distracted her from the rather absorbing lab work she was helping her thesis supervisor conduct on bromodomain inhibitors. (Science, the one dependable thing she was willing to admit she needed.) It was that very work, carried out in crazy, self-denying shifts once they finally got back to Chihuahua, that would in a mere six months garner her advisor some serious international recognition and Big Pharma buzz, and Ana herself a prestigious two-term research fellowship at Oxford, where she, among the clinking of the beakers at G3 in the Chemistry Research Laboratory, would meet, fall head over lab clogs in love with, and not too long afterward marry an Indian boy named Rithvik, who was six months her junior, had a real knack for saying the wrong thing at the wrong time, and as fate would have it hailed from a Bengali family who made the Portillos look like middle-class retirees and the governor's mansion like a quaint country cottage.

Ultimately, Ana had taken the trip as a way to make Larissa happy. By letting her feel good about supposedly helping her. It was, perhaps, the kind of small sacrifice and well-meaning deception real friendships were full of, something Ana could always find the energy for where Larissa was concerned. Even at a time when the world spun off its axis. Which is why she was currently pretending to put her foot down on nixing the road trip with the boys, so that Larissa could win her over with affectionate pleas, and she could feel good about herself once Ana turned out to really enjoy the sights of the snowed-out Arizona desert. Like they were just what she needed.

Her bag almost full, Ana retrieved the discount Armani dress Larissa had insisted she get from the big heap of Ross Dress for Less purchases on her bed. Larissa's passion for bargain-hunting, while potentially insufferable coming from someone in her condition, was so earnest and unfabricated that it ended up perfectly endearing. It was Larissa's special talent, her complete blindness to the undercurrents of extraneous bullshit everybody else seemed to read in people's words and actions. She wasn't naive, not exactly, and definitely not stupid. She knew how other people saw the world and was, in fact, particularly considerate of their right to. She just never did it herself; it never occurred to her. Guileless, yes.

It was a good thing she had Ana to look out for her.

Out on the faux outside balcony with the glass screens, Larissa hung up the phone. She worried about her parents, a bit. Now that she was moving to the DF, she worried they would lose the last thing they had in common, that they would feel even more alone in that big empty house. She wished she could take them with her, hear them talk very serious-faced about what set of dishes it was best to buy for her new apartment with Ruiz.

She picked up a lemon and brought it to her nose, letting herself be swept up in its surprisingly strong scent. It was a strange magic of Las Vegas that you could have buildings this massive and this beautiful and have breakfast above the water holding a lemon that smelled this good. It was the best of two worlds: the desert and the city, the natural and the man-made. She remembered being shuttled along on her dad's official visits when she was a kid and Chihuahuan metals were freighted over by the kiloton to construction sites all over the just-then-booming Las Vegas Strip. There must be a lot of her family's work went into this very building.

Of course Ana would think it wasn't, but this trip had been really good for her. Not in the intended sense, maybe, no. But Larissa realized Ana would know how much it made Larissa happy to help her, and that because of that, she would decide to go along with the trip, and pretend it was making her feel a little better. And in doing so, in pretending, and in allowing herself to do something good for someone else—even just letting Larissa believe she was being a good friend—she actually *would* feel better. Making Larissa happy by pretending to enjoy their silly trip to Vegas was perhaps just the kind of outward-focused labor of love she needed to start realigning the world after the accident.

She stepped back inside to start packing her bags. The ceramic tiles felt nice and cold under her bare feet. Ana was folding the dress she would one day wear on her first date with her husband, Rithvik, who would spill soy sauce on it.

It was going to take some convincing, but she knew Ana would say yes to the road trip in the end. It was Larissa's unshakable belief that humans were ultimately wired to connect with each other, and do each other good, that would one day get her through the rough days of her parents' divorce and later, ten years from now, her own, with Ruiz. We seem so distant, and closed off, and so alone, but deep down we just want to reach for one another, to help and be helped. It was only a pity, she thought sometimes, we could never just tell each other what we really feel.

Interlude VII

(the story of a day at work)

from: zachromero@gifty.com
to: lvgifters@lists.gifty.com
subj: 'twas the season
January 13, 2015   9:42 AM

Howdy Gifters,
Holiday season is over, and thanks to our collective hard work, I'm
glad to announce it's been the best Holiday season yet for us. By,
like, a mile. I don't exaggerate when I say we've doubled our most
optimistic projections (guess I should probably fire the guy who
made the projections huh?—just kidding, love you Mark). But so
I wanted to take this time to thank all you guys personally for
everything you've done, for all your efforts in making Gifty the
number one gift service in the world, and for making it all happen
here, in Las Vegas, our home.

With the benefit of hindsight and years passed I can now tell
you that many people—overpaid Silicon Valley knowitalls and
such—had advised strongly against the move. They said we would

drift right off the map, fade into irrelevance. Well if there's one thing this Holiday Season tells us it's that—as far as gift-outsourcing is concerned—we ARE the goddamn map, and they are tiny irrelevant dots at the corners of it. Gifty is a Las Vegas company, now and forever. The rest of them better learn to deal with it.

Back to business, we've got a really exciting year ahead of us. We need to start strong and stay on course, keep up with the impressive numbers we've posted so far. Which we are totally going to do, I feel sure of it. Here's the part were I should caution you against post-peak-season relaxation and sleeping on laurels and whatnot, but I know my Gifters, and I know I don't need to. The world will come a-calling for gifts in Spring just as it did in the Winter, and we'll be there to choose them, make them, and ship them for them, won't we? Relax is not what we do, except when we want to.

Speaking of, I noticed Friday's Mario Kart tournament in the arcade is overbooked. Since I want everybody to have a chance, and since y'all can sure try to chase me down Grumble Volcano but there's no way your catching me, we split the tournament into two flights, with the finals in the afternoon. I call Bowser, it's only fair. Winner (that is second place: I'm winning) gets a Budget++ Personalized Algorithmically Generated Gift, plus a ride on the company helicopter over the Grand Canyon.

This will be an incredible year. We have insanely cool projects percolating just about now, you can probably smell the smell of innovation already. Sick announcements coming up in the next months, stay tuned. Let's make this our best year ever. Thanks to all of you, It's already been the best start we've ever had, and I can't wait for what's to come.

Keep gifting,
XOXO
Zach Romero
CEO—Gifty Enteprises

from: ImCEObitch@gifty.com
to: tariqwilliams@gifty.com
subj: ten o'klonopin
January 13, 2015   10:02 AM

Seriously these were the worst two weeks of my fucking life ffs.
What a shitshow. How can we be behind on EVERYTHING? Is it
possible, like statistically? You're the math whiz, you tell me.

Warehouse on Centennial will be operative by 2020 at this rate,
and I don't even have time to go check it out. And it's ten miles
away. Just so you know, your next vacation is also in 2020.

And since when do I have this side gig nursing all the nutjobs in
the State? Is it because I'm the only rich guy in town who's not a
hundred? All week this campaign manager dude's been pestering
me about selling them use of our algorithm for strategic political
marketing or some shit, they want me to meet their tech guy who,
get this, is fucking *seventeen*. Got a call from the goddamn
governor about it too. And that's like the normal ones. Last week a
"paranormal activity expert" wanted funding to conduct "research"
inside Strip casinos. Swear to God I'm not making this up.

Anyway, speaking of crazy, can you make sure Wiles's lapdogs
leave me alone for like 24 hours? I don't need this in my life right

now, honestly. Besides, I don't know what to say to them yet, so I don't know, stall them or something.

Love you long time,
Zach

from: zachvader82@aol.com
to: anita.romero@gmail.com
subj: Re: It is no longer affordable housing if your Project Manager forces me to build McMansions
January 13, 2015   10:28 AM

Hi Mom, yes, okay, I'll see what I can do. Come to dinner tomorrow?

Love you,
Zach

from: zachromero@gifty.com
to: hendrikvogelsang@wilesgroup.com
subj: Re: Meeting
January 13, 2015   11:23 AM

It is such a pleasure to hear from you directly. I'm glad my assistant was helpful, but I wanted to apologize personally for not being able to arrange a meeting before the 26th. We have a crucial day coming up this Friday, after which I'll be flying to NYC to inaugurate our new offices in TriBeCa and will be taking meetings there all week.

I do look forward to meeting with you and your associate, though. And in the meantime, my entire team is at your disposal, starting with my Chief Advisor Tariq Williams (tariqwilliams@gifty .com).

Talk soon,
Zach Romero
CEO—Gifty Enterprises

from: ImCEObitch@gifty.com
to: tariqwilliams@gifty.com
subj: Fwd: Meeting
January 13, 2015   11:25 AM

I will have your head on a silver platter.

Love you a little less,
Zach

from: ImCEObitch@gifty.com
to: skunkworks@lists.gifty.com
subj: You're It
January 13, 2015   11:48 AM

Alright listen up kids, are we doing this thing or what? This is, like, #1 priority right now. Stop whatever it is you pretend you do around here and focus; call your wife, your husband, your poly triad, your dog, your dealer, and tell them you won't be home for a while. We are going in the trenches.

This is happening.
Zach

from: zachvader82@aol.com
to: anita.romero@gmail.com
subj: Re: It is no longer affordable housing if your Project Manager
forces me to build McMansions
January 13, 2015   12:10 AM

Mom, can we talk about this tomorrow? At dinner? I know it's
important, but can we maybe agree that it's not life-or-death urgent
right now? I swear I care about this too, and I want to be involved,
but now is really not a great time. You'll tell me all about it over Due
Forni tomorrow, how's that?

Also, Mom, why do you keep emailing me on here? Is it like a
nostalgia thing? I have *two* work emails, pick either one.

from: zachromero@gifty.com
to: lvgifters@lists.gifty.com
subj: Hopping for freedom
January 13, 2015   12:33 AM

Hello again,

It has been brought to my attention that some of you more
regulationist Karters are asking that the technique known as "fire
hopping" be banned from Friday's tournament, as it is quote an
unfair exploit of an unintended game mechanic and basically a

glitch unquote. You argued that it penalizes players who don't know of its existence or can't pull it off properly in game.

Now, I've been giving this issue some thought over the last twenty minutes. Your voice was heard. The fact is, the imposition of rules restricting the liberties of a free market is really not my thing. Like, fire hopping is an added layer of difficulty, granted. But don't we, as a society, value meritocracy? Don't we feel like the best hoppers *should* be rewarded, instead of a meddling authority (i.e. yours truly) stepping in and telling them to stay with their wheels on the ground? Whether fire hopping was intended by the game developers or not, the fact is it *can* be done, and banning it means restricting the ability of the individual to use their hard-earned skills to win. And that's downright un-American, if you ask me.

Still, while I don't much believe in regulation, I do believe in sharing. A free race needs to be a fair race, where we all have a shot at making it, if we put in the work. In that spirit, here's a couple of videos explaining fire hopping for beginners, so that the playing field is level. Should anyone feel the need to practice ahead of the tournament, the consoles in the game room will be available 24/7 until Friday.

https://www.youtube.com/watch?v=9zC519Ned_8

https://www.youtube.com/watch?v=hLE16Go9piY&frags=pl%2Cwn

And on Friday, when you watch my beloved Bowser's spiked green shell disappear in the distance, get ready to watch him hop like a bunny after every turn. For Freedom. For America.

May the best Gifter win (or, you know, get second place).

Cheerio,
Zach Romero
CEO—Gifty Enteprises

from: ImCEObitch@gifty.com
to: skunkworks@lists.gifty.com
subj: Re: You're It
January 13, 2015   12:52 AM

Good stuff, good stuff. I like the vibe in this thread.
Keep it coming.

Unfortunately, as you can see from the Mario Kart email,
government regulations and restrictions are the the bane of my
existence, so yeah, preaching to the choir dudes. But we're
treading a very fine line here, and this intersects a bunch of tricky
issues, issues of labor, issues of civil rights, issues of privacy, so
I can't promise you total freedom with this. Which, like, bummer,
I know, but this is not a game.

There is a lot at stake, I mean. This could change the future of our
company, and let me be a little grandiose about this, the future of
the world. It's like the next evolutionary step in a truly *free* market.
You guys are making history here. We do this at the Positano, it
will become the standard literally everywhere.

As for your question, I'm thinking early Spring, I mean why wait.
But we'll see how the next couple weeks go.

Now get coding, my lovelies. It's time.

Excelsior,
Zach

from: zachvader82@aol.com
to: anita.romero@gmail.com
subj: Re: It is no longer affordable housing if your Project Manager
forces me to build McMansions
January 13, 2015   12:56 AM

Mom we bought like half of 89031 for the project already, do you
think maybe that's enough? You can't just singlehandedly fix the
housing market, you do know that, right?

from: zachvader82@aol.com
to: anita.romero@gmail.com
subj: Re: It is no longer affordable housing if your Project Manager
forces me to build McMansions
January 13, 2015   12:59 AM

I'm sorry, this is why we shouldn't be doing this over emails.
I really do have a lot going on, and I I'm overworked, and I'm
stressed. I'm sorry.

I'll see you tomorrow.

Love you,
Zach

10

Two Road Trips

Every Italian has a personal America. An ocean and a fingerprint scan away from its shores, America is to an Italian at best an act of translation, shapeless and patched together over time by television, music, and distant uncles. Miscommunications are frequent and inevitable. There isn't a single Italian who doesn't hold a strong idea of what America is, an intense idiosyncratic relationship with the strange far-off land Italy remains compelled to measure itself against. It's like a civic duty, to imagine America. To picture it, manufacture it, long for it, despise it, dismiss it, to dream of it; to recognize oneself in what's different; to discover one's identity by contrast. Growing up in Italy requires it, this recurring travel of all collective thought to America. A vacation home for the national subconscious.

Landed by the fickle stork of chance in a two-bedroom in East Rome brimming with Bic lighters and his mother's hand-painted pottery, little Tom too dreamed of America. He didn't dream of himself there exactly. The thought of escaping the squalor of his neighborhood felt fundamentally ungrateful: you had to deep-down believe you deserved more, that you were better than the place you were born, and who in all honesty could say that? Besides, plotting their transoceanic move wasn't doing wonders for all his peers, who just added the frustration of being stuck in the wrong place to the strife of being young and poor in an expensive city during a major financial crisis. Tom's dreams of America didn't involve him. He was just glad it existed, this other place he knew to be big, and beautiful, and full of contradictions, glad people lived there. He had formed a tentative mental map spanning from the skyline of Manhattan to the hills of Hollywood, with large stretches of Texas in between. Over the years, he filled it with tidbits of information through circumstantial evidence: there was a city called Bloomington, Indiana, because he'd once met someone from there; units of measure had weird, fanciful names, like yards, gallons, and Fahrenheits; if a policeman stops you and you get out of the car, they are allowed to shoot you.

Yet in all his American dreaming, it never occurred to Tom that tubular fragments of America, bluish and emblazoned on the front with a sprinting greyhound, would shuttle daily from Tucson, Arizona, to Las Vegas, Nevada, in twelve hours flat. And that such fragments, leather-seated and air-conditioned, would be the domain of travel-pillow-wearing seniors in running sneakers, snoring their way across the desert. And that within this domain Tom would find himself sitting one winter Friday, and that his charming accent, and willingness to listen to long stories about nephews, and share his bounty of Jack Link's Spicy Beef Jerky (he was out of Original), Almond Joys, Snickers, Hershey's chocolate bars, Reese's Peanut Butter Cups, and M&M's—all stashed in a big gas-station plastic bag—would make him the life and soul of their movable geriatric party.

"Rome? Oh, that is . . . lovely!" said his neighbor, a lady with an almost perfect sphere of silvery hair, pausing to chew on a Peanut Butter Cup. "You are so lucky! Italy must be so"—bite—"*beautiful.*"

"I am a lucky, yes," said Tom.

"My daughter's husband," she said, "ex-husband, he used to go to Europe on business. Once for Christmas he brought us two bottles of this lovely red wine from Tuscany, Brunetto, I think. It was delightful! So flavorful and rich! Of course I know nothing about wines, I must sound very ignorant to a real Italian!" She windshield-wiped her tongue across her front teeth to clean up the remaining peanut butter.

"In truth I don't drink wine," said Tom. "But what work did the husband do in Europe?"

"Oh, he worked for Best Western," she said. "The hotels? Their head-quarters are in Phoenix, but they have them all over. I'm sure you've stayed with them, a European traveler like yourself. Of course that was before everything that happened." She lingered on the last sentence with the wist-fulness of a storyteller waiting to be asked.

"Hotels are fascinating," said Tom. He had seen a hotel room for the first and only time in his life a little more than a year ago, at the Rio Hotel & Casino.

"Well, there is such a thing as spending too many nights in them, even if you're in that business, if you know what I mean."

"Expensive, yes," said Tom with a nod. "Almond Joy? Similar to our Bounty, but an entire almond concealed in the chocolate. Very delicious!"

"Italians are such charmers! You must be quite popular with the ladies over here!"

Tom shook his head and raised his hands as if to fend off an accusation.

"What brings you to Tucson anyway? Go to school here?"

"We slept in the school in Tuxon this night, yes," said Tom.

"And you decided to take a bus to Vegas for the weekend."

"I had a car," said Tom. His neighbor opened her mouth wide to let in the entire remainder of the Almond Joy, and didn't seem to be listening. Tom finished: "But the road trips, they don't go like you plan."

In spite of the stir Lindsay's article had caused, getting an interview with Al Wiles had proven impossible. All inquiries, both stemming from her @lvsun.com address and from her personal, embarrassing (and there-fore maybe endearing, unthreatening?) @aol.com one, had elicited polite idiosyncratically worded replies regretting to inform her that "Herr Wiles does not concede interviews since more than ten years." In fact, months had passed since her piece had gone locally viral, and Lindsay could feel its promise to turn her into the kind of reporter who could bargain a move to any A-list Bay Area publication evaporating quickly. She needed to keep the momentum going. Still, it seemed all her editor Steven had to offer were bids for local-color pieces of zero big-picture import: maybe she could profile young graduates of the new Desert Coding School? Or how about an interview with the kids who run the pick-up artist group downtown? Not exactly inspiring stuff.

The media cycle had run its course on the waitress story. WHOA had issued conciliatory statements about good fruitful meetings with management. Amends had been nominally made. And shares on social media had steadily decreased amid townwide speculation about whether Al Wiles could really bring the Raiders to Vegas once they ditched Oakland. Interest, in short, had waned. On top of that, it didn't help the credibility of Lindsay's piece that the thirty-six-year-old waitress who'd been the key witness in her exposé had subsequently elected to parlay her overnight notoriety into a flash career in the world of MILF porn, starring in more than two dozen productions already, including a terribly tasteless clip in which a cocktail waitress convinces her boss not to fire her, appealing to something other than his firm, hardened sense of social justice. (Links to this had poured in on Lindsay's email, all of them still unclicked-blue, the irritation they produced thriving just on hearsay.)

"What if I just did the pick-up kids piece instead?" Lindsay said to Orson. They were driving north on the stretch of I-515 that skirts Paradise and East Vegas before cutting west all across downtown to the interchange known as the Spaghetti Bowl, where US 95 resumes its lonely way toward Reno, northern Nevada, and the Pacific Northwest. They were heading out of town. "I'm never getting to Wiles anyway, and I need to work."

"Please don't," said Orson, from his reclined position.

To their right, the northeast Vegas neighborhood of Sunrise Manor was a brownish beehive of low buildings. Far east, where Bonanza met North Hollywood, the white box of the Mormon Temple rested in the shade of the mountain ridge between the city and the lake. On the tallest of its white pinnacles, the golden statue of the angel Moroni called out with his trumpet for all the righteous to gather for the coming of the Lord.

"But why?" said Lindsay. "I've done nothing but paragraph-long news bites since the waitress story came out. And at this point it's pretty clear Wiles just won't talk to me."

"Why don't you ask Aunt Ada to get you the interview? You know she could."

"Because you don't use family connections to get ahead in your career," said Lindsay. "That's not how it works."

"Yes, it is, that is exactly how it works."

"Besides, it would be pretty rude to call Aunt Ada just to ask for a favor, don't you think? I mean, when was the last time we even *saw* her?"

"Then ask Uncle John to ask Aunt Ada to ask Wiles," said Orson. Lindsay rolled her eyes. "Or better yet, ask Aunt Clara to coax Uncle John into persuading Aunt Ada to talk to Wiles. There have to be some perks to being a journalist in the most interconnected community in America."

"You don't understand."

"What don't I understand?" Orson frowned.

Lindsay paused to give her thoughts shape. The story was instrumental to her secret dream, and as such suspicious, of course. But that wasn't all it was. There was an urgency to it—a sense of honesty, something she believed in. Could it be both?

"Look there is clearly something bad going on in town," she said. "Something corrupt. And the way you uncover these things is investigative reporting, not asking for favors. You can't owe people favors when you're after the truth."

"You sound like a forties film noir detective."

"If I take the pick-up kids piece, I could at least go back to doing some actual work. And keep going after Wiles on my own terms in the meantime."

"Well, you shouldn't."

"But why not?"

"I'm asking you not to," said Orson, a note of urgency in his voice that surprised Lindsay.

"Care to offer a reason?" she asked.

"Not particularly," said Orson. On his lap, he held what was likely the most extensively underlined, dog-eared, Post-it-ed, and bookmarked copy of Gary Magnesen's *The Investigation: A Former FBI Agent Uncovers the Truth behind Howard Hughes, Melvin Dummar, and the Most Contested Will in American History* existing in the world. The jacket had been removed, and the black hardcover underneath bulged with the added thickness of extraneous paper inserted throughout the text. Making a production of this conversation-ender, Orson opened the book and began to read.

Lindsay glanced at her brother. His seat was so nearly horizontal that he had to hold the book practically parallel to the car's roof, both elbows lifted up, his skinny arms tense with muscular exertion, like a weight lifter bench-pressing obscure nonfiction. He was obstinate enough to stay like that all the two hundred miles to Tonopah, if it came to that, just to avoid a question. Lindsay now regretted having brought up the subject altogether: truth was, she had already agreed to do the article about the pick-up artist community—just this morning, in an email to Steven—and was waiting for his reply to get to work on it. She bit her lip.

"So once we get to the junction today, what is it exactly we're looking for?" Orson closed his book and lowered his arms.

The story was famous, and old news, but Orson loved it. In the last days of 1967, or early in '68, a service station worker from Utah pulled up his car on a side road just off Highway 95, about 150 miles north of Las Vegas, and found the richest man in America lying semi-unconscious on the packed dirt. The man, Melvin Dummar, picked Howard Hughes up in his car and drove him back to the Desert Inn Hotel in Vegas, where he claimed to live, all the while not knowing (or at least refusing to believe) who his celebrity passenger was. Nine years later, when the reclusive billionaire kicked the thoroughly sterilized bucket without naming an heir, a holographic will dated March 1968 conveniently showed up on a desk at the headquarters of the LDS Church in Salt Lake City. The will benefited several universities, the Mormon Church itself, and a certain "Melvin DuMar of Gabbs, Nevada" to the tune of one-sixteenth of the Hughes estate (something in the otherworldly region of $150 million, give or take a few lifetimes of median American income). High jinks ensued: a trial, a ruling against purported hoaxer Dummar, many years of nationwide derision, a pretty good Jonathan Demme comedy with an Oscar-winning performance by Mary Steenburgen. And years later, when Magnesen's investigation gave an aged but undeterred Dummar a taste of a much-awaited vindication: a new lawsuit, a new trial, a new dismissal.

What interested Orson was not the story itself so much as its role in a specific Nevadan and Mormon mythology he cherished and found sadly underrepresented. That, decades after the court ruling, a former FBI agent would still scour the landlocked wastelands north of Vegas for evidence to substantiate Dummar's long-expired claims only reinforced his belief that the stories of the desert and its people were an untapped mine of American meaning. Truths as profound as they were untold. The success of the strange, quite possibly spurious, certainly romanticized story of the Mormon Will had been a source of constant validation whenever Orson went through those times of disillusionment and complete, disheartening lack of faith in himself that he assumed were inevitable and universal to the writerly experience. It told him that people *did* care, that they *would* read. It spurred him on. Without it, quite simply, his book wouldn't exist.

Today was the day he would finally pay it his homage.

EXT. HIGHWAY OUTSIDE KINGMAN, AZ.—DAY

Aerial shot captured by a DRONE flying above the highway.

A thin layer of powdered-sugar SNOW covers the DESERT. The rocks that look red in the summer months have turned a bluish glow. Arizona is like a too-large dinner table where people have to stretch to pass each other salt. Few CARS roll by, engine-sounds muffled, tires sloshing in roadside puddles of brown-gray.

TITLE

24 HOURS EARLIER

INT. TOM'S F-150 PICKUP—DAY

TOM is driving. Seating shotgun next to him is LARISSA, hair tied in a ponytail, eating the last pieces of an old Jack Link's Beef Jerky bag she found in the truck. On the narrow flip-bottom bench serving as back seats, TREVOR sits on the left, tinkering with his video equipment: he has a GoPro camera mounted on the roof of the truck, and a second one in the trunk, pointing inside. A third camera is in his lap, and it's the one he's fiddling with. To the right, ANA is looking at her phone. Tom's driver's seat is no longer stuck obliquely, but the space in the back is still a bit cramped. Trevor's window is cracked open: he doesn't mind, but cold gusts are getting in.

TREVOR

Did you know that the top YouTuber last year made $4.9 million unboxing toys?

LARISSA

Unboxing?

ANA

Could you close the window please?

TREVOR

Unwrapping. Opening.

LARISSA

Just open the toys?

ANA

I mean there's actual snow outside.

TREVOR

Yes, she just unwraps Disney toys, takes them out
of the box, and shows them to the camera. You
never even see her face.

LARISSA

Who watch that?

TREVOR

Kids, I guess. Tens of millions of them. She has
this very soothing, singsong voice. You just see
her hands crumpling the wrapping paper, ripping
the cardboard open, getting the toy out.

ANA

Do these cameras need to be on?

TREVOR

Tomsky would watch it, right? He watches all kinds
of crazy crap on YouTube.

TOM

Indeed Trevor, could you off the cameras?

TREVOR

Like people playing games, or writing code. That kind of thing.

ANA

I didn't know we were going to be on camera the whole trip. I mean it's nice you guys are driving us home, but—

TREVOR

I'm just getting raw footage for a montage of the road trip. Chances are I won't use any of it. And definitely not the stuff we say. It's just more practical to leave it on.

LARISSA

Is easy to watch a lot of videos on YouTube, no?

TOM

Very easy.

LARISSA

Just next, next, next, yes?

TREVOR

That's why it's so profitable to be a content creator.

                              ANA

Is that what this is about? Are you going to make
millions with your vlog?

                             TREVOR

Nah, no way 50 million people would watch a video
of me and Tomsky eating cereal at 3PM while I talk
about a hand I played! I just enjoy it.

                              TOM

                             (beat)

I don't think it's strange to watch the unboxing.
I understand it.

                             TREVOR

See? Told you!

                              ANA

I mean it's making children watch someone else
open a present, over and over and over. Not really
subtle there.

                            LARISSA

Como Christmas, no?

                              TOM

Yes.

                              ANA

It's just getting children high off their memories
of Christmas mornings and new toys. It's pretty
terrible actually.

TREVOR

But I mean it's more than that, right? All those
sounds of crumpled paper, toys rattling inside
chocolate eggs, a soft voice speaking. It's very
soothing. You guys know what ASMR is?

LARISSA

Sí.

TREVOR

ASMR is an internet-born term for the tingling
sensation some people get when triggered by
certain sounds or visuals.

LARISSA

Sí.

TREVOR

There's a whole industry of that, videos, podcasts,
that kind of thing. Except this is for kids.

ANA

And that makes it better? So there's a physical
addiction on top of the psychological one. The joy
of Christmas and a tingling of the spine all
wrapped up into one. It's like visual crack. And
we give it to *children*! No wonder she gets
millions of views.

TREVOR

I mean this woman made more money on videos than
Taylor Swift last year.

LARISSA

Can we stop us? I need pee.

ANA

And you don't think that's bad?

TOM

I could stop for gas too, yes.

TREVOR

Depends on how much you like Taylor Swift.

LARISSA

(beat)

I really like persecution shows.

TREVOR

What?

LARISSA

Videos of persecution, you know? On YouTube?

TREVOR

Persecution?

ANA

She means car chases. Like cop shows.

TREVOR

(laughs)

Oh, I mean, yeah. Car chases. Those are fun!

LARISSA

Sí!

TREVOR

Kinda like us, you know? A gang of outlaws making a run for the Mexican border.

TOM

Trevor, man—

ANA

This is gonna be in your vlog, isn't it?

TREVOR

I mean it was kinda funny.

TOM

I'll stop at this one now, okay Trevor?

TREVOR

Sure. We can go get you more beef jerky.

LARISSA

(to Ana)

No se dice persecution?

TOM

Maybe you can off the cameras too?

The TRUCK turns right into a large highway GAS STATION. TOM pulls up at pump number 5, halfway from the doors of the establishment. LARISSA and ANA get

```
out of the truck and walk toward the store, talking
in barely audible Spanish to each other. TREVOR is
about to follow them.
```

                              TOM

```
Can you stay and speak a minute?
```

                            TREVOR

```
Sure, we're in no rush. Tucson is not that far.
```

                              TOM

```
Can you off the cameras though, Trevor, man, bro?
```

Trevor thumbed the controllers, and the screens went dark. Outside, the air was crisp, the smell of cold and snow overpowering the sweet sickly tang of gasoline. On the road, cars passed by with the high-speed noise even slow cars make to a static observer. Tom was having trouble getting the nozzle out of the side of the gas pump. He had a foot up against it, and was pulling on the nozzle with both hands.

"You know it's not a matter of strength, right?" said Trevor. "You just need to figure out the release mechanism."

"I am frightened, Trevor," said Tom.

"Dude, it's definitely not dangerous. You probably need to press something before you pull the nozzle out is all."

"Are the cameras on off?"

"Yes, yes, I turned them off see?"

"Trevor, man, are you sure this is going to work?" said Tom. Trevor looked like he was going to make another joke about the nozzle. "Going to Mexico, I mean. Returning in some days to respawn my tourist visa from the border police. I fear I will be apprehended."

Trevor got out of the truck and walked up to Tom. He grabbed the gas nozzle, effortlessly pulled it out of the pump, and started filling the tank. He spoke without turning around, facing the car and the highway.

"My friend, do you really think I would have suggested this if I didn't know it works? That I would risk this?"

"But aren't I the only one at risk, man?"

"We're doing this together, Tomsky. We're a team. You've known me for a long time. If I tell you I've done my research, you better believe I've done my research. On our way out they will barely check our passports, because American police will never make it hard for a foreigner to *leave* the country. Like they give half a shit if an Italian tourist goes to Mexico."

"But my passport—"

"And on our way back, you will just be a tourist, who's been to the US once almost *two years ago*, because they won't know you've just left, and they will just stamp you a new tourist visa. We do this a couple times a year, and problem solved! You're fine."

"But what if they do control the documents on the exit?"

"They won't. You and I will go first, two white American alphas with—"

"But I'm not American, is the question!"

"Two white American-*looking* alphas with our glistening first-world passports, walking up to the customs officer in long confident strides like—"

"Like Tom Cruise in *Top Gun*."

"Exactly. Like Tom Cruise in *Top Gun*."

"And he won't inspect our documents?"

"If we were alone, maybe," said Trevor. "But it's at that point that two hot Latina girls in miniskirts will walk up to that very same Dorito-munching customs officer, you see? The sad beta orbiter who's wasting his best years languishing away in a tin box under the scorching sun of El Paso/Ciudad Juarez—"

"Is quite cold today. There is snow."

"Not in El Paso. Two hot Mexican girls will walk up to him to ask him a question."

"What question?"

"A question about immigration. Procedural. Something he would know." Trevor had the knowing grin of a movie villain reciting his plan. He pulled out the nozzle from the side of Tom's pickup and placed it back on the pump with a satisfying clunk.

"A question," he said, "that will make him feel important, and knowledgeable, and in control over the hot girls. You know what happens to a man's neurochemistry when—"

"Would he not," said Tom, "want to impress the girls by pwning another male around him? Like me? To show his strength? Trevor? Man? Bro?"

"We won't be even an afterthought in that guy's sun-fried brain at that point, believe me." Trevor started walking toward the store.

Tom followed, then rushed back to lock the car, then back again. "I fear I will be apprehended," he said, breathing heavily from the sprint. "I don't think I should do this. I think I need to get back."

"What you need," said Trevor, "is to get yourself one of those Almond Joys you really like. They're like the Beauties you used to eat at home—"

"Bounties."

"—but with an almond *concealed* in the chocolate. Am I right?"

"Yes."

"And tonight, when we're at the frat house in Tucson, I will go over this again with you. Promise. We will go online and do more research too, if that makes you feel better."

"I would feel better, yes."

Trevor put an arm across Tom's shoulders.

"Tomorrow will be great. We will get insanely cool footage in Chihuahua."

"We will—"

"And Tomsky—" Trevor smiled. "Nobody has said 'pwn' in like five years."

To her right, Orson had dozed off. To her right and down, as a matter of fact, flat on the operating-table flatness of the passenger seat. With nothing impeding her view of the passenger's window when she turned her head, Lindsay felt completely alone.

Late winter and early morning, Las Vegas was as much of a quiet southwestern town as it would ever be. Dull colors, few cars, vast orange brandnew malls noosed up by swirls of highway exits, waiting for rush-hour traffic. It was a glorified parking lot, a souped-up rest station on the great east-west motorways of America.

Yet once they were out of it, driving north on Highway 95, Lindsay could feel the gravitational pull of her hometown behind her, and the nothingness ahead. Las Vegas was the southernmost tip of the triangle that encased Lindsay's life, with Salt Lake City to the east and San Francisco to the west. The pleasant disappearing act of life at home, the warm melting of her individual self and her frustrated ambitions in the gelatinous comfort of family, quivering but intact. She could do nothing, perfectly nothing, and be an integral part of a larger structure, her existence provided with meaning with barely anything asked of her at all. A smile. Belief. Love for others. That's why the call of Utah (academia, extended family, the spiritual and political center of all things LDS) had never been strong enough to drive her east for good. Not because she didn't feel it, the holy beacon personified in the trumpeting angel Moroni atop the temple in Sunrise Manor (the northeast corner of town lying smack on the pencil line connecting Las Vegas to Salt Lake City); but because, in the ingrained communitarian spirit of the Church, her contribution would not fundamentally increase if she pursued a career there, however successful and difference-making that career might be. Home, and family, and community in Henderson being as joyfully, suffocatingly important as sounding the golden trumpet of the angels, so to speak. And so in the incessant triangulation of her thoughts about the future, it was always westward that her longing ended up traveling. Because San Francisco *did* promise a paradigm shift. A chance to follow her own individual desires, to pursue this need of hers to connect to others via stories, and what was so bad in that? There was a power to it, something true and deep—the magic of reformulating the world through words. And all of it available, possible, in a city filled with people who shared her interests and values. A city where people launched literary magazines and opened independent bookstores, went to readings, discussed politics, books, movies. (In Henderson, the video store she used to work at every summer survived solely on the revenue of the candy they sold from barrels as large as bathtubs—but still short enough for an average middle-schooler to sink a ravenous arm into.) A city, after all, which, however fully Peterson-less, would still allow her to be a practicing, committed Saint, still offer her community. Where she could tell people she was working on a collection of short stories without being looked at with puzzlement (at best) or thinly veiled suspicion (more often). A place where she could one day publish them.

North of Las Vegas, Nevada quickly transformed into a vast expanse of mostly uninhabited emptiness designed to test the faith of men. It was a harsh terrain, a lawless land of mines, Area 51 conspiracy theorists, and several generations of cattle ranchers arguing over the little forage available for grazing. There was nothing here Lindsay felt a real connection with, nothing she would call home. Yet Orson loved the desert. He found something meaningful in its inhospitable dourness, something deeply personal in the stories of the men who had roughed their lives out here. It may have been because he had never been away to Utah for school like Lindsay and their brothers, but Orson seemed to consider himself a Nevada Mormon more than anything else. Uninterested in the spiritual comfort and guidance the present Church could offer, he was fascinated by the pioneer spirit of the early Mormon settlers, and the constant struggle, compromise, and loss that had haunted their descendants ever since. A hidden idealistic society in the middle of America where everyone agreed to have a little less and help each other out. A religion of survival, the devout soul of the American frontier.

"We're looking for a small dirt road in the desert, going up the mountains out west," Orson had told her earlier about their plans for the day. They'd been out of town over an hour, heading north. "A forgotten mining road deep in the heart of our desert."

Lindsay frowned. The idea of driving a Hyundai up a mountain dirt path seemed less than ideal. Right now, they were cruise-controlling through the early four-lane stretch of Highway 95, the two traffic directions separated by a slightly dipping, clean-shaven swathe of sand and lined with short orange-and-white phosphorescent top hats.

"And this is where Dummar met Hughes?"

"Allegedly, yes," said Orson. "He picked him up just off the road, close to the highway. According to Magnesen, Hughes had been driving his car up the mountain to survey some mines he'd bought. Maybe the car broke down and he was trying to walk back to the highway but couldn't make it."

Lindsay shot Orson a concerned look.

"Lin, it was the sixties. I promise you car engineers have made *some* progress in the last fifty years. We'll be fine."

"So Magnesen has already been there to investigate?" said Lindsay.

"Yes, here," said Orson, opening his book and turning it toward his sister. "Chapter eight."

"And he didn't find anything, whatever it was that he was looking for?"

"Nothing there, no." Orson met Lindsay's doubtful gaze. "But see this isn't about finding stuff."

"It isn't?"

"It's about *us* going there. In the desert, where it all happened," said Orson.

"You said this was *research*. That you needed help with your *research*."

"Or where, you know, it didn't."

"So you don't care if your story is true," said Lindsay. "It makes no difference to you?"

"It doesn't need to be true to mean something."

"Not a great pitch for a reporter there." Lindsay sighed.

"Perhaps, but I still couldn't do this without you," said Orson.

"Right, who else would drive you a hundred and fifty miles into the desert to look at an empty dirt road?"

"Who else, you mean, could understand an empty dirt road in the desert," he said, "if not a deeply sensitive fiction writer?"

Nobody in the world was allowed to read Lindsay's short stories except Orson. They were fifteen, thirty pages long, mostly set in big coastal cities, though the characters were usually from Utah or northwest Arizona (almost never Nevada), and took place sometime in the '90s—predating the story-killing advent of cell phones and ubiquitous internet connections. It was almost always summer.

She'd been writing them for years. In a sense, her attraction to story-telling had been the one constant in her ever-changing set of ideas about her future. Yet it was only lately that she had accepted that *this* was what she really wanted to do, that writing fiction was the real Calling she was asked to embrace, or refuse. The way she thought of it, her fiction was moved by the same thirst for truth that made her a good reporter, though on a largely different scale. Where journalism was tied to the investigation of external experience, fiction ventured inside, reporting from a different, truer world. Yet both were about morality, both ultimately asked the same question: How should we live our lives?

But there was something suspicious about it too. As much as she enjoyed the process of writing—the excitement of ideation, the early-stage hypo-dermic tingling of complete creative potential—her thoughts about fiction all too often morphed into an imagining of her life as a writer. A vision of herself, accomplished, listened to. An individual. And this, any way she looked at it, felt like a betrayal of her values, her conflicting instinct to pour herself out into a community—harmless, helpful—something ingrained deep within her sense of self. And so Lindsay remained in Henderson, her mind remained torn, and her stories remained a secret, except to her brother.

Orson's notes were kind and encouraging, but at times quite frustrating. When Lindsay started asking him for feedback, a couple years ago, he had taken the job very seriously. He had spent the following weeks studying fiction and screenwriting manuals, from John Gardner to Robert McKee, and had cultivated a plot-centered, jargon-heavy editing style that was the polar opposite of Lindsay's spontaneous, character-driven narrative technique. He kept insisting she outline her stories first, or that at least she know her ending before plunging in, only to find herself trapped in a directionless act 2. In a story about a struggling vegan window decorator faced with maternal pressure to come home and join the family's leather tanning business, Orson lamented the absence of a real inciting incident, and suggested the story could benefit greatly from the insertion of rotting flayed rabbits, teacup pigs, badgers, and gradually larger and more ominous animals mysteriously appearing in the main character's displays, making her lose the few jobs she'd been able to get. In a story about a former nationally ranked collegiate track athlete reconnecting in her late thirties with her now old and cancer-stricken school coach, he had commended the sweet relationship developing between the two—culminating in an intense hand-holding scene in a ramshackle Oldsmobile overlooking the Golden Gate Bridge at sunset—but had advocated for disturbing shadows (maybe allegations of old sexual misconducts with other student-athletes?) to emerge from the coach's past as a midpoint reveal, raising the moral Stakes, generating Conflict, and giving the main character more Agency in her decisions. And so on.

As for Orson's own writing, Lindsay had read enough to know it was getting out of hand. What had started as a one-page statement of purpose for his PhD application in anthropology had already grown—applications postponed—to *Moby-Dick*–size and counting. It was a sprawling chronicle of the history, economics, and geography of Nevada (mainly southern; mainly Mormon), a projected thirteen-section toner drainer spanning from prehistoric times to present-day Vegas in a frenzy of hypertrophic attribution of meaning. Everything was a symbol of everything else: the desert, the pioneers, Life, God, money, Howard Hughes's planes, casinos, the gilded Angel Moroni and his trumpet, the frontier, water bears, Death. The mineralogical concept of pseudomorphism in certain formations was also the persistence of the older forms of civilization and the struggle of new, inspired ideas to gain shape. The diamond-blue waters of the Colorado river insinuating underground and, through millennia of erosion, piercing an oozing wound in the dry skin of the soon-to-be-so-called Meadows, were at the same time an image of the arrogance of Mankind, a metaphor for the porousness and ultimate arbitrariness of borders, as well as—since the construction of the Hoover Dam—an overarching symbol of the history of Man's efforts to subjugate Nature as the history of Man's subjugation by Man. And this just from the excerpts she'd read.

According to Orson, this kind of work was right up the speculative alley of professor William T. Abendland, of the Graduate School of Anthropology at Stanford and of Viking Fund Medal fame, and would all but guarantee him a spot in the ruthlessly selective program regardless of his less-than-impressive BA at UNLV whenever he decided to finally apply. Still, another year's application term had come and gone, and while *Perspectives of Mormon History of Nevada* had now crossed the quadruple-digits page mark, no admissions committee, Viking Fund Medaled or not, had so far heard word #1 from any maximalist autodidactic scholar from Henderson, NV.

"And speaking of highly sensitive fiction writers," Orson said, head already leaning right, cheek resting on the folded headrest in a clear statement of soporific purpose, "feast your writerly eyes on the glorious expanse of the Nevada Test Site! We should be skirting it just about now. Holy Mother of all that is contaminated, muse of a thousand-and-one conspiracy theories, munificent and highly symbolic giver of cancerous fallout winds to a joyful patch of southern Utah swept under the national attention rug for a good three decades. Ain't that pretty?"

"Not very," said Lindsay, looking out at the creosote-speckled flatland to the east.

"Not kidding, though," said Orson. "Did you know St. George, Utah, has both the oldest continually operating LDS temple in the world *and* is the country's unofficial record holder for nuclear-testing-related cancer? Don't you find that truly remarkable?"

"Look at all your time on Wikipedia finally paying off."

"If it were a hundred years ago and I'd spent it in a library, I'd be called erudite."

"Seriously, is there anyone who knows more of these factoids than you?"

"Besides, I've written a lot of those entries myself, thank you very much."

"It's a shame you never considered TV quiz shows, really."

"Okay, maybe not the *big* ones, but, like, some."

Orson pulled the hood of his sweater as far up as it would go, shielding his eyes from the bland sunlight of a winter midmorning. His mouth made watery sounds as he clicked his tongue against his lips like a baby about to fall asleep. His eyes were closed. When he spoke again, his voice was a drowsy slur.

"And up ahead and to the right"—yawn—"ou should soon be able to see Yucca Mountain itself, America's sinkhole of shame of nuclear fuel and radioactive waste." More yawning. "Our secret subterranean closet of Death."

"Man, you really are the Arthur Schopenhauer of tour guides, you know that?" said Lindsay.

"Oh, thank you!" said Orson.

He'd fallen asleep smiling.

Soon, as Lindsay's Hyundai glided by in silence up the now-two-lane loneliness of Highway 95, she could indeed see a low, unremarkable mountain ridge stretching for miles to the east along the sun-fried sand. And though she didn't know or couldn't tell which one of those misshapen triangles of brown-red rock was Yucca Mountain—and didn't want to wake Orson up to ask—she couldn't help but imagine the hidden town-sized receptacle of toxic waste in one of them, and ponder for a few minutes her brother's perhaps-a-bit-heavy-handed image of America's dirt and shame, buried here to rot forever, forgotten, a leisurely two-hour drive away from her own personal hometown. It was these thoughts, then, that the white envelope flashing on her smart watch—representing a white envelope on her smartphone, representing a white envelope in her in-box, representing the white envelope that would have hosted the letter she'd just got from her

editor, Steven, if it had ever occurred to him to send her an actual letter—
it was these thoughts that the message interrupted.

The Tau Kappa House was massive. Not just compared to the drafty
empty classrooms students at the University of Rome would occasionally
repurpose for quick get-togethers or half-assed political consultations.
Massive as actual buildings get massive. The American concept of collegiate fraternities had of course filtered through to the outer margins of
Tom's awareness, but it only took a few minutes on University of Arizona
property in northwest Tucson to realize that the scale of his imagination
had been way off. The building was nothing like the little Victorian
cottage he'd been picturing. It looked, instead, like a large roadside hotel,
one of those perpetually empty-looking beasts you drive by, wondering
how they've stayed in business long enough to grow all those windows,
swimming pools, three separate parking lots. A ten-meter-wide staircase
led up to the entrance, elevated on an upper deck that ran a white girdle
all around the red-brick perimeter of the house. Bulky white doors
opened from the bottom floor onto a yard where sandy red gravel was
bedecked with yellow flower spreads, paling cacti, short palm trees. The
roofs were pointed and maroon and lined with tiny rounded windows
suggesting dusty, haunted attics. In fact, the place reminded Tom of
certain similar off-off-Strip giants you would see in Las Vegas along the
edges of the bigger golf clubs: same sun-bleached faded colors; same
tendency to sprawl horizontally rather than vertically, as if melting from
a solid cube of building-dough; same unadorned linearity of design he was
starting to identify as broadly southwestern.

They had arrived in the late afternoon, and Trevor's appearance in the
vast first-floor hall had been received with as much enthusiasm as he'd
predicted. At the height of his former career, school-aged Trevor had
brought the fraternity a good deal of secondhand coolth when he was
featured in a seminal documentary about PUAs, his interviews having

been shot in their entirety at his chapter house. According to him, the sheer quantity of collateral tail that had subsequently befallen his chapter brothers was enough to earn him hospitality in any TK House in the country in perpetuity. Sure enough, the gargantuan undergrad Tau Kappas seemed to genuinely revere the guy—who came announced by an email chain with the UCLA chapter—and by extension admire his attractive female travel companions, and even extend the benefit of the doubt to the lanky dude with the ugly scar across his lips and his big bag of beef jerky.

"Trevor fucking Silverback," said the peroxided linebacker who greeted them past the TK-emblazoned front door. "It's an honor, bro. I'm Patrick, mi frat house es su frat house. Come in, come in!"

"Thanks man, we appreciate it," said Trevor. "These are Ana and Larissa, and this is—no, that's fine, Tomsky, we can go back for those in a minute, there's no need—and this is Tom."

Patrick's handshake hurt. He wasn't quite handsome so as much as impressive, the kind of strained good looks that betrayed a very conscious project and a lot of work. His voice was a low confident rasp, as if he resented the effort of emitting words and had mastered a way to do so with the least possible bother. He articulated slowly, deliberately lingering over certain unexpected syllables in a way Tom had never heard before.

"You couldn't have come at a *better* time, bro," he said. "There's a major party at the House after the game tonight. We play Stanford, last home game of the year. Plenty of refreshments. UoA insanity all the way. Some serious *quality* guests, if you catch my drift."

"Awesome," said Trevor.

"We set you up in two bedrooms upstairs, in the top floor, so if any of you guys are too tired from the trip, you can sleep undisturbed," Patrick said, and Tom could swear he'd moved his eyes slightly toward him for the last sentence. "But I'm sure my man Silverback won't say no to a bit of legit Tau Kappa fun."

"We'll see if this old man here still knows how to party," said Trevor, pointing a mocking thumb to himself. His tone was less extravagant than Patrick's, more effortless and plain, but Tom could see how the confident croon he'd learned to know and envy belonged to the same performative genus as their host's.

"I would bet on it! Trevor *motherfucking* Silverback! But first, we prepared quite the feast for you all, you guys *must* be starving." Tom and the girls immediately nodded. "Only thing though, bro, I hate to ask, but we have a pretty strict no-video-*policy* inside the House, you know—"

"Dude, don't sweat it, I know," said Trevor. "I was never going to film inside here."

"No, yeah, sorry man, didn't *mean* to—"

"All good, all good."

The dining hall was a big-windowed room overlooking a back patio with a brownstone fountain. Inside, faded hardwood and orange-brown walls gave it a warm, welcoming feel in spite of its spacious proportions, its vast rows of tables sparsely populated by a dozen or so intimidating Tau Kappas in slim-fit shirts and studiously coiffed preparty hair. At the center of the wall opposite the windows, a polished glass displayed the lucky steel ruler that, Trevor explained, had been passed down the Tau Kappas from generation to generation since the founding of the fraternity in 1852. The original ruler had been lost during World War II, but to this day every new chapter was gifted with an appropriately rusty copy upon foundation, and instructed to keep it safe at all costs. Beneath it, a heavy gold plaque was etched with the fraternity motto "ἄνθρωπος μέτρον," translated below in dainty serif as "Man is the measure of all things." The whole presentation was quite impressive.

"You guys are not seeing the big picture here," said Trevor. Once they were alone, Patrick having excused himself to attend to party-related business in the main hall, Ana and Tom had both quickly expressed a desire to call it an early night. They were now being submitted to bilingual attempts at persuasion by their respective roommates. "For both of you, this is likely to be the last chance in your life to attend a real American college party!"

They were walking sideways in single file along the food spread. Farm-to-desert-to-market greens languished in aluminum foil trays to the left of the table, transitioning to carbs and beans in the middle, and climaxing as glorious buckets of fried chicken to the right.

"Is true!" said Larissa. "*Ven a la fiesta Ana, realmente quiero ir!*"

"I'm tired, and we have a long day tomorrow," said Ana.

"Come on, Tom, come to the party!" said Larissa, a sweet dimply smile pointing like two upturned arrows to her mint-slushy eyes. While Ana would barely look at him and conducted herself with a distant, attractive haughtiness, Larissa was consistently nice to Tom, which of course made her even more terrifying.

"Besides," said Ana, "what makes you think we would even *want* to attend an American college party in our lifetime, anyway?"

Something in Trevor's expression changed. He still looked cheerful, but Tom could now see something strained in his friendliness. It was something automatic, reflexive, his alpha training kicking in as he autopiloted a response to this textbook shit-test by his opponent.

"Cool," he said, lingering back among the broccoli and baby kale. "Not everybody likes to have fun. If you just want to sleep, that's what you should do."

Plates full, the girls headed back toward their table in rapid-fire Spanish conversation. Like most Italians, Tom had always felt a mixture of curiosity and shame hearing this language so close to his, with so many words he would recognize as his own, but that for the life of him he could never understand. From the way she stretched her vowels, it looked like Larissa was pulling some kind of playful whining angle to either guilt or coerce Ana into going to the *fiesta*. It would perhaps not be impossible to think that, if he did go to the party himself, and allowed cheap frat-house booze to melt his fears and inhibitions, and he loosened up a little, maybe danced some in her general vicinity without actively engaging her first, and then organically ran into her at the refreshments table (would there be a table? Did they have an actual bar?), nonchalant about his sweaty hair and casually unbuttoned shirt, refilling his glass with yet more alpha juice on the rocks, a hero at rest, like Tom Cruise in the bar scene in *Top Gun*, it wouldn't be impossible to think that Larissa's kindness could eventually escalate to something more right there and then. Wasn't that what college parties were for? He'd need to relax, though. Breathe. Just go, and things would take care of themselves.

But parties were not Tommaso's jam. While he knew that in order to become a Man, he needed to question such preconceptions, and while he did indeed owe to a long-ago night at a club the only romantic incident of his young life, the truth was he couldn't even dream up an ideally successful party scenario without feeling beads of cold sweat lean over the balcony of his forehead lines, threatening to jump. It scared him, as Americans said, without shit. The crowd. Everybody moving, dancing, seemingly knowing what to do, while he stood in corners counting seconds in his head to space his obviously fake phone checks at least a couple minutes apart, in case someone was looking. People happily surrendering the keys to their mental cars to alcohol while he clutched the wheel, fearing his drunk self might make an ass of himself and crash. The horror of people watching him, and the pain of people ignoring him.

"Dude, what the hell?" said Trevor, walking up to him by the fried chicken. "You're not coming?"

"I am tired," said Tom. "From the driving?"

"That's fine, go take a power nap now, but then come to the party."

"I feel I should not come."

"Man, you can't miss this, trust me," said Trevor. His plate was brimming with greens, and he wasn't even looking at the glorious display on the other side (golden crispy chicken, tiny single-portion cups of brown-red sauce in staggering numbers, huge Gatorade jugs full of a mysterious liquid called "jungle juice"). "Things get *wild* at parties at frat houses. Something memorable *always* happens. To come all the way here, and be this close to a party like this, and then *not even see it*? Dude, it would be crazy."

"But, Trevor, bro, I really don't *like* parties. Please," said Tom. It was starting to look like another one of their all-too-frequent one-sided arguments, inevitably ending with Tom conceding and Trevor having his way. Tom was aware of this; it was a trend he'd observed since early in their friendship. And yet, hundreds of conversations in, he still didn't know how to alter the script, how to flip the dialectical tables. He was utterly powerless.

"College parties are a founding experience for the adult American man, a cornerstone of our growth as individuals in this nation." He paused to pick a piece of broccoli from his plate and bite it. "They teach us to dare to want things, to truly believe we deserve happiness, and to act upon this belief."

"There are multitudes."

"Yes, and you are no longer a man who's afraid of that," said Trevor. "You've braved the crowds of America on Saturday nights in Vegas, you've—"

"But I only play poker!"

"—learned to exploit the masses to make a living above ordinary life, above conventions, above the Law!"

"Trevor, bro, man, I swear I will be fine in the room," said Tom, trying to stand his ground to the best of his abilities. Why did Trevor care so much that he come, anyway?

"Man, I'm saying this for you, Tomsky! You know I've been to a million of these. You know I don't like to insist."

"No, I know, I'm sorry."

Trevor smiled.

"I really think you have a shot with Larissa," he said.

"I do?" said Tom.

"Absolutely you do, you should just go for it."

"I don't know."

"Tonight, you should go for it tonight—"

"I am no good at that."

"—at the party."

"I am *a louse* at it."

Trevor turned over to the table on the far side of the room, where the girls still looked deep in their own version of the Recursive Roommate

Conversation. Even from a distance, it was clear that Larissa had over time developed a kind of counterstrategy to Ana's charisma that seemed to be based on cute neediness, on vulnerability. Something Tom should consider, maybe.

"She's cute, right?" said Trevor. "Curvy, sweet eyes, just your type."

"My type?"

"I think she really likes you."

And finally Tom saw what was going on. It dawned on him instantly, in a single electric-shock-like flash, the reason why Trevor really wanted him at the party.

"She likes *you*!" he said. "And you want Ana!" He couldn't believe he hadn't noticed it sooner, in the car. "You only want me at the party to distract her, so you are free to be with Ana. I am . . . the bounce!"

Tom glimpsed a look of surprise appear and vanish quickly from Trevor's face. "What?" Trevor said, composing himself to a tone of amused curiosity.

"Yes, yes, is the reason you need me. Like a distraction."

"Tomsky, are you high? You do remember that we're here for you, right?"

"In fact! We are here because *you* decided is good for me. And now you decide what I do tonight, because it serves *you*!"

Tom's raised voice was starting to elicit looks and snickers from a pack of Tau Kappas who were pregaming nearby with cupfuls of juice from the Gatorade jug, something Trevor noticed with obvious irritation.

"You need to calm down now, bro," he told Tom in a whisper.

But Tom couldn't stop. He felt once again trapped in a bad situation because of Trevor's selfish decisions and his own pathetic fear of confrontation, his failure to keep his promise to himself after the eye-opening shortcut on the freeway overpass in the sweltering Vegas sun. He was letting it slide again, letting his friend take the upper hand. It was time for a new Tom to make his voice heard.

"You don't care that I will fail. Maybe you don't care if I get apprehended. It's enough that things work out for *you*," he concluded, surprised at his words even as he was saying them.

"Dude, control your woman," said the largest, jockiest of the nearby frat boys, to uproarious laughter from the others. Trevor, about four years older and twenty centimeters shorter than most of them, turned over with the look of a caged lion, unable to do the mauling and maiming he'd be certain to enjoy.

"Whatever," he finally said, turning around and leaving Tom alone by the chicken buckets.

The Cottontail Ranch was the first planned checkpoint on the journey. Once they'd reached Esmeralda County, Orson opened up a folded piece of paper from his book, revealing a highly annotated pencil map of the area. Lindsay laughed, pointing at her phone, but sure enough, once they got to the desolated airstrip in Lida Junction, no amount of two-fingered zooming on the screen seemed to provide any new information. Just a single line for the highway, a thinner one for SS 266 heading west from the junction, the tiny white segment of the airstrip, and blank gray nothingness all around. Looking outside, she couldn't really blame Google Maps: aside from the mountains at the horizon and the small patch of cottonwood around the abandoned low house that an orange-and-silver billboard still garishly announced as Cottontail Ranch, there appeared to be nothing whatsoever worth signaling to any driver. Desert.

Orson's creased slip of paper, however, overflowed with scribblings alongside the vertical line of HWY95. Information he'd collected from Magnesen's book, cross-referencing satellite data with old atlases, simply asking people on the internet for help. All to find an abandoned mining road that led nowhere, to go look for something that wasn't there, to prove that something that had never in a million years happened, happened. According to the map, the road started west from the highway some seven and a half miles south of the ranch.

"So why are we stopping here?" Lindsay asked, after Orson made her pull over in the empty parking lot of the obviously abandoned

house. "Shouldn't we just head back south and look for this Mystery
Road?"

"Magnesen named it Howard's Road," said Orson. "I think we can
respect that."

He slowly got out of the car and looked at the building in front of them.
The walls of the house were vertical wooden panels with a shoddy coat of
white paint and a couple of faded murals and tags. Most windows were
broken or boarded up, and next to the door on the front porch a small
yellow sign covered in dust listed the property for sale. It was as forgettable
and sorry-looking a building as Lindsay had ever seen, yet Orson seemed
to be taking in the view like a tourist in Venice or Rome.

"And the reason we are stopping here is to go inside."

"In *there*?"

"Hughes's people claim otherwise, but there's pretty strong evidence the
guy used to come here often in the late sixties to meet a sex worker he liked.
Pilot says he would fly him to this landing strip all the time, pick him back
up hours later. Well worth taking a look around, I think," he said, with the
resolution of a kid acting a role in front of the bathroom mirror.

"You want to go inside a *brothel* in the middle of the desert to take a
look?"

"Lin, it's been abandoned for over ten years. It's fine."

"Oh well, if it's an *abandoned* brothel in the middle of the desert, then
sign me up!"

Orson's ability to overlook the practical for the sake of the theoretical
was starting to get worrisome. Withdrawal from the world of bodies into
the world of ideas is all fun and games until you end up looking for symbols
and metaphors at a highwayside crack den. It was strange, having to play
the rational world-savvy relief to her brother's scholarly obsessions. Lindsay
felt like she'd been cast in it unwillingly: left to herself, she suspected she
would reveal reserves of impulsiveness she hadn't been able to access in
years. Yet Orson's impractical, self-indulgent inclinations had always been
encouraged by the family, while hers had been kindly, passive-aggressively

curtailed since childhood. Or at the very least, that's what it felt like. She stuck to the script for now.

"Ors, I'm going to have to put my foot down pretty hard on this one, I think. The place will be at best disgusting—"

"Hold the foot, Lin, please."

"—and at worst very, *very* dangerous."

"Just five minutes." He held out a hand.

"It's not an issue of time, Ors. Once you're in, you're in."

"I thought you were itching to do some researching," said Orson, again with his mirror look. "Come on, this will be fun."

"I wasn't itching, it was you who . . . look, it doesn't matter. Can we just get back to the car, please? There's just no way I'm going in there."

Inside, the floors were littered with bits of plaster and wood and broken glass, and the walls were aggressively pink. They'd come in through a loosely hinged chipboard door, the sun cutting a crude sliver of light in front of them. Orson went first, but for all his enthusiasm, he'd slowed down to a heavy-breathing tiptoe once in. They held hands, each hoping the other would think they were doing it for their sake. Neither of them said a word.

The room was small and seemingly empty, save for a green armchair in the far corner, covered in dust and ripped cloth. Taking her first steps in, Lindsay fought the desire to run back out through the open door, back to the car. She felt her senses awaken to emergency-mode sharpness: her eyes level, scouting the premises for any hint of movement not coming from the two of them; her ears straining in auditory sentry. She had imagined an onslaught of disgusting, paleobiological smells, but the room smelled like nothing but darkness and stale air. Her heartbeat was fast and seemed to come from two or three inches above where it usually came from.

Up ahead, the hall opened into what must have been the bar of the defunct establishment. A single stool survived, though missing a limb, upside down in front of a large counter, a sturdy shoulder of polished wood turning 90 degrees around the empty shelves once stocked with liquor bottles. The wallpapers had a hauntingly ugly pattern of coquettish girls in French-looking turn-of-the-century postcards. Dust looked thick enough to hold the walls up on its own. It was hard to imagine Howard Hughes, the man who could buy anything, willingly choosing to spend his time here. The place looked legitimately abandoned, though Lindsay kept her guard unflinchingly up. Orson, in turn, seemed to have relaxed a bit, or at least he made a show of it. He reached for the limp stool and turned it back to its version of up, and sat at the bar counter, a smiling, silent customer. They looked at each other, desire to speak their minds coming up just shy of conquering their fear of breaking the decade-long silence of the Ranch. Orson wobbled oddly in his seat.

Even if she could find the courage to speak, Lindsay wasn't sure what she would say. It wasn't just how scared she was of this B-rate, carny-less haunted house ride, but how much she resented Orson for putting her through it. Even if the place were empty (and of course it would soon turn out it wasn't), they'd still put themselves in completely gratuitous danger. She didn't understand Orson: What could he possibly be getting out of this? He had to be faking it. Maybe the idea had sounded interesting in his head, and then the minute he'd walked through the door, it had dawned on him just how stupid it was, and now he didn't want to admit it. Moved by fear, or perhaps finally honest with herself because of it, Lindsay felt a genuine sense of impatience with her brother's fantasies. What was all this, anyway? What was this useless road trip for? What were a brothel near Tonopah and Howard Hughes doing in a book about Mormons in southern Nevada? And let's be honest, was an unpublished lump of LDS lore really ever going to win him a PhD from Stanford? It was all self-deception (or just deception?), a fantasy to buy himself years of bedridden refusal to face life and deal with it. Breaths seemed to hurry out of her lips as her rib cage expanded and contracted like a crazed bellows. She thought she'd seen movement coming from the hall behind them, but it turned out to be the front door, moved by the wind and shifting the light inside. As much as she loved her brother, in the pinch of real-life fear she found her ability for empathy coming up miles short of basic decency. She was not being fair. She walked slowly up to him by the bar counter.

"I thought Hughes was supposed to be a germophobe," she whispered.

Orson smiled back. "The place was open for thirty years after he died," he said. "Let's go see the rooms." He looked happy.

The bedrooms were diminutive, wood-paneled, and sad. Lindsay immediately regretted leaving the main escape route to enter these tiny odorless cells. Some were dark, others white with clinical sunlight from the broken windows. But above all, the rooms were full of mattresses. Piles of them, single and full and queen, white and striped and floral. In corners, stashed against the walls, triumphant at the center of a larger master-type bedroom. Multifariously, messily stained. Here, felt Lindsay, the ghosts of decades of sad, lonely men who had sought the sinful comfort of paid strangers seemed to linger in perpetual moaning repentance. Still horizontal on the beds, arching their backs up in desperate striving to see the light. A Spirit Prison, hell as a cellblock of dusty brothel bedrooms. But while her eschatological vision was taking shape, a second, more down-to-earth thought pulled her back: in a house in which anything remotely resalable or reusable had been stripped away—sometimes pried full force from behind the plaster of the walls—the presence of the occasional mattress still fitted on its shabby plywood bed frame, even sheeted sometimes, strongly suggested that someone had kept using them well after the place was left to rot. Perhaps even *recently*. Abandoned my apologies-about-this *ass*.

She grabbed Orson's hand and pulled him back into the corridor in a hurry. They were leaving, *now*. They were already most of the way in, and since strong sunlight was coming through an open door in the back of the house, she decided to just push forward. It turned out to be a semi-open office space, partially delineated by a still-intact glass panel starting four feet off the ground. Orson looked like he wanted to issue some kind of complaint, but there was no time to argue. She pulled him through the open arch that led into the office where the back door was, and there it became finally clear they weren't alone. Rifling through generations of trash, two brown-furred and very much alive, cutely white-striped, hideously long-clawed American badgers turned to look at the Peterson siblings for the longest of seconds. Lindsay froze, the shock of someone else being in the ranch both mitigated and backed up by that someone being two 30-inch-long mustelids. (The trivia Orson had attached to his flayed-mammals-in-store-display story edits came uselessly back to her now.) She felt her brother's hand pull her back toward the hallway. But the badgers reacted first. They snorted a startled, hostile nasal scream, sprinted out of the ajar back door, and disappeared into the desert.

"That was Steven," said Lindsay, back in the parked car, after pausing conspicuously to check her email on her phone. "He wants me to do the pick-up artists piece. It's settled."

He could hear echoes of the party. Barely muffled by the thin walls, scratchy bass thumped from downstairs, where a couple hundred students must be jumping and pointing to the ceiling in a bout of unchecked coeducational American fun. The party had spread through the house like a disease. The first outbreak had been located in the professionally DJed lounge on the first floor, but the infection had soon spread to the entire lower level of the building. By now, the first cases were being spotted on the upper floors, in the form of rackety drunken flare-ups in the hallways, or couples and possibly more-than-twosomes keening sickly behind bedroom doors. The rhythmic bass made the floors vibrate too.

Tom was sitting at a desktop computer in a common room upstairs that had been spared by the contagion, slowly eating beef jerky, watching a woman on YouTube open boxes of glittered Play-Doh. All you could see were her hands, studiously tearing at wrapping paper, cardboard box, plastic lids. She spoke English with a light accent, and used the word *adorable* a lot. The hands were small, childlike, with lime-green nail polish decorated with painted blue flowers. They had the weird disembodied

quality of extreme closeups. Tom figured her accent was much less perceptible than his, and probably far less unpleasant. He had started watching
videos from her channel over an hour ago. He'd chosen toy cars at first—
the ones you pull back with a rattling sound to charge them up with
kinetic energy and then release for a sad little burst forward—but had
soon moved on to Play-Doh and lunch boxes, chocolate eggs and Disney
princesses. Ana was right, there was something obviously narcotic at play
here. But given the circumstances, being taken for a neurological ride by
this pseudo-Christmas felt more or less appropriate.

What had happened was clear. He was scared. Scared of tomorrow,
scared of getting caught, scared of America, scared of college parties, scared
of getting rejected by Larissa. Scared of everything. In spite of years of
efforts, he was still a sniveling, frightened kid. Tom Cruise, my ass. And
what was worse, he'd grown so comfortable in his fear that he would rather
lash out at his best friend than take a chance for once. A friend, let's be
honest, who had been spectacularly generous with him from day one.
A friend who had seen something in him, stuttering and lame at a $1k
WSOP table, and had put in a real daily effort to help him build a new life
for himself. He figured it had something to do with the way Trevor made
him feel about the future: like there was always something better right
around the corner to look forward to; like what they had was fine, but things
were about to get *better*. Not just optimism, but *hunger*. There was no need
to settle for anything, you had the right and the freedom to want more. It
was, in many ways, the opposite of what Tom had been brought up to think:
sitting by his mother's couch, in the apartment in Rebibbia a few blocks
from the penitentiary, the future was something you had to defend the
present from. Life was about making it through, finding contentedness in
what you had. Even Mom's brilliant (and entirely theoretical) ideas to make
money, her pottery, her idyllic agricultural fantasies, were never real dreams
of success: they were minor wishes at best, quiet hopes to find ways to pay
for groceries and a handful of weed for another year, then the one after that;
then who knows. Tom couldn't go back to it now. He had internalized Trev-
or's teachings a lot more than he'd realized at first. Maybe he wasn't yet

the alpha Trevor had promised he would become by sticking with him, but he really did *want* things now. He wanted with the intensity a child craves a toy. The wanting was a hollowness in his chest, a pain that made him ravenous, restless.

The woman was unboxing a *Frozen*-themed Play-Doh "sparkle snow-dome." The thing involved several plastic subcontainers and small cans of glittered Play-Doh to be shaped in figurines of Olaf the comic-relief snowman and such. The woman's nails were now shine-polished and stenciled with tiny Hello Kitty cats. Tom felt the queasy remorse of overeating, like he couldn't take a single more of these distilled moments of pretend happiness from a pretend child. But the pull of the ripping cardboard was intense.

Any way he looked at it, anything positive that had happened to him throughout his life had not been his doing. It was Francesco who had brought about the first and only love of his life, by dragging his reluctant, twenty-two-year-old-virgin brother to one of those clubs in central Rome that cater almost exclusively to tourists. And it was again Francesco who had taken him to play poker on that fateful night in Rebibbia, when he'd won his golden ticket to America. And then it was Trevor who had convinced him to stay, convinced him that this flirtation with independence of his didn't need to be over. Take them away, and you're left with a lonely, pathologically shy mamma's boy whose only credentials at twenty-six are an unfinished, mediocre education, and a part-time job bathing pugs and Yorkshires in the suburbs of the suburbs of the world. He knew there was probably something to this need he had to find male guiding figures. The feeling of loss and directionlessness he'd felt ever since his big brother had taken his talents to Shanghai. A certain void to fill. Like, didn't take a genius. And yet aside from facile and useless self-diagnoses, what was becoming clearer and clearer—as he stopped pretending to be just checking out a video or two and flat-out pressed the unboxing playlist loop on the right of the YouTube page, and fell back on the chair's comfortable backrest in unabashed spectatorial stance, legs stretched forward, bag of beef jerky open on his gut, chewing—what was now clear was that beneath it all, *he* was the problem. Not his circumstance, his upbringing, the people around or not around him. But *him*. (The woman was still ripping, tearing, assembling.) Him and his fears, him and his fundamental, unshakable laziness, his ineptness, his cowardice. (Her soothing voice now somehow lower, suddenly feeling like a whisper, soft.) And *that* was what he had just blamed Trevor for. Not any fault of *his*, but Tom's own paralyzing fear. (He felt a warm, staticky shiver at the back of his neck, a gentle, downward tingling sensation spreading to his shoulders, arms, and along the curve of his spine.) He could see it now, and he was sorry, he was verily frightfully sorry, and needed to apologize to his friend, and be a better friend from now on. He felt a haze envelop the empty room, and the room itself recede, disappear, as his chair at the desk traveled on a current of mild electricity, back to something childish, and womblike, and liquid, a place safe with the memories of Christmas mornings, of pastel-colored wrapping paper neatly ripping along its crease lines, of new toys, better toys, toys that were now *his*, emerging from the darkness of their boxes and into his hands and into his life, and he felt the tingling sensation move along his skin, and wrap his body like a blanket or a warm warm hug, and his eyelids drop, and the sound of a now genderless, ageless voice giggling and repeating that it was all *so adorable, so lovely, so sweet.*

Orson was in a bad mood. She could see it, even if he didn't say anything. All along the old mining road, during their 12mph ascent up a barely discernible path, he had kept taking notes and looking around outside the car windows. In a clear effort to pretend nothing was wrong, he'd even related two or three factoids about the mining history of the region, Howard Hughes's land purchases, and the Mormon Will trials. But there was no mistaking the fact that he was surly. In fact, this whole display of half-hearted unaffectedness seemed to Lindsay meant to underline just how bugged he was. How much Lindsay had managed to ruin his big day.

"I'm sorry I lied before," she said after a silence that had lasted way too long. They were on their way back along the dirt road, downward and eastward and toward the highway, and Lindsay didn't dare ask if they'd found whatever it was they had been looking for. "I should have told you I'd said yes to the piece already. I just didn't expect you would care at all."

"I don't," said Orson. "It's your job. Your career."

"But you do, though, you clearly do. I don't know why, but it matters to you that I don't interview those kids."

"It doesn't matter to me at all. It's your life. I don't ask you what I should be writing in my research, do I? It's fine."

Lindsay wanted to say something, but Orson was again scribbling in his notebook. She really was sorry about lying to him. More than the simple issue of it being sinful—which any way she looked at it didn't seem like a big spiritual deal in this instance—there was the fact that she really did seem to have struck a nerve with Orson, and hurting her brother was something she worried about a lot. It was tricky business. On the one hand, their mother was always quite clear on how their living together for the time being was felicitous happenstance, but in no way implied parental responsibilities for Lindsay. She was in no way, *in no way*, to assume that her parents were tasking her with "taking care of" Orson, and should absolutely not let this perceived duty hold her back from living her own life to the fullest. Say, answering the Callings of the Church, or planning a future for herself, finding a husband, starting a family. Yet on the other hand, her day-to-day life with Orson told a different story. While he didn't need help in the physical sense—he was more than capable of getting by on his own—the personal consequences of his secluded lifestyle were hard to overlook. It is a special kind of loneliness, that which is suffered out of pride. And so her life ended up involving a lot of the caregiver's balancing act: assist because you want to, not because it's needed, while fully understanding the extent to which it's needed, while still allowing yourself to think of your needs first, all the while seeing the whole thing as spontaneous, unscripted, as natural as any relationship between two people can be. A paradox in motion.

The road was packed dirt and small shy rocks peeking their rough edges through. The sagebrush and dry brown scrub along the way were in the same state of near-death they go their whole parched existence in: a perpetual old age, the single lifelong act of getting ready to die. You really needed Orson's gift for agile symbolism to see anything here other than emptiness.

They ended up breaking the silence almost at the same time.

"Steve thinks it could be a really good piece for me—"

"Did you know their whole theoretical structure is based on a fully disproven lie?"

"—an opportunity." She clutched the wheel firmly with two hands on the bumpy road, feeling the friction of her skin on the leatherette when she rotated her grip slightly.

"The whole alpha male thing, I mean," said Orson. "Simply not true."

"And you know I really can't go back to writing about *What's New in Henderson This Week*."

"The evidence against it is overwhelming."

"That's the only reason I thought to do it, really. It just feels like I'm *so close* now—" Their eyes met when she turned to her brother. Her plans to move away from home were a secret hidden like nuclear waste festering inside a hollow mountain. She suspected he knew, on some level, but like classified military activity, the whole thing remained to her brother shrouded in mystery, with a distinct sense that it might have never existed after all. There was no point in having that conversation before it became inevitable.

"Pull up here," said Orson.

To the left, an abandoned cattle ranch flanked the road with its toothless graying fence. The small steel windmill tower that had once provided water to the farm still stood, bent and dry. Orson stayed close to the car, looking around. It was a pleasant fifty outside, but Lindsay knew the temperature could sink as far as the low teens once the sun went down. She made a show of looking incredulously from the decrepit house to her brother, but he didn't seem to notice.

"You want to go in to track down those badgers?" she said in a playful tone. "Maybe this is where the rest of the gang hides out."

"It's just a word they used in some studies about animals," Orson finally said, ignoring her olive-branch joke. "And it was in *Brave New World* too, I guess. There was a best seller about wolves that came out in the seventies, the leading male fighting other males to assert dominance and gain preferential access to females to mate with, that kind of thing. Then they used it for primates, gorillas mainly, saying we are just like them. And then this feminist advisor on the Al Gore presidential campaign said he needed to become more *alpha*, like Clinton, to win. And the media loved it, they went nuts with it."

"Orson," said Lindsay.

"Except then it turns out those wolves had only been studied *in captivity,* like, groups of random unrelated adult wolves. The same scientist who wrote the book in 1970, in 1999 he corrected himself. Wrote another book after decades of live observation, said that in nature wolves don't do that at all, their packs are based on family units. But it was too late, the idea was too popular, too marketable."

"I would ask why you even know all this, but I'm sure—"

"And then it also turns out that, genetically, we're not *that* close to gorillas, you know? And for example we're much more similar to bonobos, who are matriarchal, so go figure."

"I actually *did* know that."

"And what-do-you-know Gore's campaign consultant, who like *of course* her name was Wolf, said that her description of Gore as a beta male who needed to become more alpha had been 'pure imagination.' But the media, that is, you guys, had done its thing already, and there was nothing left to do. They started selling it to shy dudes and nerds as the secret trick to human interactions, the unacknowledged axiom that explained why women never looked at them, and what they could do about it. And of course in a matter of a few years the whole thing exploded, and now an intelligent professional editor is telling an intelligent professional reporter to go write a story about a bunch of former Gold Valley High geeks who've discovered the power of straight backs, showers, and protein shakes."

Orson's voice wavered when he named his old school, his cheeks flushed. Lindsay watched him sit back in the passenger seat, the door open, reaching for the cooling bag containing the sandwiches she'd packed for their lunch with effortful nonchalance.

"Is that was this is all about?" she said.

Orson shrugged. "I thought maybe this would be a good spot to eat before we head back."

Back in high school, Orson's only friends had been a small clique of studious suburban dorks. Lindsay had never liked them much when they'd been in school together, she as a senior, they as freshmen. They were status-obsessed. The kind of quiet, seething nerds who see tiers and social rankings everywhere. But Orson doted on them. They were important to him.

"Anthropologically speaking," he said now, "humans are multi-hierarchical, unlike animals. We belong to many different groups, and display different traits in all of them. We play different roles, wear different masks. Universal alphaness is a flat-out myth."

It was during his senior year, long after he'd chosen UNLV over BYU mostly to stay with them, that they'd ditched him. Lindsay had been at home from Provo for spring break when her brother's best friend Ben, who'd lost fifty pounds since she last saw him, came over and told Orson point-blank that he was detrimental to their social aspirations, that they could no longer afford him, that he was holding them back. He said he was making an executive decision. Orson's years in college had been particularly lonely until Lindsay had come back.

"Besides," Orson went on, his mouth full of the last bites of a spinach-and-cashew-mozzarella slider, "even if we give credit to evolutionary psychology—which we shouldn't, it's mostly disproven reactionary propaganda—then it's still pretty clear that dominance is at best a vestigial trait. The advantage humans historically have over other animals is their ability to cooperate, their sociability and friendliness. Telling each other stories and giving each other cooking tips has made us smart, not fighting over who's top ape, the Mac Daddy of the nonexistent pack."

It made sense that Ben and his clique had got mixed up with the PUA world, that they would be the ones running the Las Vegas "lair" Lindsay had committed to report about. It was just really bad luck.

"Ors, I didn't know it was your friends," she said. "I had no idea."

"Well, you never asked, did you?" said Orson.

"What was I supposed to ask? 'Hey, by any chance did your former high school friends start a large semi-underground operation in downtown Las Vegas and make lots of money teaching other nerds how to pick up girls?'"

"Believe me, you wish that was all they're doing."

"But it's still a relevant story, no? And I can give it any angle I like."

"It won't matter, you'd still be giving them attention. You'd still be helping them."

"Ors, I'm sorry," said Lindsay. "I really am. I didn't know you had nemeses—it's kind of cool, actually. But this is *my job*, you see? They pay me money to do it. It's what I buy food with."

She said the last sentence just as Orson reached inside the bag for another slider. An unlucky coincidence, admittedly. He drew back his hand as if the sandwich were scalding hot, and it was immediately clear to Lindsay that he had misunderstood what she meant, or how she meant it, or that something crucial and potentially irreparable was on the verge of happening to the careful balance of their relationship.

"You know, it wouldn't be hard to admit it," said Orson.

"Admit what?"

"That what you care about is being a big famous writer. That you'd be willing to sell out like Grandma Peterson, if it came down to it. That you want to *leave*."

Lindsay sighed. "You know I want to write," she said.

"Lin, I'm not a speaker at the LDS General Conference, you know? I'm not telling you to Ponder the Path of Thy Feet. It's fine with me if you have selfish dreams."

"Wait . . . you watch the videos from the General Conference?"

"And I don't care that you turned down a Calling."

"That one was actually pretty good, I thought."

"I just want you to be honest about it, at least with me. Look, I appreciate that you've driven me all the way out here today, I really do. But then we come here and all we talk about is what your next career move should be. And you don't even try to really invest in what we're doing here—"

"Orson, I came with you inside an *abandoned roadside brothel—*"

"—and you lie about asking for my advice, when really you've already made your decision—"

"—I was assaulted by badgers, Ors, wild *badgers!*"

"—and of course it turns out the thing you've decided to do is the one thing I've asked you as a personal favor to please *not* do."

"That's not fair. I didn't know you felt that way when I accepted it."

"And the badgers didn't assault us. That was a scream of fear, they just ran for it."

"And I didn't know it was your friends. And I said I'm sorry."

"I just want you to admit it, Lin. Just admit it."

She could feel Orson staring at her, even with her eyes fixed on the dry brown dirt. With the tip of her black running shoe she kicked up the edge of a small rock, trying to loosen it from the ground. She was aware of her breathing, in a way that made it uncomfortable and oddly mechanical. She felt a need to take a big breath, but didn't want Orson to see her. She didn't want to look like she was bracing herself for what she needed to say.

"You know it's not *you* that I want to leave, right?" she finally got out. "I'm not trying to get away from you. Come on, Ors, you feel this too. It's our town. Everything outside our community is greedy and shallow and infuriating. Everything inside of it is small, and quiet, and nothing ever changes. And nothing we do will ever matter. Come on, I know you see this too."

"If you know I see it, then you know I like it," said Orson in a somber voice. "Or admire it, at least," he added after a pause. Lindsay saw this as an opening.

"What about you, then?" she said. "Don't you want to write too? Be a famous scholar? Have Professor Habermas tell you how good you are?"

"Abendland."

"Don't you want to leave too?"

Orson finally reached inside the bag and fished out a broccoli and roasted chickpea slider. He took a very slow, theatrical bite, and chewed with a satisfaction in which Lindsay suddenly glimpsed what she had somehow failed to see in months. And a very clear, very improper four-letter-word appeared in a puffy cloud of thought above her head as she figured out exactly what her brother was about to say. That there was a reason he was so keen on getting a PhD from *Stanford*, and Stanford alone, out of all the great anthropology programs in the country. A reason he had waited on his application this year despite already having about thirty times more pages than necessary. That for all his recondite, manifold interests, all Orson really cared about was not to be left alone. Not to lose her.

He had met Vanessa that night at the touristy club near the Pantheon. It was Francesco who had spotted her, alone and hippie-looking, with open sandals and the air of someone who's not quite sure what people do in clubs anyway. She was from Bloomington, Indiana, and was backpacking alone through Europe with no set itinerary, just figuring stuff out as she went along. The three weeks that followed, a toxically hot Roman July, they'd spent in the un-air-conditioned attic laundry-room-turned-studio overlooking the Verano graveyard his brother lived in at the time. Francesco offered to let Tom stay there, and he just moved back in with their mom for as long as Tom needed the place, no questions asked. Vanessa had loved it there. Out of the window and six floors down, you could see the tramway-tracked square flanked by the huge graveyard on one side, and the University of Rome on the other. She'd thought it was a funny idea. The collegiate vibe of the neighborhood reminded her of home. She told Tom he should take over the lease once his brother left for China, and just because she'd said it, he knew he would. With Vanessa, Tom had discovered everything at once. Not just sex, though certainly that too, but everything. He'd entered their summer romance a blank slate, and the patient, understanding girl had shown him everything two people could feel, or say, or do with each other. A crash course in human interactions. By the end of July he'd felt competent, adult, unafraid, and like a specific corner in the life of a young man had been decidedly, irrevocably turned. Like he would never be afraid anymore. But then Vanessa had left, hippyishly distrustful of the emotional binds of keeping in touch (to what end?). And in a matter of weeks Francesco had left too—his job starting mid-September, and apartment-hunting in Shanghai while only knowing *nǐ hǎo* and *wǒ de míng zì shì Francesco* being no walk in the Gongqin Forest park. And all that Tom thought he'd learned, everything wonderful that had happened during the summer in the little attic above Piazzale del Verano, this first new life of his as an adult, all of it evaporated so fast he didn't have the time to see it happen. The owner of the studio had already agreed to sell it to the family who owned the apartment downstairs as soon as Francesco's lease ended. Without the magic apartment above the graveyard, he couldn't summon the courage to leave his mom's. Without his brother, Tom found himself once again utterly unable to bridge the mysterious, selective gap that separates unacquainted humans. Nothing had changed, everything was back to what it was before. He'd gone back to the club at the Pantheon once, by himself, and had spent such a horrifically lonely and soul-crushing forty-five minutes there, he'd given up on ever trying again. For a brief, dreamlike moment he had seen a path to a better life. But left alone with his fears, he had failed to go through with it, and had woken up to his same old useless self.

"Party must have been *wild!*" said a low male voice somewhere near him. All his life, Tom's consciousness had always come back to him like a bang. From deep sleep to full wide-eyed awake in one horrible instant. "I mean, I've done pretty sick shit, but I don't think I've ever woken up covered in beef jerky in front of Tinkerbell Wooden Magnetic Fashion Dolls. That's pretty intense."

"I wasn't—," said Tom, feeling his heart sink at the realization that YouTube was still on, and that the disembodied voice with the sparkly nail polish was indeed trying little magnetic outfits on a winged fairy doll. "This is auto-play? Fall to sleep; suggested videos, you know?"

"Yeah, no, that's a playlist," said Patrick. "You need to click on it to start it. But it's okay, man, I don't judge. You do you."

"But no, verily—"

"Looks like we've made a Tau Kappa out of you after all," said Patrick, with a friendliness not unlike the one he'd used to address Trevor yesterday.

"But I wasn't there."

"You old-timers really know how it's done."

"I wasn't at the party," Tom finally managed to say. "You were not at the party too?"

"Oh," said Patrick. "Weird then. But no, I mean I was, but I left right away. I had work to do. A thing we're doing with another chapter. Being a Tau Kappa is no joke, believe me. It's a full-time job."

The light coming through the large windows of the common room was pearl-white. Tom had no idea how long he'd slept.

"What time is it?" he asked.

"Early," said Patrick. "Like seven. Do you want some coffee?" He produced a pint-sized plastic cup complete with a lid and cardboard holder. It was only at this point that the strangeness of the interaction began to register with Tom. Patrick hadn't said a word to him yesterday, at all. If anything, he'd seemed mildly hostile toward him.

"Thank you?" he said, extending a hand to grab the coffee he found himself really craving. He took a long, gratifying sip. It was full of sugar, just like he liked it.

"My pleasure," said Patrick. "You awake yet? I need to talk to you."

"You need to talk to *me*?"

"It came to my attention that you're Silverback's roommate," said Patrick.

Trevor! Memories of yesterday's shameful dining hall outburst came back to Tom at once. His heart was still cantering from his rough wake-up call. He mitigated the bitter taste of guilt with another gulp of Patrick's sweet, sweet coffee.

"He's my best friend," he said.

"Cool," said Patrick. "Even better."

Well guys, thanks for watching my videos, and stay tuned for a lot more (a beat; then, in an upward inflection) *magnetic dress-up!*

"I will off this now," said Tom, stretching his arm toward the desk. The mouse was gone, though, somehow. He must have been clutching it when he'd fallen asleep, and it had tumbled off the table during the night. He was still reclining on the chair; he'd barely moved since waking up. The videos kept playing.

"Silverback is a *hard* man to get a hold of," said Patrick. "Always doing his own thing, unpredictable, free. Truly a man going his own way, you might say. We like him for it."

"We?"

"We're just thinking about the future, you know? We've got plans, big plans. Something exciting. And who wouldn't want Trevor fucking Silverback as an ally? And him being in Vegas, I mean it's just too—"

"Patrick, bro, man, I don't follow," said Tom.

"It's just we're a little concerned, is all. A little worried."

"For Trevor?"

"Well, with the vlog and everything. I mean let's be honest, what's his endgame there?"

"Endgame?"

"It's like, you're Silverback, for chrissakes, is that what you want to be seen doing? Play penny poker and live like a nerd, no offense?"

"But he likes the poker! And he plays bigger than I! Is no penny game, two dollars/five dollars, I don't know if you know, but a very serious mental—"

"Exactly! And all for what? A few tens of thousands subscribers? At best? In a completely unscalable market niche that's pretty much peaked a couple years back anyway? That's why it's really in *his* best interest too."

Patrick's way of getting the words out by exerting the fewest possible facial muscles made his already twangy English quite hard to follow. Over time, Tom had grown used to a certain amount of feigned understanding at the poker tables, where players with the weirdest accents took him way out of his linguistic comfort zone on a daily basis. But this early-morning conversation had caught him off guard, and the voice of the woman talking about Lego Frozen Fever Arendelle Castle Celebration (all 477 pieces of it) further complicated things. He felt he had no choice but to come clean.

"I humbly apologize, Patrick, bro, but I don't know what you talk about. Could you consider to ask Trevor instead?"

"Dude, I *did*," said Patrick, with a whiny stress in his voice Tom hadn't noticed before. It was remarkable, really, how much expression the man accomplished with such a limited array of sounds. "Like, of course that was Plan A, no offense. That's the whole reason I even went to the party yesterday. But then he kept trying to push this girl on me, every time I tried to talk to him."

"He was pushing the girl?" said Tom.

"Yeah, like he *really* wanted me to hook up with this six, six-five tops."

"What was the girl?"

"I don't know, the Latina girl, who cares. And like in a different situation I would be *down* to wing for Silverback any day—I mean, sure, I'll take the six, fine—but we really had much bigger fish to fry, and the man just wouldn't listen."

Tom's heart was doing some serious galloping now. It was the kind of hard knock against the ribs that makes young men believe with absolute certainty that they'll be the statistical anomaly and get a cardiac in their mid-twenties, at least for a minute or so.

"I think maybe he was mad at me for not letting him shoot video inside the house, I don't know. Maybe it kinda ruined his plans for the project. But of course I couldn't be expected to bend the rules, right? It's not like it was another *legit* TV crew like last time—"

"But the project? With the girl?" said Tom.

"Yeah, no, I'm sure you know all about it, but I only heard of it yesterday. The border thing." Tom somehow found the strength to shake his head no, to make him go on.

"I think the Latina girl is an illegal immigrant, and he wants to get her out and then back in again or something like that. He was telling me about some business at the border, I think that's what he meant, I don't know. Which of course would be batshit crazy. But the other girl, the American, Hannah I think her name is, she's pretty hot, right? So it's not like I don't understand. Even though I have to admit it seems like overkill to have the other girl deported just to ditch a cockblock. But hey, the man's an artist, gotta *respect* the skills."

Tom had never tried harder to understand human speech in his life. It was infuriating, to be this certain to be hearing life-or-death-type information, and still be unable to parse what from all indications was plain English. He hated his brain with a passion. Even more so because the slow fucker was having no problem understanding the YouTube woman in the background as she talked about something called Snowgies.

"Batshit? Cockblock? *Deported?*" he said. There a was a pleading tone in his voice that must have sounded real pathetic to Patrick.

"I mean yeah, the whole get-out-of-the-country-and-come-back-in thing is an urban legend." More pleading looks from Tom. "A myth. It *doesn't work.* I think *maybe* it may have worked like twenty years ago or something, which is how the bullshit idea originated in the first place. But there's just no way in hell they're not gonna check her documents and catch her in a split second if she tries to make it to Mexico. Talk about 'No way, José,' right?" He laughed. "I mean, the girl's as good as deported. I guess Silverback wanted to make sure she had a good time on her last night in America ever, am I right?" Still laughing. "But seriously, like *ever* ever."

Tom felt like he would die. Right there, it seemed reasonable. He was going to be the statistical anomaly for heart attacks after all. His hands were shaking, his skin was sweating cold, and his brain was playing the fastest, most terrifying game of connect-the-dots of all time.

"So man, like I was saying, we're worried for him, sort of," said Patrick. "And since you guys are *best friends*—"

"No no, you need Trevor, talk to Trevor," said Tom, rushing to get up from his chair. As he did, dozens of chunks of beef jerky cascaded from his chest, where the Jack Link's bag must have opened and fallen off while he slept. He got up with a single, awkward jolt, excusing himself in the broken English of his fear-stricken mind. "I go . . . get Trevor."

"Convince him to come talk to me before you guys leave, we got exciting stuff going on!" said Patrick, surprised by the sudden vitality of his interlocutor, and forced to cut to the argumentative chase. His voice had raised two full octaves of urgency, and vibrated now an off-pitch, childish treble. "*Exciting stuff!*"

But Tom was already dashing off. With his first step he dropped the coffee cup, which landed miraculously on the chair, the lid still safely on. With his second step he kicked the wireless mouse that had been on the floor next to him the whole time, sending it forward across a maze of dried beef, toward the same door he was himself sprinting to, but just enough off-target to crash loudly against the nearby wall, plastic body and buttons and AAA batteries and everything. With his third step he turned his head just for a second back to Patrick, his eyes begging for forgiveness, his brain burning a forever memory of this Arizona morning. Turns out Snowgies were some kind of small armless ugly snow creature.

The Spaghetti Bowl is the largest freeway interchange in the Las Vegas area. On one axis, it's cut straight by the I-15, coming in from the northeast and Utah, and getting out toward the southwest and Los Angeles. On the other side, Highway 95 comes back from the northwest, while the I-515 starts its way down southeast, all the way to Arizona and Mexico, and back again. From high above, it doesn't resemble a spaghetti bowl much. Like, you would get why they would call it that, but it's just not that accurate. The Tangle of Cables Behind the TV would be a more appropriate name.

In the Hyundai, Lindsay was anxious to get home. She had no idea how she would go about asking Aunt Clara to talk Uncle John into getting Aunt Ada to talk to Wiles to get *her* an interview Wiles clearly had no intention of ever giving. But at this point, it seemed like she had no other option. The pick-up artists piece was a clear no-go, if she cared about her brother at all. She had emailed Steven to call it off before they'd even started the drive back, and now the envelope on her watch (representing the envelope on her phone, representing the envelope in her in-box, representing the history of all ill-news-bearing envelopes in the annals of the postal service) looked positively ominous. It was definitely back to *What's New in Henderson This Week* now. She could feel her next slideshow loom above her like an unpaid bill, the hills of San Francisco fade at the horizon. She *needed* to get that interview now. She had to. All around her, the Spaghetti Bowl was vegan-meatballed with cars. She looked at the ones leaving town, on the other lanes, with a sharp sense of longing. In the ones coming in, the silent army of identical copies of her sedan, the sad vision of a Greyhound ladling seniors into the depressing pot of her hometown, she now saw nothing but despair. To her right, to her right and down, Orson was sleeping again.

In the Greyhound, the neighbor lady with the spherical head of silver hair had finished most of Tom's sweets while badmouthing Best Western Hotels representatives and praising Italian wines and men. It was just as well: Tom had bought them the day before when they'd stopped for gas with the girls, but he was in no mood to eat them now. After leaving the common room where he'd talked to Patrick, he had rushed to his bedroom to find Trevor, but the room was empty. He had knocked for a while on the girls' door, which was locked, but no one had answered. Downstairs, the house was a postepidemic wasteland: few bodies lay on couches, floors, tables, but mostly the place was deserted and littered with remnant traces of agonizing human life. Neither Trevor nor the girls appeared to be anywhere. Tom evaluated the frightening possibilities: Trevor and Ana in the girls' room, Larissa successfully pawned off; Trevor and Larissa in the girls' room, Ana disdainfully somewhere else; Ana and Larissa mysteriously unresponsive in the girls' room, Trevor missing in action; *all three* in the girls' room, the most horrifying option of all. He was pessimistically settling on this last option—he wouldn't put it past Trevor—when he noticed it. The first one hidden above the inside frame of the front door. The second one on a window behind the DJ station. On a hunch, he ran back to the dining hall: sure enough, the third of Trevor's newly acquired GoPros rested above the glass case containing the Tau Kappa ruler. The ultimate middle finger. Let nothing, no person, law, or symbol, stand in the way of Trevor fucking Silverback. Man is the measure of all things. Tom had left him the keys to the truck with a note on the desk in their bedroom, then had gone out to make the first Greyhound to Vegas. The note just read, "I'm sorry."

11

Two Meetings

On the thirty-eighth floor of the Reef, the suites had individual names. Disco Room, Space Room, Fear and Loathing Room. Aside from the iMax theater downstairs, the thirty-eighth floor was the only reason the Vegas regs could possibly have to carshare their way to the Reef, an off-Strip secondary Wiles Group property on Flamingo, about half a mile west of the Pos. The party suites here were brand-new, fully equipped, and considerably cheaper than their Strip-side equivalents. No traffic, ample availability, and the kind of management courtesy and attention to detail that stems from the need to make up for suboptimal location. If you'd just won a million dollars in a poker tournament and wanted to throw a party for your friends, the Reef would be the place.

Inside, the Frat Room was a spacious, fluffy-carpeted mishmash of bro-ish paraphernalia, a glitzy Vegas rendering of a Google image search for "frathouse + partyroom," or something like that. To the right of the door, in the vestibule area of the suite, a massive bar was rather disappointingly provisioned with vodka, gin, some kind of soda, and a bathtub-like transparent blue bowl full of ice. The plastic cups, stacked in red and blue towers, outnumbered the guest list 20:1. The large living room/party area had a pool table, a dartboard, two arcade games, a wall-mounted removable LCD tablet to control lights, AC, and entertainment system via Wi-Fi, and glass walls affording a semi-stunning view of the Strip (partially obstructed by the inland back of the Positano compound). On the left side of the room, black leather couches formed an L around a black coffee table that looked like it had been designed to cut white lines on. To the right and opposite the window walls, two discreet steps climbed to a red-lit pole-dancing station. Even by Vegas standards, the tackiness of the decor was visibly *too much*, and was maybe meant to be ironic, playful. What it did was look like the work of some lazy interior design algorithm taking a guess at what a human party would look like.

Not that it mattered. A considerable percentage of the humans inside, world-class poker professionals, had similar trouble approximating how a real-life partygoer was supposed to act, and loitered in more or less isolated clusters, waiting for the alcohol to kick in. The upstairs regs, whose dominant role was taken for granted, played silent rounds of pool with each other and poured couchside drinks for the five or six girls present (two cocktail waitresses, a wife, some friends of same). The downstairs regs represented a small contingent of $5/$10 players (the closest to the high stakes, the best of the bottom feeders) and had set up camp by the arcade games on the right side of the room. Their deal was that nobody knew who'd invited them, they weren't really friends with the upstairs guys, but seemed generally cheerful and innocuous. Plus two of them actually *were* girls, which at a poker players' party solves an always somewhat thorny liability. Though both groups were made up of well-off-to-rich young pros, the high rollers had champagne and designer cake, while the $5/$10 regs had BYOBed IPAs and shared cab rides. Something about consumer behavior and perceived relative wealth.

Standing by the window wall looking out, sipping from a blue cup of vodka-on-the-mostly-melted-rocks, Ray admitted to himself that he was drunk. He then asked himself when was the last time he'd gotten drunk. He then ignored his own question, and asked himself why on earth Logan had showed up in the first place. Smile, fancy watch, pointed shoes, and all. He came up with nothing. He chose not to ask himself what he would do tomorrow, nor how the offer changed everything, whether he liked it or not. He asked himself instead if he'd ever noticed how pretty Las Vegas looked from up here, its lights like a set of variables along the axis of the Strip, and if things always looked better, and nicer, and simpler to understand from high high high up.

Down deep beneath the Positano, the Shadow Union meeting was assembling. Hushed conversations echoed softly against the cave walls, the giddy murmurs of a roomful of students moments before the start of a class. Committee mates took seats next to each other. In the damp chill of the cave, Mary Ann and Erica wore work uniforms, as did almost every one of the over fifty participants: Mary Ann in black and silver and heels, Erica in turquoise and green and fins.

The caves had been designed as part of the expansion that created the Sorrento. The outer cave, which could be visited in $25-per-person guided boat tours, had opened to the public together with the new hotel building in 2012. It contained real rock formations, stalactites and stalagmites, obtained through a process of accelerated calcification patented by a small company from Tulum, Mexico, capable of reducing wait times from millennia to a few months. Its success, paired with visitors' feedback lamenting not being able to frolic in the cave outside the confines of the guided tour, prompted further excavations and openings in the following years. A second, larger cave, where visitors could disembark and walk around. The Sorrento Hot Springs (All-Cave Pass including boat tour *and* access to the all new Spring Pool available now for only $40). The inevitable and romantic, if slightly gloomy, grotto-restaurant La Grotta.

The Cavea, where the SU held its meeting, was to be an even more ambitious enterprise. Modeled after ancient Greek theaters, the arena would feature a half moon of surprisingly comfortable limestone seats,

and impeccable sound thanks to state-of-the art acoustic engineering—
the perfect venue for an unforgettable and intimate concert experience.
Scheduled to open the following winter (think Celine Dion Christmas
Special inauguration, think sub-lithic seat warmers), the grotto was presently in a phase of *sedimentación controlada*: droplets of precalcinated
water trickled down stumps of hyperabsorbent limestone and pooled on
the floor in rapidly accreting corresponding stalag stumps. While this
patented procedure was, from a geological standpoint, staggeringly fast, it
was still slow enough to be imperceptible to the naked eye, thus making
the Cavea, for the time being, just a large subterranean structure inaccessible to tourists, with no Donut-monitored security system yet in place,
and completely unsupervised at night. The perfect venue for an undetect-
able and clandestine meeting-experience.

Still, as they took their seats close to the center of the semicircle, Mary
Ann felt immediately that there was something wrong with the place. Or
maybe not with the place itself—this strange candelabra-lit cave with its
quiet, still waters encircling it on three sides, and its distinct *Phantom of
the Opera*-ish vibe—but with *herself* in this place. It made her uncomfortable. Nervous. According to Erica, this was going to be a particularly important meeting.

"—As a result of which, the plan devised by the colleagues of the Intel
Committee was approved with a seventy-five-percent majority, with only
six abstentions—"

In the impossibility of gathering the whole cell in one place at the same
time—with the Pos working 24/7, someone was always on shift—the SU
had to schedule meetings at different times of the day to allow all members
to keep up with the comings and goings of the rebellion. As a result, the
Board was forced to start each meeting with a lengthy recapitulation of
every seditious thing to occur since the last meeting in that shift. It was
boring and, in an age of constant internet communication, weirdly anti-
quated. But then again, thought Mary Ann, the whole so-called strike felt
like an echo of a different time. That was part of its charm, too.

"—And I'm glad to report that the Intel Committee has come through most excellently, and we are now in possession, colleagues, of the preliminary numbers we all agreed we needed to see."

The woman speaking was Carla from HR. As Erica explained, when the Positano first opened, Carla used to work most shifts at the old high-stakes blackjack lounge, left of the main cashier. With the unveiling of Club Nero in 2004, a new cocktail bar/gambling hideout for the high rollers, Carla's name just happened to disappear from the rotation, her shifts reassigned to afternoon keno and slots in the morning. She was a mother of three, her oldest, Ricardo, just six years old then, and the reassignment massively hindered her ability to earn from tips. And yet she'd stayed the course, getting more and more involved with the union to demand more transparency in shift management, until she'd been chosen as one of the waitstaff representatives overseeing the task (and, according to the rumors, more or less running it). Her son Ricardo was now the star of the Eldorado Sundevils soccer team up in Sunrise Manor—*State Champions '13!*—while Carla still worked her keno shifts, out of pride, despite having the power to give herself better ones. She was a member of the Board, but the Board, like the strike, had no one leader.

"The numbers, I'm afraid, are not good," she said, pausing to let her words bounce around the elegant acoustics of the cave. "The strike is not working."

On the night of the party in the Frat Room for Eike's big score (he'd just binked the WPT LA Poker Classic for $900k+), Ray had arrived at the Reef alone, fifteen minutes early on his calculated twenty-minute fashionable lateness. On a Monday evening in February, a peripheral off-Strip casino like the Reef traded in emptiness. Although smaller than the Pos, the place looked twice as large now, the deserted aisles of the gaming area like the barren avenues of a nighttime metropolis. It didn't help that the color patterns, dull purples and browns and oranges from the carpets, reflected against the sides of the slots like a neutral-colored hall of mirrors. The air itself smelled different, lighter, like it hadn't been inhaled and exhaled by countless others before, and reached his nostrils pure, clean, fresh off the massive filters and the air ducts above. In the seldom-interrupted silence of the halls, synth-heavy Muzak seemed to blush at the unusual attention, almost muffling its snares and violins, coy.

Coming alone had been a mistake. He had figured tagging along with JJ and Calvin, as they'd suggested, would create a kind of partygoer bond that would force him to hang out with them once there. He would have to make conversation, meet the people that they'd meet, possibly stay as late as them in a come together/leave together–type implicit deal. Back at Stanford, such unspoken covenants had been the bread and butter of the socially anxious geeky cliques he orbited, and Ray had soon learned how to resist their call. Showing up to parties alone provided him with the freedom not to commit to the night, the cool image of someone who's just *dropping by*, may even have plans later, *we'll see*. A solid strategy, just not this time. This time it was a mistake.

His first thought had been not to go at all. A party for the regs meant an empty poker room at the Pos: if a good spot happened to pass by, there'd be good chances of starting a really juicy game, an absolute rarity lately. Still, the most likely outcome of the night remained that no game would start at all.[1] Besides, Eike's invite for the first time qualified Ray as a Positano reg. Given the circumstances, Logan poaching players and the poker environment at risk, publicly siding with the others seemed smart. Even factoring in Ray's dislike for parties, attending Eike's looked like the clear-cut optimal play.

---

1   As a rule, spots tend to dislike starting new games, which often involves playing shorthanded (4–5 players) for a while before the table fills up. Mostly, they'd rather sit down at a table that's been running for a while, joining a game in progress. Reasons unknown, but a statistically proven fact nonetheless.

But the reason why coming alone had been such a mistake was the elevators. The guest elevators open to the public only went up to the twenty-
second floor; the VIP elevators for the upper floors required a room key to
operate. Stairs didn't seem to be an option in Vegas casinos. Of course he
could text JJ or Calvin for help, but after telling them he'd just "drop by
later" on his own, it seemed borderline pathetic. He figured his best bet was
to wait it out, go sit somewhere in full view of the elevators, and just walk
up to the first known faces and go up with them. But until that happened,
he was alone, stuck downstairs in a mostly empty casino, unfashionably
on time.

After his trip to the Shibuya, Ray's thoughts had taken a turn for the worse.
Logan was running a private game. Hiding away in a smaller poker room.
Out of sight. And he had somehow wined and dined all the best spots in
town into playing with him, and him alone, twice a week. The very premise
of the game, that the best players, the ones closer to mathematical perfection, would rise to the top and make more money, was rendered moot by a
short-armed smooth talker who'd found a way to game the system to his
advantage. The games that were left at the Positano were terrible: eight
decent regs per table trying to feed off mediocre spots, spots with no money
to reload if they lost, spots who didn't drink, even spots who were okay at
the game. And Ray was losing.

Not that the two things were necessarily connected; he knew he was still
the best player. But he was losing, and he kept losing, and his financial situation had deteriorated so much that he figured he couldn't take another
month like this before having to move downstairs. Tragic.

Whenever he thought of Logan, he recognized the same sense of power-
lessness he'd felt toward Cardanus. Logan was playing a different game,
and at that game, Ray just couldn't beat him.

The house advantage in slot-machine play in Las Vegas casinos can get
as low as 4 percent, sometimes even 2 percent when played at maximum
bet (usually $100 per round). On cheaper spins, though, so-called penny

slots give the casino as much as a 15 percent edge. Meaning for every dollar the player puts in, they will get a long-run return average of 85c distributed in the most topsy-turvy standard deviation in town. So even though the Iron Throne seats of the Game of Thrones slots to the left of the elevators looked quite comfortable, Ray opted to wait at one of the derelict old video poker machines to the right (only 0.46 percent house edge, less than half the standard deviation of common slots). Even for trivial amounts of money, playing a negative EV game was gambling, and Ray *hated* it. But with no bar available in his designated elevator-sentry area, and since Ray hadn't yet discovered the very common tourist practice of using slots seats as public benches (i.e. not playing), video poker offered the cheaper, mathematically less taxing option.

He played slowly, doing his best to minimize his rounds per minute, and therefore his expected (penny) losses.[2] He pulled his body as far back against the seat as he could, a foot defiantly resting on the coin slots of the machine, in a rigid figure of disinterest and relaxation. He was wearing a dark blue shirt, the first couple of buttons opened over a white T-shirt, and tight mustard-yellow pants with brown loafers and short white socks. He'd felt he needed to differentiate his party attire from his everyday clothes, but he regretted it now, uncomfortable in his clumsy approximation of business casual. His pants looked tighter at the ankles than at the waist, and when he bent his knee they ran up, revealing brown shoe, white sock, pale pinkish skin. He was already down $2.48.

When was the last time he'd felt confident, really? A year ago? More? When was the last time he'd felt on top of things, like he knew exactly what he was doing, and reality took the shape of his reliable

---

2   To be fair, since Ray had no idea what the optimal playing strategy for jack-or-better video poker was, chances are the house edge was considerably higher than the advertised 0.46 percent, which took into account theoretical perfect play. At $1 per spin, he was quite possibly losing one or even two theoretical cents with every press of the button, something he was piercingly aware of and that sent an unpleasant tingle of electricity as he pressed and pressed, slowly but methodically, like a lab rat or a pigeon in a Skinner box. Cent by cent, one inch closer to Tragedy at every press. Something very neat about it.

predictive imagination? A winner? The worst part about getting used to losing is forgetting how you ever won in the first place. He was doing the same things, he was sure, playing the game right, making the right choices based on the information he had, and yet the outcomes were no longer the same. Maybe if he zoomed out on the stock-chart of his life, his early success would look like a minor upswing, destined for a sudden and painful correction. Maybe it wasn't just a rough patch, but a rightful reversal of his fortunes and the start of a long bear market. Maybe—he tried to smile, turning his eyes toward the Game of Thrones slots past the elevators—maybe winter was coming. The $5 he'd put in to play had run out, so he slid in another one.

Just that morning, when his father asked how he was doing on their monthly call, Ray had realized that if he honestly tried to explain his present predicament, an unenlightened observer like his father might jump to the conclusion that Ray simply couldn't beat the games anymore, and was lying to himself about it. Which was infuriating. Thankfully, old Howard was constitutionally incapable of taking a real interest in Ray's poker career, and he'd soon tried to bring up "that thing" they still needed to talk about, "remember?" Ray had parried by asking about his father's eyes, and in the end he'd settled for hearing about a "fiendishly funny" bit about a blind man in some Nabokov novel, which had concluded the call. Still, the thought that, at least to the uninitiated, he might already be facing full-fledged Tragedy had been enough to fuck up his whole day.

Yet all his reflections of this kind in the past year had invariably reached the same conclusion: he needed to go on. There was nothing to fix, no choice to make, nothing needed to change. He was still the best in town, and still had a good edge over the games. His problems had a simple technical solution: just play the game right. Ignore the noise, focus on the signal. That was the paradox of a life as a professional variance-tamer: you didn't want things to happen, at all. The ideal was a string of affectless iterations of the same day, over and over, slowly accruing, through meaningless peaks and valleys, to an overall positive trend. Happiness as the positive remainder shaved off the daily grind. He just needed to go on making the correct plays, as he'd told himself in Toronto, and back home, and here in Vegas. That was the modicum of control he possessed, his focus on making the best decision consistently. The rest was noise.

"Drinks, cocktails, bevar'ges?" said the woman. Cocktail waitresses at the Reef wore gold-glittered dresses.

It occurred to Ray that by taking a free cocktail and tipping $1, he could probably scale back the house edge very close to the breakeven point, maybe, who knows, even profit slightly. He needed to raise his bets a bit to qualify for the comp, but a quick math check told him he was still better off, EV-wise. He ordered a vodka and tonic he didn't want.[3]

"Thanks, dear," said the woman as he produced a crumpled-up dollar from his pocket.

Now how was this game played anyway? Was he supposed to discard low starting hands to try for the bigger multipliers of flushes, full houses, and four-of-a-kinds? Or was it more profitable, or less unprofitable, to hold weaker but nonlosing combinations and wait for better starting sets? What was the absolute least amount of clicks per minute that still entitled him to the free drinks? Could he finish his cocktail by the time the waitress circled back for her next round? Winning and losing is an illusion. It means nothing. This was all that mattered: What was the optimal way to play the game at hand?

After an hour, when Ray was two and a half vodka and tonics in a $56.34 up, the first person he clearly recognized as a party guest approached the VIP elevators. It was Logan.

"The Board will now listen to the motion brought forward by the colleagues of the . . . Pantsuit Subcommittee? Really?"

---

3   As a matter of fact, Ray quite disliked drinking, and hadn't done much of it since college. But the math was unequivocal.

"That's what we landed on, yes."

"Whatever. Do you have a spokesperson?"

"We do, colleague."

The woman who stepped forward was indeed wearing a gray pantsuit over a black shirt. She worked the check-in desk in the hotel lobby, like the other members of her subcommittee. In her first months at the Positano, Mary Ann had been surprised to learn that suit jobs didn't necessarily entail higher remuneration than waitressing or dealing. Office staff, hotel concierges, and the like barely got any tips from the guests, and their salaries were not high enough to cover that difference. They might have cushier, more respected jobs, but chances were this woman made less than she did, suit or not.

"It is with a heavy heart that we present this motion, colleagues. You know us, we know you, we all know each other. It pains us to say what we are here to say." She took a deep breath. "But we believe the Shadow Union should suspend the strike. Revoke it."

The cave gasped and murmured. Erica sneered. A man in a white kitchen uniform whistled with two fingers on his lips. It looked like the Meeting Director had no intention of hushing the crowd, letting the well-reverberating discontent voice the collective feeling toward this buzzkill of a motion. Among a group of bartenders in full work uniforms, Mary Ann noticed a young man, not older than herself, who looked oddly out of place. He was wearing a black hoodie, with two white earphones coming out of it and wrapped around his neck like a poorly effective scarf, and she was fairly sure she'd never seen him anywhere around the Pos.

"If I could go on," the woman said, waiting for the white noise of disagreement to subside. "It's not just that we are facing reckless amounts of danger, all of us, relying on this dubious theory that Wiles will be quote 'too fucking embarrassed to do anything' unquote. Which I don't know about you, but I haven't slept two good hours since this whole thing started, just thinking of that. But now! Now that we know for a fact our strategies are simply not working—"

"We'll make better ones!" shouted someone, to widespread cheering and approval.

"We find . . . ," said the spokeswoman gravely. "We find that the strike has been from the start marred by a lack awareness of our situation." She paused. "Of our privileges."

More loud murmuring.

"We are, my colleagues, a group of very, *very* lucky people. We have good jobs, *desirable* jobs, we make *good money*. Yes, the hours can be bad, and yes, we've been mistreated in the past . . . and present, yes. But we cannot pretend we don't have it real good here, colleagues, *real good*. My subcommittee mates and I have had a number of hard conversations lately. These last weeks have been hard on all of us. We found that since the strike started, our lives are coming apart at the seams. We are living in fear, making ourselves (and our families!) miserable, and for what, I ask? To give Wiles a zero-point-two-percent *increase* over last year's revenues in the first month? We can't ignore the fact that whatever we do, we are small fish here, small, small fish, my colleagues, and our ability to affect these figures is nothing compared to a new direct flight route from Shanghai, or the Lakers having a good season."

"Or maybe you're just a coward!" the same voice from before, somewhere far to Mary Ann's left, yelled. Thunderous applause and laughter.

"All right, all right, hush now," said the Meeting Director. "Do you have a proposal too, other than just ceasing our activities and going back to our perfect little lives?"

More laughter.

"We do," said the spokeswoman.

"Let's hear it."

"We propose to write a comprehensive and uncompromising draft for a new Collective Bargaining Agreement, to be submitted to WHOA through official channels, and approved by management when the time comes. Wiles can be hard to negotiate with, yes, but his people will eventually listen to us. Good things *will* happen."

"Yeah, they'll make the water bottles even smaller, that'll teach them," yelled a voice Mary Ann recognized as Gabrielle's. She hadn't seen her in a couple weeks, and hadn't known she'd be here today. Erica must have chosen not to invite her to the meeting with the two of them, a fact she registered with both guilt and pride.

Gabrielle's quip got scattered laughs, presumably only by fellow waitresses in on the joke. The decision to replace 500 ml Fijis with 330 ml had been a management initiative to get the waitresses more money, and while it did bring in a few extra bucks, it had been widely received as a lame compromise to appease the more intransigent voices in the union.

"We cannot act rashly," said the pantsuited speaker. "We need to think strategically. We need to think of how this *looks*. We don't like what Wiles is doing any more than anyone else here, and it's true that he's proven less than welcoming toward labor voices lately—" ("He fucking hates us!" someone yelled.) "But time is on our side. We need to be patient. We need to stop this madness before we all go to jail for nothing."

Mary Ann's discomfort hadn't abated. Her stomach felt strangely hollow, a cave with walls eroded by winds and water. Cold too. Her thoughts had a sense of impeding danger, the odd feeling of having done something wrong. She couldn't quite place it. Conspicuous among the bartenders, the silent man (boy?) in the black hoodie kept smiling, amused.

"Thank you, uh . . . subcommittee. Your motion has been received, and will be given careful consideration. We will now listen to a response by our Ideological Committee, if you ladies have one? Maybe? Yes? Very well, then."

A young woman walked up in tentative steps to the center of the stage. Mary Ann thought that the speakers, standing there in front of a half-moon audience in an electric-candle-lit cave, looked a lot more like stage actors than political agitators. The girl was wearing what was pretty much a bikini, with sparkling glitter round her neck and shoulders, high heels, and a flamboyant faux-diamond-encrusted hat topped with yellow, green, and purple plumes. Mary Ann had seen her before: she was in the locker room the first time Gabrielle told her about the Shadow Union. The day of Aunt Karen's episode. She was a Big Wheel girl, whose only job was to spin the huge *Wheel of Fortune*-ish wheel at the entrance of the Positano gaming pit, while a dealer raked in the players' bets. Mary Ann had heard that of all casino games, the Big Wheel was the worst for the players, the one where the casino margins were the widest. That's why they put it right at the entrance. The girl was very attractive too.

"Yes, huh," she said, clearing her throat. "Yes, so well, no, colleagues, the Ideological Committee would . . . perhaps we would wish to be informed of objections that are . . . well, *ideological* in nature with . . . with a little advance notice, maybe? Next time? Haven't quite had the time to . . . but yes, a response—"

The cave was quieter than it had been since the start of the meeting. One could almost hear the sound of water drip-pause-dripping its rock-forming impurities on the floors. The plumes above the girl's head wavered as she shifted her gaze in deep concentration. Glitter sparkled from her bare shoulders in the pseudo-candlelight.

"It's totally no surprise," she began, finally, "that the colleagues of the Pantsuit Subcommittee should advise for caution and dialogue with the oppressor. Say we are oblivious to how good we have it. It is . . . I think, yes, it is a well-known fact that . . . uh . . . the underling sublimates, that is internalizes, the commands of her master. Domination becomes internalized for domination's sake. It's like . . . uh, those who are too weak to make a stand against reality have no choice but to obliterate themselves by identifying with it. They bow to it, secretly accepting the identity of reason and domination, forcing themselves to accept the rule of the stronger as the eternal norm. Uh, pretty much."

Mary Ann turned to Erica, who winked. Low, indecipherable whispers ran across the cave. The man in the hoodie looked intrigued.

"Las Vegas is our town. There's a lot of good in it, in its families, in its workers, in its unions. But its industry is sick, colleagues—outdated, dying. It is a cancerous incarnation of an old perceived notion of what entertainment is, and . . . and I would add *male* entertainment . . . yes . . . and it needs to change. And they know it too. But instead of changing their product, the people in charge look for new customers who will like the product they have already. New markets to—"

"Isn't she great," said Erica, with a nudge.

"She . . . she is," whispered Mary Ann.

"She's my friend," said Erica. "Maidon. Told you you should meet her sometime."

"—so that domination can perdure. Look around," the girl said, gesturing with a hand at the artificial spectacle of the Cavea, as if to encompass the entire city. Her plumes now trembled with confidence as she turned a smiling face to both wings of the auditorium. "We cannot let ourselves be fooled. All of this is just a show. It is . . . superstructure. Beneath it all, always, are the forces and relations of production. Money, my colleagues, and power. It doesn't matter that we make 'good money,' it doesn't matter at all. Besides the fact, I mean, that not all of us do, to be honest, like, speak for yourself, right? But every time we allow complacency to distract us, every time we let our anger be redirected toward someone other than the real culprits, we are just helping the rich maintain the status quo. And of all places, we cannot let that happen in Las Vegas, a town where we have to smile and look pretty as ninety-year-olds gamble a year of our rent on the spin of a wheel."

And she hasn't seen the kids in the poker room with those water bottles, thought Mary Ann. She would *love* those.

For its first hour, the party had looked like an awkward high school dance: two distinct social groups on opposite sides of the room, not mingling, stealing glances at each other from time to time. Muffled laughter, stilted conversation. The rich on one side, the slightly-less-rich on the other.

The downstairs regs seemed to be having way more fun: they took turns playing *Street Fighter II* on the arcade, shouting encouragements, chugging their IPAs, watching in excitement as two-dimensional stereotypes beat each other senseless. Years ago, Ray had briefly held a world-record speedrun for this very game, and he was pretty sure he could still play a top-notch Chun-Li if it came to that, even a bit drunk. No more than two hours ago, stranded alone at the Reef and feeling like an idiot, he would have welcomed a chance to impress a bunch of downstairs regs for a free ego boost. But things had changed now, and he had much bigger quasi-literal fish to fry. Decisions needed to be made.

Ray stood by the window walls in the middle of the room, drink in hand, doubts on his mind, looking out at the city below. Isolated from both groups. The neck of his T-shirt had a dip right in the middle, he could see it now. Like a small valley, or a little gulf reaching downward, revealing a little crescent of hairless skin on his chest. At the top of his game, VFlnd3r used to get so focused on the action unfolding on his monitors that he'd start involuntarily chewing on the neckline of his shirts. It happened all the time. He'd rest the thinly striped cotton on his lower lip, fold it out, and bite on it with his incisors, pulling, sucking. For hours on end, feeling the moist fabric under his teeth, relishing the taste of his saliva, while his brain was rapt in advanced game theoretical computation. So many of his shirts must be ruined like that, he figured, with that little dip right below the mouth, the mark of his nervous cotton-chewing. Had he ever checked? He bit on it now, pressing his tongue against the hem and wetting it with spit, trying to re-create the sensation. It didn't feel the same.

"Here he is, the man himself!" said Calvin, smearing a sweaty arm around Ray's narrow shoulders, other hand gripping the neck of a half-empty Belvedere. "Tell JJ here what online wizards think of players who can't beat the games anymore and can't even admit it."

"I . . . what?" said Ray.

"JJ's having a fit because Logan's here," said Calvin.

"The fuck's *he* doin' here?" slurred JJ, who looked already pretty far along.

Ray wondered that too. But Eike, who was reclining on the couch and laughing with two girls, didn't seem to mind. And after all, this was his party.

"And I keep pointing out that he should just pity him," said Calvin. "Having to do something so shady and pathetic because he can't admit he's just not good enough anymore. Isn't that sad?"

"He's taking our money!" said JJ. He shot back the last of his drink.

"I don't . . . I've barely seen him play," said Ray. "I can't really—"

"That's 'cause the motherfucker's never there!" said JJ. "Plays fifteen hours a week with a bunch of fish and makes five times as me!"

From the pool table nearby, Bryan shot them a look. He was playing by himself, resting the cue on the conch shell of his hand with great care and deliberation, and Ray couldn't really tell if he was disturbed by the content of their conversation, or just by its volume.

"Dude, don't yell," said Calvin. "You need to relax. You're just having a bad month."

"Try three months," said JJ. "And the games are fucking garbage, c'mon."

"I'm up a lot this month," said Calvin. "And I'm sure VF1nd3r here's crushing too, amirite?"

JJ looked up at Ray.

"Wait, did you and Logan come here together?" he said. "Thought I saw you two come in together. You guys buddies now?"

"No, no I just . . . ," said Ray, ". . . at the elevators—"

"Speaking of people who can't beat the games anymore," said Calvin. "You guys seen that kid's vlog?"

"What kid?" said Ray, eager to change the subject. "No, I haven't. What vlog?"

"It's bullshit," said JJ.

"This kid Trevor Silverback, I remember him from back in LA," said Calvin. "Used to run into him at Commerce all the time. Everybody's talking about him, he must be getting crazy views."

"Kid can't even beat two/five," said JJ.

"What is he doing?" said Ray.

"Oh, he has this vlog about being a poker pro in Vegas, he's got maybe five-six episodes so far," said Calvin. "But I'm telling you, he's *good*. He's funny. And the production value's gotten really awesome in the last couple episodes."

"It's just a dude walking around the Pos doing what we do every day—"

"Yeah, and turns out tens of thousands of people wanna see that."

"It's stupid," said JJ.

"You forget that to, like, normal people, what we do is fucking *wild*," said Calvin.

"His hand-analyses are bullshit," said JJ.

"Dude, that's not what people are watching for," said Calvin. "In the last episode he did a whole road trip to *Mexico*."

"A two/five reg is analyzing hands?" said Ray, incredulous.

"Just watch it, you'll get what I mean," said Calvin, while JJ grabbed the bottle of vodka from his hand to pour himself a shot.

"Wait," said Calvin. "Let's all do one."

He poured into Ray's cup an unshootable amount of vodka.

"To bad regs who can't beat the games anymore and are desperate to find ways to make money!" said Calvin, as he and JJ downed the drink without effort. For Ray, any fleeting awareness of the subtextual irony at play was immediately washed away by nausea, a sense of disgust so strong that it felt like the drink had gone down merely to bounce against the floor of his bowels, and come right back up like a ping-pong ball. He put a hand on his mouth and struggled to keep it shut, then worried about the others seeing him. But JJ and Calvin were looking elsewhere.

"Dude, don't!" said Calvin, holding JJ by the arm.

"No, fuck it, *enough*," said JJ.

"Why do you even care?" said Calvin, now full-on restraining JJ in the unchecked intimacy of a drunken hug. "Just relax."

"Y'all keep saying that, 'Relax, relax,' but he keeps fucking with us and nobody does nothing."

"It's just not worth it."

From what Ray could understand, while they drank their shot, Logan had grabbed one of the unopened bottles of champagne and was about to pop it open, proposing a toast "to Eike, and to the continuing success of the Positano regs, the best players in the world!" He'd picked up the long, flat knife that rested next to the still-uncut cake, and looked like he wanted to saber the bottle open in true baller fashion. The cake was a giant wall of $10,000 bricks stacked on top of each other, a heist-movie-like pile of sugar-paste money laid out in unsubtle celebration on the coffee table.

"The fuck it isn't, he's not opening that bottle," said JJ, then yelling: "*Don't open that fucking bottle!*"

As everybody turned toward JJ—even the downstairs regs, looking up from their game midfight and letting a defenseless Ken get pummeled to simulated death by strongman Zangief—Ray took his hand off his mouth. The vodka would stay down now.

She remembered about the cave. Back when she was little, her mom was in a strange play. It must have been one of her last, somewhere in New England, or Long Island in the summer. She played the tragic princess, illicit loves, solemn monologues, and all. Except the story started and ended in a cave just like this one. A man went there to meet a wizard, asking him to find his missing son, and out of the cave's bluish gloom the wizard would conjure this huge mirrorlike contraption—which was really a smaller stage within the main stage—and there the son would appear, and the princess with him. And so the whole story happened in this like magic mirror where the man could see his son, root for him, worry about his misfortunes, the entire play technically still taking place inside the wizard's cave. Little Mary Ann found the cave real scary.

"But isn't it sweet?" her mom would say to her on rehearsal breaks, while Mary Ann sat alone on a black flip-bottom chair in the empty stalls. She had on a giant puffy princess dress, and Mary Ann would sink her whole body in it, holding, squeezing. "Isn't it sweet how parents can always see their children, no matter how far away they are?"

And remembering it now, Mary Ann realized what it was about the cave that made her so fretful. This forgotten, precocious establishing of a life-long desire to be seen, through some enchanted mirror, somewhere. Her life unfolding in front of a loving audience. And while she didn't quite buy this all-too-neat attribution of causality—she couldn't help seeing, for example, how her mother had bent the truth quite a bit in consoling her, since in all her childhood recollections *her mother* was the one being watched, and Mary Ann the one quietly doing the watching—still this memory, loosened by the echoing humidity of the Positano caves and fluttering about her brain while exotically dressed speakers deconstructed the motives of late capitalism, this memory now reverberated with a strange sense of significance and not-too-small psychic import.

She found it particularly important and telling now, because her first weeks as a saboteur had made her feel more *seen* than ever before in Vegas. Not by the cameras, or the supervisors, of course—it really was true that nobody cared about waitresses at all. But working with Erica had estab-lished between them the roots of what seemed like a real friendship, born out of shared danger and mutual trust. Born out of *doing*.

The blackjack sabotage had gone smoothly. She wasn't sure they were making any actual difference to the players—and the strike report now suggested otherwise—but there was something exhilarating in the simple effectiveness with which they executed the plan, day in and day out. Every time she delivered her drinks, she would look up at the pole: if Erica was dancing the low-count signal (squatting or twirling at the base of the pole), Mary Ann would linger with the players a bit longer, make jokes, engage in charming, distracting conversation: if the count was average (Erica standing up, dancing normally), she would deliver the drink and leave; anytime Erica was upside down on the pole, Mary Ann smiled and said something like "I wish I was luckier, so I could bring you good luck while I'm here," to which all male players invariably responded by tripling their usual bet to show that they trusted her. All very easy, at least on her end. What Erica did, that was the hard part.

What fascinated Mary Ann was how their friendship seemed to be rooted entirely in the practical. They didn't talk for hours about the traumata of their past, or theorize endlessly about the most moral way to live. She barely knew anything about Erica's life, and Erica knew precious little of hers. In many ways, hanging out with Erica was the opposite of talking to Walter. She didn't worry about whether she was being honest enough, or whether her honesty wasn't perhaps itself a stratagem to win over her friend's sympathy. She just *did*. And in doing things—outward-directed, engaged, helpful things—she did feel better.

And so, now that the cave had unlocked the distant memory of her mother's rehearsals, Mary Ann understood the uneasiness she'd been feeling. Because her nascent friendship with Erica, in which she'd sunk the whole of herself, holding and squeezing, was at its heart a product of Mary Ann's role in the strike, of how *seen* this free, unexamined praxis had made her feel. As such, it probably meant a lot more to her than it did to Erica. Erica had other friends, remarkable, one-of-a-kind friends, who had center-stage roles in the rebellion. (Maidon was concluding her remarks down below.) Mary Ann's peripheral involvement—not taking any real risks, just watching Erica perform from behind a curtain of plausible deniability—made her disposable, uninteresting. Their circumstantial friendship would dry up as soon as the sabotage was over, alongside any relief she'd felt for the past few weeks.

She was going to lose Erica too.

"We are all getting *replaced*," shouted one of the bartenders, in full Positano-mandated speakeasy attire. Gray vest, white shirt, black satin sleeve garter, class, class, class. "We are going to disappear. A fully automated bar opened last week at the Diamond, drinks are all machine-mixed start to finish. This is happening *now*, colleagues. And this lady tells you we have it too good to complain! Well, let me tell you, I'm not losing my job to a goddamn cyborg or anyone else. I'm not getting *replaced!*" Cheers from the bartending clique.

"AI advancement threatening our job security is a real concern," said the Pantsuit spokeswoman, who'd lingered at the edge of the stage, hoping to get a chance at a re-rebuttal. "And we really would know, since automated check-in booths could put us out of work in months."

"But you still wanna do nothing!" yelled the bartender from the stands, to widespread cheers.

"Go gentle into that neoliberal good night," added Maidon, to awkward isolated giggles.

"Look, we are not 'internalizing the commands of our Masters' here," said the woman. "We do want things to get better. We are just trying to be realistic, and consider how our actions look outside our little circles."

"You want things to get better without risking anything you have," said Maidon. "Compromise, even mildly advantageous, is nothing but appeasement and perpetuation of the status quo."

A beat. It felt like the other two speakers were now more or less in agreement to ignore Maidon's wordiness and directly talk to each other.

"Listen," said the bartender, a red-faced man who couldn't be a day older than thirty. "My friends and I have been talking too, lately. We may be kind of new here, and we may not know a whole lot about this union stuff and, uh, *internalizement*, but we know where we stand." He looked around, as if to include the entire congregation in his remark. "We are not going to get *replaced*. We know who's to blame. With permission from the Board, we submitted a request to invite a guest speaker today. My friend Greywolf is here to offer us an alliance, and I really believe we should hear him out."

"Yeah, about that . . . ," said Maidon, as the young man in the black hoodie stood up and moved toward the center of the Cavea stage.

"Ever heard of the tragedy of the commons?" said Logan.

In the end, JJ's drunken impetus had resulted in not much more than slurring and a threatening, booze-breathed proximity. Maybe held back by

Calvin, maybe in response to the host's Terminator-accented "It's a party man, it's okay,"[4] or maybe because, deep down, even these well-adjusted nerds retained the natural aversion to physical confrontation of their kind, JJ just stood there.

"Tragedy of the Common?" he said, regrouping after his aborted attack.

"Commons," said Logan. "It's a British thing."

"You gonna lecture me too now?"

"Just listen. Until the nineteenth century, rural land in England was considered 'commons.' It was available to everyone, you know? All this land, you could just go there with your herd of cattle and have them graze away at it, total freedom."

Logan was settling into a speaker's stance, champagne bottle firmly in one hand, the knife in the other tracing small circles and curves in the air while he spoke. He clearly relished the room-wide attention, the clear-cut intellectual superiority over his opponent, the electric silence around.

"But see, what happens with freedom is that then every herdsman starts thinking: What's the most rational play for me here, you know, to benefit myself? How can I better my individual situation? And the answer is: add more cattle. Because if the land is not yours, the only thing that matters to you is how you can improve your situation and make more money. Uh, you know? You see? No interest in the land itself. And so, and so every rational English herdsman starts thinking for himself, and they bring more and more cattle to the commons, just a tremendous amount of cattle all around,

---

4 Though it was hard to say how much of Eike's bonhomie could be ascribed to a personal character trait, and how much to the fact that he'd just won just shy of a million dollars in a tournament (i.e. a crapshoot), thus effectively solving for him the problem of the decline of poker's profitability and of Logan's endangering of the entire ecosystem, at least for a while. For what it's worth, he'd always seemed nice enough to Ray, but then again Ray had come to suspect that all social behavior in the Positano poker room (and, by extension, outside, like at the Reef) was inherently performative in nature, the profit opportunity represented by the money in play vastly outweighing the potential benefits of any human relationship one might develop at the tables.

because for them that's the right play, and the pasture gets overgrazed, and over a little time everything goes to shit. Freedom in a commons brings ruin to everybody involved."

"Are you saying we are the cattle?"

"No, you are the herdsmen."

"So the fish are the cattle?"

"What? No. The fish are the fish, I mean the pasture, the land, the commons. Ain't you kids supposed to be smart?"

"So you are saying you are the rational herdsman, and you don't give a shit if the land gets wrecked?"

"No, I'm saying *you* are the rational herdsmen, and you all think that you can keep bringing your cattle to the commons day in and day out and things will stay the same."

"So who's the cattle?"

"Forget the cattle, no one is the cattle, okay? The cattle is your greed; it's you playing more hours to increase your monthly, it's Calvin staking all the *Street Fighter* nerds back there for five/ten at sixty percent, it's everyone trying to get something more for themselves and pretending we're this happy commie state with shared pastures for everyone."

Back at the window, Ray's vodka-diluted thoughts tried in vain to keep up with the scene unfolding in front of him. His internet-famous quick brain limped comically a lap or two behind the action, offering momentary flashes of insight that felt obsolete as soon as he gave them shape. He thought: that it suddenly made sense why all those downstairs regs were invited to the party; that the fact that Logan would muddle up a perfectly simple game-theoretical group dynamic with a useless parable about nineteenth-century English herdsmen was so perfectly in character that he wished he had someone to scoff at it with; finally, that he had all this while been chewing without noticing on his shirt's neckline, which was now soaked and all crumpled up.

"And who are you in this scenario?" asked JJ, the long *s* coming out as one spitting whistle.

"I'm the guy," said Logan, wiping his chin, "who understood that enclosures are a *good* thing, and that the land benefits from having one owner who takes care of it, you know?—really takes care of it, not just showing the fish that you gamble on a bottle throw once in a while. Look, the bottom line is, the number of poker players grows faster than the amount of dead money the fish bring to the tables day in and day out, and that's a fact.[5] If you don't see that, you're blind. Do you think these guys have *fun*? Coming to the Pos, being surrounded by seven or eight kids who dress like they're at the gym, who pretend they're not there *only* to take their money. These are smart, successful people we're talking about, way smarter and more successful than we are. Our yearly income is the pocket change they're willing to dust off at a card game. At my game, they fuck around with people their own age, they hit on the waitresses, they talk about business with someone else who's actually, you know? seen the world outside of a poker room. They have *fun* there. If you don't see how this is *their* choice, how this is better for *them*, then you're just a hypocrite. There is not one of you who wouldn't do what I'm doing if given the chance, you all are just pissed that I got there first."

The loud bang of the pool cue hitting the green lamp above the table alerted the room to Bryan's presence. He wore a black T-shirt stretched out by muscles, khaki cargo shorts, and a murderous scowl.

In heavy steps, dragging the cue behind his back like a rifle at rest, he walked up to Logan.

---

5   Or: the growth rate of the poker player population, Ray found himself reformulating, is exponential, while the growth rate of the resources is linear. Every poker player has the potential to produce several more, either indirectly—positive example, envy—or directly—coaching, staking—while the money fish X, Y, and Z are going to lose is always just the sum total of how much they have. Within these parameters, catastrophe appears inevitable.

"He's one of those downtown coder dudes," Erica explained. "From that Desert Coding School."

Down below, the man in the hoodie had reached center stage. He was a good-looking boy, blond, broad-shouldered, and didn't fit Mary Ann's mental image of a "coder dude" at all.

"Hello there . . . comrades," he said.

"Colleagues," corrected the Pantsuit Subcommittee spokeswoman.

"But . . . I'm not your colleague."

"You're not my comrade either," said the woman.

"Please, colleague," said the Meeting Director. "You've had your turn to speak. Mr. Greywolf is an authorized guest, and his invitation was submitted by the colleagues of the Beverage Committee days in advance. We will listen to what he has to say."

"Thank you," he said, pausing to shoot one last conciliatory smile at the woman in the suit. "Colleague it is." He cleared his throat. "Because we are colleagues, after all, aren't we? We are in the same boat, we want the same things. We believe in this city, and in the idea of this city. We want to defend it from the forces that threaten our very survival, and we are prepared to do all it takes so that we won't be *replaced*. There is a group of powerful individuals in this city who think—"

"Who decided it was okay to involve these people?" whispered Mary Ann.

"The Board decided it was safe," said Erica.

"Seems pretty unsafe to me."

"It was a close vote. Even Maidon voted against. I don't know, I think it's good that we look around. Between you and me, Maidon's super smart, but I think sometimes she can be a little out of touch with reality. She's really, really good at telling you what the problem is, but it's like she just talks about it, over and over, never actually *does* anything."

Mary Ann felt a rush of sympathy for the thin woman in the plumed hat. But maybe Erica was right. Maybe now it was time to *do*.

"So what happens today?" she asked.

"We listen to his offer," Erica whispered back. "Then he leaves, and we take a vote."

"What if we rule against, and he turns us in?"

"He's got nothing. No names, no proof, and we are legally allowed to have union meetings on casino property, which for all he knows, this is." Erica smiled. "Don't overthink this, Mary."

". . . that same automation can be used *against* them!" Greywolf went on. "I'm talking about getting back at Wiles without risking your jobs, your freedom, anything really! But in order to do that, we need your help. It's just *one* easy task that we need performed from the inside, and then we can pick it up from there. What we need"—he paused for a beat—"is a volunteer." He looked around the cave with a salesman's smile. Or a stage magician's. In the semicircle of limestone seats, all the Shadow Unionite looked down at their laps and avoided eye contact, even though no one knew what they were being asked yet.

"If our goal is to, uh, *strike* the Positano, hacking their security system is just a no-go. You'll have to trust me on this one, it just can't be done. When it comes to protecting their money, these guys know what they're doing. The Donut has a three-layer intranet system: the money is in the Hole, the deepest level, which is better shielded than most government secret data—don't ask me how I know." He winked. "Next is the Dough, which is where all security is set up, and that too is as impenetrable as a . . . it's very well guarded. So ever since we started working on this idea, we've been focusing on the Glaze. The outer level. This is where most of the service software is. Restaurant reservations, automatic seating in the poker room, casino lights and A/C, that kind of stuff. If we had access to this layer, we could destroy a whole bunch of valuable resort data, and deal Wiles a pretty serious financial hit. The money itself is untouchable, sure, but who cares about the money?" (Awkward silence.) "We're not trying to rob them, is what I'm saying. This isn't a heist. And that's why it will work. You know that first part in every heist movie where the robbers get access to the target's mainframe to get into their security, fiddle with the cameras and stuff like that? That part never goes wrong in the movies. It's later on that things go pear-shaped, when the robbers actually get in to steal stuff. But we'll never even get to that part!

"So anyway, we tried hard to bite into the Glaze on our own, but that baby's tough. Turns out Wiles is so paranoid about being robbed that even his buffet line has FBI-level software. Bummer. We were all out of options. And that's when we heard of your nice little operation, and we thought, hey, that's just perfect, for the both us. Because, colleagues, we can't hack Wiles's systems *from the outside*, but what if someone from the inside could *open the door for us?*"

He looked around again. An edge-of-the-seat-type feeling seemed to take hold of the crowd, in between fear, discomfort, and excitement.

"Does anybody know what the Internet of Things is?" he said. A few half-raised hands here and there. "Well, it's very simple really. The IoT is the network of all the devices, appliances, *things* we own that connect to the internet. You know, like at first the internet was only computers. Then they hooked up laptops to it, then phones, and then *everything*. Your TV, your car, the mall's escalators, the gym's treadmills, your grandma's toaster. Every time you turn on your washing machine remotely with your phone, the IoT is what you're using. And here's the cool thing for us. All the computers connected to the Positano security system are just bulletproof. Can't get through there. Nada. But what about their *toasters*? What about all those new internet-ready appliances that were installed in the last couple years that go online for something stupid and innocuous and link up to the Glaze? Are those impenetrable too? The answer, I'm happy to say, is no. There's just no way they've secured every new device they have. And if we can hook one of these"—he reached into the pocket of his hoodie to produce what from a distance looked like a black matchbox—"onto a vulnerable device, then we are in. So all we need to do now, with your help, is brainstorm. You know the place better than anyone else. What could we use?"

"The front desk staff can use the check-in software in the main lobby!" Erica shouted right away, making Mary Ann jump in her seat.

"We can't plug a box to it," said the woman in the pantsuit. "Are you crazy?"

"Man, you really *are* a coward!"

"There's cameras right above it, seriously—"

"Colleagues, colleagues," said the man in the hoodie. "It's okay. Chill. I appreciate the sentiment, but the check-in software is on a computer, I would presume, and we can't hack those."

"What about the slots?" said a voice. "The ones with progressive jackpots."

"No, nothing connected to money." He shook his head. "Those machines are heavily monitored with Hole-level security. It'd be crazy to try anything there."

Colleagues from the SK Committee exchanged nervous looks.

"Think . . . different. Think outside the box."

Mary Ann knew the answer. She'd figured it out as soon as she'd heard about the toasters, and now she felt her cheeks flush with a tingling, burning feeling. Speaking up would immediately qualify her as the perfect volunteer for the sabotage, should the motion pass. It would put her in an unprecedented amount of danger. And yet Wiles needed to be stopped; he needed to learn that his workers would fight back if he went too far. She tried to summon the anger that had led her to this ragtag group of rebels in the first place, the righteous fury against the rich and powerful of the world that had followed Aunt Karen's own episode so naturally, but the pressure of the moment froze her. She was not sure what to do. And yet that was it, wasn't it? Just *do. My friend Mary Ann was the key to the whole thing,* Erica would later say. *You should really meet her sometime.*

The cave was silent for an oddly long time. Greywolf was obviously comfortable in his role, at ease with the palpable tension airing from the crowd. He didn't mind the silence. Mary Ann was hoping someone would say something. If they had another idea, a better idea, then she would be off the hook. But nobody said anything. Even the murmuring had stopped. She felt she had no choice.

"I guess," she whispered to Erica, so low it was barely intelligible, "the harpsichord at the lounge goes online to get the scores for auto-play."

Erica turned to her, beaming enthusiasm, then raised her hand to speak to the whole crowd.

"My friend," she began, "says—"

"First of all," said Bryan, "I can't fucking believe you're actually saying you're doing this for the good of the fish, or the land, or whatever you wanna call your little poker buddies, you greedy piece of shit."

"Well, look at that," said Logan. "First time I hear the man's voice in like a year! Love you too, buddy."

"Fuck off. Second, the tragedy of the commons, like the prisoner's dilemma, only works in an environment where the herdsmen don't all know each other and hold each other accountable. Where if you game the system, there isn't shame and punishment to be faced, and you can just get away with it. It only works in an environment incapable of self-regulation."

"Self-regulation?" Logan smiled defiantly.

"Self-regulation," said Bryan, gripping the pool cue with both hands. The room was silent.

"Look, buddy, your silver-star-sheriff bullshit could maybe fly at your home casino in Butthole, Montana, but self-regulating communities only work when they're *small*, you know? This is Vegas, thousands of poker players through this town every year. Are you gonna shame and punish all the ones who don't live up to your little honor code? Huh? The little knight in shining Armani? The selfless hero of the oppressed who drives a fucking Tesla? Give me a fucking break. It's over—there's just too many of us, and many more will come, now that online sucks balls. You said so yourself back when these kids started showing up," said Logan, turning around forty-five degrees and pointing his chin at Ray, who was very glad to see Bryan's threatening stare remained fixed forward and downward at his knife-wielding interlocutor.

Logan turned back. "This is poker, adapt or die." A beat. Logan grinned. "And as for your self-regulation, *bring it*: I'm right here, you fucking hypocrite."

Everything stood still for a second. Calvin: unaware of holding JJ in what could technically no longer be described as a restraint—since JJ wasn't moving or even trying to—but something closer to an actual hug; JJ, more or less aware of being held; Eike: forgetting about the girls; the girls: forgetting about Eike; the downstairs regs: forgetting about their game, and staring rapt at the pros they looked up to and sort of aspired to one day become getting as close to an actual fight as any one of them had ever got; Bryan and Logan (and everybody): suddenly, irrevocably, tragically aware of the fact that Bryan was holding a heavyish pool cue, and Logan was holding a long, sharp knife, and that the equipment-to-skill-set ratio of both prospective fighters was so left-leaning and scary and weird that some unreasonably heavy shit could be about to go down right about now.

And Ray, with so much of his T-shirt chewed up in his mouth that his cheeks looked puffed, and realizing now that the involuntary, tension-induced nature of the gesture was maybe integral to its enjoyment, as in one of those things you can never catch yourself loving without breaking the spell, like getting lost in a movie, or solving for x, or playing a really intense rally of ping-pong, Ray sucked through his teeth and through the wet fabric of his shirt so hard that he triggered a second and stronger anti-peristaltic bounce, and barely had time to clasp a useless hand against his mouth this time before he erupted in projectile squirts through the slits of his fingers, spraying gastric filth all over windows, floor, self, in loud pathetic wide-eyed gasps.

Everyone turned. Logan turned. Bryan didn't turn. He pounced forward, hands clutching top and bottom of the cue like a bō staff, and bent downward to shoulder Logan between the sternum and the neck. It was a precise hit, noiseless, angular. Logan stumbled, losing balance. Bryan pulled his staff forward and spiked it almost delicately against Logan's chest, then pushed him hard, making him trip and fall on his back. He landed nape-first into the cake, sending high-flying wads of green sugar-paste cash and white creamy center all over the couches and party guests. The bottle flew sideways, smashing against the floor right in front of Bryan. The knife, accompanied by the collective worried stares of the room, now suddenly back on the fight after Ray's momentary distraction, the knife mercifully flew backward, drawing a long, elegant arc, and stuck itself rather theatrically a couple wedges off the center of the dartboard. As for Logan, the whole little of him seemed to disappear into the stacks of hypercaloric currency, polished pointed dress shoes coming out at one end, the gold-on-black octagon of an Audemars Royal Oak emerging with a disembodied hand from the top of the glucose mess.

Collective laughter is rarely an expression of simple mirth. In sharing hilarity as a group, individuals invariably express a wealth of social vectors that go well beyond mere enjoyment, addressing human desire for communication, belonging, safety. And so, to an observer not covered in vomit and kneeling on a sticky-carpeted floor, the laughter that filled the room next would have revealed a stunning complexity of layers. They laughed at the scene, sure: between Logan in the cake and Ray crouching in his puddle, people really didn't know where to turn their phone cameras first. In relief, of course, at the seeming departure of the eventuality of someone getting stabbed or pool-cued to death. But on a deeper level the room's laughter had an *active* role, an agenda, a desire to defuse the tension of the fight and tell the interested parties *Enough, this is over. Everything is okay.*

But Ray didn't laugh. Even in the rush of gastric well-being that follows a good puke, finding himself, if not at the center, at least as one of two focal points on this ellipse of slapstick was not something he was programmed to make light of. His clothes were like a sad brown Pollock, and he could feel the wetness seeping everywhere, even inside his shoes. He'd made himself ridiculous in front of a group that, in terms of size and potential for outward social reach, more or less equated with the whole world. But all that, he could have lived with. Even the prospect of having to walk through the gaming pits at the Reef, and find a car willing to take him on in that state. All of that he could have lived with, if it wasn't for what had happened in the elevator. If the small man who was now breaststroking, panting, out of a car-sized dessert hadn't, just a few hours before, offered him an unexpected, perplexing, wonderful solution to the problem that had made the last year of his life hell. A man who was now openly at war with all the Vegas regs and, in a way, the poker community at large. Logan, cheating, universally despised, shortcut-taking Logan, had invited Ray to join the roster of his private game.

PART III

SPRING 2015

12

Tom

It's a nasty thing about time that we are never able to see its shape, moving forward. We trudge blindly through darkened rooms, tripping on wires, stubbing our toes against the furniture, and only when we get to the door to leave can we finally hit the light switch and look back: Ha, that's the path I walked! That's what that thing was over there, boy did that ever hurt!

The way it seemed to work to Tom was that time only existed looking backward, lumping together stretches of experience once they had ended. He'd just wake up one day, and find himself in some new situation, something entirely different from what he remembered from before. And only there he'd suddenly see the serpentine road that had led to wherever he was now—a road he'd never been aware of walking in the first place—and measure it. He'd had a father for five years. He'd had a girlfriend for three weeks once. He'd had a friend named Trevor for eighteen months.

It was this line of thinking he found himself entertaining in early April, sitting cross-legged on a large flat rock overlooking the emerald detour in the Colorado River known as the Horseshoe Bend, holding the dog in his lap. A cool Navajo Arizona wind was blowing from the East. The grip of his ringed left hand on Pepperthedog's side was perhaps overtight, but the gusts were strong, the cliff was like three hundred meters high, and the jittery little thing had already proven without a doubt to have a bit of a death wish. How had Tommaso Bernardini from Rebibbia got here? How had his life swerved its riverlike way to such an unlikely destination? And honestly, how had so much happened in so little time?

He turned around, facing the elevated boulder behind him, and smiled as his wife took a picture.

Truly exceptional change had occurred in the months following Tucson. Back home, Tom had used what turned out to be his weeklong head start—while Trevor shot, in the Chihuahua region of Mexico, his most successful vlog episode yet—to acclimate himself to a sleep schedule at polar opposites to his roommate's. Trevor woke up every day around one thirty p.m., hit the poker rooms by three, and played until ten or eleven, enjoying his free time out and about on the nighttime Strip or at the apartment. Fairly consistent, since the start of their cohabitation. It was therefore easy for Tom to craft a new schedule that involved the fewest possible interactions with his former friend: wake up at three a.m., get to the casino at four, play until one or so. Then afternoons off, bedtime at seven. He started out calling it "the baker's shift," but he soon picked up from the floor staff that worked it the official, and rather bleaker, "graveyard shift."

While his F-150 climbed up and down the greenish slopes of Las Barrancas del Cobre, in southwest Chihuahua, Tom ended up reacquainting himself with the small-time magic of the Las Vegas bus system. Sitting in the upper level of the Strip-bound double-decker known as the Deuce, he rediscovered the town. Las Vegas, in its sparkling evening dress. Or during the day, the palm trees and fountains and sky-high buildings.

Driving a car, reaching the Positano or the Shibuya from their less-trafficked entries on Flamingo, you could forget the Strip was even there. Entire weeks could go by as you commuted directly from an unglamorous residential neighborhood to the dark innards of a casino and back, and the notion of living in Las Vegas could start meaning next to nothing. But the Deuce didn't take backroads. It plunged into the slow-moving convoys of the Strip, stopping at every attraction, allowing Tom to take in the Indiana Jones fantasy jungle of the Mirage, the amber curves of the Wiles Tower. It made him feel lucky again.

Then Trevor came back. Or so it seemed. Tom's truck simply reappeared in the driveway, tank near empty, wheels yellowed by the dried mud of true outdoors adventure, keys on his nightstand. For three whole days Tom failed to see red hair #1 out of Trevor. Then finally, on a Saturday at dinner-time (for Tom), that is, breakfast-time (for Trevor), that is, late lunchtime (for the rest of the world), he saw all of it at once. Trevor was eating Lucky Charms in the living room, just like old times. He was wearing his trade-mark five-toed shoes, the blue-and-gold UCLA Bruins Basketball shorts he slept in, and a Mexican serape with fringes and horizontal stripes so garishly multicolored it added to the short list of human artifacts visible from space.

"'Sup," said Trevor, lifting his head from the cereal bowl in a perfect poker face.

"Fine thanks," said Tom.

And that was it. Tom took his free club sandwich from the Positano Café to his room and ate there alone. Trevor left for work in an Uber, still wearing the serape, using his GoPros to capture the scene.

And just like that, a new daily routine was born. One that didn't neces-sitate Tom's crummy old pickup, or him holding the camera as Trevor walked out of the apartment. A routine that didn't include Tom at all, just like Tom's didn't include Trevor anymore.

The following baker's morning, Tom awoke to an email notification from his YouTube subscriptions page. "Trevor Silverback: 'South of the Border, Down Mexico Way' - 3 hours ago." The new vlog was out, and as a subscriber to Trevor's channel—his first ever, as a matter of fact—he was being duti-fully informed. Automated algorithms have really poor taste.

Eating his 3:00 a.m. Lucky Charms in the living room, he contemplated the situation. It was hard to predict what would be in the video. On the one hand, he was convinced that Trevor must feel guilty about what he'd done. Whatever had happened after Tom left, Trevor must have spoken to that idiot Patrick at some point, and put two and two together. And if that wasn't enough, Trevor had definitely seen footage of Tom discovering his hidden GoPros in the morning, the unmistakable scales-dropping-from-one's-eyes look on his formerly trusting roommate. Could the new vlog contain some kind of apology? A heartwarming tribute to his best friend, who he'd mistreated? An admission of guilt even?

On the other hand, from a filmmaker's perspective, Tom's sudden off-screen disappearance two-thirds of the way to the border was a tough plot hole to fill. And, knowing Trevor, finding a way to fix the overall arc of the episode had probably been more of a concern to him than fixing his friendship with Tom. And so the content of the video—teased in the YouTube email by a *Breaking Bad*-type image of pants flying out of Tom's truck in the middle of the desert—remained impossible to foretell.

The funny thing, though, was that Tom didn't care. Amid the sugar high of his delicious American breakfast, he barely felt a thrill as he selected the email from his feed and backarrowed it into oblivion. He felt no interest in watching the episode, or any new one after that. He lifted another rainbow spoonful to his mouth. Could it be that without planning for it—perhaps exactly *because* he hadn't planned for it—the adventure in Arizona had finally started him on the path he had been trying to embark upon for almost two years? Had he turned the corner? He had risen from the ashes of shameless fear, and now he stood, ready to become a self-sufficient, zero-shit-taking, true-and-tried alpha. Which like take *that* Trevor, you poncho-wearing weirdo.

The graveyard shift came with a few unexpected perks. Contrary to what happened at high stakes or even Trevor's $2/$5, at good old ecumenical $1/$3—the people's stakes—most rooms could flaunt hell-or-high-water round-the-clock action. Coming in late, Tom would join tables where a few players had been gambling through the night. While he was fresh and well-rested, many of them were drunk, tired, just waiting to lose it all and go home. Twice in the first week he saw someone fall asleep on their chips. He saw tourists so far gone casino staff had to cut them off from bar service, and once a player so rowdily drunk they had no choice but to ask him to leave. It made for pretty interesting games.

The rooms themselves were better. With fewer people to take care of, graveyard-shift floor staff looked more relaxed, approachable. Tom couldn't yet pull off Trevor's effortless rapport with the pantsuited ladies at the podium, but for the first time he felt like they remembered him, like they knew he existed. At the Positano, where he played most nights, staff started calling him by name. The sense of belonging felt almost overwhelmingly warm.

In the uncrowded room, sipping coffee with cream and double sugar, Tom found he could play longer hours, and still feel less tired than before. Without Trevor constantly suggesting breaks, or needing his one-man camera crew for a shoot, his focus had improved too. He was winning more money, and for the first time since he'd started playing regularly, his earnings seemed to stack up at a much higher clip than his expenses. For the almost two years since his tournament score, his net worth had stayed more or less level around $15,000 (the WSOP money, minus a few expenses like the truck); now he'd climbed back to almost $20,000, and the money kept coming. If this kept up, it wasn't unrealistic to think he could afford his own place before long.

And that couldn't happen a minute too soon. Trevor had been back almost two weeks, and things at home were starting to get tense. It was cold war. The apartment's seventy square meters seemed to have stretched to continental proportions, and the hours of the day had dilated to accommodate two whole mutually exclusive lives. Tom and Trevor barely saw each other at all.

Yet, in keeping with the praxis of subzero warfare, a number of small but almost daily incidents threatened the balance of their cohabitation, causing the nuclear alarm sirens to moo their omen of imminent total annihilation. Silly little things. A silent, heated, wholly imaginary debate about milk (it seemed implicit that whoever finished the existing carton would have to buy a new one) rarefied to such complex strategic consequences that at one time both factions stopped drinking milk at all, and the thing expired. Acts of low-level domestic terrorism were carried out in key sensitive areas—female shoes, purses, and once even undergarments appearing on the living room couch for Tom to find in the morning, retaliation by thermostat-tampering being swift and unforgiving. Toilet paper consumption became a terrifying game of chicken.

It was a war old Tom would have never been able to fight. His need for reassurance and peacemaking would have made the ruthlessness of conflict impossible. He would have caved, for sure. But what he found now, in his first weeks as a lone wolf (and he would go entire days speaking no words out loud other than "Call," "All in," and "The number forty-two with the hot sauce, please"), was that life without the approval of a guiding figure was not the emotional wasteland he had always feared it would be. That he really could be content with being his own man—how had Patrick put it?—*going his own way*. Wasn't that what true alphas did? And as for reassurance, does it come in sweeter, more concentrated form than the sight of bills growing in his desk drawer to little currency turrets, slowly but surely, indicating without a doubt that one is doing things right?

Things were going well, great even, and the troubles at the apartment were a small price to pay for his good fortune. Besides, he would probably move out soon, at this rate.

His only real problems, then, remained on the citizenship front. Even with everything going on at home, he didn't think Trevor would go so far as to rat him out to Immigration and have him deported. He might be selfish, and he might be too proud to ever apologize for the Arizona fiasco and mend cohabitational fences, but he wasn't a complete psychopath.

And it's not like Tom had done anything to him (other than maybe screw up the continuity of his Mexican road trip docutainment).

Still, Tom remained undocumented and uninsured. He had a foreign social security card for a driver's license, and had now overstayed his tourist visa for so long that simple deportation would seem like a fantastically lenient sentence if he ever got caught. Which could happen any second, anywhere he went.

Yet even about this, Tom was feeling better. He couldn't explain why, since the problem seemed as unsolvable, and pressing, and teeth-rattling as ever, but he wasn't scared anymore. He was calm, instead. He was resolute. In control. Like Tom Cruise getting his confidence back after Goose's death in *Top Gun*. He just needed to stay the course, be ready for anything, and a solution would soon present itself. His magnetism would attract it, or something.

On a Sunday afternoon, alone in the war-torn apartment, Tom was getting ready for bed. He'd had his dinner, tidied up the thirty-five square meters on his side of the Iron Curtain, loaded up a piratical stream of the Roma-Inter soccer game from earlier that day—which he'd carefully avoided spoilers for—all while the sun was still up. The poker had been good today: a rich, bored Belgian was going all in every hand without looking at his cards, and Tom had managed to benefit from such donations twice.

In a Viva Las Vegas souvenir T-shirt and loose elastic-banded briefs, he was slipping under the covers—three Almond Joys and a Snickers bar lined beside his laptop for midgame consumption—when the doorbell rang.

"What do you mean, *not here?*" said the man in the leather jacket. He was middle-aged, with salt-and-pepper hair, and gave Tom a clinical stare-down. "He knew I was coming, where is he?"

His gaze lingered for a second on the oblique scar on Tom's lips, the train of thought forming in his head almost visible—discarding threatening options, inferring the lame truth. Tom felt as exposed as the one time he'd been body-scanned at International Departures, Fiumicino Airport. Like he should step on the yellow footprints and lift his hands up.

"I am sorry," he said, already teetering on the edge of the confidence wagon, ready to fall back into his old apologetic self. "I don't know where Trevor is. In a casino, I think?"

"Don't care where he is," said the man. "I care where he ain't. And he ain't here."

"I am sorry."

"He paid for the shit already, but this is not how this works, okay? I'm not his delivery boy."

"The . . . shit?"

"Like I'll just show up and drop his shit off, and he don't even have to see me?"

So this must be Trevor's Adderall dealer. He'd heard about him, of course; Trevor was quite fond of saying he "had a guy." He had a casual way of bragging about his minor drug addiction and familiarity with small-time criminals that made him edgy and cool, or at least that was the intention. But Tom, who had grown up around small-time dealers and petty criminals, had never quite got the point of it.

Now, in the Spring Valley sunset, he was starting to feel bad for this guy.

"Trevor is made like that," he said.

"This is not how this works," repeated the man, almost to himself.

"He is always like that."

"The hell's he thinking?"

The note of frustration in the man's voice. It dawned on Tom that this dangerous-looking man was just another victim of his roommate's selfish manipulations. He'd probably driven his van on the rush-hour beltway to drop-ship Trevor his rich kid's drugs. He could relate.

"I know," he said. "Is bad."

It occurred to him that this missed connection might even be intentional, an ill-conceived attempt to put Tom in an awkward, even scary situation.

"Maybe just leave it here for this time," he said calmly, proving himself above Trevor's clumsy stratagems. "I can take care of it."

The man looked at him with a combination of gratitude and suspicion. He seemed to be evaluating the humiliation of accommodating a spoiled kid's bad manners (and trusting a stranger with his drugs) against the pain of having to drive all the way back here some other time. He nodded with a grunt, then walked back to the van.

Two things became immediately clear. First, the man was not Trevor's drug dealer, or at least not *just* his drug dealer. Judging from the heavily Scotch-taped boxes he was examining, selecting, and finally unloading, the mystery of where Trevor had got all his expensive video equipment (and how he'd been able to afford it) had finally been solved.

Second, not only had Tom successfully asserted himself—stood his ground and whatnot—he'd done so with a rough, dangerous stranger. He'd won the respect of a man who trafficked in drugs and stolen goods and who knows what else, a man who quite clearly had a very low opinion of Trevor. Out of the two of them, he was unmistakably the tough one now.

Back in the van, Rick was stacking the goods the kid had ordered and prepaid. From the pretty basic toys he'd ask for at first (pawn-shop-level cameras, a couple GoPros, all easy-to-get stuff), he'd soon graduated to heavy-duty, very specific and pricey gear that took Rick heaps of time and effort to procure. A professional Canon HD camcorder. A top-of-the-line drone. Two different camera tripods, one traditional and one with bendable, variously attachable legs. And, this time, a wearable real-deal HD spy camera and microphone set. Which Rick wasn't even trying to guess what the kid wanted to do with *that*.

But this wasn't the time to pick and choose: Rick's main wholesale supplier, a brothel-owning kingpin from Reno he'd known for thirty-five years, had recently one-eightied, found the Latter-day God, and now steadied his fat sinning hands to feed scalding rice soup to starving children in Vietnam. To atone. Or something. Safe to say business had slowed down. In the meantime, Karen's mood was not improving, and in that state, even Rick's connections couldn't help get her a better job than that Hawaiian shithole. Rick's plan was to take her to Paris for a week or two—real Paris, that is, not the hotel—take her mind off things. They would go to a real nice hotel, eat at real nice restaurants, and he'd surprise her by ordering their food in good French the whole time. All of which would take some serious cash. So he wasn't gonna turn down work from this kid, was the thing, as much as he pretty much hated him by now.

Kind of better the kid wasn't here, even if it pissed him off on principle. Roommate seemed all right.

"The people like Trevor," said Tom, when the man came back, carrying two smallish boxes, "they don't care about other people."

After the initial scare, he now felt a sense of elation, a strange new thrill at his ability to interact with the intimidating man as a peer. Maybe even a superior. He was on a confidence high. He wanted to keep talking.

"Always like this," he said. "I think maybe they never needed to work, no? So they don't understand?"

"Look, kid—," said Rick, who was holding the boxes and trying to get Tom to take them.

"I try to tell him, I do, but it doesn't serve anything."

"Sure, can you—"

"Useless, you know?"

"All right, here." Rick dropped the boxes by the front door. When he turned around to leave, Tom saw him notice the pickup parked in the driveway with some mixture of surprise and pity. Then he started walking away.

And it was then that Tom had an intuition.

"Hey, could you get me a passport?"

Rick doubled back with a perplexed, theatrically raised eyebrow that gave him a Looney Tunes-like look.

Tom checked the residential side street. A plump, mustachioed man in slacks was wheeling a heavy trash can from his garage to the curb outside his driveway. The sky was bright orange. This was the opportunity he'd been waiting for.

"Where's that accent from, anyway?" said Rick. "You French or something?"

In the end, what Trevor's dealer could get him was way better than a fake passport. Tom had to insist, because it was clear the man wasn't in the organization himself and had at best a passing knowledge of what they did, but he finally convinced him to get him in touch. It was amazing what Tom could do with a little confidence. He'd talked right past the man's last-minute resistance ("Look, kid, I can't vouch for this guy, *comprend*?") with the ease of an expert seducer, eyes on the prize, and an hour later he was texting back and forth with the head of some sort of criminal network on a securely encrypted app. It was like a superpower.

What the network did was arrange green-card marriages for cash. It was all highly professional. Nothing half-assed or amateurish or Trevor-like; these guys didn't take chances. For a substantial fee, they provided a year of assistance (about a month to set up the wedding, plus all the crucial keeping-up-appearances period to follow), extensive one-on-one and couples training for the possible (though not altogether likely, he was assured) Fraud Interview, and, best of all, a wife. Marital Citizenship Facilitation ("Green Card Scam" being a derogatory media buzzword) was a very ordinary, thriving business in this part of the world, did Tom not know?

The whole thing was very carefully scripted to ensure the highest degree of Safety and Comfort for all parties involved. All Prospective Spouses were age-appropriate (no clumsy textbook-immigrational-red-flag deals with the elderly), and were set up alone in apartments large enough to theoretically (stress on the *theoretically*) host a couple of newlyweds living together. All paperwork was taken care of. Success rates? This is not the kind of business where you can settle for 9 out of 10, son. As for prices, there was a good deal of fluctuation tied to the cost of the wedding itself. Big close-knit families called for big traditional weddings, no getting around that, narratively speaking. A Chinese man recently had to fly twenty people to Guangzhou for the ceremony just for the sake of realism, and his Arrangement had altogether come in at more than $50,000. In Tom's case, though, a seat-of-his-pants Vegas gambler with minimal and conveniently far-away family ties, a simple casino-chapel overnighter would work just fine. In fact, given an equally unattached and provably impulsive PS, it might just be their best bet. In that scenario, cost could shrink to a simply-too-good-to-pass-up $14,999: just the bare-bones attorney work and, for the most part, the Spousal Compensation Charge. He was, he would be happy to find, their ideal candidate: minimum work, minimum risk, maximum satisfaction.

For about a week he pondered the possibility. With Trevor's advice unavailable (though more than once, running into him in the living room—pride be damned—he was tempted to ask), and his brother best kept in the dark to ensure a Genuine On-Record Reaction to the news later on, Tom was left to figure this one out all by himself.

Moneywise, it was a huge decision. While half the payment could be conveniently doled out over the course of a whole year—and with his new schedule, he was sure he could make it work—the $8,000 advance was a daunting sum. He'd be cutting his net worth by almost half. Even with his very few expenses (comped food, low rent, gas so cheap in America they were practically giving it away), he'd leave himself very little room to breathe.

Still, the real issue was risk. Could he really do something like this? Come out of hiding, shine a huge spotlight on his years of illegal status, challenge USCIS head-on for one final all-or-nothing showdown? The old Tom would call him crazy. Rome Tom, the frightened child who just wanted to be left alone. Yet this wasn't about the old beta Tom, not anymore. Now: what would alpha Tom do?

They could deport him either way. Except, presently, it was a *passive* risk: always depending on someone else, always at the mercy of chance and other people's whims. If he took the MCF gamble, it'd be all on him. *He* needed to prepare for the interview. *He* needed to stick with the Narrative. *He* decided when and where the battle was fought. *Active* risk. A highway to the motherfucking danger zone.

As soon as he said yes, things sped up and blurred like a VHS on fast forward. They texted him instructions. There were things he needed to do: (1) prepare the money for the advance; (2) avoid being seen in public with other women; then, once a PS was pre-selected for him, 3) go through her social media accounts and check for Aesthetic Agreeability. In case he found her satisfactory, he was to (4) friend her *just on Facebook* (other, more intimate social media connections would be staggered at strategic stages of their "relationship" later on).

Other than that, they took care of everything. Tom's legal situation was thoroughly studied, scans of his documents sent to the network's attorney (a different number on the same encrypted, self-deleting text service), and quickly deemed 100 percent compatible with the MCF procedure. He needn't worry. The PS selection process was speedy and effective, as apparently Tom's ideal Premarital Status (which he still wasn't sure he fully understood) made him a highly desirable match for swift, no-fuss Arrangements. Everything seemed easy, streamlined. In good hands.

He attacked his duties with excitement. Positano chips were agreed upon over text as a viable payment form. In six smaller installments (cash operations over $3,000 were rumored to arouse unwanted fiscal attention) he picked up the money from the poker-room cage.

He'd never owned $1,000 chips before. Bright yellow circles with red-and-black spots around the rim, the gray center brimming with figures and letters (ONE THOUSAND DOLLARS). Now he had three. But it was the flag that gave him goose bumps. It looked just like any other chip. Like a $1 chip. Same weight too. Except it was shiny white, with the red-blue motif around the edges that gave it its nickname. And that number, $5,000, at its heart.

He thought back to the Rio, when he'd kept his $1,512 in bills—all the money he owned in the world—in an envelope paranoiacally wedged between his underwear and his perspiring butt-cheek. He thought of how, getting his huge tournament score from the cashier, he'd immediately stashed the whole thing in his pants, scared someone could see it. But now, holding the flag, he really *wanted* to be seen. It was strange. He felt a real desire to be seen fiddling with his high-denomination chips, like it was a mundane, everyday thing to do for him. It was—he figured as he lingered at the empty table right next to the cashier, the yellows and the flag in front of him on the felt, pretending he was waiting for someone—it was like the money being in chips, or the chips being in the casino, or the casino being in Las Vegas, somehow took away the shame he'd always associated with showing off wealth. The ugliness of having more than your share. The trick, of course, being that others would assume someone toying about in a casino with $8,000 in chips would have *a lot* more in his bank account. Which made it even worse.

"Can I touch it?" said a young man standing in line to change a couple stacks of $1 chips back into cash. "I'm really sorry to ask, but I've never seen one."

Tom feigned embarrassment. "I . . . sure," he said.

He handed him the flag, which the kid received in his joined hands like the sacramental host. He was younger, and truly childlike in his appearance. He must have been playing one of the limit tables in the back, with the old people. He handed the chip back almost in a hurry, afraid of holding it too long.

It was weird to admit, but the kid made his day. He'd never been in a position of such undeniable power over another human being before. It was exhilarating. Even more rewarding than his interaction with Trevor's dealer. Pure, distilled dominance. The kid had obviously assumed Tom to be a high-stakes reg, and Tom hadn't bothered correcting him. The result had been a perfect little moment, one that immediately left Tom wanting more. Was this how Trevor felt all the time? Was this how *Tom* had made Trevor feel for almost two years? He got his chip back and, with some reluctance, put it with the others in his wallet and sauntered out of the poker room. At any rate, prepare the money for the advance: check.

Avoid being seen in public with other women: check.

Last up was the social media scouting of his assigned PS. It was eerie, the blue-lettered link that would disclose the identity of his soon-to-be wife. Like he'd been given the power to part the veil of Fate, his future conveniently arranged for him in web-page form. Profiled, timelined, statused. He hesitated a moment, savoring the romantic magic of meeting the girl he would marry. He took a breath and clicked.

The girl was Asian, short, full-cheeked, and frighteningly attractive. Her photos showed a penchant for bright-colored Keds, pencils used to hold her hair up in a bun, and baseball. And sweet, lovely smiles too. He sent her a friend request on Facebook almost immediately, feeling proud of how confident and unshy he was being about it. Her name was Lily.

He asked her to marry him on their first date. On his knees, in front of actual strangers, overcoming his fears. According to the Narrative, they had been going out for a while by then.

"Which of these outfits for a roller-coaster first date? #fashion #firstimpressions #vegasrollercoaster." She showed him her Instagram pic from three months ago, taking a cheeky poll of her followers while planting the idea that she was indeed seeing someone new. It was part of the PS prepping procedure, so that clients could be assured both a speedy betrothal and a convincing, slowly built Narrative. These guys didn't take chances.

They were sitting in the faux-outdoor tiki bar at the Newport, cardboard-palmed and sunset-lit, with two tall piña coladas. Tom had chewed on the decorative pineapple wedge right away, and now he couldn't balance it on the brim of his glass. The room had a postapocalyptic feel to it, like beaches and sunsets no longer existed and they had tried to re-create them from memory using cardboard and colored glass.

Lily was even prettier than her pictures.

"I used to work here," she said. "Before I got the job at the Wiles Tower, then I left. Guess that one kinda backfired, huh?"

Tom had been instructed to make small talk. Nothing too personal, just to get a feel for the other person. He'd been told to look happy and relaxed, and if possible avoid referencing the Arrangement. Not for fear of being overheard, the MCF consultant had specified, but to start Embodying the Narrative anytime it might prove necessary.

"I mean, I'm here doing *this* now, so . . ."

Lily's bluntness veered off-script, and Tom felt confused. She still smiled, but an edge appeared that wasn't in the pictures. As much progress he felt he'd made recently, Tom wasn't sure he knew how to deal with a real conversation with her.

"So," he said, following the tentative plan he'd rehearsed in the car. "You play baseball?"

"Softball," said Lily. "*Played*, in college. Hawai'i-U, go Bows! Used to really love it, but didn't have the guts to go for it. Another gem of a life decision; starting to see a pattern here?"

"I played football at home. Although I think you would call it soccer, yes?" He chuckled. "I don't think I have the body for your *football*." He was satisfied with his delivery.

"You're a poker player, right? Ever play at the Tower?"

He was reluctant to change topics. He had two more killer jokes ready on the subject of sports and US/Europe differences. But it seemed like Lily had no interest in sticking to MCF-mandated chitchat.

"Only sometimes, when we started," he said.

"Right, I guess all the bigger games are at the Pos these days," said Lily.

"The Positano has numerous tables, yes. Do you like that hotel? You know, I grew up only two hours away from—"

"I have a friend who works there. *Had* a friend, I guess. Must be hard to find time for a call when you work a fancy center-Strip job."

Tom's pineapple wedge had finally fallen pulp-first into the drink, and he tried to fish it out using two black straws as chopsticks. Except he'd never quite mastered the use of chopsticks, and the squishy yellow chunk kept slipping away from his plastic grip and sinking back into the sand-colored liquid with an awkward plop.

"I'm sure you've seen her around," Lily was saying. "She definitely had poker-room shifts. Not sure if at the high stakes, but I bet she would. Nobody's firing *her* anytime soon, you know?"

"The Wiles Tower also is beautiful though, right? All the red and the white and gold. I always think I'm inside an expensive box of chocolates."

"There's a Forrest Gump joke in there somewhere, I'm sure," said Lily. Tom was back to laboring over his capsizing decorative fruit. With some effort he managed to lift it up against the side of the glass. It looked like a plump yellow slug climbing to the rim, leaving behind a boozy tropical trail. "Which would be spot on, since they fired me with zero notice."

"I am sorry," said Tom. He hesitated to lift the pineapple, for fear it might plummet again. Then, with a sudden rush of self-assurance, he realized he wasn't here to impress anybody. Who cares if he was clumsy, so long as he was confident in his clumsiness. Old Tom would have worried. New Tom could just go for it. He reached with two fingers inside the glass and grabbed. "So, you go back to work here now?"

"No, I'm done with casinos. Enough," said Lily. "I'm never working for a pit boss again. I want to start my own thing, you know? Something local, something for people who actually live here. Like, *normal.* Like a dog wash, something like that."

"A dog wash!" said Tom, excited at this perfect setup. "When I was younger, in Rome, for many years—"

"But of course that takes money, and unless I can marry a new poker player every six months, I don't see that happening anytime soon. Which, by the way, I think we could just get on with this thing. It's not like we have to have a three-hour date or anything."

Lily's English was pharmaceutical-ad fast, and Tom cursed himself for missing his shot. Even with almost two years of practice, it still took him twice as long as anybody else to say the same stupid thing. His syntactical engine seemed to need subordinates to rev up before it could get to the main clause, in a way that straight-to-the-point Americans never did. It was quite frustrating.

"I already got confirmation that your money arrived, so we should just do the ring and go home," said Lily. "It's not like anybody's watching us anyway, there's barely anyone in this dump. I kept telling them when they said to meet here, but the guy said it was 'narratively congruous' or whatever."

Tom had paid the advance earlier that afternoon. Dropped off, rather than paid. At a red-lit slots bar off East Trop called Dolly's Place, which Tom had found uncannily resemblant to a similar establishment in his neighborhood in Rome. The place had been called Las Vegas, and he and his brother always made fun of how shitty and un-Vegas-like it looked. He figured if the MCF went well and he was able to visit home again without losing everything, he really owed those guys an apology. They'd got it exactly right.

He was to leave the money with the bartender, a sideburn-sporting, long-haired metalhead of at least forty, after an elaborate passcode back-and-forth to confirm each other's identity that had taken Tom an embarrassingly long time to memorize ("And a few kind souls believed my genius / Was somehow hampered by the store. / It wasn't true. The truth was this: / I didn't have the brains"). Even with this reassurance, at the moment of parting forever with the first and realistically only flag he would hold for quite some time, Tom felt the first shiver of doubt cross his mind re: the whole marital operation. Was this crazy? Was he seriously trusting someone he'd never met—scratch that, some *criminals* he'd never met—with half of his earthly possessions, based on a halfhearted referral by a drug dealer he'd met once, who he'd come in contact with only by accident and through the notoriously unreliable Trevor? Were they just going to disappear as soon as he dropped off the money, and he'd never hear from them again? Was he really that stupid?

Yet something about this decision felt right. It had been rash, and maybe reckless, but it was *his*. He'd taken the reins of his life back now, and it wasn't with weak, beta doubts that he was going to get his due. It was with firm, alpha choices. With certainty. With big, confident gestures.

"Okay," he told Lily, punctuating his resolve with a bite of pineapple. The fruit had soaked up a lot of rum, and a hot, sharp taste hit his mouth like he'd put back a shot. He coughed hard, and felt his face flush a hearty red. Minor setback. "Okay," he regrouped. "I am ready to give the ring now."

@lilynori

"I said YES!!! #heproposed #engaged #VegasBride"

[Picture of a woman's left hand, diamond ring on finger. Nails bitten short, gnawed-at cuticles. Ring likely figured in multiple fake ceremonies, worn by fake brides, but is itself real. Color filter makes hand look lobstery and weird.]

Two weeks later they were married. According to the Narrative, after going crazy for a while planning a big ceremony, they'd decided that a wedding was a stupid thing to fight about, and that their love for each other was all that mattered, and tied the knot in a no-nonsense casino-chapel money-saver. The whole thing took less than half an hour. An old woman Tom was almost certain wasn't in any way related to Lily was her witness. Somehow, the bartender from Dolly's Place was Tom's. (Lily tied the man's hair up in a bun with a pencil, to make him look presentable.) Tom didn't even tell Trevor.

And so another measurable portion of Tom's life had ended, and a new, unforeseeable one had begun. They had been issued a standard, shared-custody rescued Pomeranian named Pepper, who in no time had, seemingly on his own, started the Instagram account @Pepperthedog—complete with clickbaitingly cute pictures and hilariously misspelled captions—and

Tom hadn't been able to call him anything else ever since. To substantiate their claim of newlywed happiness, the pseudo-couple had to take a real life adventure-honeymoon around the natural wonders of the Southwest. This was in keeping with their mutual love of hiking and the outdoors (Lily's real and backed by years of online evidence; Tom's doctored but unfalsifiable thanks to his very sporadic social media presence). Monument Valley, Bryce, Zion, the Grand Canyon, Antelope Canyon, and of course the Horseshoe Bend. Lily showing her very European husband the stunning scenery of her homeland ("And one day he will take me to see his! Can't wait! #blessed #inlove #VegasWife"). The whole time, Pepperthedog kept running catlike along rocky cliffs, gazing longingly at the abyss below. Who knows what *his* previous life had been.

But certainly—Tom thought as he turned around to smile at Lily for his Narrative-prescribed picture—he could now look back at his own with the wisdom of passed time. Finally, he could make sense of all those years walking in the dark, in fear, not knowing where he was headed.

He had been unmarried for twenty-six years.

13

Lindsay

Finally, the day arrived. Without the theatrical trick of winter clouds parting like a stage curtain to reveal a clear spring sky, the changing of the seasons in the desert is more like an oven slowly heating up. Nothing changes too visibly, the sky stays cloudless and blue, but as the months go by the temperature rises and the air grows teeth. Horizons start to blur and quiver like Jell-O in the distance. Throughout March and April it comes on, warmer and warmer and hotter, as the city girds itself for another season of assault from the desert sun. It was the first day of May, and Las Vegas felt ready to burn.

Lindsay had felt it since morning, the importance of this day. Eight months had passed since the article she had hoped would change the course of her career—of her life—and it felt like she'd spent all of them waiting. Watching her trail go cold and forgotten by the public; writing filler pieces for LVSun.com without even bothering to ask if they would be in the printed paper; exchanging pointless emails with two German architects who she knew would politely and unnervingly string her along forever. Waiting. And now it had arrived, the day that would give all that waiting meaning. The day she would be the first journalist in over ten years to interview Al Wiles.

The office was so large and opulent, it looked utterly ridiculous. It was an apartment-sized room, Greek-columned and Vasarely-ceilinged, with a desk so heavy and wide they must have lugged it there with a helicopter. Wiles's chair was a massive, regal, uncomfortable number that clearly predated the widespread managerial preference for ergonomic office seating. White and gold windows overlooked the Positano Sea™. Everything was so distant from everything else (desk to drawers to guest chairs to door) that the room seemed incredibly impractical as a place of work. Yet for all the obvious clumsiness of its grandeur, Lindsay found the office frightening. If any place in Las Vegas had a claim as a receptacle of real, bone-chilling power, this was it. This was the inner sanctum, the Holy of Holies. The throne room.

And it was empty.

Lindsay hesitated a full minute before moving forward, half tempted to walk back through the heavy gilded door she'd come in from, half expecting Wiles to appear out of thin air. She was nervous, which was acceptable, and actually scared, which was for starters unprofessional and more than that really not fair. It meant subscribing to the townwide hero-worship of this man, giving him the advantage of a mythic status he didn't deserve. The marble floors had large octagons of yellow and aquamarine, with what was either a sun or a flower at the center in midnight blue. It was in the stories you heard in town about him, his love for his ex-wife, the Positano itself as a grotesque, out-of-scale wedding gift, the romantic tale of lost love and endless longing. Lindsay's low heels clicked audibly as she paced forward on the decorated floors. It was in this way billionaires had of crafting an image for themselves—be it the dreamer, the visionary, the philanthropist, or, in Wiles's case, the hopeless romantic—effectively curating the discourse that surrounded them, obfuscating more grounded criticism and getting away with things utterly precluded to us mere mortals. She was now more than halfway through the Olympic-pool-size room, too far to walk back. No, Lindsay wasn't going to be fooled by the narrative this absurd office was trying to sell her. She wasn't going to be scared. It was just . . . where was he?

She took a few steps forward. The thing at the center of the octagons on the floor was almost definitely a flower. There was something odd about being in this room alone, professional or not. A room clearly designed to instill fear, or at least reverence, a place meant to humble its visitors, that nevertheless had had virtually no visitors in quite some time (or so the story went). To be admitted to it, the first in so many years, and be left there alone. Was this a special trick, a strategy of some kind? If it was, she couldn't fathom which. Had the interview already begun? Lindsay turned to the row of white-curtained windows flanked with slender Corinthian columns. She hadn't noticed it at first, but a soft current of night desert air slithered through the room. She moved forward, heels clicking on a blue sunflower on the floor. The curtains of the farthest window, closest to the desk and the office throne, wavered quietly. The window was open.

There, on a large balcony at the top-left corner of the temple-sized room, leaning over a white marble balustrade and gazing pensively into the distance, was Al Wiles.

In the end, of course, the interview had materialized on its own.

The weeks following Orson's Howard Hughes safari had been a waste of time. Caught in a double bind between betraying her brother by giving his former friends the spotlight they craved and writing about strip-mall ribbon cuttings potentially forever, Lindsay had spent days trying to arrange a meeting with Wiles through the frustratingly unprofessional familial channels at her disposal. She tried her mother, who shook her head and lamented Lindsay's unfortunate timing. Apparently Aunt Clara and Aunt Ada were not on the best of terms lately, on account of a loan Uncle John had meant to ask the senator for, which Aunt Ada'd had some reservations about and found a way to veto. Quite a pickle, really.

"Of course, all this would have been a whole lot easier if you'd agreed to be Young Women president."

"*Really*, Mom?"

"I'm just saying! You know Aunt Ada loves to get involved with the Organization anytime she can. You could have just asked her for a favor yourself!"

Lindsay thought about approaching her father. On the plus side, he was constitutionally incapable of Mom's passive-aggressiveness, and he was, after all, Aunt Clara's brother. Yet persuading her to get Uncle John to bury the fraternal hatchet for Lindsay's sake required skills that Jacob Peterson—who for all his good qualities was not exactly charismatic, and more of the good natured dinosaur that the predators left alone purely because of his size—simply didn't have. She might as well save him the embarrassment of trying.

As time went by, and Lindsay's work assignments continued to tread the fine line between paying the bills and crushing her spirits, she finally considered whether she should just reach out to Aunt Ada herself. Why did she hesitate, anyway? For her story about casino layoffs, she'd had no problem calling, emailing, fake-running-into strangers when needed. Polite and respectful, yes, but eyes always on the prizewinning article to come. So what was all this about Ada Tingey-Peterson now? Why was she going to such extreme lengths to avoid asking a very reasonable favor of a woman who'd seen her splash around in an inflatable pool with her own children in her backyard some twenty-five years ago? The truth was as obvious as it was annoying to admit: if this was to be the piece that put her on the map, her ticket to leave her family behind, then the interview should definitely not come *from* her family. It was, Mom was right, quite a pickle.

Orson, in the meantime, was a puzzle of his own. It was hard to say how he had taken their desert-road conversation about Lindsay's future, and if he was offering any clues, they were cryptic, to say the least. Should she read something into the fact that, once the new chapter of his book was ready, it turned out to be sixty-five single-spaced pages (writing drafts directly in double-spaced format was, in his words, "monstrous") about the Faustian encounter between the Mormon spirit and the power of Money? The strange meeting between Howard Hughes and Melvin Dummar was now a symbol of the Church's profound ideological shift from community of survival to real market force, with LDS banks providing the bulk of the investments for several casinos on the Strip, many of which with a subsequent history of shady and exploitative business practices. Was this what Orson had meant to write all along, or had the events of Howard's Road somehow changed his mind?

Since he'd always been a reclusive stay-in-his-room loner, she couldn't quite tell whether he was doing it more purposefully now, to avoid her. There were no hints that he was resentful, or disappointed, or gearing up for a future where she would abandon him to go live somewhere else. And for what it's worth, their baby-monitor communications were just as frequent as before. As far as she could tell, nothing had changed.

What did change was the news story. After months of absolute zilch in the way of progress or new information, just when the path to Wiles had started to look as desolate as an abandoned mining road, something strange and unforeseeable presented itself, as if on cue, at the beginning of April. A new possibility blooming out of the dead desert land.

What happened was an email from a Mike Lindgren, of Lindgren Woodworks Inc., Pahrump, NV. Lindgren, who in the letter described himself as an honest hardworking God-loving patriot, was keen on letting Lindsay know that in 1999 he'd been stiffed by Wiles to the tune of $83,600 on a wood-paneling contract for one of the lounges in the newly built Positano Luxury Resort & Casino. He claimed to have since then lost his business—established by his father in the 1940s—to a combination of crooked judges and gosh-darn bad luck. What mattered, though, he could assure Ms. Peterson (who was meanwhile reading through the man's single-paragraph prose with an upturned eyebrow of skepticism, sympathy, and faint, irrational hope), what mattered was that he was still in possession of incriminating documents *collaborating* his claim, and that he was willing to share his story with the only writer who had the gosh-darn stones to stand up to Wiles in this here town. Which he would do it himself, believe me, if the system wasn't rigged such that if you go to court most you can get is the price of your bill, no damages no nothing, and the lawyer fees set you back maybe half as much, and maybe you'd done the job on a slim profit margin in the first place because you hoped Wiles would hire you again, or tell his friends or something, and then where are you? If maybe by then the company's going under, and you're in debt, and you have no money to pay for no lawyer. Or maybe you don't even *have* a company anymore, gone, sixty years of work and sweat and splinters, gone—and all the while the old crook still claiming "the job was not well executed," every time you so much as make a sound—where are you then? Bottom line is he still had the documents, ma'am.

Lindsay read the letter again a few times over the next two days, pondering her options. It seemed pretty clear that, in and of itself, Lindgren's testimony wasn't enough to go to battle with. It was a tenuous claim, from a defunct company owned by a man who—it turned out after a quick background check—had lost his father's business to craps and Wild Turkey a lot more than to judges and bad luck. On top of that, she suspected Lindgren wasn't telling the whole story: it seemed very likely the man had at some point accepted some cash to keep the whole thing out of court. Chances were he was just sensing an opening and jumping on Lindsay's ramshackle bandwagon to pay off some debts. Rolling the dice while they were hot, as it were.

Yet the email wasn't useless. If what Lindgren said was true and Wiles hadn't paid one of his contractors, it was unlikely that this'd be a one-off occurrence. The possibility that Wiles had left a trail of unpaid bills in his years of unbridled real estate ambition opened up an entirely new line of investigation she could pursue, one that linked perfectly to her original story of unfair treatment of his employees. Maybe she didn't need to get to Wiles after all. Maybe she just needed to build a stronger case against him and let him come to her.

Something was definitely up with Orson. Pulling consecutive all-nighters, he'd managed to whip up what appeared to be the climactic section of his grad-school personal essay cum multivolume study in less than two weeks. Lindsay hadn't had time to read all of it yet (134 single-spaced pages), but it seemed like the main idea being discussed was again the inevitable downfall of a communitarian, solidarity-based society infected with the germs of individualism and money. What scared Lindsay—other than the mysteriously obtained spreadsheets detailing the history of all the loans LDS-owned banks had accorded to Nevada gaming conglomerates and real estate moguls—was the resigned matter-of-factness of it all. There was no judgment. The invisible and complete triumph of evil and the ultimate meaninglessness of human existence were described with the eerie detachment of a grade-schooler chronicling the decomposition of an apple left out in the sun for a science project. There was no stopping it, and touching it only made it worse. No one to blame either, just life taking its course. The infection didn't come from the outside: the infection was us.

Lindsay was not the dramatic type. If Orson needed help, he was mature enough to ask for it. Besides, he wouldn't be the first cosmic nihilist to live an incoherently serene life into ripe and fat old age. Yet even by his standards, the bleakness of his most recent work did seem a tad extreme. Lindsay knew that seeing their road-trip argument as the real meaning beneath Orson's narrative would be an act of narcissism he would scoff at. But if "everything was a symbol of everything," then it wasn't all that unlikely she could have played a role in this pessimistic downturn. It was over a week since she'd last seen him, even though she'd spoken to him on the baby monitors often. It was hard to tell whether he had left the apartment at all in this interval, but he must have timed his excursions to kitchen and bathroom carefully to avoid running into her.

Not that she'd been home all that much. With a whole new investigative trail to follow, on top of her dull but still time-consuming work churning out right-column fillers for LVSun.com, she was slipping into an alarming routine of constant work. Wiles's contractors over the years ranked in the hundreds (he appeared to be rather promiscuous in his professional allegiances, with barely any company signed on for more than a couple jobs), and Lindsay had to approach them discreetly to avoid arousing suspicion. After compiling an extensive list of companies, she divided them into tiers of likelihood of misconduct: at the bottom of the list she put companies that had worked with Wiles multiple times, and the ones that had been hired on big, expensive projects—like populating and supervising an actual sea, or building geologically authentic caves in the middle of a city; at the top, one-off contractors hired for things like bathroom stall doors in second-rate properties, staff changing-room lockers, and so on. It was an enormous amount of work, and she had no guarantee it would lead anywhere.

What she discovered, though, before anything at all related to the story, was that as long as she could envision what she was doing as life-changing—a gateway to success—then no amount of work would ever be too much. Within the confines of the Wiles story, she was her own boss. And as it turned out, she was a mean, demanding boss who was never satisfied. Yet all the effort she unblinkingly poured into the work now felt conditional on her ability to tell herself that something great was coming: she could only accept her life as it was if she truly believed it was about to change. And as the weeks went by, and the names that had seemed the most promising got crossed off the top of her list, and her preoccupation with her increasingly isolated brother grew and grew—alongside a fear that he'd become so dependent on her that moving away from Vegas (and therefore him) would soon become downright cruel—her ability to believe in the success story she kept telling herself was starting to wane.

And then Wiles did come to her. Unsolicited. It happened with an email, a formal invitation delivered in Hendrik Vogelsang's stilted English as a response to her original inquiry from eight months earlier. As if they'd only seen it now, and hadn't already declined that one and several other requests after it. Herr Wiles, it said, would be pleased to receive her for a conversation in the evening of Friday, May 1st. Because Herr Wiles feels himself better in the nights, they would meet themselves at 11:00 p.m., in the private office in the North Wing of the Positano. They would send a car to pick her up. No photographs or video cameras permitted. Herr Wiles was eager to talk to her, he'd heard very good things about her. Friday. 11:00 p.m. North Wing. And that was it.

In the morning, in the crackling voice coming from the baby monitors, she'd asked Orson about it. She was eating breakfast in the living room, and was unsure whether Orson had just woken up or hadn't gone to bed still.

"Why Wiles, after all?" she said. "Now that this is actually happening, suddenly I'm not so sure."

"You mean the moral question," said Orson.

"I mean, what if this story I'm building is just that, a story?"

"Truth and narrative. That old chestnut."

"I'm not excusing him," said Lindsay. "What he did to those waitresses was terrible. But then nothing else happened, and I still went after him, month after month, just trying to find something. All those lists of contractors—I was really *hoping* he'd done something bad there, you know? In the end, he's just an old man who lives alone and doesn't talk to anybody. And the city loves him. Why am I so determined to prove he's a monster?"

There was a noise of ruffling sheets, something falling on the floor, indiscernible curses. Orson's voice came back after a long pause.

"Are you asking if it's self-serving? Of course it is! We've talked about this too." It was the first reference to their road trip he'd made since they got back. He must be moving around the room now, his words muffled by distance and little noises. "It's a very smart career move, and I'm sure he deserves it. Why the doubts now?"

"It's because I'm meeting him tonight, I think. Makes me afraid I don't have the moral authority to confront him. To expose him."

"Oh, but you don't, absolutely," said Orson, closer to the microphone. Lindsay rolled her eyes. "Just as I have no place whining about the failure of the communitarian dream. There's darkness everywhere, perhaps especially in ourselves. I mean definitely in me, I'm the worst."

"I doubt that."

"And recent developments in my research have convinced me that your audience too, the city itself, is a pretty hopeless case."

"Recent developments?"

"So all in all, not a lot of moral authority going around."

He came out of his room into the living room, fully dressed. He looked thin, and he needed a shave and a haircut, but he was basically himself. There was even, to Lindsay's surprise, a kind of strained cheer about him.

"Good thing is, there's definitely *a ton* of darkness in Wiles, just dying to come out. Like, really awful, damning stuff oozing out, just wait and see. So as selfish as what you're doing is, it's also probably not the absolute worst thing you could do, you know, for the world and stuff."

"You should be a motivational speaker."

He stole a piece of toast from her plate and took a bite. "Oh, I'm not sure I could be *that* bad."

The old man peered down at the fake sea beneath them with the wistfulness of a ship's captain. He wore a blue suit with a gold tie, and black velvet moccasins. Through their talk, he'd kept his back to the office window, facing the desert night.

Lindsay didn't know what she'd expected Wiles to look like. For over a decade, the man had basically been a ghost, haunting the Positano in sparse, more-legend-than-fact apparitions. He'd been portrayed in no more than four pictures, but these looked so staged and wax-museumish that it was honestly hard to tell if the man in them was a living, breathing organism or some kind of physical or digital avatar. Rumors of his extreme hermitism and agoraphobia were common knowledge in town, and who knows what that much loneliness could do to a man's appearance. In short, she was ready for anything. But if she had to be honest, she was half-predicting something unnaturally decrepit (he was only seventy-two, after all), or some secret physical shame he'd decided to hide from the world.

But here, high above the city he'd helped build, the man looked shockingly ordinary. He was shorter than Lindsay, as broad-shouldered as her, and had a full head of what appeared to be his own unruly and almost hiply-styled brown-dyed hair. The skin of his face was wrinkled, but it didn't look like he'd taken any surgical shortcuts to prevent that. Between the folds, the small, searching eyes of a man who's over time come to believe himself a preternaturally gifted judge of character, the kind, piercing look of self-aware intelligence of the true self-made man.

He turned to look at her. A cool breeze swept the balcony, and Lindsay was surprised by the odd feeling of being at the top of a real mountain. She hadn't realized how high up they were before she'd stepped outside. The little houses perched along the slope seemed distant and small. The city itself, with its lights, its streets, its faint noises down below, seemed to recede, to hide itself at the horizon past a murmuring, moonlit sea, as if it too wanted to preserve the illusion. Somehow, Al Wiles's firm belief in the reality of the world he'd created was enough to bring it to life for the people around him.

"I wonder if we could speak off the record now, perhaps?" he said.

Lindsay stepped closer to the edge, careful to remain at a polite distance from her host.

"Of course," she said. "Off the record."

"I'm glad. Because what we just discussed, I've got to be honest, is not the only reason I invited you here tonight."

Wiles's answers to Lindsay's questions had been simple but impeccable. From a legal standpoint, of course, Lindsay didn't have much of a case at the moment (not after her investigation on Wiles's contractors had led nowhere, and no suspicious layoffs had been reported in the last few months, and her once key witness had been compensated and had since defected to porn). But Wiles hadn't contented himself with merely fending off potential liabilities; he had been compassionate and well-spoken, expressing a seemingly sincere desire to give the gaming industry a more humane look in the future. There were initiatives, projects, and an ongoing, productive dialogue with the union to make sure the voices of the workers were heard. Did Lindsay know, for example, that a recent change in the Complementary Beverage Packaging Policy, in agreement with the union, had resulted in an estimated 3 percent increase in the Gratuity Revenue of all floor waitressing personnel, all of it money in their pockets? His own idea, that one, which had been described as "revolutionary" by certain union representatives. He'd always been a bit of a revolutionary, after all. He grinned.

"No, Ms. Peterson, I thought we could have a more frank conversation. A conversation about the future. Mine, yours, this city's."

She nodded.

For a while, Wiles looked intent on gathering his thoughts. Lindsay wondered if the focus and composure he'd maintained for the length of the official interview had come at a price—he looked tired now.

"Do you know what makes this balcony special, Ms. Peterson?" he said. "It's not the view, though I'd say you don't see something like this every day."

"It's beautiful," conceded Lindsay.

"It really is, isn't it? But it's something else that makes this place unique." He inhaled deeply through his nose. "It's the *air*. The breeze. See, this one, together with its twin in my private residence, is the only open balcony in the whole property. The only place where you can feel this wind on your skin. It wasn't always like this: back when we built it, every deluxe room and every suite had its own beautiful balcony, and even standard rooms had a shared outside space, one for every eight rooms. I never intended the desert breeze to be a private magic, just for me."

He paused, again looking at the sea.

"But then something happened. It was right after we opened—you must have been really young then, or you might remember. A forty-five-year-old man from Oklahoma who was staying in one of the higher deluxe rooms had a bad night at blackjack. He went back to his duplex, drank all the bottles in the minibar, and jumped off.

"It was horrible. His room was right above those jagged rocks over there. The pictures they took . . . And then it happened again, and again. Four more times within the first six months of opening. The press had a field day. Some hack in New York wrote about 'the ineffable feeling of Death in the city itself; the Venice of America.' The public had an awful phrase for it, they called it 'joining the Positano Diving Team.' It was truly horrible."

For a moment, Lindsay was aware of being alone on the balcony of a high-rise with an allegedly crazy old man, whose questionable business conduct she'd exposed, reminiscing about people jumping off. It was irrational, and yet she felt her muscles tighten and her fists clench.

"So we had to close them all up. No choice, really. My architects encased them in glass, maybe you've seen one? It was all really tastefully done, really top-class work, though of course it's not the same. But we'd learned our lesson. We make mistakes, and we must make up for them."

"Is that what we're doing tonight?" Lindsay said. "Making up for a mistake?"

Wiles looked surprised by the question, although Lindsay had just repeated his words.

"The world," he said after some time. "The world is complicated, Ms. Peterson. The future . . . see, when I first moved here, I thought the key to the future was change. Real estate, finance, politics. Things needed to move to stay alive, get bigger, better. I thought it was up to us to craft a better future, to compete over it. To build it, stone by stone. And I did, or I thought I did.

"But the more time I spent watching Las Vegas from above, the more I understood what the future is. Maybe I just got old. But I watched it for so long, Ms. Peterson, all these years. I saw the city grow, all these new people coming. You know how when you don't see someone for ten years and then you see them again, they look completely changed, a new person almost? But when you see them every day, those changes are so gradual and small that you don't notice them. They slip past you. That's what the future is. The future is not a still image of this town twenty years from now. The future is all those minutes and days slipping change past you, every day just a little bit different from the one that came before, so that you wake up one day and everything has changed. Everything has died."

His tone was different now. There was a tidal nature to his talking, an ebb and flow, coherent though slightly associative segments of speech followed by unnaturally long pauses. It reminded Lindsay of Orson's prose.

He seemed to barely hear her words, just a rhythmic counterpoint to his train of thought. Lindsay found herself wondering whether he had stopped meeting people because of how hard it'd become for him to talk to them, or if he'd forgotten how to interact with others as a result of his voluntary seclusion. Maybe it was both.

"It's a beautiful town to just watch, this one. So many stories, so many myths, so many struggles. Stare at it long enough and you'll lose yourself in it. I know I have. You will slowly convince yourself that all those stories amount to some kind of meaning. That you could find a single sentence, an idea that Las Vegas represents, a true essence this city is whispering to anybody who'll stick around long enough to hear it. You know, I had dinner with Andre Agassi once. He told me that when you grow up in Las Vegas—the town that was stolen away from the desert—you grow up believing that miracles really do happen. Don't you think that's lovely?"

"Mr. Agassi has a way with words," said Lindsay.

Wiles didn't seem to hear her.

"It's lovely, but that too is an abstraction. An illusion of meaning. The truth is that this town is just a town, Ms. Peterson, a place where people live. There is no large, overarching metaphor to it, no glorious trajectory we need to steer it along. Finally you realize that the key to the future is not change at all: it's defending what we love from the invisible force of time."

If his image as a romantic was in fact a curated project, Wiles could certainly still commit to it well. Yet something in his words reminded Lindsay of what Orson had told her over breakfast. *A darkness dying to come out.*

"I have to confess," she said, "that I'm afraid of what defending this town from change would look like. What it would imply."

"I've been afraid too, for quite some time. But my position entails a responsibility, Ms. Peterson. To what we created, to what we value. A legacy."

"So what happens now? How does one make up for a mistake?"

"A mistake?" said Wiles. "Yes, a mistake. A misunderstanding about what it is that needs to be protected. I no longer want to change this city, but I will defend it with all of my strength. And . . . and . . . with all the allies I can get."

"Allies?"

A pause.

"Allies. The people who love this city like I do. Like you do too, Ms. Peterson. It takes true dedication to wade through thirty years of my contracts and work relations in search of impropriety." Something cold went down Lindsay's spine. Wiles's focus sizzled back alive. "And what else could you be so dedicated to, if not our beautiful city?"

Cards on the table, then. Below them, the city strutted the shiny night-time dress Lindsay knew to be a facade, a diversion for the tourists. Everything is a metaphor, according to her brother. Nothing is, or so Wiles said. Lindsay couldn't help looking down at the sharp rocks where a man's body, his mind loosened of primal fears by minibar booze, had met its explosive fate.

"I'm just doing my job, sir."

"And you are good at it too. And your good work, I can assure you, has not gone unnoticed. There's something I wish to talk to you about, but . . . why don't we go inside?"

In the yellow light of the office, Wiles appeared suddenly ten years older. There was a weight to his steps, and he looked so small next to his giant furniture, so vulnerable. It occurred to Lindsay that what she'd taken as a strategy to intimidate her—leaving her alone in the room, meeting her outside, on the balcony—was probably just a mark of his own insecurity.

"Did you know," he said once he sat down, "that toward the end of his life in Vegas, all of Howard Hughes's closest collaborators were Mormons?"

Lindsay couldn't help laughing.

"So I've heard."

"He said they were more trustworthy, when it comes to cash. And God knows the old man knew from experience about people stealing money from him."

"An endemic problem in the business, I'm sure."

"You don't know the half of it. But yes, his private 'secretary-nurses,' whatever the hell those were, the CEO of his holding company, his chief of corporate PR, you name it. All Mormons. There's a long, good history of collaboration between us casino men and the Church. A long history!"

That's one way to look at it, thought Lindsay, still smiling.

"We built this city together, we and you," said Wiles. "There is even a strange story about Hughes's will and the LDS church."

"Melvin Dummar," said Lindsay. "I know that story."

"Oh, you do!"

"Maybe a myth, but a fun one, right?"

"Absolutely, Ms. Peterson, absolutely. Of course, there is a natural under-standing between us. We built this city together, you and we."

There was something exhausting in talking to Wiles. The fear and nervousness she'd felt at the start were still there, but they had been stretched through so many detours and odd skips that it was getting hard to take them seriously. She wanted to talk to the sinister billionaire, but Wiles kept slipping out of his role and, rather anticlimactically, into that of a plain old man. Lindsay could see him once again lose his momentum, but she decided to hold him in it. Whatever the point of this strange meeting was going to be, she felt they were finally close to it.

"You mentioned something you wanted to talk to me about . . ."

He looked up, meeting her eyes with a suddenly fierce look.

"I am going to save this city, Ms. Peterson," he said. "This city, its industry, my legacy. I am going to make sure Las Vegas survives me the way I built it to be. I will make sure my story, my struggle, all *this* . . ." His voice trembled as he left the sentenced unfinished. "I am going to save Las Vegas from itself, Ms. Peterson, and I would like *you* to be one of my allies."

"Me?" said Lindsay. "What could I possibly—"

"I am going to announce something big next week. Something that will change the industry forever, and save Las Vegas from decline. I am willing to give you the exclusive, in an interview for your paper, if you agree to work with me on a project that is very important to me."

"A project?"

"All in due time," said Wiles. "First, I have something I made for you, something I would like you to sign."

Lindsay reached for the stapled sheets of legal-looking print.

"This is—"

"See, I have a special talent for nondisclosure agreements. It's a bit of a hobby of mine, in fact." He grinned. "You always want to stay as far away from lawyers as you can, trust me."

"Mr. Wiles, I am a journalist, you know I cannot—"

"Only covers what you will *see* once we go down. No need to worry. The whole thing will be public in a matter of days anyway."

"Down?"

Wiles moved to get up from his incongruously large chair.

"All the way down," he said.

14

Ray

If there is one thing poker players eventually agree on, it's that the game has taught them some very valuable lessons about life. But while to the Kenny Rogers generation these lessons amounted to an ill-defined shrewdness or world-savvy, the post-online wave of poker nerds distilled its wisdom from the nonfiction of Nassim Taleb and Malcolm Gladwell. They learned to worry only about what they could control; to accept the overwhelming power of chance in all human affairs; to be skeptical of success, always looking to the other side of the bell curve. They were initiates, chosen adepts able to see through the cognitive biases that cloud ordinary minds, and look straight into the hidden matrix of reality. Expected Value was their gospel, result-orientedness their mortal sin. Emotions couldn't fuck with them.

It is therefore no surprise that, at the beginning of the spring of 2015, Ray Jackson found himself charting morality as a mathematical problem of knowable solution.

Up until now he'd taken for granted that playing by the rules was the only possible route to success. His stated goal was to be the best, and the best don't cheat. He would craft his happiness by beating his competition fair and square, prevailing through his wits and mental strength.

Yet Logan's proposition posed a dilemma: If given the chance to make a ton of money by less-than-unimpeachable means, would he take it? If he agreed to play Logan's game, making an easy living off of drunk businessmen, he wouldn't be the best. In fact, he would have qualms about even calling himself a real poker player. But his fears about the future would be gone, and in no time he would again be a wealthy young man, someone who'd *made it*. It was, he realized, a question he'd managed to keep at bay throughout his years of meteoric success, when the two things had proceeded conveniently parallel: Did he really want to be the best at poker, or did he just want to be rich?

In the aftermath of Eike's party at the Reef, Logan had spelled out the terms of his offer. All the more after the whole pool-cue/money-cake debacle, he needed to reduce his appearances in the Positano PR to the bare minimum. With Bryan involved, the other regs had quickly fallen in line, taking a vocal stand against what was becoming known as Poachgate. Floor personnel had been alerted to Logan's dealings, and strongly discouraged from taking any form of gratuity in exchange for information (by penalty of immediate tip-embargo from all the other regs). Requests to have the traitor eighty-sixed from the Pos for good had been extended and turned down on insufficient proof, but it was fair to assume he was now under special surveillance. In short, Logan had more or less officially become persona non grata.

Yet he still needed access to the poker room to cherry-pick the best spots and lure them away to his friendly neighborhood private game. It was vital to ensure a healthy turnover to his business. And if he couldn't be there himself, then what he needed was a spy. A reg. More specifically, a reg who was uninvolved enough with the others to conduct recognizance work undisturbed, but who could play daily in the high-stakes room without being seen as an outsider, someone to keep an eye on.

Ray was just perfect.

The deal was simple: be Logan's eyes and ears in the Positano poker room, in exchange for a seat at the juiciest game in town. One game per week, as soon as he found him his first player.

"He's a dick," said Bryan.

"He's *such* a dick," said Calvin.

"I've been telling you guys for months, he's a fat fucking dick," said JJ.

"Don't say that," said Calvin.

"But I have! I told you guys at this very table: 'Logan is a fat cheating short-armed dick,'" said JJ.

"You shouldn't call him fat," said Calvin.

"I scoop JJ, and I get one from you," said Bryan. JJ tossed him six green $25 chips, and Calvin slid him one.

The three of them were sitting at table 14, playing open-face Chinese poker to pass the time. OFC was a fast-paced, high-variance, rather dumb game that it was considered lame to take very seriously. Nonetheless, all players involved secretly thought themselves wizards, and long-term profitable at it. They were setting their starting hand of five cards faceup on the table for the next round when Ray found them.

"We thought you'd gone back online," said Calvin.

"Haven't seen you in a while," said JJ.

"Thought you'd realized we have it even worse than you guys on Poker-Stars and left," said Calvin.

"Hi," said Bryan.

"Hi," said Ray. "How have the games been?"

"What games?" sneered Calvin.

"That watch-collecting *above-average-weight* lying scumbag dick—," said JJ.

"Room's been dry all week," said Bryan. "Eike's downstairs playing five/ten right now."

"The horror!" said Calvin.

A slump in the games was not unheard of, but this was something else entirely. Ray looked around at the almost empty room. Four TV screens on the walls showing the same blowout NBA game; a gray-shirted cleaning lady emptying out 330 ml Fiji bottles from the wastebasket in the corner; three friends trading a few friendly thousands back and forth at a dumb card game. And a dealer, of course, though at this point he barely noticed them anymore.

He had mixed feelings. On the one hand, the physical impossibility of providing for himself by honest means would make his defection to the dark side an easier choice. No moral decision trees to parse, after all. On the other hand, if the Positano game died, his utility to Logan would dissipate, and he might not be offered that lifesaving seat in the first place.

"I'll go get money from my box," he said. "Maybe a game will start soon."

"Sure," said JJ, pointing at the woman in the corner, who was so short the trash bag flung over her shoulder brushed the carpeted floor. "See that spot over there? She wants to start fifty/a hundred in a minute."

"Dude . . . ," said Calvin.

"Right, right, sorry," said JJ, handing the woman a $1 chip as she walked by their table to reach her cart at the bottom of the steps. She nodded, but when her eyes darted upward at the players, they looked wild and scared.

"I'm in Fantasyland next round," said Bryan, signaling the huge bonus he would get in the following hand having locked a pair of kings up top. "And I get nineteen from you, and fourteen from you."

He scoffed at being paid his $825 in greens.

Ray felt his guts twist in a knot when he opened his box. In the small empty security room behind the PR cage, he turned his head left and right, like a boy who's snuck into the adult section of a video store, to make sure he was really alone. Nobody else could see what was in his box. Or rather, what *wasn't* in it.

A player's box at the Positano looked like a folder drawer in an office registry: small square metal section, deceptively deep and capacious when pulled out. They were offered as a free service to returning players at the high-stakes tables. A few months ago, before Eike had even won that milly at LAPC, Ray had casually glanced at the contents of his box while they both got ready for a session: entire racks[1] of yellows and flags neatly stacked against the outer wall of the drawer on one side, several hefty bricks of $100 bills wrapped in gold-rimmed paper bands on the other. The bankroll of a real winner. There was something hypnotic about the sight of that much money in such a physical, tangible form, and Ray'd had to force himself to look away before Eike noticed him. It may have been because he'd had large sums once and lost them, or because when he'd had money, it had always been invisible, the numerical bottom line on a dry web page, but since he'd moved to Vegas, Ray had more than once caught himself staring at other people's chips with piratical lust.

There were only a handful of chips left in his box now. According to the rules of proper bankroll management[2] online players considered little less than sacred, not only did Ray not have enough to play the high stakes anymore, he was rather short even for $5/$10. Sure, he had some rainy-day funds stashed away in a Canadian bank account, so this wasn't all his net worth. And sure, proper bankroll management for live poker probably had much looser rules than online poker did.[3] He had a hunch most of those $5/$10 regs were playing on bankrolls that would be risky for a $2/$5 player, the $2/$5 guys gambling on $1/$3 money, the $1/$3 crowd basically broke. But this was VFlnd3r he was talking about, i.e. himself, i.e. the player who could not, absolutely *could not* fail. And looking down at the meager left-overs of his empire, rattling like loose change around his box, he felt closer to Tragedy than ever before. He might as well admit it: his plan to move to Vegas to salvage his career had not worked.

Perhaps he had been looking at the moral quandary in front of him all wrong. Perhaps live poker—that brutish simplified version of the complex art he'd mastered over the years—was faced with its own solved-game

---

1 Plastic containers for casino chips. Each holds five stacks, i.e. 20 chips, for a total of 100 chips.
2 Thou shalt not buy in at a table for more than 1 percent of thy bankroll. Ideally, 0.5 percent or even less, just to play it safe.
3 Larger mathematical edge over one's opponents = lower variance = lower Risk of Ruin. In theory.

scenario, much like online poker. What did it matter that the outside threat was not the unbeatable perfection of a transhuman computer hive mind, but mankind's own inability to come up with a fair distribution of available assets? What was the difference between the immaculate Cardanus and that conniving little shit Logan, if neither could be beat? It was, yes, a more trivial, a less noble problem. But as far as he could tell, it was an equally unsolvable one. It wasn't a moral issue—how could he not see it?—but a strictly rational one. Problem: How does one beat a solved game? Consider tic-tac-toe as an example: How do you win a game of tic-tac-toe? Answer: you can't. The only way to win is to give radical meaning to the word *win*: hit your opponent over the head; drug him; or better yet, play against an idiot. Or, well, don't play at all. Perhaps live poker too had become, through the greed and incapacity for cooperation of its agents, a no-technical-solution problem, a state of impasse that no amount of thinking could overcome organically. Perhaps he needed to change the rules. It seemed to him like all the other regs, Bryan, JJ, Calvin, all the players anguishing over the environment problem and the future of the game, were all trying to find ways to avoid a shitty future *without relinquishing any of the privileges they now enjoyed*. And that couldn't work, could it? If the problem of the unfair distribution of assets in the future of poker didn't have a technical solution, then conscience was what needed to be reformed. A change of heart was due.

Logan was right. The only solution was to game the system.

He emptied the contents of his box into his pockets and headed back up the steps of the poker room.

The man was standing maybe ten feet away from the table, just up the steps to the high-stakes room. Ray hadn't seen him at first, his sepia suit matching the poker room's decor with the precision of camouflage gear. But the guys were playing actual poker now, three-handed, sloth-paced No Limit Hold'em, and the only possible explanation was that they must be advertising for a spot.

And Ray could see why. The man was probably in his sixties, and had the kind of elegance that, in just a few months as a live player, Ray had come to associate with lifelong familiarity with serious money. Three-piece suit, pocket handkerchief, understated confidence. In spite of Logan's teachings, Ray still knew nothing about watches, but he decided the unostentatious, leather-banded number the man was sporting had to be at least a Rolex. No cufflinks, no rings. And what had Logan said about shoes? Ray felt his hand instinctively reach into his pocket for his phone. Maybe this was it. Maybe he could get it over with tonight.

A blond waitress Ray had never seen brought the man a tea-colored drink on ice. She looked so young he wondered how she could be of age to even work there. The man tipped her with a bill, not a casino chip, and she folded and placed it in a cup on her small, round tray. She looked around to check the table numbers in the room, the same five numbers that hadn't changed in years. She must be new.

The transition, Ray guessed, must have been seamless and silent: Bryan whispering "Hold'em" to the dealer after the last hand of OFC, maybe a $5 tip slid toward her to accompany the request, everybody involved instantly understanding what needed to be done. An unrehearsed, perfect choreography. And now they were playing, with the patience of three fishermen in multipocketed vests, sitting by the docks in the early-morning sunlight, waiting for a bite. No one would walk up to the man to ask him if he wanted to play. They would just let him stew like that for a bit, his neck craned forward to follow the action at the table, the blood in his veins starting to boil from the excitement, an irresistible desire to sit down and play taking hold. Finally, Carol, the woman at the podium—she of the professional pantsuit and motherly smile—would accost him and let him know the table limits, asking if she could assist him in getting chips. Always a member of the staff, *never* a player. Just the kind of rule Logan would break in a heartbeat.

"It is a fascinating game, yours," the man told Ray, who was still standing behind table 14, a rack containing most of his earthly possessions in one hand, lost in thought. "One could watch for hours and never get tired."

British. Ray gripped his phone tighter, still in his pants pocket.

"It's stimulating," he heard himself improvise. "Challenging. A true battle of minds."

"How wonderfully exciting," said the man. "Do you play often?'"

"Quite often, yes. I love the game deeply."

Ray wasn't supposed to linger like that. Etiquette dictated he sit down immediately, putting as many chips in play as possible, looking happy, relaxed. Engaging a spot in conversation away from the table could distract him, bore him, even scare him off for good. He made an effort to avoid Bryan's stare, which he could feel scolding him from a distance.

"You must be quite good at it," said the man.

"People think it's about the money," said Ray. "But that's not the point. It's about the duel, the fight, you know?"

"A game of chess," said the man.

"And a test of courage and will at the same time."

"Certainly, that too."

JJ was collecting a large pot he'd won off Bryan, a flopped straight against his opponent's rivered two pair.

"Of all casino games, poker alone confronts a man with the true nature of life. The struggle for survival. A war fought only with the weapons of our brains, nerves, and hearts."

He wasn't sure what he was doing. Frozen in place, not playing while others were, he was shamelessly ad-libbing on Logan's bullshit repertoire to seduce a spot. With so much on the line, the first potentially good game in weeks hanging now on Ray's ability as a salesman, JJ, Calvin, even Bryan, would never say anything. Sure, he was out of line, but at this point they were all secretly hoping he could pull it off. Maybe they even liked him for it. Certainly they were surprised, at least as surprised as he was.

And all the while Ray could feel the man's stare dart to the flags in his chip rack like sudden bursts of electricity, so quick and heated with desire that it looked like he would melt them. And Ray knew exactly what he needed to say.

"It's not about the money," he said. "Especially when it looks like it's all about the money, then it's definitely *not* about the money."

The man raised his eyes to meet Ray's.

"How rude of me," he said. "I was so rapt in the game, I've forgone all introductions. My apologies. My name is Walter Simmons." He extended a hand, and Ray shook it, releasing his phone in his pocket.

"Ray Jackson."

"Would you like me to get you chips, sir?" Carol walked up to them from the podium in the rubber-soled pianissimo of expert luxury customer care. Ray noticed the slightest jitter of surprise in the man's composure. "The table has a twenty-five-hundred dollars minimum, no max."

"Oh, I'm afraid I can't stay long, madam," said the man. "I was here looking for a friend, but I seem to have come at a wrong time." He glanced around theatrically, as if to show that whoever he was looking for was indeed not there. Ray had never noticed that the pattern of the floor carpet was a mangrove-like tangle of leaves and roots.

"Oh, that's all right, you can stay as long as you wish, sir," said Carol. "And do come back any time. After all, we *are* here twenty-four/seven!"

Unseen from the quiet of the wooden podium just up the steps, Carol must have developed a skill of her own at profiling newcomers. Ray wondered if she'd noticed the same things he had, or if her ability to run a visual credit score far exceeded his (and maybe even Logan's). Whatever it was, she'd deemed it enough to lift the usual ban on loitering and spectating in the high-stakes area for this man.

"Thank you."

Several things happened as soon as the man left. Ray sat down and placed his rack at seat 6, with no intention whatsoever to join the game in progress. The game itself, as soon as the last hand was completed, reverted to open-face Chinese poker as seamlessly as it had changed to Hold'em. Finally, three very inquisitive sets of eyes turned to Ray, waiting for him to say something.

The right play was unclear. Technically, he'd done nothing wrong: he might have broken the rules of spot engagement, but he had been spoken to first; his words had been worryingly Loganesque, yes, but for all the others knew, he was just trying to get them all a good game for the day. Nothing shady about that. Of course what he really was doing was trying to get Logan a new toy to play with, in exchange for a seat at the table of Morally Objectionable Shortcuts. But they couldn't possibly know that, could they? Still, getting on a high horse about this was probably just asking for trouble. It was like he was being tried for a crime he hadn't committed, but had every intention of committing as soon as possible.

"Well, he's not the only one who can do it, right?" said Ray, after a long awkward pause. "Maybe we should give his way a chance too. We keep playing it fair and we stick to these codes of ethics, and look where it's got us." He gestured toward the spread of face-up cards on the table where the three regs were setting their top, middle, and bottom.[4] It took him a few seconds to notice he'd said *us*, for the first time qualifying himself as a Positano reg. One of the guys.

"That's not how we do things," said Bryan.

It took Ray no time at all to notice the tone of that *we*.

"I mean, he's right, though," said JJ.

"That guy was never playing," said Bryan.

"Well, how could we know without asking him?" said Ray.

"At least he gave it a shot," said JJ. Stirring the pot of JJ big boy's desire for action over passivity had been a good call. It seemed to Ray like JJ's whole plan in the face of adversity was merely to go on record as an interventionist, regardless of strategic considerations. He seemed cool with the demise of his only means of sustenance, provided he could prove

---

4   In OFC, players are progressively dealt thirteen cards, which need to be set in two full five-card hands (bottom and middle) and a three-card hand (top). Dealing methods and scoring systems can get fairly byzantine and tend to favor large, exciting swings (i.e. variance). The whole thing is beyond stupid, according to Ray.

he'd said all along that something needed to be done. By someone. At some point.

"He was never playing," Bryan said again.

"He was never playing because he was looking for his friend. His fat scumbag friend," said Calvin.

"Dude!" said JJ.

"No, fuck it, you're right, he's fat. He got to that guy already. How the fuck does he do it?"

"I've never seen that guy in here before," said Bryan.

"Same," said Calvin.

"I scoop both of you, eight and twelve," said JJ. "Ray, do you need those greens if you're not gonna play? Can you give me two stacks for a yellow? Cool."

"He must have some underground network or something," said Calvin. "Like, they pick them up at the airport or some shit."

"Let's not get carried away here," said Bryan. "He's not James Bond, he's a guy who can't touch his dick standing up."

Jane, the dealer, burst into laughter mid-shuffle. She was in her fifties, had short hair, and dealt extremely fast and quiet. The four men exchanged awkward looks as they suddenly remembered she was there.

"Well, he's doing *something*, though," said JJ, after a beat. "What are we doing to stop him?"

"Got any ideas?" said Bryan with a sneer. It was the same conclusion Ray had privately reached before the party at the Reef: there was nothing they could do about it. Logan had won.

"Actually—"

By the beginning of his sixth month in Las Vegas, Ray Jackson may not have acquired much in the way of monetary results or personal happiness, but he'd put together an impressive collection of habits. When it came to anything substantial—understanding of the underlying mathematical workings of the world, net worth, and so on—he didn't resemble a Vegas reg any more than he had on Thanksgiving. But in the obsessive, almost superstitious patterning of his life, he was by now a Positano reg through and through. In the PR, he sat at the same seat on table 14 every day (seat 6, facing the dealer and a little to the left), ordered the same drink (a hot green tea with mint and honey), and panicked alone in the security room by his box. At home, he ate breakfast at nine a.m. while listening to *The Singularity Is Near* podcast, patted the bronze owl mailbox on his way out, and chewed anxiously on the neck of his T-shirt from eleven p.m. to two a.m. before falling into time-wasting human sleep.

He hadn't planned for it, but this regularity turned out to give him some solace. In Toronto, at the end of his downswing and post-Cardanus, his internal OS had frozen stuck, and his brain had pressed some kind of eject button that forced him to relocate and reinvent himself. But something about Vegas seemed to easily override his emergency protocols. There was something scientific, something experimental, about all this. He was compiling a rigorous set of data, building a proper sample size detailing the existence of a theoretically winning poker player faced with the protracted whims of variance and the progressive deterioration of the poker economy as a whole. He might go broke, yes, but he would go broke with discipline. Studiously. Little by little.

That is, of course, unless he managed to sell out everything he'd ever believed in and save himself. If a rationally superior strategy presented itself—exploiting the human imperfection of the market for his personal gain—he was now ready to take it, he was sure.

He started leading a double life. At the Positano, where mediocre games were at least running again—around the occasional short-stacked sunglass-wearing Russian, or the cranky senior from Florida, complaining about how much better the games were back home—he conspired with the others to bring Logan down through an all-out smear campaign. It was JJ's idea, half-heartedly agreed upon by the others, to somehow get to Logan's spots and convince them that he was cheating, and that his private game was rigged.[5] At home, he texted Logan updates of the most recent table lineups and kept asking for a seat in next week's game.

Neither front showed much progress: none of the regs seemed to have the social clout to do any real damage to Logan's reputation; and as far as getting a seat at the Shibuya, Ray was starting to feel strung along like a backup prom date. Back at the Reef, in the elevator, Logan had explained how he needed another reg on rotation to fill empty seats and keep his game going. So why not let him play already? Why did Ray need to prove his loyalty by spying for him and betraying the others, if his presence in the game was something Logan actually *needed* anyway? As much as Ray had processed the decision through a rational lens, it still felt like a pretty shady thing, what he was being asked to do. It was a special kind of frustration, then, to be all ready and willing to stoop to a new moral low, and be stuck waiting for an opportunity to do so.

As cloudless March sunshine gave way to cloudless April sunshine, Ray was getting impatient. After a profitable couple of weeks once the game had picked back up, he had gone back to losing at a steady clip. He wasn't playing his best, that much he knew from his software analysis, but he was also running pretty bad.[6] Far from Cardanus's effortless regret minimization, he was as haunted by his daily mistakes as he had been at the time of his Canadian rock bottom. The difference being that he knew this time he'd just keep on playing, to the very end. His habits, once comforting, were starting to look like a joke at his expense, a Groundhog's Day forcing him to repeat the daily routine that was bringing about the demise of his career. He *was* going broke. Studiously. Unstoppably.

---

5   While X-ray glasses and various forms of marked decks are not entirely unheard of, even in casinos, proper old-school cheating is basically a nonfactor in contemporary Vegas poker. Spots, however, don't know this, and are by nature a suspicious and skittish species.

6   *Run* being the preferred mathematical term to express one's performance compared to the Expected Value of one's play. As in "I ran pretty good there" ("My results exceeded the statistical average"), "How bad can I fucking run?" ("I'm being remarkably unlucky"), "Goddamn fucking Godrunner piece of shit" ("I believe your performance in the last hand belonged to the upper end of the statistical spectrum of possible outcomes, as per luck"), and so on.

And session by session, April went by, breeding timid flowers out of the sandy patches in the alleys of his apartment complex, stirring dark thoughts of Tragedy: the worst month in his live poker career. He was looking at an unflinchingly downward graph on his laptop screen—chewing his shirt—on the evening of the thirtieth, when the phone rang.

"You're *calling* me?"

"Listen."

"Do people make *phone calls* anymore?"

"LQ's in town."

"Is that the old guy that was looking for you a few weeks ago?"

"What guy?"

"British guy, came to the PR looking for someone."

"LQ is not British."

"JJ called you fat."

"Dude, you need to listen to me. LQ is in town."

"So who is LQ?"

"Thought I told you about him. LQ is a whale. He's *the* whale."

"The one everybody obsesses about?"

"Right."

"Nobel Prize guy?"

"Correct."

"The guy who lost a million in a month?"

"Just the one."

"Damn."

"Hasn't been around for a couple years, at least. And now he's here. Not sure he wants to play, though."

"And you want me to bring him to you?"

"You're not ready for that."

"Okay, Master Yoda, what then?"

"I can't be there just waiting for him—they'll know. But you can."

"Define waiting."

"Indefinitely."

"But you said he might not even show up."

"Dude's like a thousand years old, wakes up early. You need to be there in the morning and let me know if he shows up. *If* he's there, and *if* he starts playing, you have to be on that table and tell me everything those guys are telling him. They'll talk shit about me, because we used to be buddies, him and me, and they'll be afraid I'll get to him first."

"You were buddies with the guy who's a thousand years old?"

"Told you you're not ready."

"Calvin called you fat too."

"So you try to talk to him as much as possible. Distract him. Stall him. Be a dick."

"Then what?"

"Then nothing, you're done. I show up, LQ and I go to Renoir or Limoncello, we catch up, he plays my game."

"What about me?"

"You play my game too."

"Won't the others know?"

"Yes."

"Sounds bad."

"You care what those guys think of you?"

"Not just those guys—everybody will know."

"Dude, who cares?"

"You don't care that Bryan said you can't touch your dick standing up?"

"Fuck Bryan."

"You don't care about the game?"

"I care about money, dude. You need to grow up. Now are you gonna be there tomorrow morning, or do I need to find someone else?"

"Not sure you're Yoda in this scenario, come to think of it. More the other guy."

"That a yes?"

"Yes."

"Cool, talk soon. Ciao."

On May 1, Ray's phone's alarm chimed its digital bells at 5:00 a.m. He sat up in bed, taking stock of the degree to which he was awake. Eyes more than halfway open; limbs responsive; impractical erection easily subdued. Acceptable. The risk of falling back asleep was minimal. He deactivated the alarms he'd set for 5:02, 5:04, 5:06, 5:08, 5:20, 5:22, 5:45, and kicked the sheets away. It was still dark outside.

He had no time to lose. If the news of LQ's arrival had spread to the other regs, there was no telling how early people would start showing up. All the upstairs regs would be there, even the ones who didn't play often. Ray knew most of them kept Carol and the other floor people on retainer with tips for just such occasions. Heads-up texts had probably been dispatched. Who knows, Calvin might even stake a few $5/$10 regs for the game, to maximize his profits. It was crucial that he be at the Pos before every seat at table 14 got taken, and the only way to ensure that was beating the sunrise out to the streets. There was a chance he was already late.

Out of the shower, he dabbed his body inefficiently with a towel and rushed to put on clothes. He pulled hard on an uncooperative sock sticking to his damp leg, and heard the fabric rip pretty bad. He looked at the hole, just over his right heel, then calculated briefly how long it would take to remove both socks, run back to his room, find another clean pair, put *those* on. He put on his shoes.

He was really going to do it. He was going to enter the Positano poker room—where the staff at the podium would greet him by name and put a placeholder for him on seat 6 while he went to his box, and the lady at the cage would smile and wish him good luck, and the regs would make jokes like "Look who fell off the bed early this morning!" and grin, and wink, and finally and definitively accept him as one of them—and he was going to betray them all. Text Logan as soon as LQ arrived. Stall the whale with conversation to prevent the others from defaming his benefactor. Take away the best spot in the world from the players who had always acted ethically and shown true respect for the game, only to deliver him to a lying, greedy, universally despised libertarian. His stomach groaned. No time for breakfast. He'd get a comp from room service later.

He hurried out of the apartment in the unreal light before sunrise. There was a dry desert chill in the morning air. He patted the head of the owl, and the thing spat out an envelope that looked like real mail. Stamps and all. From: Howard Jackson, San Raphael, CA.

He jammed the envelope in his pocket and sprinted down the stairs to his father's white Chevy. How little must he know Ray to think that an actual letter would be the best, or even a decent, way to communicate with him? With someone who, whether on his laptop at home or on his phone at the table, was in reach of a screen and his in-box almost every waking instant of his life? That letter could have stayed in the mailbox for days, weeks maybe, had Ray not coincidentally contracted this unsavory Vegas habit re: the owl, and therefore noticed it right away. That someone with so little predisposition for rational thinking had managed to run a business for several decades and that he, VFInd3r, was so close to the ultimate failure was just not fair. Ray didn't deserve it. Fucking variance.

Turning right from Rainbow onto the empty lanes of West Flamingo Road, Ray found himself driving east toward the rising sun. The Positano, its hill towering over the Strip, was still far and indiscernible in the suffused, lacteal light. To the sides of the road, residential areas lay unnaturally distant from one another, arranged with a desire for loneliness that now struck Ray as disheartening. It was like Las Vegas, the quiet suburban life of it, had been the accidental result of an explosion on the Strip, its buildings and neighborhoods scattered around on random vectors as far as possible from the origin of trouble. Nothing was close to anything. The Strip was at the center of a funnel, luring people in with the promise of closeness, warmth, community. Away from it, life rarefied, slowly dissipating into desert.

"Look who fell off the bed early this morning!" said Calvin. "Just itching to play poker at six a.m., are we? No special reason, I'm sure." He winked.

"Man, it's impossible to keep a secret in this town anymore," said Bryan.

"Oh, don't be mean," said Calvin. "Mr. Online Pro learned the magic of tips. They grow up so fast!"

The others were already there. Calvin, Bryan, JJ, Eike, Lauren—a $5/$10 reg, confirming Ray's hunch—locking up seats at table 14 in the semi-deserted poker room. There were only a couple of games running, both downstairs, soporific $1/$3 tables that must have been going all night. From upstairs, the low-stakes poker room stretched like a vast, dry prairie, dotted with thirty, maybe forty tables, empty in the morning, waiting for players. Two tired-looking cleaners vacuumed the brown untrodden carpet. A bespectacled old man sitting at a $1/$3 with maybe $90 in front of him was the closest thing to a Nobel Prize winner anywhere in sight. LQ was a no-show.

"Are we going to play?" said JJ, sitting at seat 3, chips already in front of him.

"I'm not," said Lauren. "No offense, guys, but you know . . ."

"There's nobody else in line, we can keep these locked indefinitely even without playing," said Calvin. "The advantages of a dry room."

"A dead room, soon enough," said JJ, who looked positively traumatized by his early wakeup: mouth open, facial muscles moving in the asymmetric, out-of-sync way of serious dental anesthesia. Eyes at half mast. "Let's just hope dude shows up." He yawned multiple vowels.

Nobody arrived. Within an hour, six oversize tray-carts gridlocked the high-stakes area with the players' free breakfasts. Oatmeal, fruit salads, omelets, coffee. They were all too tired to make fun of Eike's spaghetti bolognese. They ate in silence.

He's not coming, Ray texted Logan around 9.

You need to stay there, Logan texted back.

How long?

Until he comes.

"He got to him already, I can feel it," said JJ. "The fat fuck."

Ray turned his phone facedown on the empty table's baize.

The hours crawled by at geological speed. If it weren't for the dealer shifts—every thirty minutes, even with no game actually taking place, with change-of-the-guard-type solemnity—it would be easy to think the high-stakes room existed outside the domain of Time. A couple more regs showed up later in the morning, but neither stuck around long.

By the middle of the afternoon, conversation at table 14 sounded like something out of Beckett.

"We should start a game," said Bryan.

"I'm gonna die if I don't," said Eike.

"I'm dead already," said JJ.

"It'll just be the four of us," Calvin said. "Nobody else will play."

"I don't think he's even coming," said JJ.

"We should still start a game," said Bryan.

"I mean, if we could find at least *someone* to start the game with, while we wait," said Lauren. "But not like *this*." The left hemisphere of her scalp was buzz-cut, straight black hair coming down on the other side. Ray wasn't sure he'd ever played with her before, but he remembered with horror that she'd been at the Reef the night he'd made a bile-spraying fool of himself. Great.

"I'll play," he said. "I'll go get chips."

"Yeah, not exactly what I had in mind," said Lauren. As he got up, Ray felt a lame shiver of pride.

In the small private room, he rested his box upon the wooden counter. This was dumb. Wildly suboptimal. Playing a full-reg shorthanded game while low on funds, only to wait around for a spot who was probably not going to show. The risk/reward ratio was badly skewed.

But he needed to get in Logan's game, one way or another. It seemed so odd to him that only a few weeks ago he'd agonized over the decision, taking into serious consideration the idea of saying no. Like he had any other option, really. Bleed away the rest of his bankroll in shitty games in which he was a marginal favorite, playing bad poker because of stress and fear, how did that sound for a plan? He needed to do this, it was not even a real choice.

He reached for the box key in his pocket and was surprised by the feel of paper. Amazing. He'd gotten the letter through sheer luck in the first place, and he'd still managed to completely forget about its existence in just a few hours. Good thing it was probably useless paternal drivel anyway. He tore the envelope open with just a bit of cinematic pleasure, fingers sliding through the ripping edge, papery sounds echoing nicely in the empty room.

Son,

It is a father's darkest moment, that in which he realizes he has failed to provide for his family. The moment he looks at himself, at all his years of strife and fighting, and has to admit they were all for naught. The livelihood of his family squandered. The tree of their sustenance dry. It may be a father's proudest moment, nonetheless, that in which he turns to his son for help.

We are, Ray, your mother and I, the store, our home, your home, our lives and future and I fear very much our well-being too, we are ruined. We are in debt. The store has been losing money for years, ever since Amazon appeared, and instead of closing it to cut our losses, I kept pouring money into it. Our money. Your money. Stubbornly, misguidedly, blindly. I took, how shameful to say!, a second mortgage on the house, in a foolish attempt to delay the inevitable. And now we stand to lose everything, and I have nowhere else to turn.

I am, my son, desperately sorry. You were right, and always have been. I see it now. That my own son would do right where I did wrong, that he would see clearly where I stumbled in darkness, is both the deepest shame and my greatest joy. In the struggle between the Past and the Future, your instinct guided you to the right side, and I still doubted you. You were right, and I will spend the rest of my life begging for your forgiveness.

I have always been proud of you, Ray. I know I have at times been incapable of showing it. When I found on our old PC the detailed spreadsheets of all the games of Hearts! *you used to keep, I thought you were wasting your time. And yet my weak, losing avatar View-finder (how you loved hearing that Carver story before bedtime!) had under your tenure become the terror of the virtual tables. When you left Stanford to play online poker, I was sure you were making a mistake. But I never stopped admiring your courage, your resolve, your heart. I never stopped being proud. And look at you now! To the best of my limited technological abilities, I followed your career from afar. By the light of my dim, fading vision, burned the heart of your deepest, most faithful fan.*

We need, my son, your family needs money. A hundred thousand dollars, at least, to save the house, maybe more. We can barely pay our health insurance, and even that not for much longer, and without it we could never afford my medical expenses. The situation has become, I am sad to say, life or death, which is why I resolved to finally write to you. I've been trying to talk to you about this for so long, but every time I tried I felt my tongue tie up in a knot and my heart falter. Now it could no longer wait.

No father should ever ask this much of a son. But then again no father has ever had you *as a son. Fathers and sons are fated to misunderstand each other, I see that now, but that is perhaps never too late to remedy. I wonder, have you ever read Turgenev's excellent* Fathers and Sons? *It occurs to me that what you so clearly foresaw so many years ago, the foolish arrogance of the Old inevitably defeated by the mathematical disposition of the Young, mirrors with uncanny symmetry the 19th century Russian cultural landscape Turgenev set off to portray. The old values of the Liberals and traditionalists upstaged and surpassed by the rigor of Comtean Positivism. It truly is a wonderful book, if needlessly turgid on occasion. You really should read it. I would love nothing better than to discuss with you the characters of Arcady Nikolaevich, and his father Nikolai Petrovich, and the young nihilist friend Bazarov. Did you know that the famous Marxist economist and thinker Vladimir Bazarov took his name from this very novel? Isn't it fascinating, the powerful alchemy of Art and History, the small, invisible ways the world of our imagination overflows, seeping into the fabric of reality like water on a piece of cloth?*

We need money, my son. It is with love that I ask you, with every fiber in my body aching with shame, and fatherly pride, and bursting with infinite love for you, that I ask, indeed I beg you to save us.

I remain, lovingly, Your Father,
Howard Jackson

Tragedy.

The irrefutable evidence of defeat.

Even as he read it, the letter replaced the whole world. Nothing else existed. Poker, Logan, LQ, VFlnd3r. The letter was everything, and it told the story of his final loss.

He was a terrible son. He'd been oblivious to what was happening to his family—no, he'd consciously ignored his father's clear cries for help. He had, in fact, openly sided with the algorithmic forces that were ripping his family apart. He'd rooted for them, cheered them on, knowing full well what their victory would mean to his parents. No getting around that. And now Tragedy was no longer his alone, but his whole family's: his entire life and theirs and all he loved, crumbling in one fell financial swoop.

Letter in hand, standing alone in the security room's relative darkness, Ray found himself wading through a viscous swamp of *feelings*. Lame, probably harmful, but unquestionably *his*. He saw them combine and react like chemicals, morphing and altering the story of his life into something else, something new.

Within the swamp, he recognized fear. It was the same fear that had accompanied him since Cardanus, but now to his surprise he saw it dredge up childhood memories, early feelings of inadequacy, of being misunderstood, disapproved of. (Fear looked like a mold, greenish, spreading.) He watched fear infect his very rational decisions, proliferating to the corners of his life where he'd expected to find only logic, and his own iron-willed resolution. Why had he so staunchly refused to have anything to do with the writers his parents idolized? Why had he distanced himself so harshly from their world, if not for fear of failing them? He saw the mold stretch as far as Stanford, to those first terrifying months when he'd realized *he wasn't special*, not at all. His mathematical brilliance too, like ping-pong, had been a function of the circumstantial ineptitude of his environment back home, but there, there where the real math people were, he was just one of many. He had buried that discovery at the time, denied it to himself, but there it was, festering with mold. And now, in horror, he watched the mold spread its fuzzy filaments all over his decision to quit school and play poker professionally, that seemingly perfect EV computation too growing a rotten fungal coating: he'd been afraid of failure, of not being good enough. He had clung to poker to forgo academic judgment, and had found there new authorities whose approval he could win, and a whole new source of validation: money.

With shaking hands, he fumbled with the key and got his box out of the cabinet. Poker chips looked ridiculous: a foreign object, utterly nonsensical. Moldy. Suddenly, poker itself appeared to him like a childish caricature of real math, an oversimplified, rote iteration of a few key concepts disguised as serious intellectual work. The mold was there, in Pittsburgh, before he even played the bot. It was there, when he'd stared at those young PhD candidates to whom the game was no more than a party trick, a neat set of variables to let their infinitely complex software stretch its muscles a bit before it moved on to something more substantial. In the grand scheme of experimental AI things, Ray and his poker buddies were the fucking *control group*.

But the mold hadn't stopped there. Fear had led him from Stanford to Toronto, from Toronto to Las Vegas. Mathematician, to online poker player, to live pro. And now again, stooping lower and lower, a humiliating, almost farcical fall from grace, fear would turn him into a cheater. A lifetime running away. A lifetime in the mold. Fear of failure: the most useless, suboptimal, stupidly human feeling there is.

For a moment, with a hollow, liberating pain in his chest, he felt finally ready to accept defeat. He could still save them: if he put the—he counted—$62,375 from his box together with the less than forty grand on his bank account, he could still help. Save the house, at least, buy them some time to get back on their feet. He would have no money at all left to play, but suddenly that didn't sound so bad. He just needed to let go, to accept that it was over. Embrace Tragedy.

He could see it clearly: the optimal play now was to fail.

The door swung open with a torrent of outside light, and Eike barged in, rushing to get to his box.

"He's here," he said, grabbing flags by the fistful. "And he wants to play *big*."

He didn't even notice that Ray was in tears.

Upstairs was where the real money was. They called it "upstairs" out of implicit reverence, a silent nod to the distinction between ordinary tables and high stakes, and really it was a world away from the silly card games of the weekend tourists below. Up the two little steps that separated the elevated space in the top-right corner from the rest of the room, fortunes were made and lost, fates were sealed. Above the decorated opaque glass of the screens, the black-on-white inscription reading HIGH LIMIT POKER felt like an odd understatement.

Everything was at once extraordinary and dull, dazzling and quotidian. It was exotic, and tantalizing, and as inebriating as advertised to the eighty-four-year-old Turkish Nobel Prize economist in seat 5, khaki shorts and safari vest, yellow polo shirt, open Birkenstocks, hunched over his poker chips, squinting to make out the suits of the cards from the flop. His old heart still racing with childish excitement every time he played a big pot. It was daily and ordinary and mundane to the regs around him, serene in the knowledge that one day never mattered, one hand could never matter. There was only one lifelong poker session: the breaks, the ups and downs, exaltation and defeat were just an illusion.

The dynamic was at its subtlest here, the very existence of the pros bending and blurring the lines between employees and customers, imperceptibly bridging the distance between tourists and staff, between work and fun. A refined balance. It was unspoken and almost conspiratorial in the nuanced smiles of the cocktail waitress as she served a Macallan twelve-year-old to seat 5 (collecting a $5 tip), and a Fiji water to the robust reg in seat 4 (receiving a blue $1 chip and a "Hi Gabrielle, how's little Mikey?"). The game at table 14 was the biggest they'd had the whole year, but no one from the staff—the dealers, the waitresses, the women at the podium—betrayed the least amount of interest. It was just another Friday-night shift.

With his whole life on the table, and the future of his family on his shoulders, Ray Jackson knew for certain that this was the most important moment of his life. Every new hand he was dealt meant *everything*, every decision could save or damn him completely. This day was the only day that had ever mattered. It was a mistake, a crazy, irresponsible mistake, and yet at every new dealer he resisted the impulse to get up and leave, run away from Las Vegas. Go home. He posted his next big blind, two black $100 chips.

He had ended up playing. Walking out of the security room with his whole bankroll in a single chip rack and his father's letter folded in his pocket, he'd stumbled upstairs in a daze. He barely registered how quickly and silently a $100/$200 No Limit Hold'em game was assembling—like it was the most normal, unremarkable thing—at table 14. Some instinctual mathematical node in his brain lit up, seeing LQ choose seat 5 for himself, center table, thus making seat 6—the one locked by Ray's sapphire-blue player's card—by far the best at the table. *In position.* He sat down without even realizing what he was doing, rolling the chips out of his rack and onto the felt.

He didn't even think to text Logan.

After a few hours, LQ was winning big. He had sat down with $50,000, but through foolish plays and ridiculous luck he'd run it up to over $130,000. At one point he'd won an $80,000 pot against Bryan with a hand so incredibly *ugly*, Ray had felt genuinely sorry for the guy. But Bryan hadn't seemed to care. He'd smiled, reached inside his pockets, and asked Carol for a fresh $50,000 stack in exchange for ten flags. Less than two hours later, Bryan was almost back to even.

To LQ's direct left, Ray watched the man play like he wasn't an opponent but a case study, or a museum exhibit. He just couldn't understand how someone so smart—way smarter, most likely, that all of the young pros around him—could be so unbelievably *stupid* at a math-based game. He played, Ray admitted to himself, like a crazy person. He had no clue about basic strategy, and was destined to lose money at the game as long as he played. How could he be so careless and bad? And more, how could he not see how elaborate and complex was the world of professionals exploiting his innocent fun? The transparent obsequiousness of dealers, floor staff, waitresses, and pros, all trying to extract money from him with the various skills at their disposal. How could he be so blind?

Ray, on the other hand, saw everything. Glued to his seat by fear, and by an irrational, irresistible feeling that this was exactly what he was supposed to do, he played on in a state of mathematical trance. Every decision brought with it pure, piercing terror, and yet he wasn't making mistakes.

(He folded: A6 off.)

It was a sort of lucid dream, the kind of heightened sensorial experience he imagined hallucinogenics must be like, but with logic and numbers and ranges instead. What he'd felt in the security room, the sense that Tragedy had *already happened*, that he'd already lost and was effectively no longer a poker player, somehow allowed him to look at the game from the outside—to recognize it for the trivial little game-theoretical construct it was. Meaningless. He was terrified, but he was playing the best poker of his life.

(He folded: 85 suited.)

(He raised: KJ off, then folded to a 3bet.)

Maybe he was being too harsh on LQ. It wasn't that he didn't realize what was going on around him, or see that he sucked at playing and everybody knew it. It was that all of this, the chips in front of him, the game of poker, the Positano, the entire professional ecosystem designed to afford him the occasional weekend thrill, it was all so far below his radar that he couldn't be bothered to take notice. What was happening at the table mattered to him as much as a random documentary caught flicking through the channels on his TV. Ray's entire tragic failure of a life played out on a stage that this old man wouldn't allot more than a sliver of his attention to.

It wasn't about money. *Really rich people, they don't want to think about the money.*

Ray, his fingers trembling as he slid in the chips for even the most standard of calls, Ray couldn't think of anything else. He was up a little shy of $10,000.

Then Logan arrived.

Ray saw him appear on the second step as he posted his next big blind, in sweatpants and running shoes, a wild expression on his face. As if waking up from a long sleep, Ray picked up his phone, which he'd kept facedown on the leather edge of the table, for the first time in hours. He had sixteen unread messages, all from Logan. It was past midnight.

Nobody looked up from the table, not even LQ. Logan seemed unsure what to do. He stopped just up the stairs, as if an invisible wall prevented him from approaching the table, looking furious, and out of breath. He just stood there. His eyes never even crossed Ray's.

At the table, the hand was in progress. Every player folded until Lauren, in seat 3, raised to $600. Next to her, on the button, Bryan quickly put in two yellow chips, a 3bet to $2,000. On the small blind, LQ looked at his cards and shook his head in disgust, then reached to his stack and tossed in three chips, announcing "Raise!" A flag and two yellows: $7,000.

Ray looked at his cards. Two black aces.

By a mental estimate he'd run recently, Ray had played in his life close to five million hands of No Limit Texas Hold'em. Yet for all he tried, he couldn't think of another time when he'd had to face a single decision that could completely ruin him financially, bankrupt and possibly kill his father, all the while trying to outplay a Nobel Prize winner, under the eyes of a man who most likely wanted nothing more than to murder him with his own hands. All of this appeared to him so clearly, so distinctly, that the thought of crossing that line, of passing the decisional point of no return and committing himself to one specific course of action out of an infinite array of possibilities, felt downright insane. Impossible.

He had more than $70,000 in front of him now. LQ had more. If he could get him to go all in before the flop, Ray would put himself in the position of being at least an 80 percent favorite to double up his stack. He would have right in front of him enough money to save his family's house, maybe even help with the store, and still have some left for himself. All his problems could disappear within the next two minutes. But of course, he could also lose everything and be doomed.

With the storm raging in his mind, Ray hadn't moved a muscle since the action was on him. There was no shot clock in live cash games, but for all the others knew, this was still a trivial preflop decision for him, and he needed to get on with it. He tried to force himself to think like a poker player again.

Simply calling LQ's $7,000 was of course an option. Cardanus itself would certainly do it some percentage of the time. But by doing that, he would give Bryan 3:1 odds to see the flop as well, effectively reducing the statistical dominance of his aces by a considerable margin and increasing variance. Although, if LQ was bluffing, it was perhaps wise to allow him to keep doing so, letting him fire again after the flop. Reraising here, a 5bet, would show such crystal-clear strength that even a Nobel Prize idiot like LQ could not ignore it, and would probably just give up on his bluffs right away. Then again, if LQ had a *real* hand, as his pathetic disappointment act strongly suggested, it would be crazy not to let him go all in preflop, and end it right there and then. But wait, was Ray really basing the most important decision of his life on a *live tell*? On the stupidest, most unreliable form of strategic reasoning, which only feel players and amateurs kept believing? Whatever clarity he'd felt earlier, it had gone for good. Ray was frozen.

In the end, it was the thought of living with himself after fucking up this dream scenario—say by allowing Bryan to see a flop for cheap and scoop the pot—that made the decision for him.

He grabbed three flags from the top of his stack, and added four yellow chips before carefully sliding his $19,000 across the betting line.

"Reraise," the dealer, Jane, announced.

Lauren's cards were in the muck before the dealer even spoke.

Bryan didn't immediately fold, as Ray had imagined he would. He peeked again at his cards, the calm look on his face unperturbed. What the hell was he thinking about? Did he actually have a hand? Or was he just hoping that LQ would understand he was folding a big hand, and maybe think again before donating all his money to Ray on some idiotic bluff? Over the spasming, knotted pain in his stomach, Ray found himself for the shortest of moments back in his poker mindset, in mathematical disbelief at Bryan's indecision. With a calm, smooth gesture, Bryan pinched his cards between his thumb and index finger and flicked them over to the center of the table. Ray thought he saw a hint of a smile across his lips.

The action was on LQ now.

Slowly, he lowered his neck toward the table until his face was practically inches away from Ray's $19,000, counting. He looked at his own $7,000 raise, then back to Ray's flags, an operation that took so long, Ray wondered whether he was struggling with grade-school arithmetic or just putting on a show. Through the underwater vision of near-breakdown, Ray could feel the stares of all the players at the table plus Logan fixating on the old man, recognizing and easily unmasking a kind of charade they'd seen a million times, the feigned weakness of an amateur betraying real strength, and excitement, and a desire to go all in. Ray waited. Any second now, this complete stranger could say the words that would 80 percent of the time save his and his parents' life, and 20 percent of the time destroy it. It was more than the human heart was built to withstand.

Finally done assessing the size of Ray's 5bet, LQ began counting his own remaining stack. He was intolerably slow, carefully rearranging all his black $100 chips in piles of ten, then halfway through realizing he'd fucked up and made them elevens, and going back to get one chip from each little pile and count all over again. Ray had the weirdest feeling of watching his grandmother count all her change at the store's checkout line, except with the knowledge that his life somehow depended on it. What was even more infuriating was that the whole thing was completely pointless, since it was perfectly clear that just the stack of flags LQ kept in front of his black chips more than covered everything Ray had in front of him.[7] If anything, he should be counting Ray's chips.

Minutes went by. LQ was so anticlimactically slow that after a while Ray felt almost bored, if that was even possible.

---

7   In No Limit Hold'em, when two players go all in, it is the smallest of the two stacks that determines how much money will be in play. For self-evident reasons.

At the end of what was now without a doubt an act, LQ's eyes widened as if he'd had a sudden, momentous intuition, and with sloth-paced excitement he started stacking up all his chips together and gripping the sides of the resulting little chip castle, getting ready to slide them all very theatrically over the betting line, like they did on TV.

This was it. He was doing it. He was going all in.

But before he could complete the laborious procedure or speak the iconic, legally binding words, the loudest siren in the world started blaring out intermittently, and all the black bulbs of the eye-in-the-sky cameras exploded like minuscule glass confetti raining from the ceiling, and the lights in the poker room faltered, and came back up, and finally went out for good.

15

Mary Ann

The harpsichordist had long hair, longer than Mary Ann's. It came straight down the back of his tuxedo, silver and smooth, with the gloss of a shampoo commercial. When the man's hands traveled to the farther end of the keyboard following the tumbling counterpoint of Scarlatti's Sonata in B Minor, K. 27, the hair remained still, as if tethered down with a weight. Like a pendulum. She was looking at the hair as she waited for Neal to place a single old-fashioned on her tray. After the clipped metallic sound of the last bars stopped, the harpsichordist remained seated for a few seconds, facing the tables, his back to where Mary Ann was standing. He was the last player for the night, and Mary Ann knew he was programming the auto-play function on the instrument. When he got up, he bowed three times to the different sides of the lounge, as if the room had been full. The faint applause coming from Walter's usual table was the only sound Mary Ann could hear above the *prestissimo* beating of her heart. It was time.

She was about to commit a serious crime, facilitating an even more serious crime to be committed by hackers at the behest of a coalition of political insurgents, start-up techies, and disgruntled workers. After tonight, either the underlying balance of the Las Vegas gaming industry would change—the workforce proving once and for all that they had the power to run a multibillion-dollar business to the ground, if it came to

that, a new CBA being hastily drafted and approved, unjustly fired
employees rehired with sincere, wire-transferred apologies—or Mary
Ann would be in jail. Her and her alone.

If you looked up Mary Ann online, search engines would dig up a Japanese shampoo commercial from five years ago. She was the protagonist,
center-couch in the opening conversation about split ends, walking between
her two friends in a scene-stealing pearl-gold dress in the final club shot.
She smiled and ran a hand seductively across her hair, draping a brown
wave across her neck and shoulder as martini-holding men in suits leered
at her. The ad had been shot in New York, and her lines were dubbed in a
happy Japanese singsong that didn't match the strain behind the heavy
makeup on her eyes. She hadn't thought about it in years, but she remembered it now, as the silver-haired musician walked in silent steps out of the
Scarlatti Lounge. The harpsichord—ghostly internet hands already plucking
at the first lonely subject of *The Art of the Fugue*—now sat unguarded. The
black device in her purse dug a sharp corner in its shape; she could see it
from here.

The tricky thing about spur-of-the-moment decisions is that the spurring
is often shorter-lived than the consequences. Back at the SU cave meeting,
everything had looked real simple: she would plant a remote hacking device
on the IoT-connected digital harpsichord at the Scarlatti Lounge, establishing a backdoor port-binding so that a crew of North Vegas geeks could
infiltrate the outer layer of the Positano system and engage in acts of data
disruption—deleting hotel registries and restaurant reservations, messing
with guest-room key authorizations and VIP loyalty program privileges
and such—essentially dealing serious damage to the property without
touching a cent or endangering any of its guests. Piece of cake. Put on the
spot by her colleagues as the clear-cut ideal candidate once the motion had
been enthusiastically approved (though a few members of the Board,
including Maidon, had voted against), she had nodded yes, thinking the

whole thing would be over and done with in a couple of days. That was over two months ago.

As it turns out, orchestrating an untraceable DDoS attack against a multimillion-dollar security system takes surprisingly long. Not that Mary Ann had any special faith in or love for computer nerds, but she'd always assumed they would at least be very good at their job. She'd expected the brand of affectless competence one sees in movies and TV: those awkwardly dressed, unrealistic twentysomethings who seem to perceive the world entirely through the lens of logic and mathematics—perhaps misreading human interactions and group dynamics to comical extents, but ultimately coming through when it mattered. Yet in the weeks following the meeting, her exchanges with the allies from the Dot Com-mittee (it was really starting to look like the lion's share of the SU's brainpower was expended on creative nomenclature) had been limited to brief interfaces with Neal, the plump, red-cheeked bartender who'd spoken up in the cave, and had only managed to confuse her. Neal worked at Club Nero, which was why Mary Ann had never run into him before, but he promised he would set up a switch with a colleague at the Scarlatti for the night of the sabotage. He had a laid-back ease about him, and when he gave Mary Ann progress reports from his coder friends, he made it sound like they too had a relaxed, almost casual attitude about the sabotage and how long it was taking. There was something frustrating about their chats, like talking to a car mechanic or calling a plumber about a leaky faucet. Everything would be all right, everything was going to work. Just not today.

"So Neal takes the device out later, at the end of his shift?" Erica had asked over nighttime waffles with strawberries at the Teddy Bear Diner.

"Yeah, as he's leaving," said Mary Ann. "Makes more sense for him to be checking the harpsichord then."

The Teddy Bear was a twenty-four-hour diner on West Trop, on the way to Erica's apartment in Southwest Vegas and not too long of a detour for Mary Ann. It had a lovely kitschy feel to it, lined wall-to-wall with shelves of smiling teddy bears, and a friendly staff and unlimited refills of good coffee.

"But by then most of the trace removal will be done anyway," Mary Ann explained. "All camera footage gone too. It'll take Wiles's people weeks just to figure out how and where we got in, so Neal's not really doing anything dangerous."

On its own, the coders taking their time tweaking and constantly perfecting the device upon which Mary Ann's future—and the SU's, and possibly the whole city's—depended could be nothing but a good thing. It showed care and trustworthiness. Yet it also gave Mary Ann time to reexamine her impulsive decision over and over, pondering the ways her anger and desire to take Wiles down after what he'd done to Aunt Karen were leading her to such an extreme course of action. Victimless as her crime would be, she was undeniably crossing a line, a kind of ethical point of no return.

"What about you, though? Are *you* scared?" asked Erica, scooping up a mouthful of waffle and melted vanilla ice cream. Mary Ann had never met someone who ate quite so much, and with such genuine pleasure. She took a large bite herself, buying time for her answer.

"Not really. I don't have to do much either."

Mary Ann's role in the operation made her invaluable to the cause. The story of the Positano workers' fight against Wiles was now *her* story, something that gratified her in a way she had never felt before, but also made her highly suspicious of her own motives—the pretty obvious selfishness of most heroic selfless acts. But in spite of her childish instincts, the sabotage was, at its heart, really not at all about her. And in that way, her personal doubts and fears must be nothing more than the admission price of collective success. Like, seriously, suck it up. If she was to be cast in this heroic role, then she wasn't going to be a killjoy about it, complaining, worrying, or even worse, backing out.

"You're doing more than all the rest of us are," said Erica. "We're here on the sidelines, watching you take all the risks, doing nothing."

Something else scared her, though: it was fairly obvious that the SU board was having strategic conversations with the DCS coders behind her back. Whenever they talked to her, they made sure to ask her for updates and request status reports, pretending they had no idea what was going on with the plan. They acted like their days of reckless subversive engagement were over, and they now had to wait around for someone else to risk their job and freedom for the cause, while they went about their everyday unrevolutionary routine, unaware of the latest developments in the rebellion they themselves had started. Like they would ever be that careless. And so if she was right, and she clearly had to be, that the SU was still very much involved, and that the Dot Com guys, as laid back and disengaged as they strived to look, were also working hard and competently and obsessively at the plan, and that the only reason all this was being kept secret from Mary Ann was the need-to-know basis of all properly organized sedition, if she was right about all of this, then still Mary Ann was even more uncomfortable and manipulated and alone than she had expected to be. Trapped. Waiting.

"In the end, all these people here, all these women and men who are struggling, they will all owe *you* their future. It will be because of *you*. Isn't that crazy?"

And it was. For all her doubts, the thought of really, actively improving the life of others, for once, was inebriating. Mary Ann, the selfish, calamitous child who ruined the life of everyone around her. Didn't she owe this, this brave act of self-sacrifice for the greater good? Didn't she? She kept thinking about it, especially after her coffee with Karen.

In the apartment on Pecos and Trop, Aunt Karen was in bad shape. It was like decades of Vegas sun had finally caught up with her, and she was drying up like a tomato or a prune: she looked, and moved, and talked fine, but the juice inside had gone, and what was left was withering by the day. Her eyes, a yellowish light blue—unlike her sister's and Mary Ann's—looked watered down, unfocused. Mary Ann visited her as much as she could, but she was starting to question whether that really made a difference.

"Rodrigo is eating again," Aunt Karen said, early in the afternoon of that same day. "He's being such a good boy."

"What about you?" said Mary Ann.

"Haven't had to scoop up a rotting mouse from the cage in months."

"I mean, are *you* eating, Karen? You look thin."

"Oh, don't worry about me, you know I can take . . ." Aunt Karen's sentence trailed off into silence, and Mary Ann could almost physically see her mind wander away, chasing some other thought. It was like her reflexes, muscles, and even brain had slowed down to a crawl, as if her mind was getting ready to hibernate for a long winter. Karen looked up at Mary Ann again, and smiled apropos of nothing.

"Should we make coffee?" said Mary Ann.

"Yes, let me, let me."

Mary Ann had taken the habit of setting little traps at Aunt Karen's place, to get a clearer picture of what her life was like when she wasn't around. She would leave a stack of VHS tapes in precarious balance in the living room, making sure they impeded access to the big brown-curtained window; a shampoo bottle lying down awkwardly along the edge of the shower floor; a coffee-stained mug in the sink. A few days later, on her next visit, she would run a recognizance tour of the apartment to track her aunt's movements and assess her well-being.

"So how's work?" said Mary Ann. "Are you getting good shifts?"

"Good, good shifts, yes." Karen was sitting at the Formica table in the kitchen, doing nothing.

"Did you go yesterday?" said Mary Ann.

"Oh, no, I don't have weekend shifts, you know," said Aunt Karen, very much not making coffee. "It's always good to have the weekend off, it is."

"It's Wednesday."

"I saw your friend at the Newport the other day."

"What other day was that, Karen? When did you go last?"

"The cute one."

"Should I worry that you're skipping work?"

"Lillian."

"You mean Lily."

"Lily. She is so cute!"

She was wearing an oversize Las Vegas souvenir T-shirt that reached below her knees and lime-green flip-flops. There was a cartoon of a man on the faded navy-blue shirt, waking up next to a cactus in the desert with an empty bottle of Jack Daniel's and moths fluttering out of his wallet. The caption read: THIS TOWN WASN'T BUILT ON WINNERS.

Nobody spoke for a while. The old AC unit had the seashore sound of muffled waves crashing against a pier somewhere far away.

"I'm gonna make coffee," said Mary Ann.

It didn't look like Aunt Karen was listening to her. There was a focused look on her face now, as if she was finding it extremely hard to keep it together for Mary Ann's sake. This sitting down at the kitchen table, keeping a conversation going, remembering the name of Mary Ann's friend from years ago. Like any of it mattered. Mary Ann had a sudden feeling that her visits were actually making her aunt *miserable*.

"There's a dirty mug in the sink, Karen," she said. "Let me wash that for you."

"Oh, thank you Mae, I'm sorry," said Aunt Karen. "I . . . had a cup just before you came, I was going to wash it myself, but then you knocked—"

Mary Ann winced. "Look, Karen, I'm sorry to insist, but I really need to know how work is going. Are you showing up for your shifts?"

"But I am, Mae, I told you. I met your friend Lillian just the other day!"

"So you see her often, right, you have regular shifts at the same time?"

"Oh, no, she was there for a date, you know."

A date. At the Newport. Sure.

"Karen, Lily works there. She's a waitress, we used to work there together, that's how I met her, remember?"

"No, no, she was there for a date. I remember because the guy proposed to her right there!"

"Wait, what?"

"On his knees and everything."

That Lily, a depressed, cynical tomboy with a pronounced hatred for her place of work, would go on a date at the Lei'd Back was already far-fetched. That she would go with a guy who knew her so little that he would get on his knees in public to ask her to marry him was downright impossible. Clearly Aunt Karen had mistaken her for someone else.

"Okay, good for them. But when was this, Karen?" She thought for a second. "You know, so I can call her to congratulate her on the engagement."

"I think it was the day that it rained."

Rain in Las Vegas has a fantastical way of leaving a mark in the imagination of locals, especially the ones who have moved there after growing up somewhere else. A reminder of childhood, and getting soaked at the park during a sudden summer shower. Even though it's often only a drizzle, a cheap desert knockoff of real rain. It happens in spurts, sudden and quickly gone, and it's rare enough that it gives the day a specific quality, a kind of value, or relevance. It hadn't rained at all since last week.

"Karen, that was like Tuesday."

"I remember because they closed the escalators on the Strip, you know how they get slippery."

In the bathroom, Mary Ann scrutinized the medicine cabinet. Outside of the benzos in New York and the meds she'd been on since, she had surprisingly little drug experience herself. But she had been around addicts enough to recognize Aunt Karen's sudden downturn for what it was. After all, it ran in the family. Yet in spite of how out of it and distracted Karen looked, it seemed like she was still present enough to store whatever she was taking—vikes, if Mary Ann had to guess—in some less obvious hiding place.

It was awful, this weekly reenactment of fragments of her childhood. Through her years of traveling the country with her mom—their "two-girl troupe," she called it—Mary Ann had been too young to understand the implications of a thousand little daily occurrences, gestures, and details she'd been shamefully blind to. Now, as they happened again through the lens of time and familiarity, she was forced to relive them one by one, this time fully aware of everything she'd missed on her first go. Of everything she could have done differently.

There was also the issue of who Aunt Karen was buying from. Mary Ann had never met this guy Rick, but from her aunt's stories, she had developed an instinctive dislike for him. That he was back in her life—the man who'd got her the job on the Strip in the first place, who time and time again had destabilized the world of the only member of her family who seemed remotely capable of some degree of happiness—it could only be bad news.

Karen's phone, left carelessly on the edge of the bathroom sink, buzzed quietly with an incoming text. Before the screen went back to black, Mary Ann could see that Aunt Karen belonged to that trusting category of people who allow a preview of the message to appear on the lock screen. The sender was DANA NEWPORT. If she wanted, Mary Ann could read the text without even unlocking the phone, and without her aunt ever finding out. Her doubts about the morality of intruding on private correspondence lasted a good couple of seconds, then she pressed the home button:

HAVE SHIFT TMRW AFT 2-9, MAYBE TUES MORN 8-3 NOT SURE, NO MORE NXT WEEK SRY

So here it was. Aunt Karen hadn't been skipping work, she just didn't have any. Mary Ann recognized the text from her early days at the Positano: her aunt must have been placed on extra-rotation, subbing in a couple times a week whenever there was an opening available. It was usually a short training period for new hires, just to get acquainted with the system, but Karen was clearly no trainee. With the virtually nonexistent tips she must be getting at the Newport buffet, there was no way she could be making enough to get by in just a couple of shifts, and Mary Ann knew her savings were not something she could live on for long.

Back in the kitchen, Aunt Karen was staring inertly at the coffeemaker.

"Coffee's ready, Karen, we should get some."

"Oh yes. You know I never make it for myself, I'm such a lazy bum!" She smiled. "But I could use some, I'm going to work later."

As Mary Ann poured the coffee, she felt her chest seize with a dread that would stay with her through the following days, through her late-night conversations with Erica, and up to the fateful night of May 1. If there was even a small chance of getting Aunt Karen fair compensation for what had happened, she had to try. It was the right thing to do. Her anxiety felt familiar, like the voice of a close friend.

Thirty minutes to go in her shift. Behind the counter, Neal looked calm and carefree, a dorky charm in the jazzy getup of a Manhattan mixologist. Mary Ann went to her purse to fetch the device. When she'd seen it at the meeting, far away in her seat in the Cavea's semicircle, she'd expected it to be heavy and full of buttons and screens. It wasn't. It was light and seemingly hollow, with a single on/off button to the side and an ordinary USB plug on the front. It looked cheap, like a complimentary flash drive from some old tech convention in town. Yes, that her life and the town's future should depend on something so crummy-looking seemed utterly absurd.

There was something incongruous about the act. Risking her freedom to help others and committing a crime—both seemed like huge resolutions, which called for big, dramatic gestures. Yet all she was supposed to do was plug a flash drive into a USB port. Even the people behind it—both the enigmatically silent SU Board and Neal's mysterious coders—seemed determined to downplay her responsibility. It felt small, even funny. It felt fake. Only her fear was real. She slipped the small plastic box into the garter belt she'd worn for that specific reason.

What scared her most of all was how familiar it all felt. She had felt it for days, for weeks, the dread. She lay in bed, unable to sleep, thinking of the plan, and there it was. She forced Aunt Karen to confess she was burning through her savings and would be broke soon, and she felt it hurt. She took in Erica's beaming optimism and praise, and the dread turned it to nothing. It was the feeling of hurting others, no matter what she did, no matter how hard she tried, and the feeling of others seeing this, finally unmasking her as the horrible person she had always known she was. The feeling of wanting a break, of wanting to be taken care of and comforted by a professional, by someone who didn't care about her. By someone she couldn't hurt. She poured herself a glass of water from the counter and looked at the little blue pill in the palm of her hand. She hadn't taken one since New York, she'd never even looked at one. But wasn't tonight, of all nights, worth it?

Neal was working on the drink. She watched him cover a cooled tumbler with a black paper napkin and place a sugar cube at its center, then soak it with two dashes of Angostura bitters. His movements were both quick and careful, deliberate and seemingly instinctive. She thought of the robotic arm mixing drinks at the Diamond Grand, one of the newer and fancier properties on Fremont. Neal removed the napkin from the glass, letting the blood-red sugar cube slip inside, then added a dash of orange bitters, just like Walter liked it. He crushed the sugar cube neatly with the flat end of a steel straw. At the Diamond, you selected your drink on a tablet; then you watched the arm go to work, buzzing softly as it pivoted on its base to fetch ice cubes and maraschino cherries, sliding the finished cocktail forward with an android flourish. Neal added the whisky in three separate pours, each time pausing to stir the drink, then squeezed an orange peel above the liquid, twisted it lovingly, and sank it.

It was all so much bigger than her. There was so much at stake she barely understood, and yet here she was. Technological advancements threatening the future of century-old jobs, gender and age discrimination, the rights of the workers versus the owners' drive to keep an industry afloat. Thousands of families, children, lives sweated out under the desert sun, the entire economy of a region, the political balance of a key swing state in the upcoming election. And at the center of it all, Mary Ann, a harpsichord, and the flimsy plastic toy bulging awkwardly against her left thigh.

"The old-fashioned," said Walter. "A drink so old it was already the grandfather of all cocktails in the late nineteenth century. The obvious choice, really, to go alongside harpsichord music and neoclassical paintings, not to mention my incredibly old self." He chuckled. "But is something wrong, dear? You look agitated."

"I'm—it's nothing, I'm just feeling a little anxious tonight."

"Why don't you sit down with me? There's no one else here anyway."

The lounge was indeed empty. A strange, lucky coincidence, or maybe just the inevitable long-term result of the ridiculously unhip decor. The wood panels, red walls, large paintings of carriages and men in top hats with walking sticks.

"You really don't mind?"

"Please, love, it would be my pleasure."

It felt like she hadn't really talked to Walter in months. Maybe the man whose memoir he'd been writing was busy, or he'd gotten tired of baccarat. And Mary Ann too had traded in some of her lounge nights for extra shifts at the Cove with Erica. But even when he'd been there, even when they *had* talked, Mary Ann had not let herself be honest with him the way she used to. In awe of Erica's commitment to *doing* rather than overanalyzing, she'd distanced herself from the doubts and recursive thoughts that had been the bread and butter of her friendship with Walter. Of course, there was a lot that she simply couldn't tell him—the strike, the Shadow Union, the hack—but she realized now, as she sat down and told him about Karen, how much she'd missed this. Just talking. Someone who would listen.

"Did you find them, the drugs?"

"No, she was lucid enough to hide them."

"I'm really sorry. This must be truly harrowing for you."

"It would be, right? And yet every time I go there, I just—I get *angry*, Walter. I get really mad at her."

She waited for an answer, but Walter just nodded, encouraging her to go on.

"She lies to me, constantly. I know, I understand it's not her fault, and I swear I want to help. But it's so frustrating, all the lies, about the money, about the drugs, even about a stupid cup of coffee—it's like she's treating me like a *child*. And then I get mad at myself for getting mad at her. I'm starting to think my visits make us both feel miserable, but I can't help it. Am I not just the worst?"

She felt a sudden warmth spread across her chest. She'd missed this, yes. The simple act of pouring herself out to another human, with no intent to find a solution or make a plan to fix things. A calm to it. She realized that, on some level, the physical sensation of well-being moving through her chest and muscles must be the pill kicking in, the artificial serenity of drugs. And yet how could it not be Walter, too?

"I apologize if this sounds trite, but you're not, dear, responsible for your *thoughts*. We cannot be judged on the content of our thoughts. Nobody would be absolved." He took a sip of his drink. "You are only responsible for your actions. It's what you do, how you choose to act on your thoughts, that defines you."

"What I do—"

The device. She felt the odd weight of it on her thigh, pressed against her skin by her garter belt. It was almost time. She looked back up at Walter.

"What if it's my actions, too, I'm not sure about? What if I can't tell anymore, like maybe I am just programmed to do harm, or to be unhappy, or to hate myself forever, I don't know. I keep trying, but it doesn't make any difference, and maybe it keeps getting worse."

"Do you feel worse?"

"But it's not just how I feel, right? It's that my actions have consequences, whatever my intentions, and I have power, I found out I have power to really affect other people's lives. And it keeps getting bigger, and more confusing, and I just don't know anymore."

"What is it you are asking, dear?"

"I guess—am I a good person, Walter?" She paused, feeling the air vibrate with a sudden intensity—suspended, an energy she knew must be coming from within, and yet seemed to be all around her, in the wood-paneled room. "Am I a good person?" she repeated. "I need to know."

Walter looked at his glass. Mary Ann thought how disappointing it would be if he said yes, the useless rush of a hug or a pat on the back, the immediate doubts about his sincerity. And at the same time, how she craved it! Had she ever been told that, even once? As stupid as it is, maybe it's something we need, to just believe we're good people, to be told, at least once.

"I think the question is misleading," said Walter. "Unanswerable. There seems to be a desire in your generation to resolve the complexity of the world in fixed dualities. Everything is good or evil, honest or crooked, healthy or deadly. But is it so?" He brushed the tip of his white mustache, gently. "I doubt there's any such thing as a good person. Even good actions are hard to know with certainty. We do bad things for good reasons, good things for awful, selfish reasons. The more muddled and indiscernible the world becomes, the more the rhetoric of the times seems bent on simplifying it into pairs. In the end, what escapes our dichotomies is the reality of our day-to-day world, and there nothing is ever quite so clear." He paused, and Mary Ann looked up to meet his grandfatherly blue eyes. Glancing at her phone, she saw the time: 11:57, three minutes left in her shift. "But you *care*, dear, and that is more than I can say about most people I know. The fact that you even ask yourself such questions, so fervently, betrays a higher moral concern than you give yourself credit for."

"Not that that's any help to anybody," said Mary Ann, unable to refrain from self-mocking. One more of her sympathy tricks. Walter might be right about the world, but he couldn't see just how deep Mary Ann's rottenness ran, she was sure of it.

But it was time to go. Her shift was over, and a team of unnamed downtown computer geeks was waiting for her to open the doors of the Positano to invading forces. She thanked Walter for their talk, and started to get up from his table.

"I am really sorry about your aunt," Walter said. "I was thinking, perhaps there is something I could do to help. A solution of sorts. But you're going home now, I don't want to detain you."

"I—I'm sorry."

"I will see you on Sunday, of course?" he asked.

Sunday. She hadn't thought of her life *after* the sabotage at all. Coming back to the Positano, after the night that would change everything.

"Of course," she said. "I don't think I've ever left *before* you, now that I think of it."

"Oh, it's a funny thing. I am meeting someone, at midnight, in fact. An old man like me, having a meeting at midnight—isn't that utterly ludicrous?"

The harpsichord was playing the ninth counterpoint in Bach's *Art of the Fugue*. Mary Ann walked up to it in a daze, trying hard to appear as casual and nonterrified as she could, although she knew that deactivating the camera feeds and erasing all incriminating data would be the hackers' first job once they were granted access. The instrument was beautiful: two keyboards with elegant dark brown keys, a sturdy redwood case, the open lid of which was decorated on the inside with an elaborate floral inlay. Mary Ann reached inside, behind the front panel, where the necessary evil of a backlit LCD screen ruined the illusion of antiquity. She had practiced finessing the device into its port in the dark, at home, in case she wouldn't be able to see it. But with an empty room, and Walter quietly reading his book at a reasonable distance from the instrument, and the large doorframe separating the lounge area from the bar, she had no reason not to take her time.

It all looked so silly.

She slid the device into the USB port with no effort, even getting the right side on the first try.

No going back now.

A small red light started blinking on the small black matchbox, then changed to a static green. It was done.

16

Tom

The messages started as soon as Tom got back from his honeymoon. An encrypted text from an unknown number: Unexpected legal fees; additional expenditure necessary. Then, days later: Due to unforeseeable circumstances, we regret to inform that all payment is required by the end of the month. Finally: You had better pay up, son.

Tom's first instinct, born of the fear of miscommunication he'd felt ever since landing at McCarran years before, was that he'd misunderstood something. There had to be some responsibility he'd neglected, some task he'd forgotten to carry out, and now he had put the whole operation in jeopardy. It must be his fault. Even when the texts started veering from professional, to ominous, to straight-up threatening, Tom failed to jump to the criminal conclusion. It took days of contrite requests for explanations and less and less equivocal answers for him to finally wake up and smell the entrapment.

What's so hard to understand? $100,000 and you get to stay in the country. No $100,000 and you get deported at the end of the month.

I'm sorry, but maybe is a mistake? The price was $14,999, you remember?

And now it's a hundred. Things change.

And the legal fees were paid in the advance, maybe
you forgot that I paid the advance?

Seriously?

Yes, yes, I paid the $8,000, to the man
at the Dolly's. You remember, it was one
white chip and three yellow chips? From the
Positano. I asked for a receipt, but he said
it was redundant, maybe is why you forgot?

Are you really this dense?

I am confused.

https://en.wikipedia.org/wiki/Extortion

And so on.

Eventually even Tom had to admit it was possible he was being blackmailed. By real American criminals. For an amount he had never come
close to possessing in his life. It was possible, in fact, that the first entirely
individual initiative he'd ever taken, with no help or encouragement from
surrogate father figures, had landed him in the thickest mess of his young
life. He felt his confidence, whatever precious little he'd put together after
Tucson, shrink back and hide behind his fears. It was confidence, the illusion of confidence, that got him into trouble in the first place, and now that
he needed some in the face of real danger, it was nowhere to be seen. He
was himself again: poor helpless Tom.

He spent the day in bed, sweating under excessive covers, trying to wish
the whole thing away. When that didn't work, he tried vomiting it out, three
times. Was Lily in on this too? Of course she was, she had to be. His lawfully

wedded wife, conspiring against him from the start. How much was her cut? Would she make enough to open her dog business? Or was that a lie too? She did seem awfully indifferent to poor little Pepperthedog. Sitting on the bathroom floor, exhausted from retching, focusing on the cool touch of the tiles against his skinny posterior, he looked at the cheap wedding band on his finger. This wasn't going to go away.

It was clear he had no options. He couldn't pay, because he didn't have the money, and he couldn't *not* pay, because his wife and her criminal friends were going to turn him in to the police, or worse. He was going to wait until the deadline, a miserable lump of failure in a bedroom in West Paradise, and then his foolish mistakes would catch up with him, and everything would be over. His arrogant desire to change his life. His selfish dream of deserving better than what he was given.

The only possible source of hope, if not of solving the problem, at least of going down fighting, was the red-haired philosopher loudly slurping Lucky Charms in the living room. Tom hadn't forgiven him for the road-trip incident—he couldn't—but his petty betrayal seemed now sort of put in perspective by the actual large-scale scam pulled off by the MCF people. If anything, Trevor's experience in the field of being a shitty person might come in handy.

"They're bluffing," Trevor said at the end of his story.

Throughout Tom's rambling, apologetic, adverbially rich tale, Trevor's eyebrows had climbed farther and farther up his forehead, pointed, as if trying to recede into the amber-red recesses of his hair. He listened carefully. He smiled a few times, laughed at a picture of a worried-looking Tom holding Pepperthedog on the edge of a precipice, and frowned only once, when Tom admitted to backchanneling him with Rick ("You don't talk to a bro's dealer without asking him first, Tomsky"). But more than the surprise, the amazement at Tom's reckless, admirable courage, the pride in having shaped a true alpha from the softest, most beta clay in the riverbed of masculinity, more even than the concern about the inextricable cluster-fuck his roommate had found a way into, shining in Trevor's green eyes as he listened to Tom, was the joy of true friendship regained. Or his version of that, anyway.

He was eating his Lucky Charms without mentioning the fact that Tom had at some point removed all the marshmallows from them, one by one, in the last act of their domestic conflict. It was standard protocol, to carry on with one's activities without acknowledging the discomfort (otherwise the terrorists win). Now it was clear that the joy of being asked for help, of getting back his loyal disciple after so many weeks, was worth more to Trevor than any marshmallow piece could ever be. He seemed truly happy to talk to Tom, and Tom began to feel the familiar pang of guilt. Maybe Trevor cared about him after all.

"They're bluffing," Trevor said. "The sleazy fucks."

"Bluffing?"

"They're not gonna do shit, they just want to scare you."

"But how do you know?"

"First of all, you said your wife—congratulations, by the way—is involved, so they can't turn you in to the police, you see? You get deported, fine, but she gets some serious jail time."

"Is that true?"

"Yes, I told you, I've done research on all this immigration stuff."

Tom looked down, as if *he* had said something wrong. Trevor's spoon clinked against the cereal bowl, breaking the silence.

"They probably send those to every couple they marry, hoping to find some suckers who'll get scared and pay."

"But I cannot pay!"

Trevor smiled.

"Good thing you're not a sucker, then!"

The feeling of asking for help had a special warmth of comfort and shame. It was a relief from the world of action, a surrendering of one's agency. Like getting under woolly covers after being out in the rain, or peeing your pants as a kid. As soon as Trevor started talking, Tom recognized the warm embrace of letting go; the humiliating joy of having his future be outside of his control and in the hands of someone else, someone *better*. It had been so stupid to think he'd be better off on his own.

"What should I do now, man, bro?"

Trevor thought about it for a few seconds. "I think, first off, don't panic," he said.

"Right," said Tom, tasting the vomit still in his breath.

"You don't show them you're scared."

Trevor made a show of topping up his bowl with the last of the milk in the carton. He shook the empty container with a smile. Doves of peace flying in the war-torn apartment.

"But I'm supposed to see Lily tomorrow. With the dog, in the Sunset Park."

"Even better."

"I don't go?"

"You absolutely go. You go, and you talk to *your wife*"—a slight spike in Trevor's voice—"and you act normal. Like nothing happened at all."

"But why?"

"Because, my friend, we want them to believe you have the money."

Tom gasped.

"But I don't have the hundred thousands! I never had the hundred thousands!"

"That's not what's important. We are only doing it so that you can set up a meeting with them face-to-face."

"Face-to-face?"

"Face-to-face. Enough with this bullshit texting. No more talking to their henchmen. They want a hundred grand, they better show their fucking face. Whoever's in charge."

"And then what?"

"Then you show them who they're dealing with. You take down the alpha. Establish dominance."

"I mean, Trevor, man, I don't know. Is me you talk about."

"You can do it. You're ready," said Trevor, pausing for a suspenseful second to lend his sentence weight. "Don't think I haven't noticed how much you've changed. You're ready."

And maybe he was. If Trevor saw it, he knew he could be. Because in spite of everything that had happened, in spite of his selfishness, his careless disregard for the consequences of his actions, Trevor still was a better man than him. A stronger man. And as pathetic as it sounded, this investiture was everything Tom had been waiting for since he'd moved in almost two years ago.

"Will you help me, man?"

Trevor's smile was so broad with palpable glee that he looked like he could cry.

"Of course I will, man. We'll plan the meeting together, you'll eat them alive. But first, let's take care of tomorrow's thing with the wife. One step at a time."

The warm warm feeling of asking for help, seeping through. Like a hug. Like Christmas presents under the tree. Like a whispered, familiar voice telling Tom it was okay, everything was just as it was supposed to be. Everything was going to be all right.

"And Tomsky," said Trevor, as his roommate got up to go fall on his bed in exhausted relief, and sleep the fourteen hours until morning. "I'm really sorry about what happened down south. That Patrick dude is a dick, I'm sorry he scared you like that. I should have stayed with you upstairs and done more research like I'd promised. I was a shitty friend."

Tom looked down at the floor, his cheeks flushed with something he'd never felt.

"I—," he said. "I'm very sorry about the marshmallows, man."

In keeping with the preset Narrative, Tom was required to visit Lily's two-bedroom in Warm Springs twice a week for the first three months of their marriage. While a certain degree of familiarity with the apartment was required in the unlikely event of a Fraud Interview, these visits essentially boiled down to photo ops. Lily's social media presence was to wane almost immediately with married life, as per Narrative. The @Pepperthedog account, however, needed to be kept alive and #barking at least through the animal's peak stages of cuteness and puppitude. The feed was a good chance to shore up the Narrative without being too time-consuming: Pepperthedog soaked and soaped up at the groomer's, with Lily going "Awwwwww" in background (ten-second video); scampering alongside Mommy and Daddy on a trail at Red Rock Canyon (confirming the established Hiking Storyline); and, on Sundays, enjoying a chiller outing at nearby Sunset Park.

Truth was, over their weeks at the canyons, Tom had bonded a lot more with the dog than with his wife. The Pomeranian was fluffy, overly cute, and had about him a look of sadness and existential dread that Tom found quite endearing. This was no happy-go-lucky blueblood dog. He was an outcast, a fellow worrier, Tom could just tell. The buzzkill of the toy-dog gang. The two of them soon found an understanding, and Tom had enjoyed their time together a lot, in spite of the constant fear their Assigned Pet would try to end it all in the scenic surroundings of southern Utah or northwestern Arizona.

Lily, on the other hand, remained a stranger. Her passion for hiking was of a silent, contemplative nature, and through most of their long walks Tom found himself alone with the dog, drafting the conversations he would try to initiate back at the hotel. But then, when he was just about bursting with desire to talk, Lily would deflect his openers with bored disengagement, or respond in a flat monotone while chewing on her tacos. After dinner she put on pink headphones and disappeared into Netflix until bedtime, while Tom watched an unappreciated postcard sun disappear behind the mountains of Page, or Kanab, or Bryce. Then it all started again the next day.

Tom couldn't figure it out. He wasn't trying to establish a real relationship with his wife—in fact, the Arrangement's Preliminary Agreement explicitly ruled out all romantic entanglement and intercourse—but he figured if they were to share such a reckless dose of risk, they might as well be on speaking terms. Friends, even, why not? United by communal hardship, and so on and so forth. But Lily was having none of it. Alternating between cold businesslike reserve and flat-out hostility, she seemed dead set on committing as little as possible of herself to the marriage, visibly anxious to get it over with and go back to her life, whatever that was. For days Tom had tried to connect with her through shared interests, personal memories, and painstakingly rehearsed jokes, but he'd finally come to the conclusion that it was a waste of time. He'd spent the last of his honeymoon in silent admiration of the natural scenery, sharing defeated looks with the dog. Sweet, gentle, troubled Pepperthedog.

"What do you mean, gone?" he said on Sunday morning, when Lily came to open the door in her pajamas, yawning and dogless.

"Gone. Not here," she said.

The apartment was in the stretch of Paradise just south of McCarran Airport, southeast of the Strip, where Warm Springs Road runs a trail of hot, trembling asphalt from the AC of the South Vegas outlets to Sunset Park's benevolent tree-shade. Short houses with white decks and backyard swimming pools color up the secondary streets on either side, among the red gravel, but the area remains very much a province of the all-powerful sun god.

"Where, then?"

"I don't know, they took him away."

"But they can't take Pepperthedog!" said Tom, already losing his much-rehearsed cool. Trevor was clearly wrong about him being ready.

"Why do you even care?"

"Well he's our . . ." He tried to regain his composure. "He's *my* dog."

"*Their* dog, technically. They probably need him for another Arrangement. Is there something wrong, dude?"

Tom was sweating through his Caves of Positano shirt. If they were trying to scare him, as Trevor said, then taking the dog hostage was a smart, if despicable, tactic. Lily must have told them how much he loved the little thing, and now they were cashing in on those stupid displays of sentimentality of his. If he didn't go through with Trevor's plan fast, they would probably start sending little puffs of Pomeranian hair, the tip of his tail, an ear. He needed to get it together.

"No, no wrong," he said. "All good."

"Cooool," said Lily, dragging the vowel longer than necessary.

"I shall be ready for them soon," said Tom.

Lily shrugged. She was leaning against the doorframe, in her PJs, not inviting Tom in.

"You can say it, you know?" said Tom. "Quite ready, yes."

"Soooo," said Lily.

Tom forced a smile.

"Maybe we should take a photograph? For the Instagram?"

"Look, dude, I think we're fine. Those interviews never really happen. We'll be just fine, as long as *neither of us fucks up.*"

Tom nodded theatrically to let her know her message was understood. If this was how she was going to play it, then fine by him. He wouldn't let anything happen to innocent little Pepperthedog.

"No fucking up."

"Right."

He stepped back. "I should leave now."

"Yes."

"Goodbye," he said. "I am ready."

The look on Lily's face when she shut the door was in equal parts confusion and disinterest.

Trevor was intensely, scarily happy. He covered it up a little, but Tom knew him too well by now to miss his tells. He talked fast, pacing around the room in rubber-toed strides, arms swinging around as he vibrated with professorial impetus. Some men are just born to teach.

It was clear that Tom's sheepish return to his apprenticeship, after denying him and striking out on his own, had given Trevor a strong, childish joy. But more, that Tom should come back to him in the grips of such a textbook beta crisis, real-life danger that could only be solved through willpower, and fearlessness, and alpha poise, it looked almost too perfect. The situation, Tom recognized, seemed specifically designed to make Trevor's best qualities shine.

Which was lucky, because Tom was drowning. It was the night before the meeting, the night before the appointment with the criminals under the pretense of paying up the blackmail, and he was in no way ready.

As the deadline got closer, and the messages kept coming, and the chances of opening the door to a packaged Pomeranian paw grew higher by the minute, Tom had started to lose hope. In fact, he knew he'd feel completely lost without Trevor. These were criminals they were dealing with here, real remorseless American criminals, and he was still as much a clueless foreigner as he'd ever been. It was one thing to be comfortable with small-time weed dealers from Rebibbia—who, let's be honest, only put up with him because they knew his mother as a long-time valued customer anyway. But this, this was serious crime, and there was just no way Tom was going to stand up against it and live to tell the tale. He was going home. Defeated. Banned. Truly and forever trapped on the wrong side of the world.

And what would it change, anyway? He'd be a loser on that side of the Atlantic, just like he'd been a loser on this one. He'd had a streak of luck, nothing else, and he thought his life had changed. How many tourists had he seen, sitting down with $80 at the table and running it up through drunken, lucky mistakes to $800, $1,000, even more? Always in their eyes, that look of misguided confidence, the illusion of control while the rest of the world is laughing at you. Not real confidence, Trevor confidence. Alpha confidence. No. The ridiculous sense that your luck is something you deserve, that it somehow informs your life. Trevor once called it the "burned hand fallacy," or something like that. And then it always ended the same way. A big pot building, a large, oversize preflop raise by the tourist. And a reg, sitting in the big blind, looking down at two aces. Every time.

He would go home, and all of this would be a dream. He would forget America existed, forget a city where money grew like fruit from the poker tables, small round pretty fruit of different colors that anybody, even Tom, could pick up and claim. He would forget there was a time in his life when he'd had a bedside drawer full of money, enough to live on for months and months without fear, without having to *fight*. He would go home, and live the life of the masses without hope, the calm of the nonhope, the forever silence of surviving surviving surviving without hope. Because he'd just been lucky for a while. And now it was over.

"Will you cut it out with this bullshit, dude?" said Trevor. "Come on!"

"Is true, Trevor, man," said Tom. "All true."

"Well, it *will be* true if you keep up with that attitude. Haven't I taught you anything?"

Trevor kept pacing in circles around the room, at the center of which Tom sat on the floor like a wounded animal. As much as Trevor's energy was expended entirely on the didactic, Tom couldn't help seeing something vaguely predatory in the choreography of their conversation.

"I can't show them the dominance tomorrow, Trevor."

"Yes, you can."

"They will see that I am scared."

"You won't be."

"I will forget all your instructions."

"You don't have to remember anything. You just show up, and tell them you're not paying. Literally nothing bad can happen, you're meeting at the safest place in Vegas."

"Trevor, you don't understand, man, bro. I am not like you. I am no alpha."

"That's it, we're watching *Top Gun*. Right now."

Cue Steve Stevens's guitar. Cue the F-14 Tomcats. Cue the third-act resurgence of the fallen hero's confidence after the obligatory low point. See Tom Cruise, the shortest alpha male in Hollywood history, ostensibly learn the value of teamwork at the end of his character arc, regaining his cocky testosterone-addled self after like a half hour of doubt. Feel your chest swell with manly American pride. Believe in yourself.

Watching *Top Gun* with Trevor had always been a learning experience. With minimal gestures and single-word commentary—to avoid distraction—he directed Tom's gaze to the essential behavioral teachings in Tom Cruise's performance. *Shoulders. Answer. Eye contact.* Yet today, Tom's fears took time to melt. A last-minute resistance to Trevor's charms. Doubts and suspicion from their recent falling-out lingering still through "Great Balls of Fire" and "Watch the birdie!" all the way to "Tower, this is Ghost Rider requesting a flyby." Something was off.

In a month's time, it would be two years since Tom had first seen Trevor: sauntering toward his tournament table holding a brimming chip rack, pretending to be scared of the "European wizard" sitting to his left. Did he still see him in the same inspiring, enviable light, a real man ready to shuck the oyster of the world, pry it open, and feast on the quivering moistness inside? After the ups and recent plentiful downs of their friendship, Tom was still not convinced he understood the man. All available data pointed to him being the most selfish individual he'd ever met (cf. the at best unbelievably careless border plan he'd devised to get Tom to go on a YouTube-friendly road trip to Mexico with him). Yet how to explain his seemingly genuine obsession with helping others? Tom, Ana and Larissa (who he'd volunteered to drive all the way home for free), all the vlog followers whose comments he'd spent hours and hours answering one by one. Selfish reasons or not, it was undeniable that Trevor's life calling seemed to be in finding more and more situations in which he could help others. And if that's all you do, just more and more and more, day after day, doesn't that count for something in the end? Who was to say that wasn't the *real* Trevor?

As Tom Cruise stumbled through his perfunctory self-doubt and muddy parental backstory, Tom slowly found his attention shifting from the screen to his newly regained friend. This young, excited film critic in five-toed shoes, pointing an index finger at the screen with a confident nod, relishing the attention. Maybe it was crazy to still listen to him, after everything that had happened.

But here Tom realized, a thought that for the first time crawled its sticky way inside his head, that perhaps the issue wasn't about *listening* to him at all. That maybe the real lesson beta Tom needed to learn was how to *use* Trevor, just like Trevor would use him. How to give him the attention he so craved, and take everything he had to offer. Learn how to be the kind of friend Trevor had been to him, and how to truly and finally look at the world as his personal, planet-wide, lavish buffet table, rather than a high school pop quiz he wasn't ready for.

You can be my wingman anytime, said Trevor's eyes, as he teared up after the triumphant landing back on USS *Enterprise.*

Bullshit, thought Tom. *You can be mine.*

They stayed up all night, going over the plan for the following day again and again. Posture. Demeanor. Key points in the conversation. Trevor sharing lessons he learned from his father, about the power of misdirection, about the thrill of captivating an entranced audience. Tom finally understanding that the road to self-affirmation is through the subjugation of others, through the clever manipulation of people to suit our most urgent needs. He could do this. It was happening. The first truly burning sun of the year found them awake and laughing, tense but ready. Both knew what they had to do.

It was the dawn of the first of May, and Tom's meeting was only eighteen hours away. At midnight. Inside the Positano. At the Scarlatti Lounge.

He dreamed of the accident again. He didn't think about it often, and talked about it even less. He'd told Trevor the story only once, when they were both drunk, running back and forth around the fake traffic lights at the Shibuya late at night. He still dreamed about it, though—in isolated, nonnarrative flashes, or in stretched-out sequences that extended in time far beyond what he could remember. The real thing had taken place in Rome, exactly twenty-one years before. On May 1.

The stick blender was never meant to stay plugged in, covered in chocolate cream, on the edge of the kitchen sink. It's just that everybody had left home in a hurry after lunch, Mom, and Francesco, and Dad—a hand pressed against his stomach—and little Tommaso had been left behind with Grandma. There had been no time to clean up the kitchen.

Five-year-old Tom felt shortchanged. Ripped off. Mom had promised him there'd be a special chocolate dessert for their Worker's Day lunch, but after the main course Dad told him he had "just a little indigestion, it's nothing. Just wait for us here, okay?" and then they'd all left. He remembered Grandma on the living room couch, distracted by some big crash in the car race on TV Dad had turned on earlier. She never saw her hungry, foolish grandson tiptoe to the kitchen, unsupervised, alone.

Once inside the kitchen, little Tommaso couldn't find his cake. The cake was a lie. What he did find was the stick blender, easily within his short reach, its blades covered in dense, delicious chocolate. He didn't think about it for a second before he grabbed it with two hands, and was already tasting the cold sweet joy of molten chocolate on his lips when the buzzing started.

He had never been in a taxi before, but he didn't get to enjoy the ride much as he cried all the way to the hospital, his too-large white T-shirt covered in blood. Grandma talked to herself or to God or the taxi driver, it wasn't clear. The radio was on, someone talking about the accident at the Formula One race.

The really strange thing—the thing Tom had kept dreaming about all this time, and that seemed in and of itself so dreamlike and odd, he had to remind himself this was really how it happened—the surprising thing was that once they reached the hospital, everybody else was already there. He saw Francesco, and Grandma, and Mom, all there in the emergency room as the lady in white stitched his lower lip, which was split in two and flapping like an open book, or so he remembered. They were there in the dream, in the room with him, though in reality they had probably waited outside.

Only sometimes, in the dream, Dad was there too, young and laughing and all right, though that of course hadn't happened. Instead, Dad was in a different room in the ER, where they had brought him earlier, as the doctor had told Grandma as soon as they'd arrived.

"Often mistaken for indigestion or ulcer—," Grandma had repeated, to herself, or to God, or the doctor. "If not treated right away—"

Little Tom wondered what "infraction of the posterior archery" had to do with him cutting his lower lip in half with a stick blender, but he didn't ask. He wondered how Mom and Francesco had got to the hospital before them, and how they'd known they'd be there, but he didn't ask. He wondered what happened to the pilot in the race on TV, but he didn't ask. Only, those rare times when in the dream his dad was there with the others too, he asked to be forgiven for not waiting like he'd told him to, for having tried to get the cake for himself instead, because he'd wanted it so much. He was really, really sorry.

Tom entered the lounge in slow, long strides. By the bar counter, in the antechamber, he paused to survey the space around him. Not leaning, or swaying, or rocking back and forth. He stood, still and poised, aware of people's attention being irresistibly drawn toward him. At ease. In command.

Except there wasn't really anybody there, save for a rubicund bartender with plump red hands who welcomed him with a mildly surprised smile. It wasn't clear whether this was a result of his attention being irresistibly drawn toward Tom, or him simply doing his job.

The larger room past the archway looked almost empty too: just one man sitting, facing the bar, an open book resting on the marble table in front of him. His man.

Tom nodded to him from far away. He took his time ordering a daiquiri from the bartender, pointing to the table where he'd be drinking it, even though he could see no waitress around at all. Then he straightened his back and walked on to the sitting room.

"Please sit down, dear," said the man. "Hello."

"Hello," said Tom.

"I apologize for the rather desolate surroundings, this was not my intention. It was my understanding that midnight would be a livelier time in a Las Vegas bar," said the man. "I'm afraid I miscalculated how many people care for Bach these days." He lifted his chin, pointing to the harpsichord behind them, which was performing without a player. Quiet music, a melody chasing itself like a shadow. Tom realized he'd missed its existence altogether, and reproached himself. *Be observant. Be in control.* "I don't want you to feel intimidated, at all."

"Is okay," said Tom.

"We are two businessmen, after all, having a friendly business meeting here. Nothing to be scared about."

"I am not scared," said Tom, feeling not quite at the helm of the conversation.

"That is lovely to hear," said the man. "My name, as I'm sure you know, is Walter Simmons. I'm delighted to finally make your acquaintance, Tommaso." He pronounced his name perfectly: the rounder, leaned-on *m*'s, the sweet, vibrating *s*. A sound Tom had almost started to forget. His handshake was weak, his skin cold.

"Have you been to this lounge before?" said Walter.

Tom shook his head no. He was so concentrated on his lines that Walter's small talk felt deliberate, a tactic to throw him off his game. Yet the man seemed so innocuous, so jolly and harmless in his snow-white mustache and ocean-blue eyes, that he was having the hardest time reconciling him with the criminal mastermind he'd expected to meet. Walter wore an ocher suit, a round, healthy gut, and an overall not-of-this-time look. His voice was deep, and his accent so clean Tom could understand every last word. That this lovable grandpa would be out to get him seemed suddenly unbelievable. Maybe the whole thing really *was* just a big misunderstanding.

"I thought you would enjoy *that*," said Walter, pointing to the large painting above the archway separating the sitting room from the bar. "*The*

Approach to the Villa Borghese. The most beautiful park in the most beautiful city, isn't it?"

Tom recognized the gates, the monumental entrance to the quiet city park where his father had taught him how to ride a bike. Long-ago Sundays, the sweet crunch of candied peanuts. Tom's father had grown up in North Rome, among the well-to-do families and the postcard prettiness of the architecture, and even after years of living in Rebibbia had always insisted on taking the children to play there, in the aristocratic tree-shade of Villa Borghese. "Why not our own neighborhood park?" Mom would say. "What's wrong with accepting what we have?" The painting was wide and heavy-looking, and showed a nineteenth-century procession of horse-drawn carriages and top-hatted *signori*, coming and going from the park as a few token poor looked up in awe.

"I've always found it clever that they would hang that here," said Walter. "The aristocrats and the poor coming out to play at the same grand venue. Wiles's architects have a pleasantly dark sense of humor, wouldn't you agree?"

"Mr. Walter—," said Tom.

Walter raised a hand to silence him. The bartender came, bearing a round tray, and left on the table a fresh old-fashioned and Tom's tall, decorative-umbrellaed daiquiri.

"Personal delivery," said Walter. "We are honored."

"Shift change, sir, I apologize." The bartender's cheeks were lobster-red, and he looked tired from the short walk from bar to table. "New waitress taking longer than usual to arrive today, I'm awfully sorry."

"That's quite all right my friend, quite all right," said Walter.

The man left with a little obsequious bow. He looked so perfect in his Prohibition-era garb that it was hard to imagine him wearing anything contemporary. Tom tried to picture him in sweatpants and a T-shirt, playing video games at home, but still ended up with him stirring a Manhattan in Capone's Chicago.

"I understand you have something for me tonight," Walter finally said. "Yes?"

This was it. Tom felt the atmosphere at the lounge change, the air grow heavier, denser. He could swear he heard a faint beeping sound somewhere behind him.

"No need for overt exchanges," continued Walter. "I will give you instructions for a safe dropoff."

Tom took a deep breath.

"I think," he said, trying to remember Trevor's exact phrasing. "I think that you have nothing."

"Beg your pardon?"

"You have nothing," repeated Tom, in a higher pitch than he would have wanted. He tried to lower it, maybe not like Trevor's, but at least approximating Patrick's low, effortful rasp. "You are bluffing."

The man seemed surprised, but less concerned than amused. He took a long sip of his drink, then stared at the red cherry in the glass as if trying to decipher some particularly small script.

"Would you care to elaborate, please?" he said, after some time.

"Elaborate?"

"I am fascinated by this deduction of yours. I would love to know how you came to it."

"If you send me to the police," said Tom, reciting from memory, "you will lose Lily too. She will go to jail. So you cannot do that."

"Lily?"

Walter looked directly into Tom's eyes, making it challenging to maintain eye contact. "My wife, Lily. She goes to jail. Is the law, I have checked. I am to be deported, but she is imprisoned."

"And that is my problem how?"

Tom mentally scanned his rehearsed script in search of an answer. There was a chance he'd fucked this up already.

"My . . . my wife, she works for you! So you cannot deport me without imprisoning her."

"My child, you sound confused. Your wife, according to what I hear, has committed a federal crime, it's only natural that she would be . . . *imprisoned*."

"But she works for you! She is a part of your organization!"

"I'm afraid you've let your imagination get the better of you, dear. This isn't a spy movie, there are no organizations. We are just two businessmen, meeting in a very public bar: one, law-abiding and with nothing to hide; the other, unfortunately, an undocumented immigrant, with a foolish wife who committed a crime to help him. A very sad story. But criminals have to be stopped, no matter how pitiful their case."

"But I have proof!"

"Proof?"

"I have the texts! I know your name!"

Walter smiled. His smile was warm, pitying, and his eyes moved from Tom's jittery frown to the leather-bound *Spoon River Anthology* resting faceup on the table between them, then back to Tom.

"Look around you," he said. "Not only are there cameras recording our meeting, *you* could be recording us too, for all I know. Does it look like I'm concerned? Ask yourself, dear, truly ask yourself what this *proof* of yours amounts to."

Nothing. It amounted to nothing. Blinded by Trevor's optimism, he'd failed to appreciate just how truly and irrevocably fucked he was. Self-erasing texts on a completely anonymous, encrypted app. A name that was most likely fake. A wife who, he saw it now, was just as much a victim of this as he was, innocent and naive and stupid. If he went to the police, he would incriminate himself and her, just to mount a ridiculously weak case against a mysterious old man he knew nothing about. Trevor had, once again, failed to see the big picture. There was nothing left for Tom. He had lost.

"What have you done to Pepperthedog, you monster?"

"The dog?"

"Are you taking my dog in hostage?"

"In host—What are you talking about?"

"The dog, Pepperthedog, do not hurt him!"

"Why would I hurt the dog?"

"He's weak and alone, and he needs love."

"Fine, sure, no hurting the dog." Walter's voice for the first time rose in a slight accent of impatience. Tom's ineptness in his role as an extortion victim was seemingly starting to frustrate him. "You have my word. Now, if we could perhaps return to the matter at hand—"

The harpsichord's skeletal twang drifted beautifully in the air around them. But whenever the music paused, Tom could feel a haunting stillness in the wood-paneled room; a rare Las Vegas feeling of perfect loneliness, an absence of people. No one there to help. He must be hallucinating in his state of utter confusion, because he kept hearing low, rhythmic beeping behind him too, like a digital clock on its lowest setting, pulsating every thirty seconds or so, ticking the countdown to his inevitable capitulation.

There was nothing left to do.

"I don't have the hundred thousands, Walter, mister, sir. I have never had it."

Walter's expression didn't waver, staying agreeable, serene. He took another sip from his amber-colored drink, holding the liquid in his mouth for some time before swallowing. It was unclear whether he was savoring his cocktail or Tom's confession, but in either case he seemed to find the results to his taste.

"You know what I like most about Las Vegas?" he said.

"Sir?"

"Las Vegas," he began, "is the most honest city in America. Maybe in the whole world. See, in the rest of the world, the rich hide away from the poor. They sequester themselves in clubs, palaces, private parties. Overly public displays of wealth are generally seen as crass. There's a certain shame to it, being that rich, or maybe a sense that the prying eyes of the poor may corrupt one's precious beautiful things, burn them with the flame of their covetousness. You can live a lifetime in London, and only gawk at the buildings of the rich from the outside, only guess at what their life must be like." His mind seemed to wander off, his gaze lost in the melting ice cubes in his drink. It only lasted a second, then he snapped back to his jolly old self. "But Las Vegas! Wealth is everywhere, and everywhere visible, displayed, even conveniently color-coded! Nowhere to hide it. One can walk up to the baccarat room and watch the Chinese high rollers punch the table in victory or defeat, marveling at the phenomenal amounts of money in play, even stealing their delicious free cookies. One can play a penny slot right outside the Michelin star restaurants, watching ladies come out stumbling in their high heels, drunk on three-thousand-dollar wine. One can, my child, come *upstairs* to your little poker room and *count* every last penny on the table, one by one, until one knows exactly what kind of money you have or don't have. Someone might find it inelegant, the way this town forces people to carry around little colored markers of their social standing for all to see, but I say bring it. Drop the farce. Let's stop pretending this isn't all about money anyway. Let's stop *lying*."

To Tom's surprise, Walter reached inside the breast pocket of his suit, producing a big-screen smartphone that he operated at literal arm's length, with an old man's squint and an unsteady finger. After an awkwardly long silence, during which Tom wondered whether he should offer to help, Walter finally turned the phone sideways and handed it to Tom.

On the screen, sitting on the hood of his truck in front of a breathtaking Mexican sunset, was Trevor.

"Is not true!" said Tom, dumbfounded, at the end of the video. "He lies!"

"Oh, come dear, no need for modesty now."

"No, no, I swear, I am no high-stakes wizard, I play the one dollar/three dollars!"

"That's not what your friend says. And you expect me to believe you had to suddenly leave your friend alone, halfway through a holiday in Mexico with two beautiful girls, to come back to play penny poker?"

Tom's mind was racing. How did he keep finding himself in these situations, trapped in terrifying conversations with strangers where his English failed him and his heart thumped so hard he thought it would burst through his ribs? And why was the reason always Trevor?

"Is not what happened, I didn't leave to play poker!" he pleaded. "Is a long story, I was angry with him."

"In a different video he tells the story of how you met at a thousand-dollar tournament—which you routinely play. He was eliminated, but you reached the final table, as usual. Should I show you?"

"Is not true! I mean, maybe is true, but not like that—"

"More recently he explained you wouldn't appear in the videos because you were away from Las Vegas to play high roller tournaments in Florida, twenty-five-thousand buy-in, one-hundred-thousand buy-in. I am not stupid, dear, I have done my research."

His research. Him too. Tom's life was ruined because seemingly everyone around him sucked at using the internet.

"Is all a big misunderstanding," he said, with tears in his eyes. *"Come te lo spiego?"*

"Honestly, I admire you poker players greatly. I have the utmost respect for people who can carve a life for themselves outside the social class trap. You gamed the system, exploited a weakness of the rich, and took their money. Nobody else does that. Well, *I* do that, in fact."

"But I don't!"

"And that's something else that makes Las Vegas an extraordinarily honest city: because the very visual nature of these money exchanges forces us to reckon with another deep truth about our world, one we would like to sweep under our collective conscience's rug: that all wanting is a *wanting from.*"

"Mr. Walter, sir, if you can wait, I can explain—"

"A taking from someone."

"Is Trevor, he said he wanted to make a movie character for me, to protect me—" Even in his state, Tom could see the irony of this. There was a definite, very clear beeping sound coming from behind them, where the harpsichord was: it had sped up now, maybe every ten seconds or so, and got louder.

"You of all people should understand zero-sum games, Mr. High Stakes Poker. For me to finally win, someone has to lose."

"But I don't have—"

"Just like all the people who lost to make you who you are today. I don't see you worry about *them.*"

"I don't take anything! Mr. Walter, sir, maybe is because you don't know me well?"

"I know more than enough."

"But I am a good person!"

Walter burst into laughter. It was a good, hearty laugh, part childish fun, part evil genius, and part Santa Claus. Tom was surprised to notice a gold tooth at the back of Walter's mouth. The beeping from the harpsichord was impossible to miss now, and getting more frequent.

"What *is* it with your generation and this ludicrous obsession with being *good people*? Have social media finally made you incapable of discerning any nuance between black and white? You are so bloody *earnest*, it's almost too easy to take advantage of you."

"I don't have the hundred thousands, sir, I don't."

Walter was still laughing.

"If that's true, you're even more of an idiot than I thought. But that doesn't change your predicament, I'm afraid."

Tom couldn't take this anymore. It felt like the room itself, which had seemed almost eerily quiet just a few minutes ago, was screaming like a madman into his ears. The slashing metallic flurry of a four-voice *stretto* from the harpsichord. The sound of Walter's laugh. The incessant, hurried beeping, now closer to a ticking alarm. The certainty that his undeserved streak of luck was coming to a crushing, humiliating end, and that he would now have to face the consequences of two years of loud, sinful hopefulness. It was his fault, all of it, and poor innocent Lily was going to pay the price of his complete idiocy. He was no alpha. He wasn't even a man. He was a child reaching for the chocolate cream, a stupid child whose hunger for more made horrible, horrible things happen. It was all his fault.

He pushed back his chair with a screech. He needed to leave, to run away, to escape. The beeping sound, coming from some kind of black boxy device attached to the back of the harpsichord, was now hectic, almost continuous.

"I go . . . get Trevor," he said, with an awful sense of déjà vu. "He is in the casino, outside. I can get Trevor, and he will explain it was all a lie."

He rushed for the exit, but Walter sprang from his seat with a young man's reflex, and grabbed him by the arm.

"There is no escaping this, Tommaso. Let me make this absolutely clear. You can leave now, but this is not going to go away."

Tom wrestled himself free and without a word ran toward the wooden archway leading outside, below the big Roman painting.

"You know, you had better prepare yourselves, lads," Walter called out to him as he rushed out. "With all this sincerity of yours, sooner or later, someone will take you for a real ride. Someone ruthless, systematic, a real professional. You won't ever see it coming!"

It was when Tom was just past the harpsichord and under the arch separating the sitting room from the bar that the bomb went off and everything went dark.

17

A Fire

The alarm siren roused us from our dreams.

It was a blaring two-tone cry, a deafening, trumpeting terror drowning out the sounds of a Las Vegas Friday night—the chiming, the laughing, the raucous nautical background *whoosh*. We had never heard anything like it before.

Within minutes, the Positano was a blur. A rioting city raging with a maddened nighttime crowd. We kept turning from corner to corner, from formidable sight to formidable sight, disbelieving what we saw even as we saw it.

Everything was extraordinary.

The lights went out first, followed by the cameras, heated up until they popped like overinflated balloons. Suddenly, at once collectively realizing that for the first time in a Vegas casino *nobody was watching them*, the visitors were completely free. And as the room around them kept transforming, shapeshifting as if at the mercy of some trickster god of old, we saw the crowd react to a simple, unprecedented awareness: tonight what happened in Vegas would truly stay in Vegas.

There was silence in the mezzanine. Shut off from the chaos unfolding downstairs by a thick layer of steel and solid rock, the changing room where Mary Ann was getting dressed alone remained perfectly quiet.

She'd been given no instructions as to what to do with herself after deploying the device, and when she'd finally asked, Neal had sounded almost surprised. *Just do whatever it is that you do after a shift, it'll be fine.* Yet as soon as she'd left the Scarlatti, she'd been seized with a strong urge to be somewhere else, away from the Positano. She'd speed-walked straight back to the mezzanine, and hadn't even peered down from the glass slit in the hallway on her way in, like she usually did. She'd skipped showering, too, and started getting dressed right away. She wanted to go home.

There was relief in having done it. At the lounge, the device lodged underneath the satin of her garter belt, she'd felt trapped in a situation so big, so out of scale with her little day-to-day life, that all she could do was think about it, go over her options again and again, while there was still time. But now that it was done, all those thoughts were gone too, replaced by a sweet longing for home. It was a silly instinct, this wanting to get away, she was ready to admit it. It was what children did, putting physical distance between themselves and their mischief, pretending it never happened. The truth was, she could never undo the ten-second act that could potentially define the rest of her life. It was done, and whatever the night held now for the Positano— for Wiles and his precious data, for the Shadow Union, for workers in every gaming resort in town, and ultimately for Las Vegas itself—it was all completely out of her control. And yet the thought of going home still felt good. Getting to her room and in bed and sleeping. Being somewhere else.

Mary Ann buttoned her jeans and got her green Keds from under the locker-room bench. She didn't linger on the strange emptiness of the room. Without the vapor from the hot-water showers, the air was cooler than usual, almost chilly.

She was alone, and so small and unimportant. This really *was* out of scale with her day-to-day life. Las Vegas would remember this day forever, the day labor reclaimed its role in the biggest industry in the state. The day they showed Wiles he was nothing without them. If there was one thing that was certain, one thing Mary Ann could believe in, without question, it was this: this really was bigger than herself. Whatever happened to *her* was finally beside the point, and that, as scary as it was, somehow felt good too.

She was holding this rare, precious thought in her mind, like a delicate seashell found in the interminable sameness of the sand, when the door opened and Maidon came rushing in.

"We need to go," she said. "Now."

We saw it start, grow, and end, all within the seventeen minutes it took for the first firefighters and, later, police to get to the scene. It was a bubble, a momentary suspension of all social rules under the blanket of fear, survival instinct, and the promise of invisibility. A thousand seconds of unadulterated state of nature.

What became immediately obvious was that the Positano had no plan in place for a crisis of this scale. Casino staff ran around, securing all corporate property to the best of their abilities, following whatever fragment of the fire procedure they could summon to mind, though the exact nature of the emergency remained as yet unclear. We noticed most seemed unsure whether or not to fear for their lives.

As for security guards, the majority addressed the situation as a terrorist attack, an understandable though useless deduction, since none of them were trained or equipped for such a scenario, and perpetrators seemed impossible to locate, given the size of the affected area and the near-darkness, mitigated only by the neon glare of the slots irregularly scattered around the place. Moved by the all-American instinct to find the bad guys and shoot them, but finding themselves unarmed and with no one to shoot, they wandered around feeling existentially lost until the actual police arrived, some twenty-five minutes later.

The fact was, as some of us joked, that the place looked more like a haunted house than anything else. Every nongaming system and apparatus was acting up—not just the alarm and the lights but the AC, the hotel keycard readers and printers, the escalators, even the restaurants' grills—all on its own. It was like the casino had come alive and was playing tricks on its patrons. Like the building itself was attacking.

Tourists and locals, gamblers and service workers, the young and the old: nobody knew what was happening. Even *we* were taken off guard.

In the darkness upstairs, Ray remained rigidly still. It was as if—by ignoring the very obvious casino-wide crisis and remaining seated, chips and cards in front of him, the perfect, if darkened image of a live poker professional—as if he could somehow will everyone else at the table to do it too. Go on playing. Finish the hand.

Weak fluorescent lights had turned on downstairs when the blackout started, but there were none upstairs. Their distant gleam briefly irradiated the confused expressions around table 14. Then the emergency lights went out too, and all that was left were the TV screens on the walls, mysteriously unaffected, the greenish glow of bored men in white shoes playing golf. Powder-thin shards of glass from the cameras landed softly on the table felt, but otherwise nothing moved.

Commotion could be heard coming from downstairs. In the Sportsbook, on the other side, people already rushed toward the emergency exit. The alarm was still blaring. But at the table, the players sat still, like they were wrapped in some invisible film, some superficial tension no one felt ready to break.

Finally, from Ray's left, a few feet away from the table, Logan lunged forward. Caught off guard, Ray didn't know whether Logan was attacking him, or reaching for his money, or worse yet, trying to expose his two aces lying facedown on the felt and invalidate the hand in progress. Reflexively he curled forward, his whole upper body over the table, protecting chips, cards, and self in one feverish hug.

But Logan wasn't after him. He was running to LQ.

Ray turned to look, still sheltering his cards. He wondered again whether Logan was trying to help LQ, or steal from him, or maybe take advantage of the situation to get him away from the other regs. It was the same question that seemed to be on everybody's mind, players, dealers, Carol. But not Bryan.

Just as Logan approached LQ, a hand already on his Nobel Prize–winning shoulder, Bryan jumped from his seat and sprang forward to tackle him. Their bodies clashed with a thump, Logan's momentum compensating for his smaller size, and fell sideways over LQ's back. Upon impact, LQ's chair rolled away as the old man waggled his arms desperately, like a drowning man, knocking over and commingling his and Bryan's chips, and even exposing one of his cards—the ace of diamonds, Ray saw even in near-darkness—before finally sinking below the surface of the table together with his two assailants, and collapsing on the floor with a groan.

Everybody reacted at once.

From seat 3, Lauren got up to help LQ, followed by the dealer Jane, who abandoned the deck of cards on the felt in front of her. On the floor, beside LQ panting and shifting like a turtle on its back, Logan and Bryan wrestled like overgrown children, grabbing and clawing and punching and spitting. Calvin and JJ and most of the others seemed intent on hastily throwing their chip stacks into the safety of their backpacks, getting ready to run for it. The alarm was so loud even the fighting seemed to be playing on mute. In the green light of the corner TV, Carol's face was a mask of fear and consternation, vainly shouting something completely inaudible in the noise.

There was no more pretending.

The poker game was over.

Letting go of his grip on his chips and cards, Ray sat up in his chair. For the first time in months, he couldn't stop laughing.

Out in the gaming area, members of the Desert Front were making the rounds. Patrick's group, a half-dozen Tau Kappas who'd driven up from Tucson last week specifically for this, laughed and shoved and merrily punched each other on the arm as they roamed the halls in loose formation, as did the other college kids recruited from fraternities all over the Southwest. The Vegas guys were older, some of them in their thirties, and had serious looks on their faces.

Patrick and his men caught up with them in the hotel lobby, to report to Greywolf after completing their West Side recon. The lobby was meant to look like a blossoming springtime meadow, with flowers and bees and chirping birds, but now the lights were dimmed and filtered to a cemeterial purple, and the papier-mâché birds wailed faintly over the distant sound of the alarm siren, quieter here, muffled. Freezing AC wind swept across the room.

Greywolf was on his phone, giving his team of hackers instructions in a calm, resolute tone. Patrick thought it was pretty cool of him to show up for the dirty work himself, instead of barking orders from the safety of the Lair while his men faced all the risk. He respected that in a leader. What he found pretty annoying was that all the Vegas guys got to wear plain clothes, while he and his bros had to put on these ridiculous outfits and prance around like a bunch of leftist cucks, smashing stuff and requisitioning phones, making sure people saw them and remembered their flags. He was starting to suspect this misdirection was the whole reason his and the other frats were here in the first place.

"Dude, isn't that Silverback?" said Squi, who looked like a total retard draped in a black Antifa flag. "Fucking traitor."

"Yeah, that *is* him," said Patrick, a red WHOA shirt and an itchy kaffiyeh around his neck, spotting the ginger dipshit just inside the east-side hallway pits. He seemed confused, stumbling and looking around in a sort of stupefied daze.

"No cameras," said Fat Tim.

"Six against one," said Squi.

Patrick nodded.

"You will do no such thing," said Greywolf, appearing behind them, still on his phone. "Call me back in five," he said, hanging up.

"Dude, why?" said Squi.

"He's a traitor," said Fat Tim.

"We need Silverback," said Greywolf.

"Man," said Patrick, "all due respect, but the dude is *scum*. He took unauthorized video of one of our parties and *lied* to us about it, then used it on his fucking YouTube vlog."

"We have a code, you know," said Squi.

"Look kid, I don't care what you think of him, and I certainly don't care about your frat's code. I've said over and over that these Silverback types can be great entry points. He's valuable to us, so you're not gonna touch him. In fact," said Greywolf, moving a couple of steps forward, "*Silverback! Trevor!* Hey man, come here!"

Silverback finally noticed them. It took him a while to understand what he was looking at, and he seemed surprised. He was scared like a little girl. Patrick was ready to bet the little shit was gonna run for it. But he didn't. He smiled liked he'd just seen an old friend and walked up to them, all cheerful and calm. He had on a loose flappy silk shirt unbuttoned to his chest, and a huge black cross pendant that even Patrick had to admit looked kinda cool. He was still wearing those ridiculous shoes with the individual toes.

"Dude, good seeing you here," said Greywolf, offering his hand. "Glad you could make it."

"Well, it's not like anyone told me," said Silverback, looking to Patrick with a smirk of playful reproach. "I had to figure it all out by myself."

He grabbed Greywolf's hand, then went straight in for the hug, patting him on the back and everything. Patrick thought this was such bullshit.

The split second when Tom crossed past the archway to the vestibule of the Scarlatti had been the longest of his life. He experienced it in ultra-HD, 96fps clarity, a story in an instant, both synchronic and sequential, momentary and infinite.

First—it felt like first, though he knew rationally it must all be happening at the same time—the beeping from the harpsichord had gone flat, a long, whining digital note stretching and finally falling silent. Then the lights went black, everywhere, and he instinctively turned around to the sitting room he'd just left, back where he knew his blackmailer must be. And then there was light, red analog light illuminating a look of pure terror on Walter's face, as white now as his snow-white hair. It was the light of an explosion, a sudden burst of fire from the harpsichord, filling the space around it, loud, bright. Incredibly beautiful. Tom could swear he heard Walter scream, past the fire, past the smoke, a single flash of his bloodied face begging for help, while the room around him started to burn. Then, before Tom could even think of moving in either direction, the large, heavy painting above the archway fell to the floor, so wide it completely blocked the sitting room's only entrance, and exit. Walter on one side, with the fire. Tom on the other, where everything was dark again.

It was all around us. Everywhere.

We watched hundreds of smartphone flashlights crisscross darkened hallways like an EDM light show.

We watched a family of six from Boise, Idaho, sprint down a casino aisle in direct collision path with a fifteen-strong bachelor party running the opposite way.

We saw Felix Quoss, Austrian-born roulette dealer, in Vegas since '89, thirteen years sober, single-handedly help eighteen non- or barely ambulatory seniors to the nearest fire exit, each time diving back into the madness of the gaming pits for more.

Fire was spreading through the east side, or so someone said.

The Idahoan family all swerved to the side, careening around two craps tables and knocking over a zealous dealer who was locking up the daily take before thinking of saving himself.

It was exciting news about the fire, we all thought, for it is within fire that our true nature is revealed. In the east hallway, some of us even claimed to see a small heap of blue $1 and red $5 chips on the floor darken with smoke, quiver with extreme heat, and finally melt into a sad purple monetary puddle, though this remains unconfirmed.

In the first ten minutes of the crisis, fifty-seven drinks were spilled on the gaming-pit carpets, twenty-nine on table felts and roulette wheels, eight on keyboards and slot-machine screens, one frying the circuits of a decade-old penny slot that needed replacing anyway.

Fifteen different visitors tried to break the glass chip banks at empty casino tables with their fists, none succeeding, four managing to get spotted by the sparse security force and detained (thus wasting valuable security time, leaving the enormous room even more understaffed and vulnerable to looting, tourist-on-tourist infighting, and outright vandalism).

Twelve panicked patrons at seaview cocktail bar Mare jumped over the railings into the Positano Sea™ and swam to safety, reaching the shore miraculously unharmed.

After some hesitation, Emily Jensen, of New Prague, Minnesota, stuffed $53 in quarters in her sweatpants pockets before abandoning her seat at the slots, the coins jingling like Christmas bells as she speed-walked to the exit, leaving a silver Hansel-and-Gretel-like trail behind her.

In a never-before-felt adrenaline rush, 245-pound Brett Leigh, data analyst from Fort Wayne, Indiana, clambered over the Sportsbook balustrade to cut the corner in one agile leap, reaching the green exit sign panting and laughing and vowing to join a gym after this was over.

In the end, sixty-two people took videos with their phones, forty-one of which were rendered completely useless by noise, poor lighting, and shoddy camera work, seventeen requisitioned and destroyed by roaming gang members wearing syndicalist insignia under martial blond buzzcuts, the remaining four acquired by the police as evidence, discarded as inconclusive, and eventually leaked and circulated online as a kind of fodder for fringe theories and alternative readings of the events of May 1.

We saw at least two dozen women take off their heels to run the hallways to the exits, and we worried, watching them scuttle barefoot over vodka puddles and crushed ice cubes and mercifully no glass, other than the harmless powdered fallout from the exploded cameras above.

Temperature in the pits rose to 95°F, and even higher in the east hallway outside the Scarlatti Lounge. As the minutes passed and the alarm kept screaming, even the bravest visitors let go of their sangfroid and joined the crowd dashing for the exits in tumultuous fashion.

The Positano was in complete chaos.

"The Positano is entering a new age," concluded Wiles, pressing the gold button to summon the Master Elevator. The office was the only intermediate stop between Wiles's hilltop residence and the deepest level of the Donut below. The Master Elevator offered Wiles a private connection to the maximum-security area and the vault without having to go through the fiendishly elaborate security checkpoints required for all other staff members, even at the highest clearance levels.

It was hardly a new age, thought Lindsay. Just the old one coming up with new tricks. Wiles had found a way to extend his market reach to previously nonmarketed externalities, making a powerful new friend in the process, and relieving public pressure from his employment policies all at once. The creation of new jobs was at best a happy coincidence.

"I really hope you'll say yes," said Wiles, as they waited for the elevator. "But don't make your mind up until you see the system for yourself. It's a real beauty, if I dare say so myself. Real top-shelf stuff!"

The big reveal, the secret plan Wiles wanted Lindsay to unveil to the world, was a surprise partnership with Gifty's Zach Romero. Romero was the most beloved young businessman in Las Vegas, so different from Wiles in age, aspect, and demeanor that Lindsay was having a hard time picturing them in the same room. Yet now the two richest men in town were joining forces, and would revolutionize the hospitality game forever, or so it seemed.

Gifty would provide the digital platform, a clever reimagining of their social media algorithm as an opt-in service for hotel visitors; Wiles supplied the infrastructure, his entire network of Vegas resorts available for capillary microcustomization of the tourist experience; an army of dedicated workertainers (as a sly PR initiative, job offers would be first sent out to Wiles Group personnel made redundant in the last two years) would strive to bend the confines of the collective to the benefit of the individual, constantly repackaging Las Vegas to suit each visitor's algorithmically determined tastes and needs.

Retired, looking to rest, favorite color blue, baseball fan, and into jazz? Here's a blue-walled room in the quietest wing overlooking the non-DJed swimming pool, Miles Davis from the speakers, preset reminders for all Red Sox games, and taste-tailored in-room brochures and even daily news. Young, single, and ready to mingle, but introverted and worried you won't be able to meet new people? Welcome to your weekend in a cluster of rooms allocated to similarly neurotic unmarried fun seekers, balanced for sexual orientation, political leanings, and matching interests to spark conversations while waiting for the elevator to one of the clubs where tables arranged for mutual compatibility await. All automatically handled via software at the moment of booking. All provided by staff before guests even know they want it.

Las Vegas would become the first user-determined city in the world. The slogan practically wrote itself: "What would Paradise look like *for you*?"

It was a win for Wiles, who could prove he'd taken to heart the union's remonstrations without having to spend a cent more than usual (the software did most of the work, and extra staffing cost would easily be offset by added revenue), while at the same time creating new profit channels for his struggling business without rethinking its core concepts. It was a win for Gifty, which could start rebranding itself as a legal and trusted data-mining giant, offering high-customization protocols to businesses outside the merry world of gift-making.

But that this phenomenal display of capitalist sleight-of-hand could turn out to offer Lindsay a clear win as well, that was the real surprise. Who better than the journalist who had decried the unfairness of the recent layoffs to break the story as a great result for Las Vegas workers? With Lindsay jumping on the corporate bandwagon, Wiles would secure invaluable PR from a trusted local source, but Lindsay herself would score national media attention. It was the big story she had been looking for. And there was even more Wiles had in mind for her.

"Goin' down," said a disembodied voice from the elevator as the doors opened.

"That voice—," said Lindsay.

"Clint Eastwood," said Wiles. "A little gift from a friend for my seventieth birthday."

Wiles stepped in and offered his right thumb and retina for inspection to the scanners on the elevator wall. The cabin was smaller than Lindsay had imagined, but it was impeccably decorated, with nineteenth-century art on the walls and plush velvet benches on two of the four sides. It looked like a small, fancy living room. Wiles offered Lindsay a seat, then sat himself on the opposite side, waiting.

The elevator started its descent.

Lindsay looked at him. How did he know? This frail old man, shut away from the world of the living for almost two decades, how had he figured out the only truly tempting offer he could hope to sway Lindsay's journalistic integrity with? She considered the absent look on his face, scolding herself for having been fooled by a facade. Beneath it lay a sharp, calculating mind, one she'd been wrong to underestimate.

(The physical sensation of void as the elevator plunged deep inside the artificial rock around them, and eventually deeper still inside real Nevada soil, down and down and down, was going to her head.)

Wiles had thought of everything. A deal with Gifty to secure an enduring influential role in the new, tech-centric Las Vegas. A tell-all interview with a labor-friendly local reporter announcing massive job creation to appease the union and win over municipal support. And as a cherry on top, a million-dollar book deal for an authorized biography to be offered to Lindsay herself, as a reward for choosing the right side in this fight. *Eccentric billionaire moved by young Mormon journalist's piece about him ends up hiring her as personal biographer.* An option for a second book already penciled in her contract, no strings attached, whatever Lindsay felt like writing after. What Wiles was offering wasn't just a good news story. It was a real writing career. It was a life. How could he possibly know?

(It seemed like the cabin was gaining speed, like a real free fall from a dizzying height, and Lindsay was suddenly glad to be sitting down.)

And yet she was going to refuse it. She had to. Of course she thought of Orson, and his words about ambition, and money, and selling out. She thought of his grad-school statement of purpose growing into an unnecessary tome, probably even detrimental to his chances, simply because he felt like doing it. Because he believed in it. But more than Orson's example, more than his cautioning about people like Wiles—*awful, damning stuff oozing out*—it was her own instinct that told her to say no. She didn't trust Wiles, and she didn't trust his ideas. He was once again casting himself as the benevolent god the only way he knew how, by expanding his business. By benefiting himself more than anybody else. His plan was not a solution to the city's problems; it was a shiny, sparkling patch, the real cost of which they would only understand years in the future. And what was worse, Wiles really did seem to believe he was acting for the common good.

(Faster, deeper, the elevator like a golden projectile through the innards of the earth.)

She could say no, and still have the life she wanted. This was how they tempted you, by presenting the way of the market as the only way to achieve what you want. *It's me or* What's New in Henderson *forever, honey*. But she could move to San Francisco on her own, she could finish her stories, query a few agents, wait the excruciating months or years before someone at the gates decided to let a young woman from the forgotten periphery of America inside the secret world of Letters. She could forget all this even happened.

She would say no, because she had to. Didn't she?

The elevator stopped like it'd hit a wall, abruptly, the inertial thrust so strong that Wiles fell forward from his seat and landed on the floor like a wet rag. It took a couple of seconds for Lindsay to realize something was wrong. They hadn't reached their destination. Somewhere on their way, far below the surface, surrounded by solid rock, the Master Elevator had shut down.

He was alone. At some point between serving Tom and Walter their drinks and the explosion, the red-cheeked bartender must have left.

Outside, past the lounge's door, the pits were a black region punctuated by distant neons. Tom cried for help, but none of the frenzied figures he caught glimpses of running up and down the siren-howling corridors could hear him. Smoke filtered over the fallen painting that blocked the way to the sitting area. Beyond the archway, the lounge had turned into a fiery cage. A man was dying in there.

According to Trevor, it was guilt—and Catholic guilt at that, even though Tom wasn't even baptized and could barely describe what the inside of a church looked like—it was guilt that constituted the key to Tom's fragile beta psyche. The one solution to the puzzle. He was the child who had reached for the forbidden chocolate cream, and on the same day watched his father die. The physical and emotional scarring. The inevitable suggestion of correlation. There was, Trevor argued, something inherently feminine—in the scriptural, archetypal sense—something weak and submissive about Tom's entire idea of himself. A certain sense of sin and chaos and passivity ingrained in his conscience from the earliest age. What he needed, clearly, was to *take responsibility*. How many times had Trevor told him that?

Without a second thought, Tom turned back toward the archway, determined to push down the painting and save the man who was threatening to turn him in to the police. He grabbed the double crossbar that ran along the back of the canvas, pushing with all his strength. The frame felt warm, and Tom had tears in his eyes from the smoke and from a confusion of guilt, and fear, and shameful weakness he would probably, he might as well admit it, never finally overcome. He pushed, but the painting turned out to be incredibly heavy, and possibly stuck between the archway walls and what must be heaps of detritus from the exploded harpsichord, and maybe even adjacent tables, chairs, and who knows what else. The frame had fallen down guillotine-like and wedged itself at a perfect diagonal slant, rendering Tom's efforts frustratingly useless. He tried again, shouldering the crossbar at an awkward angle with his scraggy bicep. The hit sent a shiver of pain along his nerve endings, reminding him of high school bullies punching his arm as penalty in a circle game he'd never asked to be a part of. The painting didn't move an inch.

He was weak weak weak weak. He couldn't even move a stupid painting of his stupid city to save a man's life. He was inadequate, constitutionally unable to measure up to American standards. If Trevor were here, he would rescue Walter in no time, coming out of the burning room like a fireman in a movie (had Tom Cruise ever played a fireman?). Even Patrick, or any of his friends, as young as they were, would rise to the occasion and lift the heavy frame like it were made of Styrofoam. Or maybe they would punch through it, heroically, and save the day.

Punch through it. As soon as he thought about it, he knew it was the thing to do. Tear through it, rip it apart. Destroy a nineteenth-century work of art depicting the Roman park where he'd spent so many Sunday mornings as a child. There was no time for doubts now, and nothing else he could try. He punched and scraped and clawed, feeling the canvas bulge and stretch but not give. It was thick, and yellowed in the back, scratchy. There were pencil markings in a corner, dates, places, names. The name Francesco was at the top, his brother's, and probably the painter's, though Tom couldn't make out the last name (Di . . . something?). He punched and kicked, desperately. He shoved his whole body against the canvas, no longer trying to push the painting down, only to pierce through it. The smoke from the adjoining room now filled his nostrils and fogged his vision. He wasn't thinking straight anymore. The canvas stretched. Maybe if the crossbars weren't there, he could apply pressure to the center of the canvas, its weakest spot. Maybe that's exactly why the crossbars were there to begin with. He pushed again. He wished he knew how to pray.

He wasn't going to let a man die. Not if it killed him.

"So, do you guys mind filling me in here?" asked Trevor.

Patrick's men were still around, as were Greywolf and his guys. All the other Desert Front brothers were roaming the gaming pits, requisitioning all higher-res phones, stealing from the slow and the elderly, and generally terrorizing the already pantwettingly scared crowds, making sure to create the indelible memory of a gang of savage union members on the prowl. Once the cameras were destroyed and the lights went out, they'd produced red WHOA shirts and black balaclavas from their backpacks, and now they looked positively demonic in the polyphony of fluorescent lights coming from the slots, the only source of illumination left on the main casino floors.

"You know, you'd know all about it if you'd listened when we—," Squi started.

Greywolf shot Patrick a stern look. His face was uncovered, an act of defiance and alpha confidence that Patrick had found inspiring and promptly imitated, so that now all the Tau Kappas too had ditched their balaclavas out of sheer masculine peer pressure.

"Shut up, Squi," said Patrick.

"Our intel," said Greywolf, "learned that a socialist cell was organizing workers here for some kind of protest. Some girl got fired, something like that. The usual deal, bunch of libtards and feminists arguing, lots and lots of talking, zero action. Nothing new. But then we thought—well, I thought—hey, what if this time we could convince them to do something really, really stupid? What if we could tell them we'll help them do a peaceful software hack and get them to hand us control of a whole fucking Vegas casino instead? That'd be cool, right? So we infiltrated them."

"That's dope," said Trevor. "So what's up with the commie gear?"

"Diversion," said Patrick.

"It's a heist!" said Squi.

"Think every news outlet in the country," said Greywolf, "talking about violent union workers and radical feminists taking a Vegas casino hostage come tomorrow morning. 'Socialist terrorism on the rise, NEWS ALERT.' 'Terror group responsible for attack claims Las Vegas casinos are sexist and degrading.' 'Survey shows eighty-three percent of Americans are scared of a bolshevik revolution.' 'Have SJWs finally gone too far? We asked moderate conservative Mike Cernovich to find out.' Plus, yes, we get to actually replenish the Front's finances, which we really needed to do anyway. Next year is gonna be *big*."

"Shit, that's genius," said Trevor. "How did you guys even pull this off?"

"I mean, they're so fucking easy to trick, honestly," said Greywolf.

"It's almost sad," said Patrick.

"Pathetic," said Fat Tim.

"Fun thing was, we didn't even have to lie. We said we're allies from the tech hub in North Vegas, which is true because most of my men are DCS grads. And then we just convinced them we'd take care of everything, and they were on board. These people, they don't really want to *do* anything, you know? They just want to show people they '*really, really* disapprove of things.'" Greywolf pouted as he spoke the last sentence in a mock-childish voice.

"God, they're so dumb," said Patrick.

"We convinced them that 'trace removal' was our top priority, so the whole thing wouldn't link back to them. And look, even that is not really a lie—"

"Yeah, nothing *removes traces* like a bomb." Squi laughed, getting a venomous look from Greywolf.

"Wait, you're gonna blow a *bomb* in here?" asked Trevor. "For real?"

Greywolf looked displeased, like Squi had screwed the punch line to his story.

"We *have* detonated a small explosive device already, yes," he said. "To wipe all traces of our hack from the harpsichord. No big deal, the place is deserted this late: absolute worst-case scenario, a couple waitresses die. Now, let's talk about what's important: Are you going to do a vlog covering tonight's events?"

"A couple waitresses . . . ," Trevor muttered.

"Silverback, you there? Are you going to vlog about tonight or not?"

"I . . . I mean maybe . . . eventually?" said Trevor, in his stupid nervous stutter.

"Good, then what we need you to do is to say you were here, and tell folks how scary it was, and that you saw people in black masks performing such and such acts. And then you'll say you have no political agenda to push, but that violence is never the answer, and that these people are dangerous and wrong. We'll give you some footage too."

"We got a lot of, uh, *footage*," said Squi, showing the inside of his backpack, containing several smartphones with cracked screens.

"So, can you do this for us?" asked Greywolf.

"I think . . ." Trevor looked lost. "Wait, did you say you blew up a *harpsichord*? Where was this?"

"I don't know, some cocktail bar nobody goes to, what does it matter?"

"I . . . I need to go," said Trevor, wide-eyed with lame beta fear.

And just like that, the sneaky cuck just up and left. He turned around and ran away in his stupid five-toed shoes, which, turns out, are fucking perfect for running on sticky carpet floors full of ice and vodka spills and maybe glass. He had this like faggy spastic run, all jerky and weird, and Patrick couldn't believe he'd once looked up to the man. He even heard him talk to himself as he ran away, like a crazy person. It's really true you should never meet your heroes.

Something had changed.

Watching Logan and Bryan fight over the fallen LQ like hungry hyenas on the upstairs floor; watching Calvin and JJ and the others hasten to protect their money by stashing all their chips haphazardly inside their backpacks; watching Carol, and Lauren, and Eike, and Jane, alternatively try to help LQ back up, or ease the mess of cards and chips and bodies tussling on the floor, or prevent downstairs invaders from climbing up the stairs to steal flags off the high-stakes table, Ray felt somehow something had changed.

He didn't care anymore.

Slowly, no longer laughing, he stacked his chips neatly inside a plastic rack, retrieving his now-voided $19,000 5bet from past the betting line but not even bothering to argue that the rest of what was already in the pot should be assigned to him, as the last raiser. It didn't matter.

Unhurriedly, he slid the rack inside the torn envelope that had held his father's letter so that any spills could be contained within whatever was left of the paper, carefully placed the whole thing in his backpack, and closed it. At the last moment, he took his two black aces from the table and put those in as well. It came to him like a punch: it was the last poker hand he would ever be dealt. He was done.

He walked to the glass dividers and leaned over to witness the chaos happening downstairs. It looked primal and unregulated. Irrational. He smiled, as it occurred to him that a fire in a casino (if that's what the emergency was, as he'd finally heard Carol shout over the blaring alarm) presented a unique case study in the field of human decision-making, a complex clash of data and desires: (1) the presence of abundant, life-changing, potentially unguarded money; (2) the impunity granted by the absence of cameras and relative darkness; (3) the fear of imminent death and the instinct to run to safety. The whole thing conjured up the kind of fascinating group dynamic and game theory problem that would ordinarily excite Ray a great deal. It was the same irresistible computational urge he'd felt in front of the pedestrian crossing at the Shibuya.

Meanwhile, another strong, more urgent train of thought battled for his attention. He still felt the thrill of intellectual curiosity tug at his mathematical heartstrings, but there was something else there too. It was a feeling, that same all-powerful feeling of loss and defeat he'd finally experienced in the security room, and which the sudden arrival of LQ had found a way to stall, to divert. His father's letter was still in his pocket, a simple, ordinary piece of paper the presence of which he could no longer ignore, now that the absurd dream of saving his family with one single hand of high-stakes poker had lifted. Whatever crazy thought had led him to join the LQ game, it was over now, and so was his career. He didn't care what would happen to Logan, Bryan, and LQ, to the regs, and to the Positano upstairs game, and to the poker economy at large. He didn't even want to know. His entire adult life so far had been one unequivocal, hopeless mistake. There would be no more poker. VF1nd3r was dead.

Downstairs, two hundred people ran and screamed in the vast space cluttered with tables. Most players seemed intent on running away, but almost none seemed willing to leave their poker chips behind. This triggered several angry disputes, at least two of which Ray saw escalate to full-on fights, suntanned men in flip-flops punching each other over $100 while the world collapsed around them. He watched several players try to steal from the table banks before dealers could lock them, some even succeeding. Several dealers seemed to prioritize securing casino property over helping patrons, and a few even ran away, but many stayed, pushing wheelchairs and holding wrinkled hands. With some surprise, Ray observed groups of people spontaneously band together, some with malicious intent, but more for the purpose of helping each other, leaving the poker room as a compact unit, guarding each other's backs.

It was as he watched this kaleidoscope of rushed decision-making unfold before his eyes—staring at the downstairs room like at an ocean from a silent peak, his father's letter in his pocket, his poker career finally and truly ended—that the two conflicting problems he was trying to process at once finally short-circuited. In the resulting spark, Ray Jackson found the realization he had been waiting for his entire life.

The way fire spreads from the ignition of a single piece of furniture in a room is a thing to behold. From the harpsichord's flaming wreck, fire grew against the lounge's cherrywood paneling. It was bright, neat and contained at first, like a wood-burning fireplace, except there was no enclosure delimiting the hearth, and the flames looked bold and cheerful, ready to pounce. Soon a layer of hot smoke had spread across the ceiling, thickening, bounded by the walls of the elegant sitting room. The smoke was black, a dense layer of storm clouds gathering, ominous. Flames lapped at it like a child's tongue at a puff of cotton candy.

As the smoke radiated heat, combustibles beneath it started to give off flammable gases through thermolysis, hotter and hotter. Tables and chairs and wall panels coughing thinner, whiter smoke, delicate clouds rising to join the growing cumulonimbus, so massive now it descended more than halfway down the walls. No one had installed a fire sprinkler in the sitting area, and the one in the vestibule, a light-hazard head right past the archway, couldn't reach the tables even when it finally turned on, blocked by the makeshift wall of the fallen painting.

Finally the temperature reached a critical point, and the gases ignited, and the entire room was engulfed in flames. The flashover was like lightning. Waves of fire spreading diagonally across the ceiling, lashing at the walls from side to side. Sudden blinding white all over. A silent, blazing explosion of light.

In the end, it took less than a minute for the Scarlatti Lounge to disappear. Less than a minute for the elegant, quiet, secluded nook Wiles had envisioned to turn into one solid body of fire, raging, screaming. It was in less than a minute that Tom shoved away two decades of fear and guilt, clawing at the oil-on-canvas image of his hometown, finding in the smoke-filled depths of his desperation a force purer and stronger than the one he'd aped and yearned for all this time—compassion.

But if he ever saw it—maybe for an instant, one second before the fire finally bit into the canvas, and the whole room past the archway burned, and the black smoke poured into the lounge's vestibule where he was, like floodwater through a cracked dam—if he ever glimpsed his newfound power in the end, the flashover took that too.

We were excited! We were thrilled! For the first time in so many years, the extraordinary in Las Vegas was meant for *us*. The dazzling, the exotic, the uncanny, finally arranged for *our* viewing pleasure after so many dull identical nights in the casino darkness.

Panic in the gaming pits.

Packs of unmanned vacuum carts whizzing along the hallways, knocking over blackjack tables, and chairs, and people, and each other.

Well-dressed visitors, sobered up by fear, stumbling out of high-end restaurants and bars.

And the fire. *Real* fire, sparkling, devouring, beautiful. At last, something truly original.

Those of us who were around then say we hadn't seen anything like this since that night in 1980 when the old MGM Grand burned down. What a glorious night that was for us! We made so many new friends! It is a pity, in fact, that fire safety in Vegas casinos has improved so much since then. We can still remember the light, so much light!, racing through the casino floors in burning bright waves, flames like golden rays from the sun we haven't seen in so long.

We are starved for light.

We *crave* it.

From inside the darkest heart of the Las Vegas casinos, we yearn endlessly for real light, the light of nature, the light without control.

Only fire shows us for what we truly are.

We had been waiting for this night for a long long time.

In the months after their trip through the desert north of town, Orson had fallen into a bad habit. He'd still produced work—more work, in fact, than in any of the months preceding it, digging deeper and more effectively into the millennial relationship of mankind with nature, and finally leading the meandering narrative of his predoctoral dissertation to its climactic present-day crux—he really had. Yet in the meantime he'd let his mind wander elsewhere too. He'd been, at times, distracted.

It was hard to admit, but the truth was, he'd been online-stalking his former friends a whole lot.

As he wrote, he kept their Facebook and Twitter pages open in separate tabs, and it was all he could do not to constantly refresh. As he read useful stuff for his project, he watered it down with large, befuddling swigs of their viral bullshit. He couldn't help himself. What was worse—and there was a legitimate chance he was entering full-on tinfoil-hat crackpot territory here—he'd grown convinced that something serious was going on. That the high school friends he'd once played StarCraft with were up to something.

Entering the cyber realm of a man like Ben "Greywolf" Richards, of Henderson, NV, was a maddening enterprise. The forestry of pernicious thought and ill will that had encrusted itself over what he still recognized as his former best friend's wit and razor-sharp irony was painfully hard to read through. Ben was no longer merely a person, it seemed, but some kind of intellectual entity looming at the putative center of a spiderweb of lies and anger, connecting to the most disparate and bleakest corners of the internet. He had become a leader.

Moving his investigation in a widening spiral out of Greywolf's social media accounts, Orson ended up wading through content so dense and dripping with hate and hysterical laughter that he was tempted to just forget about the whole thing forever. And he would have, had it not been for what he secretly perceived as his own responsibility in the matter. He had, he felt, a moral obligation to pay attention. This was his mess too.

There was something here, something slowly coalescing over the furious screams of propaganda of the anon shitposters and the deceptively composed arguments of the more serious theorists. Some massive secret plan, bouncing and echoing in codes and whistles from the pages of *Numenor News* to the forum posts on UltraFront, from the tweets of Eton Mess and Michael Damato to the YouTube videos of ThePUACoach, Simon Gobineau, and The Demystifier. It was there, Orson was sure of it. He could almost see it. He just couldn't understand what *it* was.

Through the month of April, after waiting for Lindsay to leave the apartment out of the irrational fear of being found out, Orson had left twenty-two anonymous tips to the FBI about some kind of imminent far-right threat in the Las Vegas/Paradise/Henderson area. But every time he came to the section of the online form where he was supposed to input the information, he realized he had nothing real to report. What he wrote in were just hunches, a confusing tangle of interconnections that might well be all inside his head.

There were tiers, different shades, even overnight drastic transformations. Diachronically, Ben's clique's philosophical stance had evolved a lot, to the point that it was hard to pinpoint exactly what they stood for at any given time. But synchronically too, within the loose boundaries of their community, the range of ideas was so nuanced and stratified that Orson never felt like he knew anything sure about them.

Somehow, though, it all linked back to Ben. And Ben, of course, linked back to him. The regret Orson felt about their early conversations, the burning shame of having introduced the future Greywolf to the philosophy of history and the history of political thought—innocent Saturday-afternoon topics for two suburban nerds in desperate need of meaning, and ones that Orson himself had picked up as an act of defiance and rebellion to the stiffness of his Mormon upbringing—it physically hurt him to think of it. And with it came the awful suspicion that Ben might have picked ideas conflicting with his own just to have something to debate with him, the way more mainstream nerds pick Batman versus Superman or Kirk versus Picard. Summer afternoons in Henderson can feel unbearably long sometimes.

And so he had kept researching. On his own, convinced that in talking Lindsay out of her interview with the so-called pick-up artists, he had done what he could for now, or at least bought himself some time. Telling himself that his online tips to the FBI might find willing ears. He was a reader, after all. Research was what he did.

It was only on the night of May 1, when Twitter started buzzing with the news of some kind of situation developing at the Positano, that Orson realized the enormity of his mistake. In a perverse twist, his former friend seemed to have chosen to reveal his power to the world at the Positano, on the one night of the year when Lindsay would be there.

He was in bed, wearing black UNLV shorts and a large BYU T-shirt that was either Lindsay's or somehow one of his brothers', his laptop resting on his stomach. The tweets were vague, a few rushed words posted by terrified tourists from inside the hotel, followed by a sudden deluge of contradicting comments, retweets, and memes by a hoard of quick-fingered fools, making the information very hard to parse. Something bad was happening, though, that much was clear. Something Orson had feared might happen for weeks, but that he had still failed to foresee and maybe help prevent. And now Lindsay was in danger.

He picked up his phone and called his sister. Once, twice, ten times. Her phone was off. No amount of reading was going to fix this.

Orson jumped out of bed.

The Strip was a four-mile-long cluster of immobile, honking, angry car lights. There were weekend visitors just arrived from LA, trying to get to the Paris or the Mirage or the Shibuya for a late check-in, stuck in traffic on the stupid Strip after midnight for some goddamn reason. Some of the drivers got out of idling vehicles to wave in frustration at the unfair spectacle around them, *Can you believe this shit?* There were workers finally off their Friday-night shifts and ready to go home, who because of an urban design flaw had to drive exactly one block on the Strip to make a left on Spring Mountain or a right on Sahara, and were now trapped as a result. In the electric cool of the desert air, and on the white ribs of pedestrian overpasses crowded with tilted phones Instagramming the moment, and in the sharp sawing sound of the first Clark County Fire Department engine finally rushing to the scene, the city buzzed with sudden collective awareness that something was definitely wrong.

In the middle of it all, sitting upright in Lindsay's blue Hyundai and with both hands on the wheel, Orson cursed himself out loud again. He really should have seen this coming. How could he not see this coming?

Maidon walked fast ahead of Mary Ann, talking. She had thrown her street clothes back on in a hurry, without changing out of her uniform. Her hair was still done up, and she had glitter all over her skin. She had talked nonstop since they'd left the changing rooms, but her rapid-fire words were mostly unintelligible over the alarm siren, as they made their way through the disaster area Mary Ann barely recognized as the Positano gaming pits. Something had gone horribly wrong.

"The Reef . . . need to get to the Reef with the others . . . ," she said, speeding past the craps tables, kicking fallen dice and on/off pucks across the aisle floor. "Tell you about . . . later . . . at the Reef."

"Maidon, wait. Please," said Mary Ann, struggling to keep up with the woman's hurried gait as much as with her words. She almost tripped over the wooden curve of a craps stick on the floor. She bashed her knee against an upside-down chair, and kept walking with tears in her eyes. "Please, tell me what is going on."

Maidon began to answer, but the screaming of the alarm was almost unbearable in the tables area.

". . . Got to our people . . . didn't realize . . . let them do it . . ."

All around them, the Positano was a war zone. It was dark, and loud, and visitors were terrified and running and in danger. There were knocked-over wheelchairs on the floor, old people holding each other as they stumbled toward the exits, incalculable damage to property. The alarm malfunction was supposed to be just a diversion, little more than a prank to keep security busy protecting the money from an imaginary threat while the hackers perpetrated the real sabotage, but it should have been over by now. This looked more like a terrorist attack.

". . . fucking fascists . . . ," Maidon was saying. "But . . . they've pulled off . . . is not real . . . not a win . . . you know?" Her words remained maddeningly feeble in the noise. ". . . vulnerable . . . seeking each other's help . . . not our weakness . . . it's our *strength*." She went on, harder and harder to hear. "They think . . . to be won . . . but it's about . . . people . . . decent life."

With great effort, Mary Ann finally managed to grab Maidon's hand, and pull herself close to her as they kept stumbling fast past the poker room and the Sportsbook, on toward the restaurants and the Flamingo exit.

"You can believe me when I say this," Maidon said, now close enough that Mary Ann could hear. "We will *never* stop fighting for you. Whatever it takes. If this goes to trial, you will have the whole group behind you, always."

"To . . . trial," said Mary Ann, narrowly avoiding collision with a fallen barstool. "But Neal . . ."

"Fuck Neal," said Maidon, flat-out running now.

A roaring, stomping crowd was amassed by the North Valet exit, squeezing out of the four heavy doors like cream through a pastry bag. They were almost outside. The Reef, the meeting point where Maidon was apparently taking her, was about a mile west on Flamingo. A cool desert wind blew through the open doors and disappeared in the unnatural heat inside the casino floor.

"Maidon, please, wait!"

And finally they were outside. Outside the Positano, outside the building Mary Ann had naively, unwittingly, recklessly plunged into an all-out crisis. Outside and away from the enormity of what she'd done. Outside like the others, running away like the others, pretending she wasn't herself the very evil they were running from, the root and ultimate cause of their suffering. Like there was any escaping what she'd done now.

"Maidon," she said through her tears, finally catching up on the steep downhill alley leading to West Flamingo. "Please tell me what happened in there."

Maidon turned to her, the glitter and heavy makeup giving her expression an inscrutable sadness.

"Someone died."

On the parquet floor of a secret private elevator, deep below the surface of the world, a young Mormon journalist was holding the hand of an old casino magnate to help him through a panic attack. The elevator had stopped dead at an unspecified distance from their subterranean destination. Pale fluorescent emergency lights had turned on. The emergency button yielded no human response on the other end, and both Lindsay's and Wiles's phones were unresponsive. They had been stuck for over ten minutes already.

"Everything is going to be okay," she repeated, as the old man hyperventilated on the floor. "These things happen. Everything is fine."

Al Wiles was not handing this well. For a man who'd chosen to live his life in voluntary confinement, he was surprisingly ill equipped to withstand ten minutes in a closed space. He'd got up, shaking and calling for help and pressing the alarm button incessantly, to no avail. Lindsay had managed to comfort him a bit since, and he'd fallen back down, exhausted, but still with a wild, lost look in his eyes. Lindsay wondered if the elevator had simply malfunctioned, or if the whole building was experiencing some kind of brownout. The cabin lights were still on, and the alarm system seemed operative, but there were no signs anybody knew they were there.

She pressed the button again.

"A distress signal has been dispatched," said Clint Eastwood. Then, like each time before, the voice went silent, and nothing else happened.

On the floor, Wiles started quietly sobbing.

Trapped deep within miles of mountain rock as they waited for the small army of Wiles Group rescuers who would soon free them and prostrate themselves before their boss, imploring mercy for their tardiness, Lindsay thought of darkness. She understood how Orson saw darkness everywhere around them. In her story about a Mormon woman holding her dying old coach's hand, he'd seen the darkness of his past looming. In the meeting of Dummar and Hughes, a humble service-station worker helping out an old man in need, the darkness of corruption putting on the mask of kindness, tricking the naive. Her brother's world was shrouded in it, encroaching, threatening. But it wasn't just Orson's fantasy. Feeling her breath getting shorter, the red-velvet walls of the elevators closer, Lindsay thought of the wide world outside. Locked away in the sunken depths of Yucca Mountain, the darkness of America festering, biding its time. In the forests and deserts and seas, a coal-black darkness spreading, the cinder world of tardigrades. And the real face of Mormon hell, the eternal damnation reserved to unpardonable sinners after the Last Judgment: an Outer Darkness, worlds without end, the never-ending blackness of being left out, forgotten, away from.

There really was a darkness in the man trapped with her. Perhaps not the conspiratorial evil genius we tend to ascribe to the ultra-rich—after all, there seemed to be a solid chance he was himself being manipulated by that fake man-of-the-people Romero into handing over the reins of his empire without even realizing it. But even then there was darkness in his blindness, in their going through life convinced their selfishness is just the way of the world, the grace of an invisible hand brushing away their sins.

There was a deeper darkness still within Lindsay herself. Because for all she knew and believed, it was the light of a Golden Gate Bridge sunset she had imagined at first when Wiles made his offer. Her life as a real writer in San Francisco, Wiles's biography as the concrete, attainable gateway to all she really wanted. Her moral disdain, Orson's slightly simplistic ideas about "selling out," the black-and-white nature of morality as it had been painted for her, growing up, in Young Women's and Sunday school—all of it had come later. At first it was the light.

Yes, there really must be darkness inside her. And in spite of how clear the right answer was, Lindsay didn't know what to do.

There were no slot machines lighting the east hallway as Trevor ran breathlessly in the dark. Only the bright light coming from inside the Scarlatti Lounge. From a distance, he had the absurd image of the lounge as a wooden cottage with a crackling fireplace, a merry little house warming itself in the cold rural night. A stormy night, in fact, as it seemed to be inexplicably raining in the hallway. Thick, hissing rain that vaporized into mist, pooling in puddles along the carpets and soaking the nearby pai-gow tables. There was nobody else around.

Drenched in his white shirt, but with his rubber soles still maintaining excellent traction, Trevor ran toward the lounge's door. The alarm siren was extra loud here, screaming from the ceiling among the hollowed-out remnants of the eye-in-the-sky cameras. Once he got closer, Trevor saw that the water came from three of the hallway's sprinklers, triggered by the heat radiating from the lounge. There was smoke coming out too, and the air around had an indescribable tang to it, like a hot tar pit in the rain. It must be hell inside there, but it didn't matter.

He just hoped he wasn't too late.

The front room was dark with smoke. There was another sprinkler inside, which had soaked the red carpets and the bar counter, the pressure of the water enough to topple a few bottles from the higher shelves. From the front door, Trevor had trouble seeing more than a few feet ahead of him. He stepped outside again, took a deep breath, and stumbled back inside, holding a hand against his nose and mouth, walking toward the main room. There was fire there, that much he could see: real, blazing fire, burning behind some kind of dark mass where the archway used to be.

He made his way toward it.

He found Tom just this side of the archway, lying on the floor. He was alone in the empty bar, wet from the indoor rain that had prevented the fire from spreading to the front room. He looked unconscious. In the darkness, amid the wreckage and the noise, Trevor couldn't tell if he was breathing. His body looked so frail, a delicate, foreign object in the smoke-filled room, but when Trevor tried to lift him, the weight was more than he had expected. Trying his best not to breathe in the smoke, he dragged Tom by the shoulders, clumsily and wetly, more than halfway to the lounge's door, but no further. He shook him, then slapped him twice on the cheeks, nearly exhausting his limited repertoire of resuscitation techniques with no real result. There was no one in the hallway. No one who could come for help.

Finally, it was as he leaned in to attempt a desperate and completely improvised mouth-to-mouth that his best friend coughed twice and slowly opened his eyes.

"Tomsky!" Trevor yelled.

"T-trevor," said Tom.

"Fuck, man, you scared me."

"I'm sorry."

"Are you okay? What happened in here?"

Tom's eyes widened, like he'd finally realized where he was. "I'm sorry, Trevor, man, I'm so sorry. I tried to help, I tried to save him." He was crying.

"Save him?"

"Mr. Walter. He . . . in the other room. I'm so sorry."

"You mean, the guy who blackmailed you?"

"The piano exploded, it was making a sound all the time, but I didn't understand, and then there was the fire."

"Dude, it's okay, as long as you're okay. It wasn't your fault," said Trevor. "We need to get you out of here, the police will be here soon."

He grabbed Tom, who seemed still utterly confused, but more or less unscathed.

"But what happened?" he asked, as Trevor got him back on his feet.

"It was them, it was Patrick and those guys, they are fucking *crazy*!"

"Patrick?"

"They planned a whole thing, but I got them. Can you walk? Try not to breathe until we're out now."

"I—I can, I think," said Tom. "You . . . got them?"

"On camera. Oh, you'll love this. Remember when you got that . . . delivery from Rick for me? That package? Well, today I did the first livestream episode of my vlog! With this!" He took off his necklace, holding in his palm the black cross of his professional spy camera, thankfully fifty-feet waterproof. "I was gonna get footage of you and Walter leaving the lounge, you know, in case we might need evidence, and then I thought, Why not? You know? Everybody's doing livestreams these days, they're really great for viewer engagement. So I got those fucking idiots on camera explaining their whole plan, live on YouTube with thousands of people watching, can you believe it?"

"It was Patrick?"

"Yeah, I mean him and a bunch of people from here that knew me from way back, in LA. My vlog will be on fucking national news. But then they said they had put a bomb at the lounge, and I was like, 'Fuck, Tomsky's at the lounge.' This way," he said, with Tom's arm over his shoulder, supporting as much of his weight as he could. "We need to go. I think it's better if you don't talk to the police for now, you might still get in trouble."

"But Trevor, man, bro, is the livestream still on?"

Trevor smiled.

"No, man, I turned it off when I came to save you, I didn't want you to be on camera and have a lot of explaining to do. Thought it was a bad idea."

"You . . . turned it to off? But if you were in livestream, everybody could see you were a hero. Why did you turn it to off?"

"Dude, you are my friend. Do you still think a couple more views on YouTube matter more to me than you?"

They walked side by side toward the exit, Tom leaning on his friend, limping among the Positano ruins like two cowboys riding off into the sunset. Like action heroes in the third act, wounded and scarred, but alive to fight another day. If it weren't for the siren, and the screams, and the omnipresent background noise of all Vegas casinos—somehow heightened today, almost excited, frantic—you could have almost heard Steve Stevens' guitar play their victory song.

It is us. It's always been us.

We are the sound you hear beneath your weekend fun. We are the voiceless cry on which the city was built.

We are the dead, the losers, the gamblers, the suicides, the forgotten, we are the ghosts trapped in these halls.

We are the restless souls doomed to an eternity in Paradise.

Every night, we tell our stories to the air-conditioned wind. Our tales of luck and loss, both extraordinary and dull, laughable and sad. We tell our stories to those who stay and those who go, trying to warn them, trying to help. But the music is too loud, the lights too bright. We never amount to more than faint background noise. Oftentimes we just listen to one another, for nights on end, just to give us some relief. We will listen to the one who joins us too, our new friend. He will sing with us, here with us, one of us, forever.

We are what happens and what stays here.

Dario Diofebi

He saw it in an instant, watching the frenzied crowd downstairs. From above, Ray saw them fight, cower, help, sacrifice, exploit, take, share, hope, despair, run. An unsupervised cluster of agents exploring endless possibilities, changing, learning. How could he have missed it, all these times, how much clearer and more truthful everything looked from up above, the agency of all life without himself at its center? The realization was like light, a ray of sunshine burning away the mold, warm.

He finally saw that he'd looked at the Cardanus incident all wrong. He'd focused on his own mistakes, obsessing about the ways he was different from the computer. But that wasn't the important part. What mattered was how *similar* they were. The computer hadn't played some radical new style that had taken them all by surprise. It had played more or less like they did, just better. So what was impressive wasn't that a reinforcement learning system had gotten really good by playing trillions of hands. It was that *they*, the Brains, the simple, flawed humans, had been going in the right direction all along. That decades of slow, dumb, suboptimal evolution of the game—from the cowboy-hatted romantics to the number-crunching nerds—had gradually led humanity as a whole to the level of play Ray was able to express: not perfect, but pretty goddamn good. What mattered, that is, was not the fight between a multiagent AI and *himself*—an individual, discrete consciousness. What mattered was the discovery that *humanity itself was a multi-agent system*, and that each of us is but a node, a single agent, both fundamental and useless at the same time. And since humanity didn't act like a supervised system,[8] but much like Cardanus, a self-governing one, that meant that exploration of all possible policies was as important to it as the exploitation of established knowledge. To the whole huge system—Humanity—failing was *good*. It was vital.

With a grin—as he started moving toward the stairs, backpack on his shoulders—it occurred to Ray that the very concept of evolution is just a feel player's unrigorous description of a reinforcement learning system. He,

---

8   I.e., there's no input telling us what to do.

Ray Jackson, was a single turn in an endless game of Life (the most complicated and as-yet-unsolved game ever conceived—or happened), and as
such his agonizing about the consequences of his own individual actions
was just misplaced. It didn't matter that he'd failed, it didn't even matter
that he hurt, because he was ultimately just testing out one of the finite but
astoundingly numerous possible paths for the good of the system. And the
system—as proved by the convergence from feel-based Mississippi-barge
poker to online top-reg near-GTO, and by the clear prevalence of mutually beneficial, helpful policies in the downstairs chaos—the system was
moving toward good. It would take a long time, and humanity was a lot
farther away from life-GTO than Ray and his buddies were from Cardanus,
but the trend was undeniable. And as soon as you stopped caring about all
those useless lives as discarded, flawed policies, billions of lives whose main
contribution to the system was weeding out one of myriad ways *not to do
things*, then things didn't look so bleak anymore. Ray's whole life was a
single experimental move in a self-play sequence of a large reinforcement
learning system.[9] And it was okay.

Ray turned away from the downstairs scene, facing the Sportsbook and
the closest, optimal emergency exit. Inside his backpack were the remnants
of his poker career and the letter indicating his next move. He would set
out to test a new possible path. He would go home. If humanity was a multi-
agent system, slowly refining itself over time and countless mistakes, then
it was in the connections between its individual nodes that the progress
occurred. The sharing, the correcting, the *forgiving*. That's all there was to
it: we are just a large neural network, connected by *feelings*, striving toward
good.

---

9 His self-awareness, most likely, was simply a strategic choice the system at some point in its
history had found winning, and rewarded.

Interlude VIII

(the story of a victim)

What a load of rubbish! The man is inside a burning building, surrounded by hundreds of people running, screaming, and possibly dying, and he thinks of computers! Someone detonates a bomb, and he tells us humanity is *good*. Let me tell you, of all this parade of solipsistic monsters we call a society, these techno-utopists are the absolute worst. All those pathetic reformulations of the very religions they feel too cool to embrace, just to validate the reach of their egos. What a sham!

And so I died. In a small fire contained to one small room, while everybody else panicked for nothing. The only victim of this whole mess. I suppose you will be happy now. After all, I am the bad guy in this story. Evil old Walter (that's not my real name, by the way). It wouldn't matter if I told you that I didn't know the boy was poor, that I was genuinely fooled, that I wouldn't have done it otherwise. What would it matter to you, when my death wraps up the plot in such a neat little bow? I mean, look at me, an effete old Englishman: I'm practically a Disney villain! Just blame it all on me. Isn't that convenient?

And don't think, incidentally, I haven't noticed who ended up looking like the hero in this abject farce of yours. That loathsome boy who saved his friend and foiled the terrorists by virtue of being a sliver less of a fascist than the actual fascists. My compliments, really. What a wonderful, edifying story this was!

What angers me the most in this whole affair is that I should have seen it coming. It was right there under my nose all along, and I missed it. There is no worse sin if you're in my line of business than overlooking the signs of another con taking place—underestimating the competition, so to speak. Yet here I am, but a small-time grifter in comparison, no more than a good-hearted swindler who never meant any harm, and I get the worst of it, while real evil endures. In case you're wondering, they will only arrest that deranged Greywolf fellow and those other fools who showed their face to the camera. All the rest will get off scot-free. That is how tragically unfair our world is.

And now I join the rabble of the phantasm world, this drove of spirits too vulgar to haunt the attic of a London terrace or a wing in a country estate, cursed to moo this poorly plotted tale to crowds too self-involved to listen. What happens in Vegas *stays* in Vegas, get it? What a painfully crude twist. And please spare me the jokes about calling myself a "ghost-writer" earlier, this campy Dantean afterlife is humiliating enough as it is. God, I can already feel my ghostly vocal cords strain at the thought of reciting all that mathematical drivel until the end of time.

So here is what happens after you die. When your soul peels off your body, it doesn't do so in one clear rip, but rather like the flap of an envelope tearing in jagged fringes. There's bits of paper everywhere. It's messy, and highly inefficient. You'd think we'd have figured out a better way by now. And it's this grotesque liminal state—rather like the dizziness of getting up too fast, or the first hints of drunkenness—that poets and holy men have romanticised for ages as a glorious moment of transcendence, the letting go of earthly concerns to embrace the serenity of the eternal beyond. It is nothing like that. You feel alive and you are not, which is infuriating enough, and then there's nobody here to explain to you what you need to do next. Only schools of purposeless wraiths floating around through some incorporeal trick I haven't figured out yet, whingeing about their deaths in ghastly accents. I wish I could tell you this is just some sort of preliminary limbo, that you ascend to some puffy-cloud heaven or descend to some kinky hell afterward, but the truth is, nobody has bothered telling me yet, and some of these spectres look like they've been here a while. Honestly, the service in this place is just unacceptable.

So while I'm here, figuring out how to leave behind these charred remains (incidentally, nobody even *tried* to save me, other than a boy so dim he couldn't move a painting from a bloody doorframe), I might as well tell you what I've learned from all this. The one nugget of wisdom I've acquired too late and that I'll soon forget, as I transition into another one of these poor forgotten howling souls. (Trapped in Paradise! Whoever's in charge here must think dramatic irony is the definitive form of poetry. I bet they're from Los Angeles.)

What I've learned is that we've largely misunderstood the highly significant dictum that "the house always wins." That it extends far wider and deeper than we're comfortable thinking. That humanity is not a network striving toward good, but rather an inextricable tangle of hierarchies of evil, and that within this tangle we are so powerless and meaningless, so ignorant and frail, that the house is to us every last thing outside our weak little selves. That we are not connected by *feelings*, as our starry-eyed transhumanist would have it, but by layers and layers of interlocking narratives. By stories, in short, that is to say *lies*. Convenient little parables to pretend we're not always talking about power, and money, and death. The pursuit of happiness, which my adopted countrymen seem so keen on extolling, is but a euphemism for fratricide.

You'll have to admit, I was the only one to see things clearly in this whole affair. The only one who didn't fight uselessly against the current, but tried to float gently with it. I knew that fighting meant losing, and that believing in the goodness of the system meant losing with a smile. I thought that if I never played against the house, if I hustled at the margins, relinquishing all hope and ambition and that unnatural burden, morals, too, then the house would spare me. Leave me be. Yet even I overlooked something crucial. We have eyes only for our little narratives, our dull stories of individuals, while the tide brews and finally sweeps us away. I even tried to warn the girl about it, if you remember, in words she could understand. But I forgot how much the house loves its little stories: these harmless tales in which the innocent monster of the day is dispensed with, the dead are forgotten, and everything stays the same. Mediocre action, perfunctory moral dilemmas, even bloody ghosts!

And now they come for me, asking me to join their third-rate choir, to relate how this pitiful story ended. Here they come, and I don't feel ready. My God, it's like feeling underdressed for a party one never meant to attend in the first place. I feel human, and alive, and angry, and please, please let me stay. There is evil in this world, real evil rising, raging, hungry. Listen to me! Enormous, frightening amounts of evil, and you don't see it. I need to stay. Please let me stay. This was all wrong, all wrong from the start. I was only doing what I could. Why won't you listen to me? There is so much evil, and so much pain, everywhere, so much of it. Please! I am guiltless, guiltless, guiltless . . .

Epilogue

Aunt Karen giggled as the waitress left. Whatever the reason, the name *tarte tatin* never failed to make her laugh. Sweet, warm smell of apples and sugar rose to Mary Ann's nostrils from their plates. In the middle of the afternoon, the sun was still going strong, high above the tables of the bistro. It was too hot out today for apple pie, but it was good to see Karen like this again.

There were tourists around them. An elderly couple, two women laughing, a family of four. Mary Ann grabbed her phone and tilted it sideways to encompass the desserts, the simple metal cutlery, and their glasses of red wine. Pictured on the screen, the perfect sphere of ice cream to the side of her tart had already begun to melt in a glossy pool of white. She tapped around to adjust the color settings.

She'd got home after the fire, and hadn't left the apartment for three weeks. The story all over the news, Maidon, and Erica, and even Gabrielle checking up on her and updating her as much as they could, the townwide murmurs about the progress of a confused, at times farcical police and FBI investigation—none of it mattered. It was only a matter of time. Mary Ann was going to go to jail.

While the midday darkness of her Strip-side condo turned the place into a makeshift cellblock, somewhere beyond her closed curtains the investigation that would condemn her to a real one unfolded. It was a strange affair. On the one hand, the Positano bombing was a perfectly simple, open-and-shut case of domestic terrorism, in which the perpetrators had extended the police the courtesy of detailing their plan like Bond villains, but on camera and during a YouTube livestream of the event. Greywolf and four of his men, plus a handful of college kids from Arizona, had been arrested before the night was out, the evidence against them overwhelming, the copy/paste reproach from across the political board swift and noncommittal.

On the other hand, it was clear that the men hadn't operated alone. Someone had to have been working the vast amount of software tampering behind the night's events, and that someone was obviously not in custody yet. When Greywolf's lair was raided by the police, mere hours after the attack, the place was deserted, hastily emptied out of all equipment, literature, even furniture. Another matter yet was the identity of the person or persons who had planted the bomb at the Scarlatti: if Greywolf was to be believed—and he was in fact innocent of the physical act of pulling the trigger on an attack he was very much guilty of masterminding—then whoever had done it was still at large.

In the grips of her self-administered Dostoyevskian punishment, Mary Ann waited. They would put the pieces together, infer, deduce, *see*—and they should. She had killed a man. His name might not be in the news yet, due to the complications of identifying the body, but Mary Ann knew it. The name missing from newscasts, press releases, and police files, the name forensics professionals were scrambling to find, was Walter Simmons. Dead. It didn't matter that she'd been an unwilling instrument in the hands of the real criminals—that she'd thought she was only facilitating a simple, victimless software hack—it was still her fault. The trajectory of pure evil she'd been on all her life had finally reached its inevitable climax. She slept sixteen hours a day, and still woke up to the same miserable world, a murderer waiting for justice to run its course. They might as well get on with it already.

But they still didn't. Something was wrong. The investigation was taking way too long to follow what must be the fairly unmissable bread-crumb trail leading from the ashes of the Scarlatti to the quiet beige condos on East Flamingo and Koval. In an unlikely chain of coincidences, every lead tying Mary Ann to the fire seemed to have gone cold almost simultaneously. Neal, the natural link between the convicted terrorists and the Positano staff, had quickly disappeared, alongside every other remaining member of the Desert Front, and wherever he was, he didn't seem keen on facing justice himself just to turn in Mary Ann and the rest of the SU. He dropped away from national attention almost overnight, and got a brief mention in the *Las Vegas Sun* only two years later, when he turned up dead in a botched bombing of a Partido dos Trabalhadores rally in Porto Alegre, Brazil.

As for Greywolf, the only other Fronter to have actually seen Mary Ann, if only once and from a distance, it turned out he'd never bothered to learn her name. Pressed for details, he wasn't able to describe the alleged bomber to the authorities with anything more specific than "She was hot, like, movie-hot, you know?" Ultimately, the theory that he'd made this mysterious perpetrator up to lessen his culpability took hold pretty fast.

The final path leading to Mary Ann went through the woman whose job it was to oversee and file the waitressing shifts at the Positano. Police reports indicated several rounds of questionings of a Carla Alvarado, 42, of Sunrise Manor, Nevada, none of which resulted in any new information relating to the night of May 1. Mrs. Alvarado claimed not only to have "no memory whatsoever of any staff working the lounge at any point" but to have "misplaced" all physical records of the shifts as well. (Mrs. Alvarado being interrogated twice more by officials in the following weeks, and again in an internal Positano investigation, and eventually terminated with cause for her clear refusal to cooperate and deliberate mocking and filibustering of the proceedings by means of showing off impeccable memory when it came to her son Ricardo's Eldorado Sundevils soccer games, starting lineups, and scores—*State Champions '13, take that Palo Verde!*).

Days and days and days passed, the news cycle stretching the story to the limits of the country's withering attention span. It became quickly apparent that the investigation had reached true crime's least exciting stalemate: confessed culprits well in custody, and a lot of snooping left to make light of potentially nonexistent accomplices or accessories. The palpable shift from prime-time detecting to busywork. A feeling had started to grow within the SU, Mary Ann learned, that the worst was over. She might yet get away with it. She remained *unseen*.

Drinking potfuls of bitter black coffee in the apartment on Pecos, Aunt Karen and Rick stayed up all night talking. After May 1, the pendulum of Karen's odd symbiosis with her niece had swung back, prompting her to get back on her feet in Mary Ann's moment of need, much as she had done for her months ago. In a matter of days Karen cleaned up her apartment, flushed out the pills she'd been scoring off the Newport parking lot (she hadn't told Rick, who for his part had been so preoccupied with work lately he hadn't even noticed), and tentatively started going to meetings.

"We cannot tell her," she said.

The living room looked twice as big now that her records and VHS tapes had all been moved to cheap Kallax units against the walls. Rick had come over earlier that day to help with the assembling, and among the cardboard boxing and plastic wrapping and acrylic-painted fiberboard they'd rolled around like newlyweds as they put together the square modular grimness of Karen's future. She made crepes for dinner, and they watched *Love in the Afternoon* cuddling on the couch, and for the briefest of moments everything was right with the world.

"We cannot tell her," she said.

What brought them both back to earth, sitting at the kitchen table, drinking bitter coffee late at night, had been Rick's innocent question, How's the girl doing? Karen, who still didn't quite understand how Mary

Ann was involved in the events of May 1, told Rick what the women she saw coming and going at her niece's lately had told her: Mary Ann was devastated by the loss of one of her best friends, a man named Walter Simmons, who had died in the fire. Rick's expression had suddenly changed, and what followed was a thirty-minute-long piecing together of information, a conversational short-circuit strong enough to give them both a headache. Hence the coffee. And now the indecision.

"We cannot tell her," she said.

"I don't know, Karen," said Rick. "I think if I had a friend wasn't really my friend, I'd want to know. She wouldn't be sad about it anymore."

"She's not just *sad*, that's not how this works."

"No?"

"That's the kind of thing you never understand. And I know 'cause I used to not understand it either."

"What's there to understand? He was trying to sign her up for his business."

"We don't know that. Not for sure."

"I knew the guy. I'm not stupid."

"We need to think of what is best for *her.*"

"I think people should know the truth."

"You always think you can figure people out all the time, but do you, Rick? Do you?"

This went on for a while. For all her regained lucidity, Karen's conversation retained an elliptical tone, a certain recursive quality that made it really hard to ever reach the point. But whether Rick was moved by a genuine desire to help, or whether his stubborn defense of what he called "the truth" was the expression of a preexisting philosophical stance more and more threatened by a world he no longer could interpret—in the aftermath of a tragedy he had both lucidly foretold and grossly misunderstood, in which the spy camera he'd almost refused to sell to a kid he thought was a criminal ended up as the weapon that brought the real bad guys down, and which had left him confused, having sort of kind of lost that ultimate faith in the miracle of the internet that once made him feel like he had access to the hidden code of the world, and to real meaning, and truth—Rick eventually let it go. They went to bed.

On a sunny Monday morning in June, four women were at the door of Mary Ann's pitch-dark apartment, smiling excitedly. Three of them were young—one *very* young, in fact—the fourth probably in her mid-forties. Karen had seen most of them in passing in the last few weeks, leaving Mary Ann's bedside to give them privacy. This time they told her to stay.

"It's over," said the oldest of the group, who seemed to be invested with a certain spokesperson role, and treated almost deferentially by the others. "I wanted to be the first one to tell you."

"You're free," said the blond one with the glasses. "It's really over!"

Mary Ann looked around, as if surprised at the little committee gathered in her darkened bedroom. She paused on Karen with a frightened look.

"It's okay," said the first woman. "It's okay. We can all talk freely now. No more secrets. Everything's okay."

What Carla, Erica, Gabrielle, and Maidon related over the next hour, as Aunt Karen struggled to keep up, was truly exceptional. According to confidential information retrieved by the Intel Committee (which Gabrielle blushingly turned out to have been in charge of all along), Al Wiles was doing everything in his power to suppress the investigation into what he considered a "catastrophically bad PR incident." The old man's antiunion feelings were so strong and paranoid that he'd rather have some of the culprits go free than shine a light on a crime in which his workers were ultimately as much a victim as he was. When it comes to organized labor, said Gabrielle, his philosophy remained to close his eyes and sort of wish it away. Kinda like Mikey does when he doesn't like his veggies.

"It's not like that's a good thing," said Maidon. "Like, huh, frankly I still wish the man would choke on his Michelin-star dinner and die. But that's just me, I guess."

"I like your friends!" Karen laughed.

"Regardless," said Carla. "For once it seems like his paranoia benefits us, so we'll take it."

"Craziest thing is," said Erica. "In the end, he *was* too embarrassed to do anything about this. I mean, that was the plan all along, right?"

"Yeah, okay, like, I wouldn't really brag about our plan, honestly," said Maidon.

"Put that in the 'learn from our mistakes' pile," said Gabrielle.

"I'm just saying . . ."

"Ladies, ladies," said Carla. "We can talk about this later, maybe?"

As she sat upright against the headboard of her bed, Mary Ann's expression was difficult to read. Now she was freed from the prospect of external judgment and punishment, as it seemed, would her own inner jury let her go? This strange bedside gathering had an uplifting end-of-an-adventure feel to it, but Karen knew her niece enough to be doubtful.

"After all, we haven't got to the best part yet," said Carla. "We haven't told you about Walter."

Mary Ann grimaced, and Karen felt a needle pierce her chest. Both of them looked down, avoiding all eye contact, waiting.

"They've identified the body," said Gabrielle.

"It wasn't him, Mary. It wasn't Walter," said Erica.

"Whole other name," said Gabrielle.

"It's true," said Carla. "It was some other guy."

"Which, like, it's not like that's ideal—," said Maidon. The others turned to look at her reproachfully. "But yeah, it wasn't him."

Karen cheered louder than anyone else, although she knew they were all wrong. In an unpredictable turn, she now knew something nobody else did—something that could disrupt the momentary happiness that was now lighting up the most sullen room in Paradise. She alone knew the truth about the man they called Walter Simmons. *The truth.* Watching her niece smile, for the first time in weeks, at the thought of having accidentally killed a stranger instead of a friend—when she had, in a sense, done both—she surrendered the last of her ability to make sense of reality. Not with a struggle, like Rick had, but with relief.

"We can put all of this awful year behind us, Mae," she said. "We can finally move on."

Mary Ann's eyes met her aunt's. In the room's incongruous yellow lights, shut off from the first summer sun striking poses outside the third-floor windows, they looked at each other with what both perceived, for a moment, as hope.

"About that," said Carla. "There's something else we need to tell you. We discussed this, and we agree . . . we think it's better if you went away for a while."

"Not too long," said Gabrielle.

"Just until the dust settles," said Erica.

"But like maybe actually leave the country?" said Maidon.

"That'd be great," said Erica.

An awkward pause.

"But you said everything was fine," said Karen. "You said Wiles was suppressing the investigation?"

"It is," said Maidon. "And he is. But we can't tell for sure he's not going to try to pursue justice, uh, *on his own terms.* Uh, you know?"

"What Maidon means," said Carla, "is that he might conduct secret internal investigations. We've heard reports of several meetings with Zach Romero and his people ever since the accident—that's probably what that's all about."

"Carla got fired already," said Gabrielle.

"That's terrible!" said Karen.

"Oh, it's okay," said Carla. "I work with WHOA now. Honestly, I should have done this a long time ago, suits me much better. We do really good work there."

"But yes, go away for a bit," said Maidon. "Like, soon."

Throughout the conversation, Mary Ann hadn't said a word. The room had a faint smell of closed windows and dust. There was a dirty plate and fork on her nightstand, and three 330 ml bottles of Fiji water on the floor. She had been so alone, thought Karen, so alone for so damn long.

The women at the table next to theirs were the only other Americans. The elderly couple spoke Spanish, the family Chinese. There was light in the afternoon, warm #nofilter light from the summer sun. The ice cream melted on the *tarte tatin* faster than one could eat it. The bistro was Aunt Karen's favorite, and Mary Ann had over time grown fond of it too.

"I like it here," she said.

As a matter of fact, Les Deux Magots in Saint-Germain-des-Prés looked a lot like the bistro at the Paris Hotel in Vegas. The tables outside with the same checkered cloth, the menus in dainty cursive, the waiters in black vests and white shirts. It had that same air of manufactured ambience, the same postcard Parisian flair, almost fake. It was the real thing, and still it wasn't. Mary Ann had been too harsh on Las Vegas, or maybe she just had a talent for ending up in places like these. Maybe she was attracted to artifice.

They had been in Paris a month already. In the end, it turned out Mary Ann had misjudged Rick. When he heard of her predicament, he changed the name on the plane tickets for Paris he'd been saving up to buy as a surprise for Karen, and let them go together instead. When Mary Ann finally met him, and told him he didn't have to, really, that she could work out some other way to leave for a while, that this was their trip, not hers, he'd shaken his head and wouldn't listen. "Je vous en prie," he just said, in a clumsy southwestern twang.

They spent a month being silly American tourists. Aunt Karen took her to the movies in pretentious black-and-white theaters—old Hollywood films, lots of Wilder. They went to the museums and to the Latin Quarter, to the Seine and to the Tuileries. They took selfies in front of the Eiffel Tower and the glass pyramid of the Louvre.

Early in the morning, Mary Ann ventured outside alone. She spent little time at the hotel (a kitschy-romantic place Rick must have picked off some internet ad), but these hours especially—when Karen was still asleep or enjoying rich breakfasts in bed—these hours of silence and walks and photographs, she treasured more than everything else. She no longer tried to capture the beauty (or lack thereof) beneath the fake. She didn't try to unmask the city, to discover its true, unguarded essence—no longer pitied the neon lights, their endless begging for attention. Her favorite subjects were touristy hangouts and souvenir vendors, people taking pictures and museum gift shops.

"I like it here," she said.

"God, I do too," said Aunt Karen, scooping up the last of her pie. "This city is everything Las Vegas can't be. It's so real. It's magical."

Mary Ann nodded, though that wasn't at all what she meant.

"It's kind of sad we have to leave," Aunt Karen said. "But at the same time, I'm happy to go home. Start our lives again, you know?"

The American women next to them were complaining about expensive Manhattan rent. Paris was so beautiful, they said, but still *affordable*, you know? There was a *dignity* to life here. The waitress took away Karen's plate without breaking her stride. Soft concertina music came from the outside speakers, though mellow jazz was playing inside the bistro.

What remained, in the end, was a question. It was her project, the only life someone who had done what she had could deserve. A question so urgent she was willing to risk herself for it, so pressing there was no going on living but in answering it: Do we care about others, really? Not just ourselves and perhaps our loved ones, but *others*; not when we are *seen*, when it's expected of us, but truly, and deep down. Can we really care about others, when no one else is looking? Could she?

"I'm not going back, Karen," said Mary Ann. "I'm staying here."

"You're staying here?"

"I enrolled in a photography class at the Roland Barthes Institute—they can give me a student visa. I'll find a job. I can't go back, Karen, I just can't."

"But you heard Carla! There's no danger anymore. Now that Gifty's on board, everything will get better. I like that Romero guy, he looks like he cares. We can make it work again, Mae, we can!"

Aunt Karen took a large sip of wine from her glass.

"Maybe it's true," said Mary Ann after a beat. "I really hope it is, Karen. But not for me. I'm not going back. I'm really done."

A whir of foreign voices and laughter from people passing by superseded her words. How could she explain it? It wasn't about making it work, and it wasn't about surviving. It wasn't even about being happy, or even not hating herself, or even trying. She no longer craved to feel *seen*. A need to get lost, to disappear. Something bigger than herself. How could she explain?

"Karen," she said. "Karen, listen . . ."

Tommaso Bernardini was a free man. The one-man organization that threatened to have him deported had burned in the same fire that left Tom miraculously unscathed. His marriage with Lily, now unchallenged by hostile whistleblowers, had so far convinced USCIS enough to let him be, legal and undisturbed. Finally, he'd avoided the unwelcome questioning that would have no doubt taken place had he been found by firefighters or medical staff or, worse yet, the police at the Scarlatti Lounge, thanks to Trevor's selflessly off-camera rescue mission. Yes, Tom was a free man. An almost unbelievably lucky free man.

In the weeks after the fire—as Las Vegas licked its wounds and cheered the news of a game-changing business partnership in town—Tom took some time off to regroup and adjust his vision to the new, widened horizons of a post-Walter life. Anything was possible. As an American citizen-to-be, he had a name, and a signature, and could finally legally claim every portion of the life he'd had to live vicariously through Trevor, from renting a house to owning a car. He could have real expensive American health insurance, and a driver's license, and one day a right to vote, and even leave the country. The buffet of his freedoms was as rich as he could dream—or afford.

Back in Rome, his mother had some news of her own. With the help of a friend and the money she'd saved renting out Tom's old room, she had managed to expand her little Airbnb venture, creating a small single-family unit out of the abandoned garage next door. It was no Grand Hotel, she could assure Tom, but it was cozy, and tourists loved it. She took the guests out for guided tours, taught them pottery in a minuscule garden she'd cleaned up out back. *You know I've always loved to take care of people, make them feel special.* When he told her he would be able to visit her soon, she said US Customs officers are allowed to shoot you if you act suspicious, so be careful.

He talked to Francesco, who promised to come to Vegas soon, maybe after the summer, when it's not 45°C out there. Getting away from his firm was tricky, but it was about time he saw his little brother, who'd made it in the craziest city in America. Besides, there was something different in Tom's voice, Francesco said: he sounded . . . *grown up*, happier. He had to see it for himself.

And of course, there was Trevor. After the events of May 1, Tom's friendship with Trevor had a kind of postwar feel to it. With Tom at home most of the day, encounters were once again frequent, and oddly choreographed with pats on the back, overloud laughing, and more-than-occasional manly hugging. Whenever Trevor required Tom's still unpaid assistant work on the set of his booming vlog, he now asked for it so nicely—*only if you really have nothing better to do, really*—that Tom found the whole thing awkward as hell. They were at peace, but the wounds from the war were fresh, and hard to heal. And while the apartment was no longer the stage of elaborate brinksmanship, their cohabitation seemed to have lost its natural flow, and their conversations had taken on a certain stilted formality neither of them seemed to enjoy. Oddly enough, it was Trevor, out of the two of them, who seemed most scarred by the experience: he looked nervous, jittery, and as much as he tried to hide behind his meteoric YouTube rise, Tom could tell there was something off. He wasn't surprised when Trevor told him he was leaving.

"My job here is done," he said. "I think I've outgrown this town."

"But where will you go?" asked Tom.

"Brooklyn, for a start. That's where the content creators go. You know, there is *one* thing that idiot Patrick was right about: turns out poker is not a scalable business, after all. I mean, it's great for you, don't get me wrong, you can really make a life for yourself out here. But I want to expand my channel, and poker just ain't gonna cut it. The exposure I got from the livestream is an opportunity, but it'll dry up fast if I don't go for it."

"New York is far."

"It's a great market. And it's the place to be if you want to be a serious travel vlogger."

"I mean, is far from Las Vegas."

"I guess it is, yes," Trevor said with a hint of what sounded like relief. "It'll suck not getting to be roommates anymore, Tomsky, let me tell you. But it's something I have to do now."

Tom nodded knowingly. For the first time in over two years, he felt like he could finally read his friend. See through him. It was, perhaps, now that he had no skin in the game, and their friendship seemed poised to fizzle out like one of those rare and memorable desert rains, that Tom possessed the calm to look at Trevor with dispassionate eyes, and see him for who he really was. Or maybe Francesco was right, maybe he *had* grown up a lot lately.

What he could see now was how *weak* Trevor really was. Even within the transactional marketplace of human relationships Tom had come to accept as a reality—perhaps an American reality first, but who was he to judge?—Trevor was not the winner Tom had always tacitly assumed he was. Even when he'd hated him, even when he'd blamed him for his suffering. No, the Trevor he saw now was a haunted man. He wanted to move to Brooklyn, putting as much geographical and ideological distance between himself and the still-at-large members of that brotherhood of hatred and deranged rhetoric he'd been—willingly or not—enmeshed in for a while, only to betray them all in the most damning and public and retweetable way. Meaning: he was afraid they'd come for him. And yet even that—this puerile and arguably very beta fear of retaliation—wasn't his true weakness. Even when he finally and after so long dropped his time-honored "Silverback" moniker (which Tom was stunned to discover wasn't his actual last name) and moved to "pivot his personal brand" toward something more "attuned to mainstream audiences," even that wasn't it. What Tom began to understand now was that the same *wanting* that had looked to him like a sign of confidence really made Trevor a slave. He was a single-minded machine of desire, a straight arrow of want. He had an urge for something outside himself, constantly, endlessly. He'd wanted *people*, of course (and what was there more explicitly telling of an unquenchable thirst for people than the life of a pick-up artist?), he'd wanted places, he'd wanted recognition. Maybe that hunger, that need to engulf more life within himself that had seemed foreign and blissful to Tom, maybe that hunger wasn't *good*. Maybe it wasn't even pleasant. It made him shiver to say it—especially since it seemed to imply the opposite was true of himself—but for a brief, lucid moment it sounded undeniably true: people like Trevor would never be happy.

And so once Trevor finally moved out, rather in a rush, Tom thought, it was with a real sense of moral superiority that Tom calmly looked for a new place, and eventually settled on a small but homey one-bedroom in North Vegas, off Osiana Avenue. It was a new residential complex built by the Anita Romero Foundation as part of a Let's Make It Right campaign to provide "well-designed, energy efficient, and affordable homes" in the infamous 89301 zip code, the veritable heart of the colossal housing market bust that had precipitated the 2008 GFC. While recent *Las Vegas Sun* reporting suggested that not all that glittered was true affordable housing, Tom wasn't much of a newspaper reader, and the apartment represented his first time truly on his own. The money was still a bit tight after the $8,000 he'd given Walter, but he would make it work. Everything was fine. And as he resumed his ordinary Vegas life—he drove his truck, more often than before, to the Wiles Tower or the Shibuya, now that the Positano triggered in him some dark, primal fear—something else began to find his way back to him. At the end of his own emotional rainbow, he spied again the glimmer of that truth he'd held and lost during the fire, as he rushed in to help the one man who stood between him and all he'd ever wanted. A mind free, unclouded by guilt, unshaken by fear, Tommaso Bernardini was on his way to rediscover that treasure buried within himself: love.

By the time Lily called him to tell him they needed to talk, Tom had been legally married to a U.S. citizen for three and a half months. She said that the ponytailed metalhead from Dolly's Place, the man Tom paid the money to, had been in touch, and that Tom needed to come see her right away. She sounded angry.

It was the hottest day in Tom's life, 47°C (or 117 fake American degrees). As he got out of his truck, the sun hit so hard it had an almost physical quality to it, as if it were actively pushing Earth away from itself. The white driveway at Lily's place glared in Tom's eyes like a mirror, and the reddish pebbles to its sides gleamed like coals glowing in a fire. Las Vegas itself was a citywide replica of the sitting room at the Scarlatti Lounge, deluged in white light, waiting for the flashover to take it away.

Walking the few burning steps to Lily's door, Tom wasn't sweating because of the heat. He had been naive to think it would end with Walter's death. There were others aware of the proceedings, others who could turn him in, and now that Walter was gone, others who could blackmail him and Lily in his place. How could he think Walter wouldn't have made copies of the incriminating evidence and given them to his henchman? The guy from Dolly's had been his goddamn *best man* at the wedding, how could he forget about him? After all he'd been through, this was how it ended. He was walking to his doom, and he had only himself to blame. All he wanted was for this to be quick.

"We have a serious problem," said Lily, leaning against her doorframe in her PJs, still not inviting Tom in.

"I know," said Tom. "I'm so sorry."

"Oh, you already know, good. So what do we do?"

Tom shook his head.

"I don't know, Lily. I don't think there is something we can do."

"Well, we need to do something. I mean, I can't just take it, that wasn't the deal."

"I know, I know," said Tom, recognizing in his wife the first stages of denial and rage he'd felt when the first threatening texts started pouring in. "Is very unfair. But maybe there is no choice except to take it. They are very evil people."

Lily nodded.

"I didn't know you felt this strongly about this too," she said.

"I tried to stop them before it arrived to you, and I thought that I had won, but it seems they vanquished me. I am sorry. Is my fault."

"Okay, well, it's no use playing the blame game now," said Lily. "Let's just figure out what we are going to do about it."

They stood by the door in silence, Lily at the very edge of the AC chill of her living room, Tom still outside in the blazing heat. Between them, invisible walls of hot and cool air crashed into each other, fighting and gradually combining. Lily looked so pretty in her white shirt and green shorts. If she weren't his wife, maybe he could have told her. In the end, it was a such pity they had to meet in such trying circumstances.

"You know, I didn't get any sleep last night," she said after a while. "All that crying, and crying, like nonstop! These annoying, whiny moans, all night long. I really can't do this, Tom."

"I was like that too," said Tom, moved. "When it started, I cried a lot."

Lily looked puzzled.

"Is no shame," he went on. "I am sorry you have to feel like this too, you don't deserve it."

"I'm . . . I'm glad that you agree."

"Is unfair for you."

"Yes."

"I wish it can be just me."

In spite of the situation, it was heartwarming to see a smile appear on Lily's face, that beautiful smile of hers.

"I'm so happy you understand," she said.

"I have had a long time to think about this."

"I'll be right back, then."

She closed the door to block the sun from flooding the microclimate of her house. Tom was still outside, drenched in the sweat of his existential fear and the anxiety he still got from talking to a woman, regardless of the outside temperature. His heart, the weak, frail, hopeless heart that constituted his sole inheritance from his father, had the unmistakable accelerating rhythm of a ticking bomb just before its explosion. He stood there, waiting for Lily to come back with whatever version of Walter's horrible threats she'd received, waiting for their scam to be found out and everything to end.

He stood there, so ready to lean in to read a text message or a threatening letter made out of newspaper cutouts that the sudden yips coming from the pink cat carrier in Lily's hands startled him. It was a familiar sound. It was the sweet high-pitched bark of little Pepperthedog.

Tommaso Bernardini was a free man. And Pepperthedog too, skipping in what looked like the burning, boundless happiness only the severely moody can ever experience, he too was free of his captors, united at last with his true companion. In the tree-shade of Sunset Park, in a breathable four by four meters away from the implacable sun, the last of their problems finally evaporated. It was such a lovely day.

So in the end what Lily had called Tom about was not, as he'd assumed, a sudden recrudescence of Walter's blackmail through an informed collaborator. The man from Dolly's, wholly unaware of the extortive portion of Walter's scheme, had simply been stuck with a clingy Pomeranian when the old man died, and after a brief moral struggle with the idea of just ditching the noisy thing in the parking lot of the East Trop Walmart, had resolved to unload him on Lily, i.e. the last person and address he remembered driving him to a few months ago. "Change of plans," he told her in his most professional and matter-of-fact tone, "you actually get to keep the dog. You're welcome." Lily's "serious problem," then, was nothing more than a gambit to get naive Tom to volunteer to take Pepperthedog instead. Which he'd readily done, without even realizing it. Problem solved.

The fact was, of course, all of this was completely unnecessary. Tom loved Pepperthedog. In fact, Tom *wanted* to get him back. And as he petted him, and laughed, and hugged him as his new and forever best friend, in the emotional drunkenness of the heaviest weight lifting from his chest, he realized something else too: he really liked Lily. He *wanted* her. Why should she be his fake wife, when he liked her, and they could be together, and live happily ever after? And surely there was time, and there would be time, to settle into his new life, in his new home, with his new friend—a friend he would never doubt, or argue with, or feel neglected by—and time to properly and skillfully court his wife, now that nothing threatened their future. There would be time to get the things he wanted, and freedom to want them.

Pepperthedog licked his face frantically, and Tom felt his heart swell in a rush of real pursued-and-attained American happiness. In the blissful shade of a city-park tree, the wounds of his recent past healed, and a new and distinctly Trevor-like understanding began to spread through him.

Yes, he had been too harsh with Trevor, once again. There is more than just unhappiness in wanting, so long as we get what we desire. What we deserve, yes. Every Italian has a personal America, and this was his, at last: the realization that he *deserved* all that he had, not through luck, but as a just consequence of his own individual will. As the memory of the fire and his near-death visions of compassion grew opaque, distant—like a scene from a movie or a recurring dream—the lesson his daily (very-far-from-death) experiences validated was of a different nature. It impressed itself on his permeable mind with perfect clarity over the next months, and it remained there. Yes, yes, this was what he'd learned. That he was right to want, and right to claim what he wanted for himself. That real freedom was freedom from doubt. That he could eat the cake—the chocolate cake that had eluded him all his life, as he waited without complaining, as he taught himself not to long for it, let alone expect it—that he could finally eat his cake and, as the Americans said, that he could have it, too.

FALL 2017

In the pinkish light of the Californian sunset past the windows, Ray watched a Tesla Model S park out front. He was in the tea room at Satis

House, arranging twelve rows of stylish metal chairs for the reading. The first few guests would arrive soon. Estimating an attendance between fifty and a hundred people, Ray had decided to go with twelve rows of ten chairs each, five per side with an aisle in the middle, just to be safe,[1] and had printed out eight RESERVED signs on ordinary sheets of paper for the first row, two of which carried his parents' names.

Satis House looked so different now. Under Ray's first hesitant, then more and more committed tenure, the simple indie bookstore had overcome its financial troubles, and changed its appearance in the process. While his parents' core concepts (books, readings, pretentiousness) were all still there, Ray had brought home from Vegas the notion that the money customers spend in an establishment is a function of the time one can keep them inside it. Over two years, Satis House had expanded into a quaint Bay Area coffee shop, a high-end stationery store, finally even a small hipster tapas bar. His parents had been skeptical at first, but had done their best to encourage their son's extraordinary talents, and had ultimately come around to his way of seeing things. By now Ray basked in parental approval so unrelenting and ubiquitous he was starting to question whether, in their eyes, he could ever do something truly disappointing anymore. Sometimes he wondered . . .

Ray frowned at the luxury car outside. Rich tech bros weren't a rare sight at the House, of course, but ever since he'd come back from Las Vegas, he couldn't help being irked by the kind of extravagant displays of wealth he associated with his long-gone life as a high-stakes poker player. The kind of things that would have appealed to Logan, or Calvin. Or Bryan, for that matter, who as far as Ray could remember drove a Tesla just like that one. For a strange second, Ray felt an unwelcome shiver of fear at the thought that it might actually *be* Bryan, who'd tracked him

---

1 His initial plan of nine chairs per row in groups of three, with two aisles to facilitate access, had ultimately seemed to him efficient but a bit airline-like, too formal. Human warmth toward the customers being a new variable added to his decision-making as of late.

down all the way to Marin County, and was now about to discover
VFInd3r working at an indie bookstore.

The fact was, Ray hadn't seen or heard from anybody in Vegas since
that night of two years ago. He hadn't looked for them, they hadn't looked
for him. Gone. People in Vegas disappeared all the time. As much as social
media and geotagging and round-the-clock availability made the idea of
disappearing sound rather odd these days, to Vegas regs it remained a
very ordinary reality. People went broke, they moved down stakes and hid
away, playing at the Wiles Tower or in LA. Or people just moved, they got
married, they got a job, these things happened. And they usually didn't
make a big deal out of it. They didn't announce it to the upstairs group:
they just left. The sudden disappearance of someone you'd seen every day
for the last one, or two, or even five years, someone you'd been at the table
with for thousands of hours, even talked to a lot and maybe met socially a
couple times outside the casino, it really wasn't something strange. It was
just the way things were. To the players in the poker room, the where-
abouts and plans of absent regs remained, for the most part, an extremely
dull mystery. So why the hell was Bryan here?

Ray forced a shrug. So what if it was Bryan? Quitting high-stakes poker
had been the best decision he ever made. He'd quit the game without
going broke, and he'd had enough to save his parents' business and their
home. He had learned to accept his mistakes, he'd reconnected with his
family, and he'd turned an old bankrupt bookstore into the #1 hangout
spot in San Raphael on Yelp. He was proud of himself, he was. Yet the fear
he felt as he watched the driver's door open, and two Converse high-tops
step onto the asphalt, and a figure rise from inside the car, the fear was
familiar. He knew its face, its moldy smell. He couldn't shake it.

The man in the car wasn't Bryan. Flushed with relief and suddenly
ashamed of this momentary relapse, Ray didn't recognize the youth
walking up to him until he was near enough to shake his hand.

"Hey, man," said Matthew Wong. "Long time no see."

"Matt?" said Ray. "I didn't know you were still around. My mom told
me you'd moved."

"Yeah, I live in DC now. I'm just here to see my parents for a bit. Didn't come home for Thanksgiving the last couple of times, you know? Work work work."

Matt Wong looked much older than he had the last time, which, Ray now realized, was that Thanksgiving dinner on the eve of his move to Vegas. He looked all grown up. Above his old worn-out shoes, he wore the smart-casual clothes of a young tech millionaire—good shirt, sleek black hoodie. There was something more deliberate to the way he moved, like his limbs had gotten heavier, or he'd been tethered down to the floor with a paperweight.

"I thought you were in school," said Ray.

"No, man, I never went. I'm a private consultant for political campaigns now. Been doing this for a while."

"Seriously? How old are you?"

"Twenty in a couple months," said Matt. "I know, so old, damn. But seriously, I was psyched when my parents told me you worked here now. I wanted to come thank you in person."

"Well, I mean I own the place, it's not like . . . wait, thank me? For what?"

"Dude, I owe you, like, everything. Maybe you don't even remember. Last time we met, at Thanksgiving, we played ping-pong, remember? After the game, I asked you how to make money—ridiculous, I know, I was really dumb when I was a kid—and instead of making fun of me, you gave me this whole speech about finding a field that was still dominated by *feelings* and crushing it with math."

"Excuse me?" asked a woman who'd just walked in. "Who is reading this evening?"

"I don't know, madam," said Ray, more curt than usual.

"But I mean, is it fiction?" the woman insisted. "Or nonfiction? Or poetry?"

Ray looked at Matt Wong with apprehension, but the kid seemed genuinely not to care. He waited in his confident kyphotic stand, not looking around or snickering or drawing conclusions, his stare lost thoughtfully in midair.

"I'm sorry," said Ray. "I don't know that either. You'll have to ask my mother, in the next room." He pointed.

"Man, I thought of that stuff you told me a lot," Matt resumed, as if the interruption had never happened. "Like, seriously, I was *obsessed*. I thought of every possible field, I made lists, I read so many Wikipedia entries I was afraid I would go insane. Then one day, on the way home from school, I saw this billboard for some stupid local political race, I don't even remember what it was. And suddenly it clicked. *Politics!* Man, talk about the ultimate feel players. All these stuffy men in suits trying to convince regular folks to vote for them even though they look like aliens trying to act like humans. It took me like twenty minutes online to realize I was right. Politics was the next bubble, one hundred percent."

He didn't fiddle with the zip of his hoodie, didn't rock back and forth as he spoke.

"And so I started working at it, day and night. I studied software models, I learned all I needed to know about the system, I ran simulations. Little by little I started asking around, cautiously, just to see if anybody else had thought of this. Before you know it, this private think tank got in touch: turns out I'd done better work in a few months alone than they'd managed to do in *years*. But they had the resources, and they were in talks to partner up with a huge company that had access to virtually unlimited data-mining. Like, really really cool shit, for someone who had my models. By the time my acceptance letter from Stanford arrived, I was making six figures working on the presidential campaign. Less than two years later, now I'm working on the midterms, and I'm pulling *seven*. And it's all thanks to you, man."

"Jesus," said Ray.

"I mean it, man. You changed my life. And you were right about the bubble too. I mean straight-up campaigning is cool, but it's not gonna last forever, you know? I'm already looking ahead, I'm diversifying. I could tell you all about it, there's opportunities, stuff you wouldn't believe—"

"Sorry," said a teacherly man with narrow rectangular glasses, pushing Matt aside with a certain urgency.

Dozens of people were flowing inside the store now, walking fast to secure good seats for the reading. Ray and Matt, standing in the center aisle, were being run into by geriatric men in tweeds, twentysomething book nerds, and the usual rotating clique of regulars attracted by the free refreshments.

"I think we're in everyone's way," said Matt, taking a couple steps backward. "I'll catch up with you after the thing. It'd be cool to chat a bit, sort of repay the favor."

"Sure," said Ray, now submerged by the literary flood.

"And Ray," added Matt with a smile. "Who *is* reading anyway?"

"It's Lindsay Peterson!" said a woman walking by him, with a certain disdain for Matt's ignorance. Ray nodded, laughing, then watched Matt swim back toward the exit door.

He thought about it sometimes, still. An echo from his maverick past. It was when the thought struck that he got his ideas about rebranding Satis House, maybe add a cocktail bar, expand just a little more. Meeting Matthew Wong, it was just the kind of thing to make everything around him look frail. Not tragic, maybe, but precarious, hollow. *There's opportunities*, he'd said. He thought about it, sometimes, and tried to imagine a version of adulthood where money—the acquisition of it, the lacking or abundance of it—wasn't a source of constant preoccupation. One where bankruptcy wasn't a perennial possible outcome in the next roll of the experiential dice.[2] He moved against the current toward the sound mixer, then tapped the microphone three times to test it. Maybe that was all he'd really wanted, to be free of fear that everything would end. Was that unfair to ask? To be rich and happy and secure, to be right and to know it for sure. That's all. Yes, perhaps—in the simple life of an

---

2   One, to be clear, where Risk of Ruin (RoR%) = 0.

ineffective, soon-to-be-discarded policy in a hypercomplex system—
perhaps that was enough.

The lectern was there for her, the microphone was there for her, the people,
all gathered in the small-but-not-*that*-small room, were there for her.
Lindsay walked up to the lectern and rested her book on the gray metal
top. She adjusted the height of the microphone, pulling it up a few inches
toward her face. She looked ahead at the small crowd, which appeared
shimmering from where she stood in a pearly mist of otherness, like
looking through a veil or a thin sheet of alabaster. A roomful of people
waiting for her to speak.

It was odd, reading to them about Las Vegas. Earlier that afternoon,
after picking up Orson from his graduate apartment on campus at Stanford, she'd tried to articulate the friction. At the overlook point in Sausalito,
watching traffic on the Golden Gate Bridge, sitting (or in his case lying
down) on the grass, on a day that was such a picture-perfect incarnation
of the life she used to dream of back home, it seemed pointless to hide the
intention. To be away from home, and to tell strangers about it. To have
lived through the events of 2015, have her life changed and forever marked
by the decision she'd made in the aftermath, and to be here now. Everything was at once so arbitrary and deliberate, so comforting and strange.

"We like to think we learn lessons from crises," Orson had said. "It has
a good arc to it. But I think mostly we survive them, and maybe that's
enough. Who we are is way more complicated than that."

"Sounds like an excuse," she replied.

"It's just stories, Lin, all of it. Narratives, big and small. We look for
them in times of uncertainty. They excite us, and they're great to write
books about—I should know—but it's dangerous to grow attached." He
paused. "I can see that now."

Lindsay looked at her brother. He seemed calmer, away from the desert,
almost distracted. Although he'd never made it there, something of him

had burned in the Positano fire. What it was, or whether he was maybe better off without it, Lindsay ultimately couldn't tell.

"I think most of us just learn all the wrong lessons," she said.

"Ever the pessimist," said Orson, making her laugh.

In her new life, there were days to swim through, and tasks in which to sink her energies. There was Orson, and there was a Temple here, too. There was the true religion of community, of the people around her, the meaning she'd never really needed to go looking for. There was the passing of time, and the practice of being alive, more fluid and significant than any single moment could define.

And then there were the stories. Perhaps Orson was right, and all we have is a set of contradicting narratives to explain to ourselves who we are and how we act. All falsifiable—all, in the end, false. But we still get to choose, don't we? We still *have to*. There is so much freedom, so much responsibility in that. The stories we choose to believe. The ones we choose to tell.

Lindsay looked down and opened her book to one of her bookmarks. She took one last look at the people in the room. The stories were a thing of their own, beyond her doubts and the long, imperfect project of being herself. They were small bridges between herself and others, and here, behind them, she felt happy to rest. Not bother anybody. Barely be there at all.

She began to read.

ACKNOWLEDGMENTS

This book is the product of favorable variance. As such, it simply wouldn't exist without the help of a large number people, to whom I'm forever grateful:

To my brilliant and generous editor, Callie Garnett, and the phenomenal team at Bloomsbury (Laura Phillips, Emily Fisher, Laura Keefe, and many more—thank you).

To my agent Marion Duvert, who patiently guides me through the strange world of publishing, and to everybody at The Clegg Agency, especially Bill and Simon.

Over the years, Martina Testa did more for this book than I could possibly have asked, and more for me than I could possibly deserve. I can never thank you enough, but I'll keep trying. I owe infinite gratitude to Scott Gannis, who read every draft of every chapter, and watched basketball with me, and was my friend. And to David Lipsky, thank you, for the stories, the walks, and all the books.

I am grateful to the NYU Creative Writing Program, where most of this book was written, to all the teachers and staff, and to all the friends I met there. Among them, John Maher and Hannah Gilham, thank you for all your help.

To all the people who did big and small things for this book (and for me while I was writing it): Christian Favale, Sara Consalvi, Pat Lipsky, Andrea Vezzani, Jerome Murphy, Philippa Robinson and all the staff at NYU London, Carlos Dews and everybody at John Cabot University in

Rome, Emma Borges-Scott, Sara Duvisac, Emily Barton, Katie Kitamura, Aljosa Vella, Edmund White, Michael Carroll, Darin Strauss, Susan Choi, Andrea Gale, Doma Mahmoud, Tim Glencross, Jonathan Lee, Hank Yang, Calvin Lee, Clavio Anzalone, Federico Granara, Daniele Colautti and everybody from the poker years, Drew Grauerholz, Samuel Greenblatt, Marco Cassini, Margherita Mirabella, Isabel Kaplan, Frances Ofosu-Amaah and anyone I may be forgetting. Thank you.

My unbelievable luck begins with my family. With my sister Diana, my friend Dario, and their beautiful children, Martina and Lorenzo. My parents, Flavia and Riccardo, helped me and keep helping me in more ways than I can count. Any small good thing I accomplish, I owe to them. Finally, to Francine, who shares her life with me, thank you. My greatest luck is the life I have with you.

A NOTE ON THE AUTHOR

DARIO DIOFEBI was born in Rome, Italy, in 1987. After earning a BA and MA in comparative literature from the University of Rome, he became a professional online poker player from age twenty-two to twenty-six. After that, he was a traveling high-stakes live poker player for another three years, mostly based in Las Vegas. He quit the game to pursue writing, and received an MFA from the NYU Creative Writing Program.